Touchstone

A Shards Of Fate Novel

AMY LAURENS

OTHER WORKS

KADITEOS
How Not To Acquire A Castle

SHARDS OF FATE
Touchstone

STORM FOXES
A Fox Of Storms And Starlight
A Stag Of Snow And Memory

SHORTER WORKS
All The Things We Saved You
    From
Bones Of The Sea
Christmas Miracle Is Just A
    Saying
Dreaming of Forests
Mint Grows Even In The Dark
Rush Job
Trust Issues

COLLECTIONS
And Then I Shall Transform
April Showers
Cherry Blossom And Other
    Stories
Darkness And Good
It All Changes Now
Of Sea Foam And Blood
The Inklet Collection

POETRY & PLAYS
Change Becomes Us
For A Little While
Life Had Other Plans
Where Your Treasure Is

NON-FICTION
How To Write Dogs
How To Theme
How To Create Cultures
How To Create Life
How To Map
How To Plan A Pinterest-Worthy
    Party Without Dying
On The Origin Of Paranormal
    Species
The 32 Worst Mistakes People
    Make About Dogs

**FOR YOUNGER
READERS**

SANCTUARY
Where Shadows Rise
Through Roads Between
When Worlds Collide

The Ice Cream Crown Skating
    Races

Find more about the author:
www.AmyLaurens.com

TOUCHSTONE

AMY LAURENS

AUSTRALIA

Hardcover ISBN: 978-1-922434-91-3
Paperback ISBN: 978-1-922434-92-0
eBook ISBN: 9798230094043

www.inkprintpress.com

National Library of Australia Cataloguing-in-Publication Data
Laurens, Amy 1985 –
Touchstone
372 p.   cm.
ISBN: 978-1-922434-92-0
Inkprint Press, Canberra, Australia
    1. Fiction—Fantasy—Urban 2. Fiction—Fantasy—Paranormal 3. Fiction—Fairy Tales, Folk Tales Legends & Mythology 4. Fiction—Fantasy—Contemporary

Summary: Kyla has five days to find the mythical, magical Touchstone or her father dies.

First Edition: September 2025

Cover design © Inkprint Press.

Clare & Kerryn. I know words are literally my gig, but also: I literally have no words. I'm so grateful.

MONDAY 5 DECEMBER
MELBOURNE, AUSTRALIA

EIGHT NINETEEN ON A MONDAY EVENING, AND THE LAST place on the planet Kyla would have expected to find herself was her sister Pippa's driveway, anticipating a visit with someone who—last she knew—hated her and who—last she knew—hadn't wanted to speak to her ever again.

She had no idea what in the world could have happened to change that, if not the one thing that—somehow—had happened: Kyla and Pippa's father had gotten suddenly ill, had been hospitalised, had his hold on life made suddenly even more precarious than the usual day-to-day existence of your average human being.

Pippa was a paramedic, so when she'd told Kyla that despite the hospital's more optimistic prognosis, she thought it best that Kyla come see their father while she still could, Kyla took her at her word.

Only now, that meant that here she was, at eight—well, eight twenty, now, on a hot Monday evening in early December just before sunset, sweat trickling down the back of her neck thanks to the brief walk from the bus stop, contemplating how this visit might go.

She tucked her gloved hands under the straps of her backpack and squeezed. Her hands were clammy despite the 'sports performance' fabric of her gloves, but it was a mild distraction compared to the fact that here she was right now, at number 138, stopping in front of the chunk of unaesthetic brick that passed for a mailbox and staring up at the house.

Pippa had moved since Kyla had seen her last.

That made sense, Kyla supposed, since the last place had been a tiny studio apartment Pippa had been renting while finishing university, but still: the horribly bland, horribly beige single-storey with attached double garage that Kyla was staring at in the fading light was... uninspiring. She'd always accused her sister of lacking an imagination; she hadn't known it was this bad.

The plain concrete drive led to two beige roller doors. Garage and house alike squatted under a terracotta tile roof that did nothing to offset the awful, unappealing beigeness of brick that, presumably, a builder somewhere had chosen to use solely because no one else wanted it.

Kyla couldn't think of any other rational reason to create a house so ugly. She supposed—grudgingly—that it must have been cheap, too, or else even Pippa wouldn't have stooped so low in the taste stakes.

Kyla shifted her weight, hitching up the black-and-silver hiking backpack that held the entirety of her possessions for this trip. She used one shoulder to wipe ineffectually at the sweat dripping down from her hairline; nearly sunset, but the early summer sun was still determined to fry her right into the pavement. The back of her tank top was probably soaked right through.

The air felt warm in her nose, tasted of hot brick and concrete and salty sweat from her upper lip, felt like it was wrapping around her and suffocating her.

Or was that just the fact that she was about to more or less voluntarily go speak to her sister?

Urgh.

Kyla sighed heavily, reminded herself of how much she loved her dad—the entire reason she'd run away from home at age fourteen—and started up the path to the front door.

The shadow of the lone silver birch that constituted Pippa's front garden was a welcome, if short-lived, temperature shift. Kyla glanced up at it and did a brief double take at the beautiful crystal chimes hanging from the lowest bough, motionless in the cloying, breathless evening air. A little more whimsical than she'd have expected from Pippa.

In contrast to the brief shade, which was very welcome, the shuddering screech from behind as the family across the street opened their also-beige roller door made Kyla wince— and wince again when two young kids squeaked and shouted, the sound echoing across the busy street. Hastily, Kyla shoved down memories of similar moments from her childhood, before... Well, before a lot of things.

Before she'd developed her Touch and realised that for her, self-control was going to be both a lot harder, and have a lot higher stakes.

Before she'd learned what kind of person her mother really was.

Before she'd done what she'd needed to do and seen her mother sent to prison to save her father's life.

At twelve, Kyla had desperately wanted to be attractive. Her mother had wanted that for her too. And she'd become very attractive indeed, once her Touch developed: the unconscious, unavoidable need to discharge energy from her fingertips every few days, which for most people with Touches (few enough back then, but becoming more and more common with every passing year) meant a jolt of extra good luck, or a sudden insight about the future, or the ability to briefly know what other people were thinking or influence their thoughts.

For Kyla, however, it meant death. Not hers, of course, but of someone—whoever was nearest by, usually, until she'd run away from home and her mother's pathological need to shape and direct and control this 'talent' for her own gain...

Until Kyla had spent a year out in the outback, mostly alone—mostly hungry for the first few months, too—with the space she needed to figure out the depth and extent of her Touch without worrying that someone would die while she slept—or even worse, while she didn't: the memories of her first attempt at a boyfriend still burned hot enough to give her the occasional nightmare.

Kyla sighed heavily. Slouched. Took a deep, steeling breath—*stop being ridiculous, it's not like Pippa can do anything to you*—Pippa loathed all Touches on principle, after seeing how their mother had treated Kyla, after seeing how Kyla was forced to treat the world—and strode to the house's front door.

A security screen cloaked it, and the doorbell had a strip of black electrical tape over it indicating, presumably, that it was out of use, so Kyla knocked smartly on the panel of yellowed, textured glass beside the door instead, though what the point of a security screen was if a would-be intruder could just smash the glass instead, Kyla had no idea.

She sniffed, shook her head.

Footsteps sounded inside the house.

Kyla tensed.

The door opened.

Pippa had aged.

Not *dramatically* so, but she was clearly now a woman just edging into her thirties instead of the still-gangly girl she'd been... well, twelve years ago when Kyla had seen her last.

Kyla's chest fluttered.

Pippa's blonde hair with its natural wave and thickness was always going to be a perfect camouflage for grey hair, but her face was now full and mature, with a softness around the edges that hadn't been there before and fine lines tracing her forehead and the corners of her grey eyes.

Grey eyes that widened slightly before narrowing as Pippa realised who was at the door and stiffened in response. Though she didn't, Kyla noted, wear a protective glass pendant anymore. Interesting. What had happened to make her less afraid of being Touched?

Kyla shrugged it aside: probably Pippa had exchanged the visible pendant for one of the less visible Touch-protective charms that were trendy these days.

Kyla twitched one side of her mouth in some sort of approximation of a smile. "Hi," she said.

Pippa looked her up and down, pursed her lips, and stalked back into the house.

But she didn't shut the front door, so Kyla took that as a sign to come on in and, opening the screen door with a screech, she did.

The screen smacked shut behind her and she took her time closing the front door after it, inhaling deeply of cool air that tasted faintly of lavender and the kinds of laundry powders that called themselves 'original' scented. Objectively, it was pleasant compared to the baked air outside, but subjectively...

Deep breath, she told herself, hitching her backpack. *You can do this. You've done plenty of worse things than this.*

At least no one's going to die.

That last thought jolted her stomach as Kyla considered the entire reason she was here in Melbourne at all, let alone breaching the sanctity of an estrangement that had allowed the two sisters to survive the last decade-and-change: her father, *their* father, sick in hospital and apparently in a critical condition.

She *hoped* this wouldn't end with anyone dying.

One more deep breath, squared shoulders, and Kyla dropped her backpack by the front door and set out through the house to track down Pippa.

The white-tiled hallway was breezier than she'd anticipated, wide for a house this size, with a formal lounge room to the right and to the left, the master bedroom—immaculately white in every conceivable texture, tone and variation.

Say what you would, Pippa was clearly a woman familiar with bleach.

Was it better than the bland beige of the house's exterior? Kyla couldn't decide.

The white theme was repeated in the bathroom, next on the left, and in the kitchen where the hall opened out at the end of the house. Directly ahead, a sizeable TV was playing the latest celebrity gossip show to two empty white couches (studded with grey velveteen cushions, of course, to match the carpet), while to the right...

Pippa stood at the counter in the kitchen, a Schnauzer-grey ship in a further sea of white broken only by the black door handles on the cupboards, aggressively making tea. Kyla watched as Pippa dropped a tea infuser into each mug—shockingly, one a pink stoneware and the other sky-blue ceramic—then drummed her fingers next to them on the counter, staring fixedly at the kettle (white). "I assume you still drink tea?"

Kyla realised she was holding her breath. "Yeah," she said. "Black, no sugar."

"I remember."

The noise of the kettle rose steadily, a quiet rumble at first that barely out-voiced the TV chattering away about some upcoming charity gala at the Museum, growing louder as steam began to issue from the spout. The kettle tremoured.

Louder, louder until the TV chatter was overwhelmed, louder...

Kyla rubbed at the back of her neck.

Click.

The kettle hit boiling and switched off.

Kyla forced her shoulders to relax as Pippa filled the mugs with steaming water and set the kettle back on its cradle, not quite slamming it, then snatched up one hot mug and strode to the couch.

Kyla maturely restrained herself from rolling her eyes and followed with the remaining mug, which actually smelled delicious, something sweet and rosy. Pippa had chosen the seat closest to the kitchen, and Kyla hesitated for a heartbeat, the heat of the mug radiating against her gloved fingers. Sitting on the same couch seemed a little too familiar; the far end of the other couch a little too distant, both physically and metaphorically.

Kyla took the Goldilocks option, the other couch but the end closest to Pippa. She cradled her tea, the warmth actually welcome in here as a shield against the aggressive air conditioning, the sweet scent drifting up to her on clouds of steam. "So," she began.

Pippa swirled the tea infuser from her mug, let it drip for a moment, and reached over to discard it in a small white dish on the white-washed wooden lamp table that occupied the corner between the two couches.

"So," Kyla tried again as she discarded her own tea infuser. "Tell me about Dad."

Pippa's jaw twitched. She took a gulp of tea that had to be scalding and stared for a long moment at the TV.

Kyla spared it a glance: a blonde-haired European-looking woman with glamorous makeup, an ice-blue gown hugging her curves as she posed on a carpet that definitely wasn't red, but gave off a similar sort of vibe.

"He *is* going to die."

Kyla turned around. "How can you be so sure?"

Pippa gave a small shrug and sipped at her tea again. She swallowed. "The hospital don't think he is. But he's going to die. Well, at least if nothing changes."

A slightly strange prognostication, perhaps, but hardly likely to be hyperbolic given Pippa's paramedical experience.

Kyla's chest constricted. "Why do you disagree with the hospital?"

Pippa let her gaze drift to the glass sliding door by the kitchen that led to a slowly darkening backyard, all concrete and the neighbour's brick wall and neatly edged, unimaginative lawn. "Call it... intuition."

"Intuition?" Kyla fought to keep her eyebrows from mirroring the scepticism in her voice.

"Yes," Pippa said sharply. "*Intuition.*"

Despite her resolve, Kyla's eyebrows gave a little jump. Fine. Intuition then. There was no point arguing with Pippa when she used that tone.

Kyla blew softly on her tea. So Dad might be dying. She ran her gloved thumb down the smoothly textured handle of her mug—the pink stoneware one. She hadn't seen Dad in about eight years. What would he look like now? Had he aged much in the face? ...Would she still recognise him?

That twisted her stomach, and it was her turn to raise her mug and gulp at still-too-hot liquid that scalded its way past the tip of her tongue to burn down her throat and settle in her stomach.

The black tea was rich and sweet, its soft, rosy notes a contrast to her harsh thoughts, and she took another scalding sip. "What is he dying of?" Her voice sounded fragile and polite, a stranger enquiring courteously about the health of someone else's beloved.

Pippa hesitated.

End-of-show music rang out on the TV, jarringly loud.

Pippa dug the remote out of the couch's cushions and muted it. "They're not sure. It almost looks like a toxin of some sort, but a) that's ridiculous and b) none of the tests for any sort of regular household poisons or anything else common have showed anything up."

Kyla sipped again at tea that was slowly cooling to a drinkable temperature, her fingers curled tightly around the mug, gloves pinching at the base of her fingers, the hot liquid soothing in her throat. "How... How long do they—you—

expect he has?" she asked. She'd visit the hospital tomorrow, find out for herself what the prognosis really was. She wasn't going to hastily discount Pippa's expertise... but she wasn't going to take it as gospel, either.

Pippa shrugged, her fingertips blushing red and white around the blue mug. "Maybe a week."

Adrenaline, hot and sharp, a brief lightning bolt through Kyla's chest and stomach. She made a small, wounded noise.

It's fine, it'll be fine. She said herself the hospital don't agree.

Pippa shot her a daggered glance. "I wouldn't have called you for less."

I wish you would.

Oh, there was a startling and unexpected thought.

Kyla breathed carefully, as though the very air of the room was as delicate as its faint traces of lavender and soap—and tea. "What... What do you need from me?"

"I just *thought*," Pippa said, tone sharp, "that you might want to see him. I'm not a monster."

Did Kyla imagine it, or was there a slight emphasis on the word 'I'm'? Either way, she was spared from replying by her phone ringing.

She snatched it out of the back pocket of her shorts—unknown number—and pressed the green button, angling herself slightly away from Pippa as she did. Another round of celebrity images flashed across the TV screen, the woman in the ice-blue dress featuring prominently in an ad for the upcoming gala the talk show had been discussing.

"Hello?"

There was a breathy scratching against her ear, and as a thrill of adrenaline shot through her for no discernible reason, Kyla considered hanging up.

Before she could, however, an equally scratchy, gender-indeterminate voice began in a conversational tone. "How's your father, Kyla?"

She froze, her grip on her phone turning vice-like. "Who is this?"

"Just a friend, Kyla, just a friend. A friend who happens to know exactly what is wrong with dear old Daddy, and who knows that in exactly five days from now, he'll die, unless he's given the antidote to the, uh, *very special drink* he took a few days ago."

"Who *is* this?" she demanded, phone case biting through her gloves as she *very carefully* set her tea down on the lamp table. "What did you do?"

Glamorous women paraded past on the TV, posing, vaunting.

"Disappointing, Kyla. You're asking the wrong question."

A moment of prescience: Kyla whipped down the phone and hit speaker.

Pippa opened her mouth; Kyla shushed her urgently and nodded at the phone where the scratchy voice continued.

"The right question is, of course, what do *you* need to do to convince *us* to hand over the antidote."

Kyla's stomach knotted at once, a tight ball of nausea, fear—and fury.

"To what?" Pippa mouthed, expression more confused than concerned.

Kyla ignored her.

"And *I'd* say," the voice continued, "the answer to that is very straightforward. We just want to engage your services, Kyla. One job for us, one antidote for dear old Daddy."

Kyla's free hand balled into a fist so tight the Velcro strap around the wrist of her glove tore loose. No. No no no. Never again. She'd sworn, never again… "I won't be blackmailed," she said, heart racing at her throat. Because there was only one thing they could be wanting from her, given her regular artefact-hunting services were freely advertised and available to anyone for a reasonable fee.

Murder, in exchange for her father's life?

She'd sworn, never again.

"Won't you?" the scratchy voice said, bemused. "I think it's a bit late for that. Besides," the voice continued. "I think you'll find our terms aren't so disagreeable. All we want is the Touchstone."

Kyla nearly swallowed her tongue. The *Touchstone*? "But that's... a fairy tale! It's a myth! There's no such thing as the Touchstone!"

Her father was going to die because some idiots decided they wanted her to find a non-existent artefact? She tucked her knotted fist tightly under her leg so she wouldn't punch something.

"You want to risk your father's life on that possibility? There *is* a Touchstone, Kyla, and rumour has it that it's in town for a special event, and you're going to find it and bring it to us before the end of the week so we can, uh, *address* your father's little ailment, understood?"

Her heart hammered. "And if I don't?"

"Oh, well," said the voice, thick with an overly bright kind of resignation. "I hear your relationship with your father isn't that close anyway. You haven't seen him in what, nine, ten years? I'm sure his death on Saturday won't crush you too terribly."

Something cold shivered its way down Kyla's back. They were out by a bit, but... how did they know how long it had been since she'd last seen Dad? "But I—"

The phone call disconnected.

"Wait, but—" Kyla fumbled at the phone, hit redial—and again as the first call went to a blank voicemail—and again—and again.

"Get. Out." The tightly controlled fury on Pippa's face hit Kyla like a cloud of burning steam. Pippa's grip looked like it would crack her mug at any moment.

"Pippa, I—"

"Get out. And you'd better find this *stupid* Touchstone, or they won't be the only ones you have to deal with."

Words boiled through Kyla's head—*don't kick me out— you could help—can't I see Dad first?—the Touchstone doesn't even exist!—this isn't my fault!*—but the sentences leapt and tangled around each other, and she couldn't find the beginning of one, and it didn't matter, because none of them would help her anyhow.

She stood, tucked her phone into the pocket of her shorts, and nodded at Pippa. "I'll find it," she said. "If it's here to find, I'll find it."

It wasn't. It couldn't be. An actual, real Touchstone?

It was like saying the moon had come to life and started granting wishes.

...Or like people had suddenly started waking up one day with slightly strange abilities—the Touched, they'd been nicknamed, for the way their power seemed to be channelled through the physical touch of their hands—and no one could figure out why.

Goosebumps rose on Kyla's arms. The fierce air conditioning, no doubt.

She shook her head, a single tight, tense shake.

Pippa ignored her, staring steadfastly at the B-grade celebrities like Kyla had already left the room.

Kyla strode down the hall, snatched up her backpack, and let herself out, allowing the screen door to slam loudly behind her.

Air only slightly cooler than suffocating hit her face. Her stomach roiled.

Well. It wasn't like she hadn't *expected* the meeting to go terribly. She pressed a hand to her stomach and headed back down the drive. She'd just a) vastly underestimated exactly how terrible the meeting would be, and b) been wrong about why.

In the time she'd been in with Pippa, the shadow of the house next door had crossed the front garden and was even now climbing up Pippa's garage. The shade was welcome, a dimmer on the fierce heat. Kyla ran a thumb over the protective glass pendant that hung on a black leather thong knotted around her neck, a slightly wonky glass square, the motion soothing and grounding.

The Touchstone.

Really, actually the Touchstone.

She ground her teeth. Really actually the Touchstone *if* the blackmailer's info was good. Otherwise, her father's life was in danger for no reason—*multiple* lives would be in danger, there was no way it was possible to believe that all the blackmailers wanted from her was a stone—although... Was it possible? Did she dare hope that maybe, just maybe, they'd contacted her solely because of her reputation as a finder, and they didn't know the true nature of her Touch at all? After all, what lengths had she gone to to hide it from everyone around her? It was... possible.

Most people didn't know she had a black Touch.

It was possible.

She inhaled firmly and set her shoulders, let her pendant fall back under the neckline of her tank top.

The Touchstone.

Well. There were two people in town other than herself who always had good information about magical artefacts: Alethea, and the Bloodhound.

Looked like she had more visits to make in Melbourne than she'd planned.

2

K YLA GLANCED SURREPTITIOUSLY AROUND THE TRAIN carriage before pulling out her phone. Only two other occupants sat in the carriage, by the window on the opposite side, about as far away as anyone could be in the small space: two men, talking animatedly about... whatever it was they were discussing. Kyla didn't care, except that it made good cover for the conversation she was about to have.

She'd only been on the train five minutes or so, but already her butt was going numb from the poorly padded seat, and the temptation to put one of her long legs up to brace against the seat in front of her was high. It wasn't worth the fine, though, so instead she glowered briefly at suburbs flashing past in the dark, a maze of human-made lighting outshining any attempt from the stars in the night sky (though the red light of a plane was blinking away up there, tracking time) and slipped one glove off to unlock her phone.

She scrolled to a number she hadn't had cause to use in a very long time—eight years, to be precise—hesitated with her finger over the name 'Bloodhound', and let out a breath.

The air in the train was stifling, muggy, the air conditioning fighting against the heat even at this late, dark hour. Or maybe it was broken, and that's why train stank like sweat and stale air, something that was quite a feat really given it stopped and opened its doors every few minutes.

The thought of the sweat baked into the fabric of the chairs had Kyla squirming for a moment—but she was avoiding the phone call.

She hit dial.

The ringtone blipped in her ear and she glanced over her shoulder at the two men, still thoroughly engaged in their conversation, pulling her glove back on.

"Hello?" said a cautious voice that sounded like it belonged to a twelve-year-old boy.

Blood had been nearly twice that eight years ago, just a handful of years younger than Kyla, but apparently, his voice had decided never to age.

That and his happy-go-lucky attitude, completely at odds with his nickname, the Bloodhound, had earned him a strange degree of respect in the Touched community—when you looked and sounded small, vulnerable and likely edible, you worked three times as hard to prove your worth, and Blood had proved it to the community over and over. His knowledge of the Touched and the energy that powered them was unrivalled—and he had the physical skills to make sure his knowledge was never exploited.

Kyla sniffed, briefly wondering as she spoke how *he* would react in her situation. "Hey Blood," she said. "It's Kyla."

"Kyla?" His voice squeaked even more than usual, followed by a clatter as, presumably, his phone fell to the ground. "Sorry," he said breathlessly a moment later, "dropped my phone."

"No kidding," Kyla said drily. It wasn't like him to be skittish—and she'd just been blackmailed into hunting for a mythical stone of protection. Hmm. Was the search for the Touchstone simply that? Or was something *big* about to go down in the city of Melbourne?

One more thing to ask Alethea about.

"Why—I mean... Hi? Long time no speak? I didn't realise you'd still have this number," Blood stammered out.

Kyla closed her eyes, leaned her head against the cool(ish) glass of the train's window as it rattled around a corner on the tracks. "Yeah," she said. "I didn't realise I had it still either." True, though she would have known if she'd thought of him at all in the past several years. "Listen, I know it's been a while, but I have a favour to ask you."

"You—" His swallowing was audible, even over the continued chatter of the men behind her. "You do?"

"Yeah, and I don't want you to get all judgey, okay?" Not that he would. If anyone would believe her quest for a mythical object was real, it was Blood. He wasn't quite a conspiracy theorist—if only because most of his theories about the Touched turned out to be true—but it was a close call that sometimes came down to splitting hairs.

"Okay?"

Kyla's brows drew together. "What's going on? You're jumpier than a cat on a hot tin roof."

"Nothing! Nothing, I just... I'm busy, you know? I'm... kind of a big deal these days. Lots of jobs. Important guy. You know."

Kyla's right eyebrow reached for the roof, even though he couldn't see her. "Sure," she said, deadpan. "Super important." No clue why that ought to make him jumpy, but okay then. "Look, anyway, I have a question for you. What do you know about the Touchstone?"

An indistinct squeak, another clatter as his phone dropped.

Kyla sighed, bumped her head gently against the window. Fifty percent of her leads were, apparently, high as a kite right now. What an auspicious start to this search. She sighed again.

"The... Touchstone?"

He didn't explain the dropped phone, but whatever, moving on.

"Yeah. I've been... hired to find it." Close enough, and the fewer people who knew she was blackmailable, the better. Basic op sec. Definitely not because she didn't want to admit it to anyone, least of all someone she'd once called a friend.

Blood cleared his throat. "Okay. You have. Right. Hired. That makes sense."

Kyla's eyebrows pretzeled. "Does it?"

"Well yeah, you're, like, the best artefact hunter in the country, if anyone can find it you can."

She sniffed. "Thanks for the vote of confidence. What can you tell me about it?"

If she was the best artefact hunter in the country, why *hadn't* the blackmailers just hired her?

...Because she would have said no, that's why. It was a complete waste of time, and she had a living to earn.

The train slowed as it approached the next station. Kyla ground her teeth and repositioned her butt on the pointless padding of the seat.

"Well it's all theoretical," Blood said, voice changing gears to something more animated, filled with confidence as he engaged Lecture Mode, "which I'm sure you know, but the thing is, there's been some talk about it recently that makes it, uh, more plausible that the thing exists, right?"

The train doors shushed open, letting in air that was perhaps a few degrees cooler than the train, though still humid.

Kyla peered intently at the dark platform. With any luck, the air was all the open doors would let in. "What kind of talk?"

"Hunting talk," Blood said. Was it Kyla's imagination or was his tone suddenly a bit grim? "No one's said anything about it in years, but now, all of a sudden, I keep hearing about it. Just here and there, nothing concrete, but just... you know. Mentions. And..."

A beep, and the doors of the train whooshed shut again, sealing in the muggy air, carriage still empty of everyone but Kyla and the two men.

"And what?" Kyla said. There was a dark smear of some sort on the seat facing her; she hadn't seen it earlier since it nearly blended with the dark blue and green pattern of the seat fabric.

"And... rumours that someone is... hunting for it."

Kyla sniffed again. "Someone is. Me."

"No, I mean someone... big."

"I see." She didn't mean for her tone to cut glass, but on the other hand he had just called her the best artefact hunter in the country, so if *she* didn't count as someone big... Hmm.

"Don't be like that," he said quickly. "I mean someone scary." Kyla's eyebrows rose again and, almost as though he could see them, Blood added, "You're not scary. Your Touch might be, but *you're* not."

"Right," she said drily, drumming her gloved fingertips on the hard edge of her seat. "So I've been set... *hired* to find a thing that maybe doesn't exist, except now you think it does because rumour has it that someone scary is also looking for it? I'm not sure that's the most convincing evidence." And it definitely didn't help her find it. Urgh.

"Kyla, you *have* to find it. You don't... I mean..." A hiss of frustration sounded over the phone. "Please take this seriously."

"Oh, I am, trust me." The blackmailers had seen to that. "Okay, so we're assuming it's real and I have competition. What else can you tell me? What am I even looking for?"

It wasn't always necessary for her to have a physical description of an artefact to hunt it down, but it definitely expedited the search. And in this case, something so mythical? Literally any information would be useful.

"I don't suppose you've read Mnason, have you?"

"Who?"

"Student of Plato's. The less famous one. Though if it hadn't been for—"

"No," Kyla cut in before he could launch not only into Lecture Mode, but Sidetracked Lecture Mode. "I haven't read him."

"Right. Okay. Right. Well, he theorised about the Touchstone in connection with Plato's Timaeus dialogue, thought that maybe it had come from At—"

"Will this help me find it, Blood?" Kyla said, squeezing her eyes closed and resisting the urge to pinch her forehead as the train clacked onward in the night.

He sighed heavily, the aggrieved noise of an enthusiast deprived of an attentive audience. "Kyla, please believe me: I'm trying to help. I really, really am."

She softened a little as the train rounded another corner and began to slow again. "Yeah," she said. "Sorry. I'm just... This one's important, okay?" She drew in a steadying breath.

"You don't have to tell me that," Blood muttered.

What *had* he heard?

But before she could comment, he resumed. "You're looking for a stone—obvious, given the name—but it might not be made of actual *stone*, right. Best guesses are that it's glass, or maybe obsidian. Obsidian makes more sense given the age of the references, *I* think, but not everyone in the field agrees with me. It's going to have a weird aura about it, I'm pretty sure—everyone is pretty sure—"

"Wait, the *artefact* will have an aura?" That had Kyla sitting up straight, even as her balanced rocked, the train pulling up to a stop again. It didn't matter how magical they were, how often they'd been exposed to Touch energy: artefacts couldn't store Touch energy, which meant they couldn't have an aura like a person with a Touch did. Kyla's aura was black when she drew on her Touch energy; Alethea's was red; Blood's was orange. Different colours for different skills—death, truth-seeking and people-seeking respectively, in this case—but artefacts, objects? They never had a colour, an aura.

"Yeah, I know right. But that's the one thing every account agrees on: the Touchstone has a weird vibe to it. Weird energy. Weird aura. Of course, no one knows exactly what that *looks* like, but I'm just saying: you'll know it when you find it because it's gonna be a weird one."

Train doors shushed open. Cool air tinged with the city smells of concrete and petrol flooded in, a hint of salt from the approaching ocean just detectable.

The back of Kyla's neck itched. "Blood, this is not exactly the illuminating information I was hoping for." She shifted uncomfortably on the seat as someone wearing a black hoodie—somehow not dying of heatstroke despite the fact that they had the hood all the way up, concealing their face— entered the train carriage.

"Yeah I know, Ky, but if it was easy to find, whoever hired you would have found it themselves, right?"

Right. Kyla sighed. Scratched the back of her neck. Scrunched up one side of her face as something niggled at her. "Thanks anyway, I guess. I assume that's all you have for me?"

The new arrival seated themselves on one of the sideways seats near the doors, which whooshed shut, sealing out the night air.

"Since you rejected my attempts to articulate the cultural paradigm of the Touchstone for you, yeah. It's glass or obsidian—my money on the latter—and will feel really weird. 'S all I've got for you I'm afraid."

"It's fine," Kyla said, shifting again as her neck continued to itch. "At least I know it's really real." Well. Probably.

Abruptly, energy surged and the darkness behind her eyes wasn't just darkness: it was the black aura of her Touch.

What in the...

Wait.

No.

Crap.

"Blood, I gotta go," Kyla snapped. "Meet me at the Museum tomorrow night at ten, okay?"

Without waiting for his reply, she hung up and shoved her phone deep into her pocket.

A quick, steeling breath.

She pivoted to face the newcomer.

She'd thought for a moment there that her own Touch energy had flared, but it hadn't, it was still leashed—present, it always was, but under control.

This black Touch energy now filling the carriage with the sense of it, black energy so out of control that any split second now would find a host to latch onto?

It wasn't hers.

It was coming from the black-hooded person sitting by the doors.

3

"**G**ET IT UNDER CONTROL," KYLA SNAPPED AT THE NEW-comer. "*Now.*" She didn't have to add 'someone's going to die otherwise'; a person with a black Touch this strong would know that. Why the hell they had gotten on the train in the first place with their energy so close to discharging, Kyla couldn't fathom.

The person didn't respond.

Well, they did: they hunkered down in their seat, head practically disappearing into their shoulders.

A second realisation struck Kyla: there was no scent of ozone in the air, no lemongrass—the scent of a well-honed, well-practised Touch.

Crap.

This was not a discharge, controlled and controllable by the person Touched; this was a flash, a random surge of energy that happened when someone's energy had been allowed to build up for too long, had been suppressed—and it was totally out of the Touched person's control.

The two men were still chattering away at the back of the carriage, utterly oblivious to the danger. It was a miracle the black energy hadn't snapped in on one of them already; for Kyla, it only took a split instant between the release of her power and the death of her victim.

She threw herself to her feet, sprinting for the back of the carriage. If she could get there first…

Then what? She only had the one pendant on her.

Too much energy.

So much blackness in the space between blinks.

"Get down!" she shouted at the men, who gaped as she sprinted toward them down the aisle. She waved frenetically.

One of them was a little faster on the uptake than the other—or else just knew a little more about the idea of Touches than the other; he threw himself at the floor of the train, sliding as the train cornered and braked.

Kyla launched herself at the other man, knocking him flat on the row of seats.

"What the—"

But before he could finish his cry of outrage, the black energy flashed.

Ozone sizzled in the air.

The square glass pendant hanging haphazardly around Kyla's neck shattered, shards of glass splintering into her chest.

"You…" The man stared at Kyla's shattered pendant, colour draining from his face. He met her eye. "You saved me."

She shoved herself off him, stood, brushed the shards of glass from herself with gloved hands, as gingerly as she could.

In her peripheral vision, the other man lay hunched on the floor.

Kyla turned to the black-hooded black-Touched person by the doors—and the doors slid open, letting the night air in, and the black thumb out.

Kyla just had time for a glimpse of a stricken face framed with black hair—dark eyes, Asian-tanned skin—and the girl was gone. "Hey! Hey, get back here!"

"Theo? Theo, man, she's gone, you can get up," the man Kyla had saved was saying, nudging the man on the floor with his foot. "Theo? Theo!"

Shoulders slumping, Kyla headed for the emergency intercom and pushed the bright red button with a gloved finger. "Hi," she said, throat dry. "There's been an incident. A man is—"

"Dead!" the man she'd saved screamed behind her. "Theo is dead! What happened? You! You killed him!"

Kyla slumped against the wall of the train and prepared herself for the inevitable barrage of questions—from the man, from the train conductor, and eventually from the police. She just had to hope that her other glass charm, the one tucked into one cup of her bra, would do its job and continue disguising her black Touch as merely dark grey—otherwise she'd undoubtedly be looking at an overnight stay in the local prison.

Now that would put a damper on finding the Touchstone.

T HE POLICE QUESTIONING HAD BEEN MORE EFFICIENT THAN Kyla could have hoped: her hidden glass charm successfully cloaked her Touch, making her appear grey to the testing officer instead of black (and such devices weren't common knowledge yet, so he had no reason to doubt his senses, thank Kyla's lucky stars). Which meant she was off the hook, especially paired with her testimony about the black thumb, corroborated by the surviving man.

So Kyla had made it down to her intended destination without more than an hour's delay; a miracle, all things considering. She sighed at that. There had been no miracle for Theo tonight.

She hitched her silver-and-black backpack, the movement allowing air to circulate up her sweat-soaked back for a moment, cooling her tank top before the bag resettled. It wasn't overly heavy—just a couple of changes of clothes, a few necessary toiletries, her wallet, an artefact or two—but it was bulky enough, and despite the late hour, the air was still hot and humid.

At least the streets were relatively empty of pedestrians; cafe tables and chairs had been packed away, sandwich boards no longer littered the footpath, and even the traffic had slowed to a hoarsely whispering trickle. Spicy, savoury scents filled the air and beckoned at Kyla's stomach, which grumbled in reply. A cup of tea since lunch was hardly the best way to treat it, something it was all too happy to remind her of—but she didn't have time to stop off at any of the restaurants, nor the inclination: right now, answers were more important than food.

So she strode down the street until she came to a tiny, narrow alleyway, sheltered from passersby by a metal door, currently plastered with posters and advertisements screaming in poorly chosen fonts and lairy colours. To either side of the narrow alley, a bookstore and a yarn shop slept peacefully, only their emergency lighting dimly outlining their wares in the windows.

Streetlights dotted the wide street, of course, but the shops were all old, two-storey affairs with fixed awnings that stretched out the width of the street and blocked most of the light from hitting the pavement.

There was a security light on in the alleyway, but it illuminated the door from behind, and so did nothing to shed any light on the contents of the posters—literally or figuratively. But as Kyla pressed her gloved hand against the metal door to push it open, she squinted in the dark and ducked down a little: the woman in one of them seemed vaguely familiar.

A passing car provided enough extra light for just a moment. Kyla sniffed and pushed her way through the door, dismissing the photo of the blonde B-grade celebrity she'd seen wearing the ice-blue dress on TV at Pippa's house a few hours earlier.

The alleyway was surprisingly clean, or at least, it would be surprising to casual visitors who didn't know that this was the unassuming entrance to one of the most magical trading posts in the world. The concrete floor was recently swept, bright under the fluorescent light that sat high up on the terracotta brick wall behind a protective cage.

Despite the half-full skip bin at the end of the short alleyway, the smell was mostly clean concrete and damp cardboard. Kyla's footsteps echoed in the enclosed space as she headed toward the stairs over the bin, then slapped against the brickwork of steps at least a century older than she was, worn down in the middles.

She gripped the metal railing with gloved fingers, her hands hot and sweaty despite the cooling night air.

Alethea.

She hadn't seen Alethea in almost as long as her father—seven years, now. Two years after… Well. Two years after Kyla had seen her before that. Hmm.

Once—before those other two years, so twelve years ago in total—she'd been one of Alethea's most frequent visitors, buying almost as often as she sold. Just trinkets, back in those days, before Kyla had gotten really good at her job.

To begin with, Alethea had helped her with that, too, being the strongest red thumb Kyla both knew and had heard of—and given how far Kyla often roamed across the country in search of the strange artefacts that even stranger people paid her to find, that was saying something.

The last time Kyla had seen Alethea, Alethea had thrown her out and told her to never come back unless it was a true emergency: the end of what could have been a very productive partnership.

Kyla sighed. No good thinking about what might have been.

She reached the top of the stairs. The door that greeted her had been painted teal at some point in its life, and to be fair, most of it still was—a good colour choice with the brass door handle. A brass nameplate in the centre of the door bore the words 'AA's Artefact Exchange'.

Kyla turned the brass knob, her grip slipping slightly until her gloves found purchase against the metal, and stepped through the open security web into the past.

The store smelled of herbs and leather and metal polish. Kyla strode down the long centre aisle, its shelves just short enough for her to see over (many people wouldn't have been able to), cluttered with glass objects and crystals and cutlery and mugs, the rafters above hung with all manner of herbs and dried flowers grown with the help of Touch energy to become more than your regular condiments and garnishes, ignoring the wire racks on the walls full of boots that might give you a tiny boost of good luck if you allowed them to guide your footsteps, or scarves that helped protect you from airborne illness, or any manner of other small magicks.

Nowhere in the world had such a large collection of artefacts, Touch-touched items, been amassed in the thirty or forty years since Touches had first appeared in the general population, and no one was more expert in their usage and application than Alethea.

Of course, what most people curried favour with her for was her Touch, a red one, one that meant at the most basic level that the wielder could incontrovertibly sort truth from lies, but which for Alethea, whose Touch was deep, cherry red, highly saturated, fully developed, meant all she had to do was listen with intent for the answer to a question, and if anyone in the almost ten thousand square kilometres of greater Melbourne knew the answer, Alethea would know it too.

Toward the back of the store, a pair of clocks ticked dissonantly, slicing time into smaller-than-real fragments; between that and taste of dust and *age* hanging in the air, and the dim after-hours lighting, the whole place felt like a cocoon against space and time.

Actually, Kyla observed, heading down the centre aisle to the door under the clocks at the back of the shop, something *had* changed: the scent of lemongrass, lingering in the air, sharp and warm—and strong. Much, much stronger than it had been seven years ago, a sign that Alethea had clearly been practising her Touch. (Another mystery for the conspiracists: no one had yet figured out why lemongrass, why ozone, and why only other Touched could smell them.)

The click-clack of a shotgun loading stopped Kyla in her tracks as Alethea appeared at the end of the aisle, silvered hair piled in a bun atop her head, dark eyes sharp as ever in a face creased and lined like a well-loved letter.

"That's far enough." Alethea's voice was level as a pond—and cool as frost. "I told you. This had better be an emergency."

Kyla's hands had popped up at the sound of the gun, and now she lowered them slowly, carefully. "If I don't hand over the Touchstone by Friday, my father's going to die."

The scent of lemongrass strengthened until Kyla could taste it, and ozone permeated the store as though a storm had recently cleared. In the darkness behind her eyes when she blinked, Kyla could see deep cherry red, the colour of Alethea's Touch.

"You're telling the truth," Alethea said.

"Of course I am." Kyla managed not to sound offended, but really, what did Alethea expect? Kyla had known Alethea since the first waxing of her Touch, and Kyla wasn't *stupid*. "I'm also not at full power, so you can quit waving that thing in my face." She'd have shoved her hands in her pockets if she could, but the pockets of her shorts weren't deep enough. She settled for hitching her backpack, which had the advantage of rather prominently drawing attention to her gloved hands.

One of Alethea's eyebrows, at least, was interested. "Who'd you kill?"

She'd been around since the waxing of Kyla's powers, too.

Kyla shrugged. "Couple of strays."

Her pulse pounded. It was absolutely not a lie, because there had been an unfortunate incident with a stray cat that still made her chest tug, and besides that, all the cells she killed were technically straying from their owners, right? But as far as she knew, no one else had figured out that her cursed kind of Touch energy could be discharged off onto anything other than a complete and entire human being, and although she still had nightmares about the years she'd been forced to choose who around her would live and who around her would die, she knew perfectly well that it benefited her reputation for people to... assume things.

Would the omission count as a lie to Alethea's Touch, though, that was the question.

Kyla forced her body language to remain languid and nonchalant, her breathing regular, neither overly fast nor overly deep.

Alethea sighed dramatically. "There's something you're not telling me, but I guess history's gotta be worth something, don't it." She lowered the shotgun. "Fine." Her gaze flicked to the old, square clock above the door that led out back, gleaming white in the dim light, a stark contrast to the worn, dusty aura of the rest of the store. "'Bout closing time any-ways," she muttered, despite the fact that the majority of her business was done in the hours between official closing time and midnight. "You go on back to the front and lock the door. I'll put the kettle on."

Obediently, Kyla headed back and turned the lock in the brass handle of the front door.

The sound of a kettle whistling ushered her through into the back room behind the shop, the apartment where Alethea lived. The little kitchenette looked just like it always had, with its white chipboard cupboards below a scuffed, silver sink that had probably seen more days even than Alethea. The wallpaper was peeling away from the tops of the walls in places but for the most part the peach-and-cream floral pattern was just as clean and well-kept as ever, if a little more worn in places. The same chintzy armchairs gathered around the low Queen Anne coffee table, joined by an old-fashioned grandfather clock.

The door under the stairs, papered in the same peach-and-cream floral as the rest of the walls, hid the tiny bathroom.

Kyla wondered if it would still smell of eucalyptus disinfectant.

Alethea nodded Kyla to the chairs. "Black or green?" She lifted a pair of mismatched floral teacups.

"Green, please." She'd have enough on her mind interfering with sleep tonight without adding extra caffeine. She sank into the armchair closest to the back door and let her head loll back. Tiny dark-pink roses tangled around her on the cream fabric. Idly, she traced the pattern, looking for the trio she'd always imagined as a face.

Alethea poured the tea, docked the kettle, brought the two steaming teacups over. "Right," she said as she set them on the table and herself on the chair opposite Kyla. "I supposed you'd best tell me why your father's about to get himself killed."

Kyla's gaze sharpened. "He's not. I'll find the Touchstone."

Both Alethea's eyebrows were interested this time. "Will you now."

Kyla slouched. "Honestly? Probably not. Not unless you help me, Lethie. No one else knows anything useful about the Touchstone being in town, and until this evening I'd've sworn it was nothing more than a myth."

"How d'you know it's not?" Alethea, who had covered a twitch at the sound of Kyla's old nickname for her admirably, cradled her teacup on its mismatched blue saucer with hands lined and weathered but still steady as rocks.

"I guess I don't." Kyla frowned, watching steam curl up from her own teacup, still on the table until it cooled significantly further. "I guess it could be a misinformed threat."

"Or a hoax." Alethea's eyebrows gave another little bounce.

Kyla shook her head. "Dad's in hospital. Pippa thinks he might die."

A sharp inhale, followed by coughing. Alethea set her teacup back on the table and thumped at her own chest for a moment. "Blasted pipes," she muttered when the coughing had died down. "You say Pippa thinks he *might* die? Only might?"

That deepened Kyla's frown. "The hospital disagree. Pippa said they think he's fine."

Alethea tilted her head to one side as though listening.

The scent of lemongrass and ozone rose slowly in the room.

It prickled at Kyla's skin, stirring up the urge to move, to run, to protect herself...

You're fine, she told herself. *You're safe. You know how this works. It's just been a while, is all.*

In the silence, the ticking of the grandfather clock beside her might as well have been thunder.

Was Alethea listening for anything to do with the Touchstone? With Kyla's father? *What?*

She forced herself to stay still and not fidget. Try her patience though it might, this was still significantly faster than wandering blindly around the city, hoping to stumble across something useful.

The steam billowing from her tea had slowed, so she picked it up and risked a sip.

Ow.

Still too hot, and now the tip of her tongue was scalded.

Scowling, she reached back toward the table—and looked up sharply as Alethea came back to herself with a shuddering breath.

Tension traced the lines of Alethea's body as she shifted in her seat to directly face Kyla. "The Touchstone," she said, "isn't the only thing in town."

Kyla shifted in response. Something big. That was what she'd thought talking to Blood, wasn't it. She pushed aside the sudden spurt of adrenaline in her belly. "Oh?"

Alethea shook her head, a brief, irritated gesture rather than a 'no'. "I don't know." Frustration laced her voice.

"Something's building. Something big. But people are being cagey, cautious. I don't know." She drained her teacup and set it back on the saucer with a little clink. "Be careful."

"Always."

"I mean it. Keep your allies close, Kyla. You weren't meant to do everything alone. You know what happens when you do."

The tea didn't burn her mouth this time, and she drank half of it quickly, the slightly sweet, green-tasting liquid grounding her.

What allies? All she had was a sister who hated her for what she was, and blackmailers determined to kill her father if she didn't cooperate. Did Alethea mean herself? Doubtful. In which case... "I'll be careful," Kyla promised after she'd drained her warm teacup. "So the Touchstone is real after all? It's in town?"

They'd discussed the Touchstone once, back in the day, but Alethea's extraordinary knowledge extended only as far as her Touch could reach: back then, the Touchstone had obviously not been in town, and Alethea had known no more or less about it than your average person in the community.

Alethea nodded sharply. "It's here. It's not what you think it is. I can't hear more than that. But it's going to cost you something to find it."

"I didn't know your Touch extended to foretellings."

This time, Alethea's smile was wry. "Call this one a hunch. What's *true* is that someone is looking for you."

"What kind of someone?"

Alethea frowned. "Someone dangerous. Someone good for you. Maybe someone out to harm you. Maybe they're all the same person. Try the glass stores."

That was the problem with the truth: it came to you in its own time, in its own words, and usually not all at once, or even in order.

Kyla set the teacup down crisply and stood. "Then I'd better make myself available." She took a few steps toward the back door, the wooden floorboards creaking under her feet. "Thank you," she said turning back to offer Alethea a grateful, if not overly broad, smile.

Alethea was staring at her. "Be careful."

"You said that."

"So do it."

"I will." Kyla opened the door halfway, warm night air gusting in on a breeze that brought with it the sound of traffic and the smell of gathering rain. She paused, gloved fingers curled around the edge of the door. "I'm not going to cross the line, Alethea. No matter what happens this time."

Alethea pursed her lips, then hid her face in her empty teacup.

Sadness twanged in Kyla's chest—but that was the way of life, that sometimes one mistake cost people's trust in you forever.

So she slipped out the back door and headed down the metal fire stairs to ground level.

Above, clouds were gathering surely enough, beginning to obscure most of the night sky; if it was going to rain, she might have to risk finding somewhere indoors to sleep.

Kyla stepped off the bottom step onto the gravel—and tilted her head. In the scruffy area that might have been a very narrow yard or else a very wide alley where Alethea's building stopped short and the two on either side continued to the street, a strange, large shape lay crumpled on thin, scraggly grass, poorly lit by the streetlights from the road some twenty metres away.

A few steps closer, her feet crunching on gravel...

Kyla pursed her lips. She'd seen a dead body too recently to recognise this as anything but.

Two in one night?

She was absolutely going to have to be careful.

THE FACT OF THERE BEING A DEAD BODY IN THE ALLEYWAY behind Alethea's shop was not actually the most shocking part of the whole incident. The man was probably in his thirties, with a dark polo shirt and jeans, an expensive-looking haircut, great skin—or, well, skin that would have been good if... Well, you know.

No. The most shocking part, the part that sent a little thrill of adrenaline through Kyla's stomach and tripped her pulse, was that he was covered with frost.

Kyla shrugged as cold, rain-scented air gusted into the broad back-alley, goosebumps rising on her bare arms. She hitched her backpack and took a step away from the corpse.

Yes, the temperature was cooling. Yes, rain was obviously on the way. But regardless, it was still a hot, early-summer night, thick with the smell of warm garbage and hot concrete and car engines, and even now in the dim streetlight the frost that covered the body and the patchy grass around it was melting.

Kyla had a brief but gripping longing for the quaint little kitchen and hot, steaming tea she'd just left behind: if she was still in there talking with Alethea, the body wouldn't be her problem.

She sighed deeply. Technically, it still wasn't her problem.

Technically, a mystery corpse with mystery frost on a mostly hot night was...

She gave her head a tight shake and strode over the gravel, footsteps crunching. Who was she kidding? Of course she was intrigued. Of course she was going to make it her problem, because either this was some weird new colour of Touch or else someone had used an artefact to do this—and either of those definitely felt like her business.

She crouched by the body at the edge of the frost line, tilting her head sideways as she examined his face. Could have been handsome, maybe, if there'd been the right personality to animate it. She closed her eyes and focused.

No scent of lemongrass or ozone; no lingering, greasy feeling of Touch energy in the air; no particular colour in the darkness behind her eyes. Just the shifting patterns of warm and cold air as the brewing storm slowly encroached.

Weird. So weird.

Chatter drifted to her from the narrow, one-way street at the back of the block. She straightened and darted for the shadows.

A year ago, it wouldn't have been anything more than ordinarily suspicious for her to be found near a corpse wearing gloves. But last July, a black Touch had made headlines in the USA for murdering twenty people in a week before the authorities had managed to subdue them. Overnight, Kyla had gone from almost complete anonymity in public to outright suspicion whenever anyone spotted her gloves.

It had died down, of course, the suspicion: black Touches weren't very common after all, a thing to be grateful for on many levels. And she still preferred to wear the gloves for the little additional control they gave her over her Touch.

But still.

The chatter, however, turned out to be a small knot of teens in their best I'm-definitely-of-age clubbing wear who passed quickly enough without noticing anything askance. None of them gave off any scent of lemongrass or ozone; the colour behind Kyla's eyelids in between blinks didn't change. No Touched among them, just regular teens out doing what Kyla assumed were regular teen things.

She felt some of the tension ease from her shoulders as they swung out of view—only for it to ramp right back up again as an overly loud low-riding car that was undoubtedly meant to be impressive to the right sort of people screamed past, doing at least twice the very-slow speed limit of the one-way street, doov-doov music blasting at full volume.

Kyla rolled her eyes as it too vanished into the night—and glanced up at the clouds as the first icy spits of rain struck her cheek. Dammit. She really would have to find somewhere indoors.

For a brief moment she contemplated going back to Alethea. This hardly counted as an emergency, though, and she didn't want to see the look on Alethea's face if she said no.

Kyla huffed a sigh, straightened, and hitched her backpack again. She'd head a few blocks north to a school she'd found on her maps app, see if maybe they'd left a convenient gate unlocked so she could at least find somewhere under cover. Outdoor locker bays made great emergency bedrooms and were pretty much only beaten by cemeteries for places the general public wouldn't go at night, although much would depend on the level of security the school had invested in.

The frost was nearly all melted from the corpse now, nothing but a puddle of water faintly catching the street-lights. But...

Kyla paused. There, in the soft part between the man's chest and shoulder... a dark stain... And it was sparkling.

Not sparkling as in 'something wet like blood catching the light in the night', but sparkling as in 'some sort of foreign object lies herein'.

Kyla pursed her lips. A wound there shouldn't have been fatal.

Shouldn't be *shining*, either, no matter how much blood may have been spilled.

Her pulse skipped into high gear again. She stepped closer, wincing as her sneaker splashed just a little in the melted frost that was turning the dirt into mud.

The dark stain looked like it was probably a hole, about the diameter of her finger... and there was definitely something gleaming in there, something that tugged at every sixth sense she'd honed hunting artefacts the last thirteen years.

She crouched again at the body's side—and hesitated.

Making the occasional corpse because her cursed Touch didn't give her a choice in the world was one thing. Was she really about to stick her *fingers* into this one?

A noise on the narrow street again, lightly running footsteps.

Instinctively, Kyla widened her nostrils, breathing deeply, hunting for that feeling that she wasn't really smelling with her nose but which nevertheless smelled like lemongrass and ozone, the indicator that someone else with a Touch was nearby.

The scent was missing, but there was... something.

Huh. She'd never sensed anyone like *that* before, something adjacent to Touch energy that still somehow... wasn't. Strange.

Fluidly, Kyla stood and backed away into the shadows, easing her feet down carefully to minimise noise on the gravel. She could run, of course. Or simply stride purposefully out of the alley and down the street, vanish somewhere easily before anyone found the corpse and raised the alarm.

But whoever this person was, Kyla found herself wanting to see them. So she crouched behind a cluster of wheelie bins that stood against the neighbour's fence and held her breath —not because she was anxious, but because the bins had spent the day baking in the sun and they smelled like it.

She forgot the smell almost immediately, though, as a man entered the dingy space at a jog, slowing to a halt as though this was exactly where he'd been aiming for the whole time. His features were indistinct in the night, facing as he was away from the streetlights, but he was tall and broad with dark hair and skin that wasn't dark, but definitely wasn't pale either.

Casual shorts, basic dark t-shirt—and that slightly strange feeling against her senses, not someone Touched, but... something. She squinted, not to help her see better— pointless, in this light—but to think better. Maybe someone only lightly Touched? Someone with a tiny shard of talent?

She closed her eyes all the way, but couldn't detect a colour reading. If he was Touched, it was only very slight indeed.

Kyla pursed her lips and reopened her eyes. Regardless of his magical status, he was here and he was probably trouble, making a beeline to the corpse too purposefully for his sudden appearance to be coincidence.

He crouched by the dead man's side, pulled a phone from the pocket of his own shorts, flipped on the torch—and Kyla gasped as the newcomer stuck his finger into the wound that had Kyla herself had been contemplating.

That was nothing to the small, glassy something the man retrieved from the wound, a sparkly item about the size of a coin, glinting in the light.

The man stared at it for a moment, cupped in his hand. He seemed both to have expected it and be... what? Upset? Perturbed?

Kyla realised she was frowning in response to his frown and forced her face muscles to relax.

Between thumb and forefinger, the man held the strange glass object up to the dark night sky—

And Kyla couldn't help the twitch that ran through her. *Get a grip*, she told herself angrily.

But the sparkling glass object—was that a... snowflake... pattern?—drew her attention back as irrevocably as day followed night and water followed ice, gleaming as it did in the streetlight, seeming to dance somehow in the scant raindrops even though the man's hand held it perfectly still.

The air wasn't *greasy*, per se, but Kyla's skin did prickle with energy, the scent of ozone faint in the air, indistinguishable except to someone who'd had reason to become very, very familiar with that smell as a matter of life and death.

And when she closed her eyes... Kyla breathed in sharply. *Things* weren't supposed to contain Touch energy. But the glass object the man was still holding to the sky, sparkling as though he'd plucked one of the stars from the heavens for his own?

Behind the darkness of closed eyes, it gleamed *rainbow*.

The Touchstone: probably glass (although maybe obsidian—looked like Blood was wrong about that, though) and with its own aura, one that felt 'weird'.

You'll know it when you see it.

What else could it possibly be?

Kyla swallowed and wrenched her eyes open, fighting against the impulse to lose herself in the dip and swirl of pastel colour behind her eyelids.

It was so beautiful.

Like staring at this man, with this... whatever it was... Kyla breathed slowly and took stock of her body: relaxed, fluid... grounded.

She hadn't felt like this... ever. At least, not since she could remember, not since her Touch had developed along with puberty, marking her as an outcast at best and a death-sentenced abomination at worst. So: she couldn't remember *ever* feeling so... calm.

Literally, she could watch him—it—him—for the rest of her life.

Blood had said she'd know it when she saw it. She definitely couldn't be certain—she didn't *know* anything—but this kind of calm, beyond discharging, beyond any kind of Touch energy? *What else could it be?*

The man pocketed the glass object—Kyla sighed as faint disappointment wound through her chest, not for any logical reason but just because being within view of the probable-Touchstone was magical—and he tapped on his phone, and held it to his ear. "Police, please," he said in a voice that wasn't especially deep, but managed to be both rich and grounding in a way that made Kyla sigh again. "Hello, yes, I'm ringing to report a dead body…"

That jolted Kyla back to herself.

The man was giving the details of the place, of the body, calmly, matter-of-factly—but not without empathy, she noted, as he reached out to close the eyes of the corpse.

Kyla felt a brief tug of shame that she hadn't thought to do that. She'd been too busy trying to assess the situation, determine why a body on a warm night had been enveloped in frost.

In contrast, this newcomer seemed present in a way that unfurled a tug of envy in her chest.

But, if that really *was* the Touchstone… She shivered, not daring to finish the thought that maybe one day—one day— such a feeling of groundedness might not be out of her reach.

He hung up, and stared right into the shadows where she crouched.

Kyla couldn't stop her sharp little inhale of breath, rancid vegetable air hitting the back of her throat and forcing her to fight down an instinctual cough.

"I know someone's there," the man said conversationally, not much more than a silhouette sitting back on his heels now he'd switched off the light of the phone. "And I know you're not responsible for this." He gestured at the body.

Kyla held herself rigid, allowing only the tiniest amount of air in to barely inflate her lungs, enough to keep her alive and not an atom more.

The man shrugged as he unfolded up to his full height. "Suit yourself," he said. "The police will be here soon though." And, tucking his phone back into his pocket, he left the alley.

Kyla bounced her lower lip twice between her teeth, shrugging her shoulder to wipe away errant splatters of rain from her cheek. It might *not* be the Touchstone.

But on the other hand, it might be, and her job was full of moments like this: decide to chase and risk wasting time on an object that wasn't what you were looking for (although at least some of the time those wrong objects were cool artefacts in their own right that she could even sometimes persuade their owners to sell), or risk losing something that might be the very thing you were looking for.

...He'd barely been out of sight a second before she launched herself up from her hiding place and went after him, hardly sparing a glance at the formerly-alive man on the ground in his puddle of water that was now rippling with raindrops.

The other man, the alive one, had turned right, and was even now striding along a few houses down, weaving between a cluster of parked cars blocking the street that, together with a bassline she could now hear drifting on the night, suggested a party—and the gibbous moon was just rising into sight in the arc of sky visible between the two-storey buildings that lined the narrow street.

The party was her salvation: there were enough people drifting in and out of it that it would give her some cover while following the man, at least for this block. She set off, thumbs hooked into the pockets of her shorts, shoulders back nonchalantly despite her lengthened stride.

Her hair was getting a bit damp in the light rain and the humidity had skyrocketed, but at least the temperature was dropping.

A group of people—three women in sparkling tops that caught the light and two men in jeans—laughed their way past toward the party, close on the one-lane street. Kyla tensed as they overtook her, the familiar taste of ozone-and-lemongrass and the greasy, slick feeling in the air of someone Touched tagging along with them.

She took an extra-long blink and saw soft blush-pink splashed across the black behind her closed eyes—and breathed easy again. A simple good-luck Touch, and a weak one at that, or the colour would have been darker and more saturated—although it was a well-honed, well-practised Touch, given the strength of the smell.

Nothing to concern Kyla, at any rate, though goodness knew she'd be up for some luck this week if anyone had some to spare, ha.

On the other hand... She tensed, waiting for the moment when the other Touched person would sense her in return.

Ah, yes, there it was: the woman in the sparkling rose top missed a step, staring wildly around before spotting Kyla, studiously avoiding eye contact and grabbing the arms of her companions to propel them quickly onward while her lips pursed.

Kyla pressed her upper arm against the pendant in her bra cup, grateful as ever for it. Better to be feared as a grey Touch than persecuted as a black one.

A brief kerfuffle in the yard of the party house made Kyla glance up as she passed, expecting to see the blush-Touched woman and her friends; instead, a small crowd of people had gathered in the yard who were currently screaming in apparent delight while waving around flashing phones in the manner of people drunkenly attempting to take low-light photos.

A strong scent of lemongrass flooded out into the street, with sparks of all sorts of colours flashing behind Kyla's blinks—and that was definitely her cue to leave.

Kyla high-tailed it away as fast as she could without looking suspicious.

In the distraction, she'd missed which way the man had turned at the end of the street—and something tiny and akin to relief fluttered through her as she peered left toward the school and saw him ahead of her at the end of the block, just crossing the street that shone in the wet night like a narrow black ribbon.

She flicked a strand of wet hair off her cheek and headed down the road. And if her stride lengthened again, her pulse tripping a little, as she hurried along a road now populated with nighttime traffic and lit by stronger, warmer lights? Well, that was just because it had been a frigging long day.

Nothing at all to do with the man and his strange glass object.

She glanced left and right, and spotted the man continuing on past the school, probably heading for the train station a couple of blocks on, his shoulders shrugged against the light rain.

Kyla paused as a red car turned down the road in front of her, rain-splattered paint glinting in the streetlights. She jogged across the street to the block occupied by the school, hurried along damp pavement as the scent of petrichor rose around her, eyed the silhouette of the man still fifty or so metres ahead.

She'd been planning to stop here for the night, find somewhere sheltered.

If he was really going to the train station, it wasn't like she could keep following him. He could be going anywhere.

She couldn't follow him inconspicuously on a train.

But she couldn't let an opportunity like this get away. The Touchstone, right when she needed it? Maybe she'd caught some spare luck floating around after all.

Something hit her from behind.

Kyla shouted, an instinctive cry of surprise. Someone was clinging to her back—and it wasn't only petrichor she could smell, there was ozone there too, and the faintest trace of lemongrass.

Footsteps. A shout, the man's voice.

But the person who'd jumped her was Touched, which meant it would only take the barest instant of skin contact…

A hand grabbed her upper arm, shocking in its bareness.

And there was no colour behind Kyla's eyes, nothing except blackness.

Black.

She had the slightest instant for panic to surge through her as she plummeted to the pavement—and the world folded up around her and went dark.

6

THERE WAS A CLOCK TICKING. TICK… TOCK. TICK… TOCK. Tick… tock. A slow instant of tension before the tock, a two-tone rhythm of rise and fall.

Also she was somewhere warm.

Wait, why was she somewhere warm? She remembered falling to the concrete, the dark night, the smell of rain—and, almost indistinguishable, ozone, with a hint of lemongrass.

Someone had jumped her.

Kyla bolted upright, heart smashing at her chest.

It was a bedroom, a guest room probably given the sparse neatness of it, lit dimly by a streetlight peeking around the blind and light filtering in through the open bedroom door from somewhere out in the rest of the… house?

The warmth was a fluffy feather doona, and in addition to the clock, rain was spitting fitfully at the window.

Somewhere out there in the house, a TV was playing.

No footsteps.

Her door was open, so she didn't seem to be a prisoner...

She wriggled across the bed, legs still weighted by the blankets, and peeled the blind away from the wall with one finger.

She winced as the streetlight stabbed at her eyeballs. Ow.

Ow, oh, yeah okay, that had *not* been a good idea; the view of the street outside told her exactly nothing about where she now was, other than that she'd not travelled far—the houses were all the same narrow, single-storey cottages with their tin verandahs and white cladding and picket or else iron-railing fences one found most places on this side of Melbourne—and on the other hand, she now had a stabbing headache.

Gingerly, Kyla let the blind fall back against the wall and cradled her head in her hands.

Ow.

Oh, oh and her stomach was unhappy now too, and—

She gagged.

Flung back the covers.

Staggered from the room, hoping the bathroom would make itself immediately apparent.

"Oh hey," said the not-dead man, appearing in the corridor. "I thought I heard—"

She gagged again, hands pressed tightly over her mouth. Her stomach squirmed and twisted.

"In there!" The man flung open the door to her left.

Kyla half fell into the room, just had time to angle herself over the toilet—and the contents of her stomach made their appearance.

Far *out*, was this what it felt like to be flashed? *Urgh.*

She spat to clear her mouth of chunks and sour acid, squatting on tiles cold beneath her bare feet.

Abruptly, goosebumps broke out all over her body, and Kyla shuddered.

"Can I turn the light on?"

Kyla nodded without turning to look at him, breathing slowly as her stomach calmed.

In-one-two-three, out-four-five-six.

The light clicked on.

She ignored it.

In-one-two-three, out-four-five-six.

Bloody hell.

She wiped the back of her wrist over her forehead. Took another long inhale. Decided she could risk a very slow and careful stand...

Yep, there we go, all good. Look at me, being all upright and everything without shaking—or puking again.

"You okay?"

She nodded again, still without looking at him. Flushed the old, vintage toilet with its stained bowl. Crossed the tiny bathroom to wash her hands at a sink that had seen better days sometime before Kyla had been born.

The sound of the running water filled the silence between them and Kyla surveyed her face in the mirror: pale, now, strands of her dark hair plastered limply all over her like she'd stuck her finger in an electrical socket recently—or, in fact, like she'd gotten sweaty and rain-soaked and had then been flashed and then vomited, the sour taste of it still coating the back of her throat and her tongue.

Her eyes slid to the man at the door—and the adrenaline that pumped through her as she accidentally caught his eye wasn't entirely bad. Looked like he had something Polynesian in his heritage, and like he could have been making a fairly decent living playing football for someone fairly major if he'd wanted to.

She cast around for a towel, hands dripping cold water over the sink.

"On the wall."

Kyla turned and dried her hands on the chocolate-brown towel hanging from an uninspiring hook on the wall.

And froze.

Realised what she'd just done.

She'd washed and dried her hands. Her bare hands. Her bare, ungloved hands...

Her gaze snapped right back to the man, searching his face. Did he not know about the Touched? Did he know and not *care*? Had he never heard of a black Touch? Her heart hammered generally, but at the thought of black Touches it gave a double kick.

Instinctively, her hand went to her bra.

Her tension unwound, just a fraction: the cloaking charm was still there. So maybe he'd just assumed she was grey. Still a dangerous assumption, but slightly less deranged.

"Do you need to lie down again?" His voice was gentle, concerned, matching the little furrow in his brow, the slight downturn at the corners of his mouth.

And some more of Kyla's tension bled away. "No," she said—pleased to discover her voice was clear and confident. "No, I think I'm good now."

He nodded—and left.

Kyla stared after him for a moment before collecting herself enough to follow. Surely he had to know about Touch energy, though; he didn't stumble upon that shiny probable-Touchstone by happenstance.

She padded barefoot out onto the lino that covered the floor in the hall, rubbing her arms briskly against goose-bumps that were still pimpling her skin.

Where was her backpack?

She glanced at the dim room she'd come from, contemplating longer sleeves—and her gloves.

"Are you hungry?"

He was out in the room ahead of her, a kitchen-cum-dining-cum-lounge, small and just as neat and sparse as the room she'd been in. A round dining table for four, cheap yellow wood slightly scuffed; a couple of grey couches, worn and a bit baggy; a giant TV that seemed garishly new and out of place. The whole placed smelled of disinfectant and neglect—and Kyla wasn't at all surprised when she spotted something manual-ish discarded on the second couch, bearing a photograph of what was probably this house, in the manner of all short-stay rental accommodation internet-wide.

So. Not-Dead Man wasn't from around here.

And yet he had happened unerringly upon a mysterious corpse, containing a mysterious object. And came to the aid of a stranger being attacked.

Hmm.

Abruptly, Kyla abandoned the need to retrieve long sleeves and gloves alike. *You know what? If he's comfortable with my hands ungloved, so be it. His funeral.*

Kyla worked her mouth to get rid of the last of the sour vomit and slid onto the peeling black pleather barstool at the kitchen counter, staring fixedly at the marbled black-and-white pattern of the bench as though it was the most fascinating thing she'd seen all night, hyperaware of the air movement against the backs of her hands, cool little eddies driven by the air-conditioning unit above the TV.

"Water?"

She nodded. Watched as he filled a blue plastic picnic cup from the tap, old pipes rattling out their protest at being made to do work.

Deliberately met his gaze as he handed the cup across the bench to her, aware with every atom of her body of the nonchalant way he offered it, making no effort to protect his hand from hers.

She took the cup.

Their fingers brushed—and static leapt between them.

Kyla's heart leapt after it, her whole body coiled tighter than a piano wire, waiting for him to stiffen, gasp, collapse—and die.

That was what it usually felt like, to her, to have her Touch flash accidentally against someone else's skin…

But his dark eyes never wavered, and the corners of his mouth tilted upward a little as he nudged the cup against her frozen hand.

She took it. Swallowed nothing just to steady herself. Lifted the cup and let that break her gaze with the strange and extremely Not-Dead stranger as she sculled down water like she was dying.

Her Touch energies must not have accumulated so quickly today. They did that, sometimes, when she'd had a particularly exerting day, and although she hadn't really run anywhere or pushed her body to its limits, catching a long-distance bus five hours to her sister's house, hearing the news about their father, seeing Alethea again... well, it was all an exertion of sorts, wasn't it?

She plunked the now-empty cup back on the marbled counter with the hollow thunk of plastic on laminate. A final drop of water sat beaded on the cup's rim, catching the light with a tiny glimmer.

"You want more? Anything to eat?"

Kyla glanced up sharply—and her breath caught again at his dark, careful gaze. "Actually, some more water would be great."

One side of his mouth twitched. "If I'd known you'd wake up that thirsty, I'd have left something on the bedside for you."

Wake up. Right.

Kyla groaned and sank her head into her bare hand, elbow propped on the counter. "I was knocked out, wasn't I," she said as he filled the cup again from the screeching tap.

In her peripheral vision, tall-dark-and-handsome nodded.

"You brought me here?" She inflected it like a question, but it wasn't, not really, because obviously he had.

"I hope that's okay," he said, a note of anxiety tugging at his soft voice as he handed over the cup, again making no move whatsoever to keep his bare skin protected from her. "I, uh, figured you might not want to go to the hospital, and I'm staying here for a little bit. We're about a block down from the school," he added as she peered out the window by the kitchen and tried to see anything other than streetlight and black. "Right by the—"

He was saved from completing the sentence by the sudden roar and rattle of a train swooping past.

Kyla nodded. Going to the hospital would probably have been okay—it wasn't like they routinely screened for Touches, although that day was doubtless fast approaching—but on the other hand, it was... circumspect of him to bring her here instead. And given his activities earlier this evening, she suspected circumspection ranked high among his personality traits. "It's fine," she said, and a tension she hadn't spotted in his shoulders softened. "Thank you."

He nodded.

Kyla opened her mouth, thought better of it, and frowned. Maybe he had the Touchstone, maybe it was something else (she'd learned the hard way not to make assumptions in this line of work). But either way, he clearly knew things she didn't, and in a job like hers, you collected all the information you could, because you never knew when something apparently small and unrelated would turn out to be the key that unlocked it all.

It was tempting to drum her fingers on the counter as she thought. She settled for drumming her bare toes against the textured grey lino of the floor instead.

First things first, though.

"Why did you rescue me?"

He frowned himself at that, eyebrows lowering, the skin between them crinkling so that Kyla found herself wanting to reach up and smooth the creases away. "Someone knocked you out. I kind of assumed they weren't inviting you to a picnic, you know?"

She nodded—yes yes, good Samaritan, chase away the bad guys, etc—but it was more than that. There was something she was missing. "And you didn't take me to the hospital or call an ambulance because...?"

The frown deepened. "Should I have?"

She shrugged. "'Should' is a strong word. Most people probably would have though."

He shrugged back, frown giving way to an impish crinkling around the corners of his eyes. "I'm not most people."

"Noted." She tried to ignore the way a mirroring grin tugged at the edge of her mouth. "You took my gloves off."

That was it. A stranger might jump in and save someone who was being assaulted, might even take them home to care for them if they knew the hospital might be risky.

But if they knew enough to know the hospital might be risky… why would they remove the person's gloves?

He nodded slowly, a thoughtful, glacial motion. "I did."

"Why? Don't you… Aren't you…" She swallowed, shifting her weight on the barstool. It creaked. "I have to assume you know I'm Touched."

That long, thoughtful nod again.

"So why take them off? Why put yourself in danger?"

The look he gave her hands was speculative, and Kyla found herself suddenly very aware of the way her hands sat on the bench, abruptly awkward and completely unsure what to do with them; why did her hands feel so large all of a sudden? Oh hell, was that how she usually held them? Now she couldn't tell if her hands looked awkward or not—

She inhaled firmly.

My hands are fine.

"My mum *hated* wearing gloves. But she refused to take them off, even when it was only family in the room. I…" He took a deep breath. "I didn't want you to wake up and be uncomfortable. Sorry if it made you uncomfortable. Sorry." Not-Dead Tall-and-Handsome shrugged one shoulder in an awkward sort of twitch and headed to the couches. "But also," he added over his shoulder, "I don't think you'll hurt me."

Kyla slid off the stool and followed, adrenaline skipping her pulse along. *Had* she tried to hurt him when he'd passed her the glass?

…Not consciously.

She knew the risks, though. Hadn't tried to protect him from that.

Didn't want to think too hard about that.

"So what do you do for a living?" She perched on the couch, the one he wasn't sitting on. It creaked in protest.

The smile he gave was dangerous, but in a way that included her on his side. "I find people."

"What a coincidence," she shot back. "I find things."

"Oh? Find anything interesting lately?"

'Find any*one* lately' was her first instinct. But also... Kyla made a split-second decision. "I did. But someone beat me to it. You."

His eyebrows flickered up his square forehead. "Me?" The forehead creased in thought.

Kyla bunched her lips to one side. Wait for it... Wait for it...

There: the creases smoothed as it clicked for him what she was talking about. He dug into the pocket of his shorts and pulled out the small glittering object. "This?" He held it up as he had before, between thumb and forefinger.

A snowflake. A sparkling glass snowflake with six sharp, wicked points.

And behind her eyes, each time she blinked, the swirling, whirling pastel blaze of colour.

Kyla reached out instinctively—and he folded the charm away in his fist, smiling ruefully.

"Yeah, you don't want to touch that," he said, and tucked it back into his pocket. "There's a reason I found it in a corpse. You were the one watching from the shadows?"

Kyla nodded, that same faint ache of disappointment in her chest that she'd had the first time he'd hidden it from her sight. "Have you ever heard of the Touchstone?"

Oops. She definitely hadn't meant to blurt it out just like that—that had been the distraction of the shiny snowflake with the mysterious Touch energies, a strange object like none she'd ever seen before showing up *conveniently* just when she was hunting down a myth...

But whatever. She shrugged to herself. The direct route was a legitimate questioning approach too.

"Sure."

For a second Kyla's heart burst with expectation—it was the stone! He had it! She'd found it!—but instead he shrugged. "Popular fairy tale. Pretty sure everyone in our community has heard of it."

'Our' as in his and who he came from, or 'our' as in his-and-hers, which surely meant those Touched?

Frowning, Kyla ran her senses over him again, like taking an extra close look at something, but with a sense other than her eyes. Still that strange sensation, Touched but not—calming, grounding.

Which made her realise: aside from any adrenaline roused by the possibility of finding the stone, she really *was* calm—just like she'd actually flashed him earlier when their hands had touched, calm like she usually only got when her Touch energies were at their lowest, when they ceased being a tight, anxious thrum in the back of her awareness that built and built and built until—pop!—they exploded out of her.

Kyla settled back into the soft couch cushions with a sigh that was all exhaled tension leaving her body. She'd have to leave at some point, find somewhere to sleep for the night—but she could enjoy being cool and dry and comfortable—and glove free—for just a little longer. Surely.

Especially if she counted it toward research. "I don't suppose you've heard anything else about it?" she said, almost idly, disarmingly, letting her head drop back against the couch. "Only I'm supposed to find it is all, and if truth be told I have just one single lead and I'm not super confident in his ability to stay sane in matters such as these." Blood was all well and good, but he did rather tend to get carried away with conspiracies and cryptids.

Come on. I know you know something you're not telling me.

Kyla's host raised a dark eyebrow at her. "Who says you're supposed to find it?"

She smiled wryly. "The people who poisoned my father, that's who. Also"—she stuck out her hand—"I'm Kyla"—realised her hand was bare, went to withdraw it—

He took her hand firmly and shook it, eyes dancing again. "Tane." A two-syllable name, Tah-neh, definitely not English; she must have been right about his Polynesian heritage. "Who poisoned your father? Is he dead?"

"Not yet, and I don't know. I'm working on it," she muttered in response to his look.

"So." He leaned back, stretching muscular arms along the top of the couch. "You want the Touchstone so you can hand it over in exchange for your father's life, is that right?"

"Need, not want," she muttered again, then tore her eyes away from his arms to meet his gaze. "It's not a want."

He shrugged. "Po-tay-to po-tah-to."

"No one says po-tah-to, and no one says that keeping your parent alive is just a want, either." She knew her voice had gotten snippy, but also, add that to the list of things that mattered a lot less than finding a way to save her father.

He closed his eyes, face still, peaceful.

Too peaceful.

Kyla knew looks like that, and the brain-turmoil they were designed to hide. She narrowed her eyes.

Abruptly he stood, though the movement was fluid and catlike rather than jerky. "I'm starving," he said. "There's nothing here to eat other than cereal, but I'm going to order pizza. You need to eat."

It wasn't a question.

Pizza did sound good.

Her stomach rumbled, reminding her that two cups of tea since breakfast was a pretty poor way to treat it.

Halfway to the kitchen, Tane paused, glancing back over his shoulder and then away again. "I'd feel a lot better if you stayed here the night. Someone out there wanted to—hurt you, and you shouldn't be sleeping on the streets after an episode of unconsciousness."

Kyla frequently said nothing because she preferred to, or to make the other person uncomfortable. Rarely, however, did she say nothing because she was caught so entirely off guard.

This was one of those times.

"The guest room locks from inside," Tane added in a rush before resuming his path to the kitchen and snatching up his phone.

Warmth bloomed in Kyla's chest—not the heavy, sticky heat of early summer sweat, and not the deep satisfaction of a treasure hunt making progress. No. This was a warmth she hadn't felt in many years, not since the last time she'd seen Dad: someone cared about her wellbeing.

Maybe not in a personal sense; Tane would have behaved the same for anyone he'd seen attacked in the street, she suspected.

But that made the warm glow warmer, not cooler.

She wasn't accustomed to spending nights with men unknown—but even if her Touch did take another day to build back up again, well, she hadn't survived on her own this long by being defenceless. Her style of fighting was best termed 'street'—but it was effective, and she knew how to make even an opponent his size hurt.

She watched him phone the pizza place and order a pepperoni, then he put the phone down against his chest and called out in a stage whisper, "Seriously though, what pizza do you eat?"

"What if my Touch discharges in the night?" But her heart was already sighing dreamily at the thought of a proper bed—of her own, a bed to herself, the bed in the guest room that was—and her stomach was drooling at the thought of pizza.

She really should leave. It was the right thing to do.

But on the other hand, he clearly knew things. This was as good a lead as any. Viewed from that angle, staying practically made sense.

"Would it make you feel better if I told you I have something that can protect me even from you, and I promise to use it all night?"

He knew. He knew she was a black Touch, and he'd still taken care of her, taken her in, taken her gloves off and was offering to feed and shelter her.

Gnurgh.

She was not grinning. She was definitely not grinning and that was because her lips were pursed so tightly they hurt, but she was *not grinning*.

Deep breath.

"Oh, well, if you promise to use it all night," she said—and the grin broke out of its own accord. "Hawaiian, please. I'll take a Hawaiian."

7

TUESDAY 6 DECEMBER

TANE HAD BEEN GONE WHEN KYLA HAD FINALLY WOKEN UP— she literally could not remember having slept so long in her life—though he'd left a business card on the kitchen bench with a note saying 'Call me if you get stuck'. Tane Rangi, People Found, the business card said.

Kyla snorted, but tucked it away into her wallet.

Then, after a quick breakfast of the cereal in the cupboard Tane had mentioned the night before, she was off again. No point sticking around without Tane there to question—a quick and delicate rummage through his room had revealed that he'd taken the snowflake, the possible Touchstone, with him—and she was on a deadline.

Urgh. That was another thing she'd learned early on: keying in on the first item you saw sometimes meant you missed the real thing.

How sure was she that the snowflake Tane had was the Touchstone? Well, it fit every aspect she knew of the description. She'd definitely be back to question him some more.

But in the meantime, she was going to continue her search.

Kyla rubbed the side of her neck, stretching it out as she walked down the footpath to the soundtrack of passing traffic and, behind her, the occasional train rattling past. Cute cottages far more than twice her age lined the road that was still busy with morning traffic, most of the houses rusting around the edges, a few in dire need of new paint over their previously white cladding. The gardens trended cottagey, with soft aesthetic clumps and clusters, one with its picket fence tangled in jasmine whose warm, spicy perfume seemed even warmer in the hot morning air.

Today was going to be a stinker. Already sweat was pooling in all the usual locations, her backpack a hot weight against her back, her gloves making her hands heavy, hot, swollen—especially noticeable after the contrast last night and this morning.

Another thing she couldn't remember: the last time she'd had her gloves off for so long away from home.

A shiver spasmed down her despite the heat, a regular someone-walking-over-your-grave type feeling. But it ended in her fingers, and they buzzed and snapped as the energy left her body.

Since waking this morning, she'd felt like her Touch energy was coming back slowly, gradually. But once she'd left the house, even a scant block down the road, the energy seemed to be wanting to make up for lost time. At this rate, she definitely wasn't going to make it to dark without needing to discharge it.

Kyla eyed the passing cars nervously, and the woman across the street overtaking her with a bright red jogging pram. Parkland. She needed some parkland. Although she'd worked long and hard to ensure her Touch only caused death at the cellular level, she still felt uncomfortable discharging it around other people. Just, you know, in case.

According to her phone, the nearest parkland was east: back to the main road where Alethea had her shop, onwards another few blocks, and then maybe a half hour's walk north.

Kyla wriggled her fingers experimentally. The buzz in the back of her head droned at her in time to the rhythm of her moving fingers. Yes. She'd have to discharge the energy soon —but there was time to stop in on Alethea first, a decision made a little easier by the knowledge that Alethea was, if not infallibly, at least heavily protected.

This time, Kyla retraced her steps from the night before, down the one-way road, past the house where the party had been—now empty and silent, one front window open with a gauzy curtain billowing out in the warm breeze—past hot, rotten dumpsters that left a sick taste in the back of her throat… and through the yard space where, last night, a dead body had lain in a dappling of frost.

Kyla eyed the gravel-and-grass area, scuffing her shoe across the loose surface, the sound loud in the quiet street. But there wasn't even a damp patch to indicate where the body had lain; no lingering feeling of strangeness or Touch energy, not even a chill as Kyla eyed the bricked buildings on either side and positioned herself right where she remembered the body lying.

She glanced up at the now-sleeping streetlight and was hit with a fresh memory of its light glinting off the snowflake that Tane had removed from the corpse—the pastel rainbow riot of colour, the ache of longing—and Tane's warning that if she touched it, things wouldn't end well.

Kyla nibbled at the inside of her cheek thoughtfully.

What was he not telling her?

And how important was it in relation to her father?

Surely the object was the Touchstone, right? But if so, why had it been found inside a *corpse*?

She thought of the business card he'd left for her on the bench, tucked safely into her wallet in the innermost pocket of her backpack.

She sighed and headed for the weathered metal steps to the back door of Alethea's tiny apartment.

Tane didn't seem like the type of person to let information slip once he'd decided not to give it.

Didn't mean she was going to give up trying to extract it from him, though.

Kyla knocked on Alethea's door, this one teal like the front door to the shop but with fresher paint—had Alethea simply not gotten around to painting the front one yet, or was the peeling, worn look something deliberately cultivated?—and sighed again.

She smelled lemongrass and ozone, felt the oily touch in the air as Alethea worked her Touch on the other side of the door—undoubtedly checking Kyla's identity before opening the door.

Which, that definitely wasn't how red Touches were supposed to work, inasmuch as anyone knew anything about how the different colours *were* supposed to work; the internet had done a great job at collectively cataloguing the extant abilities, and while red definitely ran the full gamut of truth-and-lies, Kyla hadn't heard of anyone yet for whom 'truth' seemed to hold such a broad definition that it might as well have been fortune telling, people seeking, and lie detection all rolled into one.

Of course, Kyla added wryly as Alethea opened the door to reveal a questioningly pointed eyebrow, that didn't mean Alethea was any more forthcoming with what she knew than Tane was—and to be fair, from what Kyla gathered, it didn't mean Alethea necessarily *understood* much of the information she did have.

"It's business hours." The look on Alethea's face said that Kyla had better have a good reason for interrupting her during said hours.

"I just want to know if you know of any other black thumbs in the area," Kyla said hastily. "I'm not here to stay."

Alethea snorted. "Not sure if that's better or worse."

"Better." Kyla grinned as she gently shouldered the door wide enough for her to enter the little apartment that, this morning, smelled of toast and fried potato. She wriggled her fingers as they zinged again. "I'll be out of your hair again in no time and you can get back to unspooling the secrets of the universe in peace."

Alethea snorted again with even more conviction. "Kyla Jewel, the day you are out of my hair and leaving me in peace is the day you're dead."

Ordinarily, Kyla would have laughed at that like the joke it was. Today, though, after last night... She shivered. "I was jumped last night."

Alethea's eyebrows shot up. "By a black thumb?"

Kyla nodded. "Well. Dark grey. My pendant shattered earlier on the train."

Alethea's eyebrows climbed even higher, aiming, apparently, for the moon. "*Two* black thumbs?"

"A black and a grey," Kyla said, shaking her head. "It's the grey I'm most interested in, though." *Given their interest in me, heh.*

Alethea shook her head. "I don't know of any in this part of the city. Which isn't to say there isn't one, or that there isn't one passing through, just that no one's mentioned it aloud."

No one's mentioned it aloud, meaning Alethea couldn't have knowledge of it. Kyla sighed, hooking her thumbs into the straps of her backpack. "I was afraid you'd say that." The memory of her consciousness fading nauseatingly away gripped her again. Maybe she should start wearing long sleeves again for a bit, despite the heat.

Ew.

It had been years since she'd been at serious risk from another Touched.

Urgh.

She slung the backpack onto the floor with a thud. Alethea eyed her warily as Kyla dug around in the bag that even to her seemed almost magical in the number of pockets and compartments it held. She drew out a thin, long-sleeved shirt, smoke blue and made of light-weight linen.

Alethea untensed.

Kyla slipped the crushed and wrinkled shirt on and did up the buttons, then replaced her backpack.

"It's like that is it," Alethea said flatly.

Kyla's pulse leapt at Alethea's tone. She shrugged.

"Well." Alethea's pursed lips and abruptly folded arms telegraphed clearly what her next sentence would be: "I'll thank you to keep away from the store, if it's all the same to you, until you're finished getting into trouble."

Once, Alethea would have offered to help rather than turning Kyla aside.

Kyla gave a curt, business-like nod that hid the ache in her chest. "I guess you don't know anything about the body in your backyard last night?" She hoped their relationship was still good enough that Alethea wouldn't hide something of that magnitude—and the little start of surprise Alethea gave seemed to indicate that Kyla's assessment was if not *accurate*, at least not definitively *in*accurate.

"Tell me."

Kyla would have told Alethea even if she hadn't been so imperiously commanding—and so she did, summarising the pertinent events of the night, leaving out the bit about the conveniently good-looking stranger and his glassy snowflake trinket. (Partly a touch of embarrassment, but more so the lingering feeling of strangeness she felt even thinking about mentioning the snowflake. Somehow, it seemed like a thing that needed to be discussed as little as possible right now. Just in case.)

"And I suppose that's when you got yourself attacked," Alethea concluded as Kyla finished describing finding the body.

"Something like that."

She was saved from having to craft a version of the truth that would satisfy Alethea's Touch without giving too much away by her phone ringing in her back pocket.

She pulled it out—and winced heavily as a tirade began on the other end of the line.

"It's Pippa," she mouthed to Alethea, who rolled her eyes. "I'd better go take this."

Kyla slipped out the back door of Alethea's apartment with a quick farewell wave over her shoulder, and perched on the top step to tune in properly to whatever her sister was ranting about this time as Alethea closed the teal door behind her. "Pip," Kyla interrupted firmly. "I'm going to need you to start again from the top and be a little more succinct this time."

She squinted as Pippa's cursing hit her, screwing her nose up. The warm breeze brought her a faceful of garbage-flavoured air that seemed to fit the moment well.

"I was on shift last night, Kyla," Pippa shot scathingly. "Don't try to deny what you did."

Discovered a dead body? Tailed a strange man? Managed to get herself jumped? Spent the night—very safely, very chastely—at said strange man's house, ungloved no less? "Sorry, which one of my actions last night is supposed to have gotten me into trouble?"

Unless Pippa had been stalking her while on shift, there was no way for her to have known anything at all about what Kyla had or had not done in the last twelve to fifteen hours, however long it was since she'd parted ways with her sister.

"The body," Pippa hissed.

Kyla's stomach contracted. Tane had called the police, hadn't he? But he'd also said 'dead body'; maybe the police had brought an ambulance escort regardless? That seemed like a thing they would have to do, right? "What about it?" Kyla said cautiously.

"*Don't* play cute with me, Kyla Jewel. You have no idea what I'm—what our training is like this days, and I know a black Touch when I see one."

Kyla frowned, her forehead crinkling deeply.

A beat-up beige car clattered its way past down on the one-way street.

"Sorry," Kyla said. "Do you mean the guy had a black Touch?" She'd never heard of anyone's Touch being registered after they were dead, let alone the colour of their Touch…

"I told you not to play cute, Kyla. I covered for you. Do you know what that will cost me if anyone finds out?"

"I'm… sorry?"

"Sorry isn't going to bring someone back to life, Kyla. I thought you were—I thought you didn't have to—" Pippa's sentences tangled in frustration before exploding. "Why did you come if you weren't going to be able to keep yourself under control? This is the exact reason I worried about calling you in the first place!"

Kyla hunched forward, shifting her weight on the metal step, her long linen sleeves brushing against her arms. "Wait, you think *I* killed him? He was already dead when I got there! He was lying on the ground covered in frost! I know I can't prove that to you but you have to—"

"What, so I suppose a dead body just happened to be riding the train unsupervised"—Kyla's pulse gave a start—"the *exact train line* you were planning to use to get into the city, at the *exact time* you were planning to catch it? Wait."

Kyla could practically see her eyes narrow.

"On the *ground*? Are you telling there was another body last night?"

A long inhale. Hoo boy. This was *not* going to end well. "I know the incident you're talking about," she said, voice perfectly even and controlled. "But it wasn't me. I was there. The police interviewed me. It was…" She swallowed. "There was someone else, on the train. I gave the police the description, I don't know why you're haranguing me about it!"

Pippa drew in a long, shaky breath. Probably, she'd had a long night. "Tell me about this other guy, then."

"I was visiting Alethea," Kyla said as a flock of sparrows flitted past overhead. The rain had petered out overnight and the sky was patchy and overcast this morning, humid enough that Kyla's skin felt slick and wet even on her bare legs. "I left just after ten. There was a dead guy in her backyard. Another guy turned up just as I got down there. He rang the police. I'm at Alethea's again now, and when I got here this morning the body was gone. I assume the police picked him up."

Out on the main road on the other side of Alethea's shop, a tram rumbled past, a low, thrumming rumble with a metallic screek that got right into Kyla's chest.

Her pulse thrummed back, adrenaline pumping hot and white through her body, setting her building Touch energy jittering in the back of her head, in her shoulders, in her fingers.

The breeze was growing hotter by the minute. If the clouds continued breaking up, the sun would heat the dull metal steps she was sitting on to unbearable temperatures; even now she shifted again on the hard surface, the metal sticking to her sweaty thighs.

"So you didn't kill the man on the train," Pippa said, flat and emotionless as the gravel lot.

"No."

The flock of sparrows, six or seven, circled back and landed down there on the gravel. They hopped around, pecking at the sparse stalks of seedy grass.

"Have you made any progress on finding the, you know. The stone?"

"Some."

Two of the sparrows got into an argument over something they'd found in the gravel, a particularly interesting seed, or a crumb perhaps. Kyla's chest contracted as she realised it was right where the dead man had lain last night.

"I'll... Look," Pippa said, her tone softening a little, "I've got to work again tonight and I'm going to need to sleep, but if you meet me at the hospital at... eleven thirty? Yeah, that works. Meet me there at eleven thirty and I'll let you check in on Dad, okay?"

Kyla's chest constricted again, half bristling at 'let', half pleased that at least Pippa was choosing to believe her about the man on the train.

She sighed, suddenly feeling very heavy. Squeezed her eyes shut, pressed the back of her wrist against her forehead —sweaty, gross. "Yeah," she said. "Yeah that'd be great."

"See you." Pippa hung up before Kyla could say goodbye— and Kyla couldn't bring herself to be too sad about it, if truth be told (which—Kyla snorted—around Alethea's place, it usually was).

Another sigh that was as heavy as her body felt, and Kyla hauled herself up by the railing that left her brushing orange rust flakes off her gloves.

She plunked down the stairs, footsteps setting the metal ringing, dull boings that echoed in the narrow space of the yard. Halfway along the narrow footpath that ran the length of the fence, she paused and stared at the gravel that, last night, had been covered in frost on a warm evening.

Kyla frowned.

What was Tane not telling her?

...Whatever it was, she wasn't going to find it by standing here staring at gravel and drab grass, and it wasn't going to get any cooler. Alethea couldn't help her any further, her meeting with Blood wasn't until ten tonight, and now she had an hour to kill before risking a train ride to the hospital—and her fingers were feeling buzzy.

She'd better find that park first; the thought of what might go wrong if her Touch discharged in a hospital gave her a sick, queasy stomach.

Shoving her hands deep into the pockets of her cut-off denim shorts, Kyla headed for the one-way street. She'd follow it north, head east across the main road, find that park a few blocks away.

Another beat-up sedan drove past, white with a crushed-in rear, likely from backing into a pole.

Something prickled at Kyla's nose.

The engine noise dopplered away and Kyla watched the car round the far corner as, tense and alert, she stepped out from Alethea's property, out from the shelter of the brick wall, and onto the street.

Behind her, someone leapt.

Kyla whirled instinctively.

Snatched.

Grabbed by the wrist girl who looked no more than thirteen at best and appeared Asian, with straight black hair, dark olive skin, dark narrow eyes—and teeth she bared as she brought her free hand around, aiming for Kyla's face.

Kyla huffed away the faint taste of ozone and caught the girl's other wrist as well.

Behind her eyes, darkness—but as she examined it attentively, if hastily, she realised her assumptions had been wrong. This wasn't a grey Touch, though it was definitely the same one that had knocked her out last night. No. The girl now struggling and tugging against her immoveable grip had a dark Touch to be sure—but it wasn't grey. It was an extremely, extremely dark blue, something Kyla intuited more than saw.

She opened her eyes. The girl was still tugging half-heartedly, staring up at Kyla with eyes that had now wide with fear.

"Hi," Kyla said with deliberately saccharine brightness. "I feel like we've gotten off on the wrong foot."

The girl glared up at her, but she stopped struggling.

"I'm Kyla," Kyla said. "Why exactly are you trying to knock me out?"

8

"I ... I NEED YOUR HELP." THE GIRL WITH THE EXTREMELY dark blue Touch had stopped struggling entirely now, going practically limp in Kyla's grip. Any limper, in fact, and Kyla would be holding her up.

"Hey," Kyla said sharply, shaking the girl's wrists just a little. Energy snapped and buzzed in the back of her mind, prickling the tips of her gloves. "Hey, none of that now. Stand up." Definitely she was talking to the girl, and not the Touch energy boiling inside her. She gave a final shake of the girl's wrists for emphasis and let go, taking a half step back out of reach. The girl might lunge for her, sure—though if she did, she was also the best child actress Kyla had ever seen, as defeated-looking as she was—but Kyla's long sleeves would buy her enough time to deflect.

Her jaw tightened. And enough time to make sure her Touch wasn't going to flash in response without warning.

The girl drew in a shaky breath—which made Kyla realise that, despite the rich, consistent colour of the girl's Touch behind Kyla's eyes, there was no scent of lemongrass in the otherwise-fuel-scented air. *Great.* Kyla groaned internally as the girl straightened herself up. Strong and almost completely untrained.

Exactly what Kyla loved running into most, especially with her own energy prickling and misbehaving. Urgh.

A dark blue car rounded the corner, engine rumbling. Kyla side-stepped off the road, dragging the girl with her.

The car passed, and looking again like she'd found a functional spine, the girl lifted her chin and shook her dark hair out of her eyes. "I'm Eirene," she said. "And I need your help."

Kyla tucked her buzzing thumbs under the straps of her backpack. "Really?" she said as the flock of sparrows finished whatever they'd been doing in Alethea's unfenced yard and flew off overhead, twittering madly. "How exactly was knocking me unconscious supposed to help you?"

"I'm not *that* dark," the girl muttered, and Kyla wasn't sure if she was supposed to have heard or not—but either way it was illuminating.

Not that dark. Kyla's breath hitched. *Not* that *dark.* Meaning her Touch colour wasn't so dark it was only unconsciousness, which meant the girl—*Eirene*—had blue abilities. Mind control abilities. She might or might not be able to knock Kyla out herself, but regardless she could apparently force Kyla's brain to do it for her.

Kyla took a sharp step back, gloved hands squeezing her backpack straps. "Stay out of my head." It came out harsher than she'd intended, but apart from black thumbs, blue was the colour people were most wary of; no one liked having their thoughts influenced, or their memories rearranged, or any of the other mental-related talents the blue-Touched had exhibited so far. "Hey." Kyla squinted at Eirene. "Hey, why are you crying?"

"Do you know how hard it is to find a black Touch?" Eirene's voice was perfectly level, despite the tears coursing down her cheeks.

Kyla's pulse skipped. "Yeah. Yeah I do." Although the one last night had been easy enough to find, swanning around on public transport... Kyla's jaw twitched. Her fingers buzzed, and in the back of her skull, Touch energy jittered. "But I'm not a black Touch." She itched to check that the cloaking charm was still in place, but it had been there when she'd left Tane's, there was no need to draw attention to it.

Eirene raised her chin, hands clenching by her thighs. "You are. I'm a blue Touch, remember? I saw it in your thoughts last night. I know your Touch is black." She took a quick breath and continued before Kyla could decide how to react. "My sister is a black Touch. If you don't help her, more people are going to die."

"I don't even understand how you found me," Kyla said as she followed Eirene along the edge of a wide, green playing field backing up against another school. They'd walked for twenty minutes or so, mostly in silence as the heat of the day built, humidity thickening the air until it felt like Kyla was breathing through a wet blanket, the clouds overhead splitting to reveal the baking, blazing sun.

Kyla was actually glad of the linen shirt; at least it provided something to mop up all the sweat.

The playing field had been mowed recently, and hot, slowly decomposing grass scented the air, a usually pleasant smell turned overpowering by the heat.

"There's a network," Eirene said, trudging along in front of Kyla on the concrete path that slowly wound away from the street it had been paralleling. "Online." She glanced back over her shoulder at Kyla. "Tracking the Touched. You can log sightings on the app."

Kyla nearly stopped short at that, adrenaline clenching its fist around her heart. "That sounds... awful."

Eirene shrugged. "We're all going to be found sooner or later."

That was a nihilistic, if pragmatic way to look at it, Kyla supposed. She'd spent the last eighteen years trying her best to hide what she was; the thought of people spying on her and just... making her location freely available for anyone to find...

She shuddered. The implications of that were too horrifying to even consider right now. But next week, once she'd found wherever this Touchstone was and handed it over to save her father? Next week, she'd be booking a long and very in-depth appointment with Damon, the glassblower who'd made her cloaking charm. Surely there must be something he could do to help her veil her Touch even more.

"In here."

The path was now screened on either side by bushland: just a fringe on her left, blocking her from the school oval. But to the right, the bushland was sizeable—a wetland, according to her maps app, though it didn't seem particularly wet. Black and white and grey eucalyptus trees mingled with tea-tree thickets, intertwined with vines; shrubs and wild grasses fought for space with squat acacias, some still in bloom with their golden round blossoms decorating the space like tiny Christmas lights. It was messy, it was weedy—and it was no doubt full of spiders and insects and creepy crawlies and birds. Some of the tension knotting in Kyla's chest eased. She wriggled her gloved fingers, Touch energy buzzing.

Eirene pulled up a branch on one of the scrubby bushes, a roundish mass as tall as Kyla covered in tiny, slightly prickly leaves, and in sparse patches, tiny white flowers. A bee visited one of them, treading circles for a moment before settling into the flower, striped behind wriggling.

Kyla's Touch energy flashed unintentionally—just a tiny spark, she wasn't full yet, but she'd have to be careful, careful, careful.

The bee dropped dead, tiny carcass freezing stiff before slipping sideways from the flower.

Kyla stared at the now-empty flower, her chest just as empty. *It's just a bee, Kyla.*

But it had been years since her Touch had flashed outside her control. Years since any whole creature had died to sustain her.

The hole of grief in her chest yawned wider than she would have thought it ought to, given it was only a bee.

Kyla sighed pushed the blade of her hand over her sweaty cheek.

Sorry, she told the bee.

Eirene's head reappeared under the branch as, impatiently, she gestured for Kyla to stop gawking at the scenery and follow.

Twigs scraped at Kyla's legs as she pushed her way into the bushland, Eirene's footsteps crackling and crunching ahead of her on the leaf litter that blanketed the ground. Eucalyptus oil from the crushed leaves wafted through the hot air.

They walked for a handful of minutes in relative silence, insects chirping and whirring in the hot morning around them.

"Eirene," Kyla said eventually, "why—"

But she stopped short as Eirene did also, Eirene turning back to face her with fearful eyes, her lip snagged between her teeth.

And Kyla didn't need to finish her question; even without her eyes closed, the sense of oily closeness in the air telegraphed the presence of someone strongly Touched—and when she closed her eyes, the depth of the blackness there made her inhale sharply.

Eirene had said her sister was a black thumb. She hadn't mentioned how strong she was.

"Are you ready?" Eirene said quietly, eyes no less fearful but her shoulders thrown back, spine rigidly straight.

Kyla nodded.

Arms held high to avoid the worst of the scratching, scraping, clawing twigs, Eirene pushed her way between two low-growing, dense acacias. It wasn't the easiest path forward; anyone casually wandering would have taken the clearer route left or right.

Kyla followed her.

And stopped dead.

In a small, hidden clearing, hands covered with dirty, dark-blue socks, both wrists wound tightly with layers and layers of thin rope that bound her to the tall white gum tree behind her, surrounded by a perfect circle of dust and gravel, grasses withering and dying around the circumference, a teenage girl snarled.

Her brown skin and clothing alike were covered with streaks and clumps of dirt; twigs and leaves matted her black hair. Bloodshot eyes rolled as she jerked at the ropes restraining her...

...And Kyla had to stop, inhale carefully, precisely, push aside the memories that threatened to surface of the year she'd spent in the bush, at about the same age, looking about the same. Only this girl? When Kyla closed her eyes, the webs of energy were so thick the colour was solid—and it was purest, infinite black.

Ordinarily, even with eyes closed there were still afterimages, or a sense of light and shadow, the movement of pixels against the darkness caused either by the brain still trying to process information from the retina or the play of light through the blood vessels of the eyelid, or something.

Now?

Nothing.

Kyla might as well have been staring into a blackhole.

The air that moved past her face, her legs, was warm and humid... but to her other senses, it was dank, oily, a claustrophobic rag over her face making it hard to breathe.

She inhaled deeply. Opened her eyes. And—"Get away from her!" she snapped, lunging forward to snatch at Eirene's arm.

"What? I brought her food," Eirene protested, jerking her arm out of Kyla's grip and waving the protein bar she'd pulled from her pocket.

"Which is very admirable of you," Kyla said, "but please trust me. She is full to bursting and if she touches you right now, you're dead." Kyla fought the urge to bite at her inner cheek. *What would life have been like if I'd had someone to bring me bars?*

Eirene glared at her. "She's never hurt me yet."

"Does she usually look like this?" Kyla raised both eyebrows, tilting her head at the girl bound to the tree, teeth currently bared as she stared intent, animal-like, at the protein bar.

Kyla narrowed her eyes again. Something about the girl...

"Yes?" Eirene answered.

Only one eyebrow quirked this time. "This bad?"

Eirene slumped. "No. That's why I need you," she added with a furtive glance at Kyla.

Kyla exhaled. Right. Yeah. Not only did she have to find a mythical object in a city of five million people somehow in the next four days to prevent her father from dying a horrible death, now she also had to deal with the teenage human equivalent of... the Black Plague? A volcano? A volcano spewing Black Plague?

What was something that killed faster than Black Plague?

...She was stalling.

She frowned at the girl. Something about her...

Eirene was staring at Kyla, the gaze practically boring into her temple. "You... You can help her. Can't you?"

Sigh. "Yes," Kyla said. She glanced at the black thumb and shivered again as the weight of all that power focused on her through the girl's gaze. "A little."

Oh.

Oh. That gaze.

Kyla recognised it, even though last time it had been little more than a fleeting look, thrown over the girl's shoulder as she'd left the train, all desperation and grief and helplessness.

Here she was: Pippa's missing black thumb, the girl who'd killed the man on the train.

Heaven help us all, Kyla mused. If this really was the same girl, she'd flashed—definitely flashed, not discharged, there was no way that had been a controlled release of energy, no way—only last night, and already she was so full that the black energy snaked around the bushland, almost tangible.

"I can help her a little," Kyla repeated, hoping she wasn't lying. Last freaking night, and already she was ready to explode again.

Eirene nodded decisively. "I'll take a little. It's more than I can do," she added somewhat ruefully.

The nuclear bomb in the shape of a teenaged girl moaned quietly, jerking at her ropes, fixed again on the protein bar.

Eirene twitched it at Kyla. "Can I at least feed her?"

Kyla pursed her lips. "Unwrap it and throw it to her from here."

Rolling her eyes, Eirene tossed the wrapped bar to her sister. "She's Touched, she's not incapable."

Sure enough, the girl snatched up the bar from the dust, held the bar in one socked hand and used her teeth to hastily split the wrapper open. She bit into the bar with another little groan.

Okay.

Okay. How was she going to approach this?

"Does she talk?" Kyla asked as she and Eirene watched the girl gulp down the bar.

Eirene shot her a dark look. "She's as lucid and you or I unless the energy's too high."

"Right." Okay, that would make things a little easier. But regardless of anything else, she was going to have to draw the girl's power down somehow first; the girl was going to have to focus, and no one in the world could focus with that much energy raging through them.

A hot wind gusted through the trees—the breeze was picking up. Eucalyptus oil and hot, cut grass; dust and the faintest, remotest sliver of lemongrass.

The black-Touched girl, now sprawled against the gum tree in the dust, a smear of protein bar joining the dirt on her face, eyed Kyla warily, a feral wolf half-mad from fighting the energy threatening to consume her.

"What's her name?" Kyla said softly.

She *was* fighting the energy, Kyla could see now. She recognised that strain around the eyes, the tight, tense feeling in the clearing as the Touch energy blistered and boiled— the clammy feeling of restraint, rather than how the energy felt when it was let free.

"Lyssa," Eirene said, rhyming the first syllable with 'my'.

Kyla exhaled loudly through her nose. The girl was fighting it with everything she had—and she'd just flashed last night—and if she didn't discharge again soon, the energy would flash of its own accord—and this time, Kyla didn't have a pendant to save her.

If Lyssa flashed, Kyla, Eirene, or both, would probably die.

Kyla wished there was wall handy to gently bump her head against. Maybe that would knock some sense into her, because the *sensible* thing to do would be to turn around and walk away *very fast*, call the authorities—or someone, any-way—and let someone else handle this mess.

On the other hand... who could possibly handle this?

...She knew what it felt like to have no allies. No one you could trust, no one to turn to for help.

And who else in the world would understand that more than this girl?

So Kyla sat down cross-legged in the dust, right at the edge of the girl's—Lyssa's—circle of death where the yellow grass prickled at her legs, took off her gloves, held her bare, pale hands up to the girl, and said, "Are you ready to learn?"

Lyssa nodded.

Kyla drew in a deep breath, and began.

9

A GOOD WHILE LATER, KYLA LEANED BACK AGAINST THE white-barked gum tree that was still tangled in Lyssa's ropes, smiling with satisfaction. The humidity was a killer and she'd just as soon get out of the heat to somewhere that felt less like a sauna, but—she swiped sweat from her temple with the back of her blue linen cuff—this had probably been the most important hour of her life, aside from the year where she'd taught herself to do this very thing: in the middle of the clearing, Lyssa stood shoulder-to-shoulder with Eirene, who had a pair of binoculars out and was busily examining the nearby tree trunks for bugs and insects, pointing them out, and cheering as Lyssa flung out a hand in the direction Eirene had indicated to let a trickle of her energy flow out and zap the bug.

It wasn't perfect. Lyssa still lacked the finesse to target individual cells, but insects were a darn sight better than people if something had to die. There'd been a hairy incident in the first fifteen minutes that Kyla was trying very hard to forget, uncertain as she was whether the amount of energy that had flashed out of the clearing was enough to be fatal to a passerby, but overall, good had been done. Lyssa could still slip and accidentally kill someone—but if she was concentrating, she could direct tiny sparks of energy out into nearby insects instead.

Luckily, she was good at concentrating. She'd had to be.

She'd also have to find an almost unlimited supply of insects at this rate, because her Touch built back up so fast she'd have to discharge out at bugs almost continuously—the Yee household would never have a mosquito problem, that much was certain—but it was something.

It wasn't perfect.

It was possible someone had died.

Probably not, but possible.

Regardless, Kyla let her head rest back against the gum's trunk and inhaled air that still smelled overwhelmingly of eucalyptus and hot, cut grass—but which was beginning to smell just a little more of lemongrass. Amazing progress in such a short space of time.

Shoot. How long *had* she been here?

Kyla pulled her phone out. Ten past eleven, shoot shoot shoot. "Guys?" she said, then repeated herself over Eirene's giggling. "Guys, I have to go. I'm late."

"For what?" Lyssa's eyes were wide with interest, nothing at all like the feral child she'd been when Kyla had arrived, though dirt still smeared her cheek and leaves tangled in her black hair.

"Never mind," Kyla said, and her stomach twinged. None of their business, especially not the reason her father was dying—especially not the *Touchstone*, though good lord, if anyone on the planet needed it, it was Lyssa, and that was a thought Kyla immediately quelched. "But I really have to go.

Can I..." She'd been going to say could she drop them somewhere, but without a car of her own here, there was little she could do, really. And they were obviously used to fending for themselves. Kyla's forehead wrinkled as she grabbed her gloves up from where they lay on the spiky grass beside her. "Where do your parents figure in all this? Shouldn't someone be wondering where you are?"

"I'm legally an adult," Eirene said with the air of someone pointing out the obvious.

Kyla blinked. Judiciously, she held her tongue and refrained from pointing out that she'd assumed Lyssa to be the eldest; thin and waif-like and half a head shorter than her sister, she'd pegged Eirene at about thirteen, but if someone wasn't paying too close attention, she could easily pass for ten.

Kyla stopped staring and gave her head a little shake. "*She* at least should be in school." She pointed at Lyssa.

Eirene folded her arms. "Where she's a constant danger to everyone around? No. I came to an arrangement with the school years ago. They help us out with resources, but formally, she's homeschooled."

"By you." Who had to be, what, two years older at most?

"And our dad, when he's at home. He works FIFO."

Kyla did not want to know. She did not—"And... your mother?"

"Dead."

Kyla's gaze slipped immediately to Lyssa...

Who folded her arms now too, a taller, broader version of her big sister. She tossed her wild matt of hair. "*I* didn't kill her. There was a car crash. When I was nine."

Kyla held both her hands up placatingly. "I said nothing." She began pulling her gloves on. "You'd better get yourself a pair of these," she told Lyssa, motioning her hands up to indicate the gloves.

Lyssa shrugged. "Why? It just paints a target on me for anyone looking out for the Touched, and unless they'd bound on I rip them off as soon as my energies get too high anyway, whether I mean to or not."

"I…" But really, what was there to say to that? Kyla shook her head, finished pulling her gloves on, and sighed. She picked up her backpack and slung it on. "Can I at least walk you somewhere? I feel weird just leaving you here in the bush."

The girls exchanged a glance.

"We literally live on the street backing the wetlands," Eirene said, still holding Lyssa's gaze. "But"—some sort of signal obviously passed between them, for she nodded and moved her gaze to Kyla—"you can walk us there if it'd make you feel better."

Kyla snorted. "Why do I feel like I'm the one being looked after in this situation?"

Lyssa grinned.

It was a good look on her.

True to Eirene's word, it was a matter of minutes to scramble back out of the bushland up onto the footpath, through the public carpark that fringed the wetland, and pass onto a cobbled street lined on the right with two-car garages, the top storey of the houses peeking down at them like interested aunties peering over their phones at the trio as their footsteps slapped down the road.

Kyla hitched her backpack and tried to ignore the feeling of being watched.

The third house on the right was the girls'. They let Kyla in through a wooden back gate that creaked gently to a yard smelling of jasmine and roses in the hot late-morning air. The pretty flowers lined a bricked path up to the girls' back verandah… where the back door stood open, the screen ajar, the door itself a yawning cavern into the house.

The girls frowned at each other.

Kyla's pulse skipped. "I take it you didn't leave the back door open when you left home this morning."

"No," Eirene said, staring at it.

"I swear, I will *kill* them," Lyssa said, leaping for the two-storey house.

Eirene snatched her back by the neck of her t-shirt. "Funny," she said. "But we are calling the cops."

Lyssa muttered inaudibly, then said, "At least let me check if anything is missing."

Eirene sighed long-sufferingly, but let her sister go.

Lyssa bounded up the two wooden steps to the back verandah, kicked her shoes off, and slipped into the house.

Torn, but burning with curiosity, Kyla toed off her sneakers and followed Lyssa into a cool, dim hall where she stood motionless, staring at a wooden side table decorated with carefully placed candles below a brass crucifix hanging on the wall. "What's missing?" Kyla said in a low voice.

Lyssa started. "Hmm? Um, yeah." She brushed past Kyla, back to the verandah where Eirene was on the phone. "Eirene?" she said, quiet but with an urgent kind of intensity to her voice. "It's gone."

Eirene stopped mid-sentence, mouth open wide.

A hot breeze wafted in through the open back door, warming Kyla's face.

"I'm sorry," Eirene said into the phone. "Just a second." She cupped a hand over the phone and stared at her sister. "Are you sure?"

Lyssa shrugged. "It's not there on the table. Who would have moved it?"

Eirene's jaw twitched as she squeezed her eyes shut tight for just a second. "Give me a sec to wrap this up," she murmured, then turned her back, uncupping the phone.

"What is it?" Kyla said, voice similarly low.

"Our mother's urn," Lyssa replied.

Something unsettling frissioned down Kyla's spine. "Oh."

Before she could think of something appropriate to say, her phone rang. A guilty twinge of relief surfaced as she juggled it out of her back pocket—and winced. Pippa. And it was half past eleven.

"Hi," Kyla said apologetically. "I'm so—"

"Where the hell are you, Kyla?"

Lyssa was standing in the cool, dim hallway again, staring at the table.

"I found your other black thumb."

"I told you to—wait, what?"

"The other black thumb," Kyla said patiently, flexing her fingers as they tingled. "The one who killed the man on the train last night?"

Lyssa shifted her socked feet on the floorboards at that, but her gaze didn't waver from the table.

"Where are you?" Pippa said.

"Ha, funny," Kyla said, drifting into a formal lounge room adjacent to the hall for a smidgeon of privacy, assuming the girls wouldn't mind. "I'm not telling you where she is so you can haul your cop buddies over here to arrest her," she continued in a low voice. "You can *barely* live with protecting me, and I haven't... you know... in years. Not that I don't appreciate it," Kyla added hurriedly as Pippa growled down the phone. "Anyway, I found her and she's only a kid herself, and I'm giving her lessons, so don't worry. I'm sorry I'm not at the hospital like we agreed. I could catch a train now...?"

"No. I've been up since forever and I'm on duty again tonight. I was doing this as a favour for you, Kyla. I have to head home and get a nap before my nightshift."

Kyla sighed. "How is Dad?"

Dark green couches that looked luxuriously soft edged the room around an intricate rug, a huge projector screen hanging on one wall. The dark curtains were drawn, giving the room a sleepy, private feel and keeping out the worst of the summer heat. Kyla scrunched her socked toes on the edge of the rug.

"The doctors think he's doing okay," Pippa said at last. "Stable."

"But you disagree?"

The room smelled faintly of incense.

"I... am not sure what I—think."

Kyla frowned. Something she'd just said nudged at her consciousness—a thought she'd nearly articulated, or a clue she'd overlooked...

"Look, I'm going to head home and hope I can catch Theo before he heads off to work, alright? I'll call you when I'm up again."

Oh, right, cops.

"Oh hey," Kyla said, only half registering Pippa's words. "Your boyfriend's a cop, right?"

"My *husband* is a *police officer*, yes."

Kyla's stomach flipped. "Wait, you *married* the *Spy Guy*?"

"He is *not* the Spy Guy, Kyla, his last name is Spyrou!"

"Your last name is Spyrou now? Wait, is it? Did you change your name? *Are you a Spy Guy now too?*"

Pippa hissed in frustration.

Right, okay, yes. She could deal with the way her stomach twisted later, could unpack the fact that her sister had gotten married without her, without even *telling* her, later, later when there weren't—something thumped out in the hall, and Kyla peeked out to see Eirene standing with her arm around Lyssa, phone tucked out of sight—weren't so many people in danger.

Far out.

"Um, okay. Right. Can he, like, you know: trace the call I got last night? See where it came from?"

"Yes, thanks Kyla, it never occurred to me to get the police involved when I'm literally married to them."

Okaaay. "Right. So, um, did he find anything? Who the caller was?"

Silence on the phone, punctuated by murmuring in the hallway.

"He needs your permission to trace the call, technically."

"Fine, yes, he has it, do I have to sign something?"

"Technically."

Kyla narrowed her eyes at the projector screen. "And *un*technically?"

Her heartbeat, thundering in her ears.

The girls, still murmuring out in the hallway.

A magpie, warbling outside the window.

"Pippa?"

An explosive sigh. "He has a lead. He's going to follow up on it this afternoon, but yes, if you can stop by and sign some paperwork he'd appreciate that."

"What lead? Who was it? Where did it come from?" Kyla's grip on the phone tightened.

"You know I can't tell you that. He can't tell *me* that."

"Pippa, if this really is about the Touchstone, if it really is real, I'm not going to be the only Touched looking for it. This could get dangerous. Quickly."

"Oh wow, gee, danger. Yeah, I guess Theo isn't used to that."

Kyla ground her teeth. "So, what? I'm just supposed to sit here and wait while your, *his* buddies, hunt down whoever's responsible for *poisoning our father*?"

"No."

Momentary hope—

"You're supposed to find the damn stone in case something goes wrong."

—crashed to the ground. "Right," Kyla said dully. "Of course." She rubbed the back of her neck, Touch energy tingling. *You just do your job, Kyla, go hunt down your plaything while the adults do the real work.* Of course, the Touchstone was hardly a plaything, and hunting it down could be life changing regardless... She sighed heavily. "Find the stone."

"That's your job, isn't it? Finding things?"

Kyla's hand went to the shattered remains of her pendant, the leather thong still hanging around her neck. She hadn't done a job that needed help from Damon in a while, and she'd need the pendant replaced as soon as possible regardless.

It was as good a place to start as any.

"Yeah," she told Pippa. "It is my job. Call me if your boyfriend shares any information with you."

"He's my—"

Kyla hung up, probably reducing her chances of Pippa sharing any information voluntarily to zero, but whatever. Pippa was right. This was her job. And damn it all, she was going to do it.

T HE TINY SHOPFRONT THAT PROVIDED THE PUBLIC COVER FOR Damon's real business glittered in the early afternoon light. If it wasn't for the fact that the kind of real estate he needed was so hard to come by, Kyla might have suspected him of renting the place solely for the way the afternoon sun slanted in through the handmade glass windows, lighting up the showroom with a thousand tiny rainbows as it bent through the glass sculptures that encircled the room.

The bell over the door tinkled as Kyla walked in; she paused for a moment, holding the door open to run a gloved thumb over the door's glass—transparent, but lightly textured, as though somehow it can been captured mid-flow and convinced to remain suspended here as a window.

The energy in her fingertips buzzed.

Damon had made the windows himself, Kyla knew, and that was why this store had roller shutters that pulled down tight over the shopfront every night: plate glass would have been expensive enough to replace, had something ever gone wrong; these handmade windows were priceless.

Well, probably not *priceless*, Kyla amended as she let the door fall gently shut, shaking her hand to dispel the feeling of static from her building Touch energies. Damon was a businessman as well as an artist, and the cynical part of her noted that the flecks and bubbles and inclusions that gave the glass its delightful character were probably also indicative of glass that had been made with significantly less care than, say, the filigree glass chandelier hanging overhead like glittering silver snow falling from a cloud of the finest-spun glass Kyla had ever seen.

"Can I help you?" An assistant appeared behind the counter, the smell of woodsmoke and hot metal flowing in with them as the workshop door drifted shut.

"Hi," Kyla said brightly. "Is Damon in? He made a piece for me a while back, as a gift. My Dad was so touched, I thought I'd see if Damon could make me another." She tucked her thumbs under the straps of her backpack and smiled broadly. The only necessary bit was the word 'touched', but Kyla never really knew how much the assistants were involved in Damon's more *custom* side of the business.

Of course, the fact that she was wearing gloves... Something twanged in her stomach; maybe Lyssa had a point about the gloves telegraphing what she was.

Anyway, that and the fact that the password was literally 'touched' meant the assistants would have to be a special kind of ignorant not to put two and two together, really.

Kyla forced her smile to stay in place, her shoulders to drop their tension.

"Sure," said the assistant with a shrug. "Just a minute."

The workshop door opened and closed again, with the brief gust of warm air and hot smells—metal, wood, paper, and of course, glass.

Kyla circled the store slowly while she waited: on one wall, metal hooks held charms and pendants innumerable, in the shape of tiny flowers or bees or hummingbirds, even a couple of vehicles in crayon red and blue. Glass-bead bracelets hung over matching necklaces, beads mossy green and spherical or ocean blue and boxy or baby pink and organically shaped, like freshwater pearls.

Shelves of statuettes, leaf-green paperweight frogs and spinning lilac ballerinas, a primary-coloured robot balancing on a stand, a precarious yellow umbrella with glass so thin it seemed impossible, a huge, gold-winged angel as tall as Kyla's waist, playing a saxophone because why not, Kyla supposed.

Vases and drinking tumblers made rustic and a little bubbly, glass shimmering green or aquamarine where it thickened around the rim and the bottom circumference.

A marble-sized mirror made of strangely dark glass, only a handful of tones shy of true obsidian, edged with green leaves and white, star-shaped flowers so fragile that Kyla wouldn't be surprised to see real bees buzzing at them. Something about it made her shiver, and she almost reached out to touch it—what was the *point* of such an absurdly tiny mirror?—but she kept her thumbs tucked safely into her backpack.

The handmade windows masked the noise of the street, the passing traffic a dull mumble that ebbed and flowed; a fly bumped drunkenly in the warmth, way up high near the ceiling.

The whole shopfront would have been pleasantly drowsy if she'd come here freshly flashed—and without her father's life hanging in the balance.

Beautiful pieces, a stunning collection, artisanal price tags—and all of it a front for Damon's real work, which was crafting objects for the Touched, or those looking to be protected from them.

The workshop door opened again, and a short, balding man, wiry and currently shiny-faced, hurried through, still wiping his hands on a soot-streaked rag. Damon, unchanged in all the years since Kyla had seen him last, face creased and lined by years of larger-than-life expressions, both bright and not.

"Kyla Jewel," he said, beaming. "To what do I owe the honour?"

This time, Kyla's grin was entirely authentic. She hooked a thumb under the leather thong she was still wearing around her neck, the silver clasp dangling where it previously had held her protective pendant, the one that had shattered on the train. "I'm after one of your custom pieces again, I'm afraid."

Damon tutted. "Kyla Jewel, if there was no one left in the world, you alone would keep me in business. Was it smashed or overloaded?"

"Overloaded." Kyla pursed her lips wryly. "There was an incident on a train."

His eyebrows lifted. "The northern line? Two nights ago?"

She nodded curtly. "It wasn't me."

"Obviously, or you'd not be here needing a new pendant." The fleeting look he gave her indicated she had clearly lost several points of intelligence since she'd last visited, regardless of whatever else may or not have transpired.

Then he nodded, the brief, satisfied nod of a craftsman appreciating his work. "Well, it did its job then. Come."

At the far end of the workshop, past the furnaces and work stations with their iron rods and forked racks, past two apprentices busy at work, one blowing through a rod as he spun it deftly while the cobalt-blue glass at the end ballooned, the other standing by with hands at the ready to do.... whatever it was she was about to do...

...At the far end, another door, old metal with a patch of rust near the bottom, covered with dings and scuffs. Absolutely nothing impressive about it—except for the trio of locks that Damon attended to, first with a key from the ring in his pocket, then with a key that hung on a string around his neck, and finally with a passcode typed into the aging push-button panel above the doorknob.

The door screaked in protest as he opened and held it for Kyla. "One day I will oil that," he muttered as Kyla entered.

"One day I'll oil it for you," Kyla murmured, shrugging instinctively at the itch in her thoughts, eyes already on the locked glass cabinets that lined the walls of the small, crowded room.

They stood practically elbow to elbow in the centre as Damon let the door fall shut with another screech of protest. It was cooler in here; not cold like air conditioning, but not the heat of the workroom either. Pleasant.

Something sweet and sharp coated the back of Kyla's throat.

In the cabinets surrounding them from floor to ceiling, glass glimmered. Large, square-shaped pendants like the one she'd worn and marbles, mostly, colourless apart from the glint of golden light from overhead—blanks, waiting to be filled—and another mirror like the flower-framed, almost-obsidian one from out front, hanging above the tiny counter space on the opposite wall, which was really just a narrow section where the glass cabinet was waist-high instead of to the roof.

"There's so many," Kyla murmured, turning.

"Demand increases," Damon said with a shrug—but Kyla could feel the tension in the way he moved.

"More Touched, or more people knowing about them?" She'd spoken about her special abilities more the past twenty-four hours than she had in the last month, and she couldn't decide if it was getting easier to say the word each time without stumbling over it, or if it was escalating her anxiety that the wrong person might overhear.

Both, probably.

"Both, probably," Damon answered, echoing her thoughts. Another shrug. "People come to me, they ask for things. They pay with money, not with words." A hard little glare at Kyla where he thought she couldn't see.

Her lips twitched, an aborted smile. "I have money, Damon."

He sniffed. "We shall see, Black Jewel. We shall see."

Her brow furrowed. "No, actually: I have money this time. I promise."

"Perhaps first we should discuss what it is you are wanting?" His dark eyebrows lifted, chiding.

Kyla shoved aside the pang of disappointment. "A replacement protection, of course," she said, tapping the clasp on the leather thong once more. "And..." She inhaled deeply, that sweet, sharp taste in the air filling her awareness again—the taste of Damon's own peculiar brand of magic, not a Touch, but something related. Her gaze slid to the mirror, the only thing in the room not made of clear glass. "I don't know. Can I brainstorm with you?"

A curt nod. "Briefly. Time is money, young woman."

Her mouth might not have smiled, but her eyes did. She'd paid for her first pendant from him in time. "Okay. Okay. What do you know about the Touchstone?"

He shrugged. "It is a myth."

"Sure, but still: what do you know of it?"

Another shrug, his head bobbing, glinting lights reflecting off his balding pate. "It nullifies Touch energy, or so they say."

"Right. Which means it either fully blocks it or absorbs it, right?"

Damon dipped his chin in agreement.

"And you..." She turned a tight circle, gaze sweeping over the array of blanks. "You use glass to attract and absorb Touch energy."

"Ehhh." He squinted one eye tight and waggled his hand. "Absorb? No. It does not absorb. Cannot get the energy to stay in place, you see. But *deflect*? Yes. My objects are good at deflecting Touch energy, as you call it."

"Okay. So you get the glass to deflect Touch energy. Maybe the Touchstone does that too."

A leathery shrug. "Who is to say what a myth does or does not do."

"Or..." In her mind's eye, a sparkling crystal snowflake, gently pulsing with all the colours of the pastel rainbow. "Damon, how could you get an object to contain Touch energy? Energy of its own, I mean, without someone there to flood it?"

"Kyla, if you discover such a thing, please tell me, because then I will become an even richer man than I am."

Her breath caught. Tell him? Don't? She bit her lip.

But if anyone was going to be able to shed light on it, Damon was.

So: "I've seen one," she said. "An object. That holds its own Touch energy."

Damon pivoted to face her head-on, eyes widening, brightening. "You have not."

Disbelief, not an accusation of falsehood.

She nodded. "The colours were pastel, so not strong, but they were there. It was..." The words hitched in her throat, and she switched to a whisper. "It was beautiful."

Her Touch stirred as though in response, and she squeezed her hands into fists.

Damon stared at her a moment, something flickering in his eyes—hunger, if she had to guess. Not to possess the *thing*, but the knowledge it represented, the answers. The hunger to *create*.

"O-kay," he said abruptly, pronouncing it as two separate words as he whirled around and slid opened the doors of the cabinet behind him. "I was perhaps not going to show you this, but it seems... relevant."

He brought out a small object, and for a moment Kyla's pulse tripped, thinking he might be about to reveal another snowflake—what would that mean, for there to be two of them? There was only one Touchstone, after all...—but the object he showed her was glassy and a similar size, but very clearly not a snowflake. Instead, this object was moulded into a stylised bee, its wings pinned against its sides so it was almost circular, light refracting through it. "It does not contain Touch energy, as you suggest, but you must agree there is something particular about it."

Kyla took the bee and turned it this way and that, squinting and trying to focus her Touch senses on it. He was right. It wasn't that it held energy, but it was definitely an artefact of some sort, something exposed over and over to Touch energy until it took on a specific function outside the realm of normal physics. She let out the tiniest spark of her Touch energy into the object. The black energy slid through the bee, a fine strand entering the glass, travelling visibly through it—and then vanishing. "I've never seen anything like this," she said, handing it back to him. "It feels kind of like a cloaking pendant in that the energy seems to be deflected through it, but what's it cloaking? It's not absorbing the energy, from the feel of it"—artefacts that did that tended to change colour to match the energy they were absorbing until they hit critical mass and shattered—"but then where is the energy going?"

Damon's eyebrows bounced up and down. "Exactly." He took the bee from her and tucked it away in one of the drawers. "And I do not know. But I will find out."

Based on the determination in his eyes as he said it, Kyla had no doubt that he would.

11

T HE DAY WAS WANING FAST, PRESSURE BUILDING IN THE atmosphere that telegraphed an impending storm, and Kyla's thoughts were beginning to turn toward food.

She'd wandered through the city, letting her instinct for artefacts lead the way, visiting three stores so far: two general antiques who sometimes sold artefacts unaware, and the third a shop something like Alethea's, though significantly less specialised. She'd let the proprietors at all three know she was on the lookout for something special—but without a physical description of the Touchstone to leave, it was hard to imagine anything useful would come of it.

This next store, though, felt rather more promising. Nestled in between a New York-style pizza place and an

Indian grocery, the long, narrow store full of second-hand glassware was completely out of place in the downtown food district. Kyla had stumbled upon it entirely by accident—it had been the scent of pizza luring her down the road when the tiny storefront had literally caught her eye, the glassware glimmering in a sliver of light falling down between the skyscrapers as the sun continued its slow afternoon descent past the edges of the quickly building storm cell.

A red-and-white sign in the store's window proclaimed its somewhat eccentric opening hours: it was currently ten minutes until closing, and an early closing at that.

Pizza could wait another ten minutes.

Inside, the store's overhead lights glimmered off glass and dust alike; the light coming in from outside had taken on a strange quality, something almost green between the early evening and the clouds; glass shelves and glass vases and glass tumblers and glass platters and colourless glass sculptures and the way the narrow, two-aisle shop seemed to bore deep into the heart of the old building... Surely the shop didn't reach the whole way through the block? But the aisle seemed almost infinite, its end indistinct in lighting that managed to be glarey and unilluminating at the same time.

Kyla glanced back over her shoulder. She'd barely left the front door, maybe fifteen steps or so.

How long was it until closing? Surely she'd been here ten minutes already...

She breathed shallowly, a tingle running down her arms.

*Some*thing here was going to be useful.

Touch energy buzzed at the back of her thoughts, louder now, like tinnitus but *inside* her head. She shrugged uneasily. She'd siphoned off a little of the energy while training with Lyssa, but as close to flashing as Lyssa was, Kyla had needed to save most of the available bug life for her.

Tonight. Tonight she'd go somewhere wild, or as at least as wild as she could get, and drain as much of her energy as she possibly could. It wouldn't be calm, not all the way, but it would be enough.

For now, something here was going to be useful. Kyla took a deep breath and, running her fingers lightly over a row of glass tumblers on the shelf, wandered deeper into the belly of the store.

Thunder grumbled outside.

It was a perfectly straight aisle, even it if did seem infinite—so why did she find herself concentrating on where she was putting her feet, glancing forward and back as though trying to memorise landmarks in case she strayed and got lost?

Sweat was cooling on her skin, under her shirt; the further into the store she went, the more ferociously the air conditioning tugged at her, eddies of cold swirling around her bare legs.

She shivered.

Where was the manager? Or a store assistant, somebody? The sign on the door *had* said they were open...

Kyla nearly called out—

Something glimmered in the middle distance. She squinted, but the glint was gone as fast as it appeared. She tilted her head from side to side, trying to re-evoke it, but the entire shop was full of glass; there was plenty here to catch the light.

Another shiver.

Kyla stopped. Eyed the distance to the back of the store.

Turned to leave—

Oof.

"I'm so sorry!" Kyla stepped back, detangling herself from the woman she'd collided with. "I didn't hear you."

Blonde hair, ice-blue eyes. The woman smiled broadly with lips that even without makeup clearly belonged on a big screen. "My fault," she said liltingly. "I walk too quietly. So many people," she added, voice lowering, "tell me that."

Goosebumps rose on Kyla's arms. The woman's smile was just a little too rigid, her eyes a little too icy...

Kyla's pulse skipped. "No worries," she said. "I was just"— she glanced at the white blouse the woman was wearing, but there were no logos, no nameplate, nothing to indicate that it was a uniform of any sort—"just leaving."

A curling glass leaf hung on a fine chain at the woman's neck, the glass thin and fragile. Surely it was too fragile to be a pendant, but something about it snagged at Kyla's senses. What was she hiding?

Her gaze hadn't left Kyla's face, a slightly bemused smile ghosting across her lips, as though she'd noticed Kyla examining her pendant and found it... appropriate.

Something about the woman was familiar.

Thunder rumbled again.

Never mind. Kyla could untangle that mystery later. She made to leave—but the woman was blocking her way.

"Excuse me, I just need to..."

The woman's smile grew wider—and she didn't move.

Kyla's heart kicked again.

The buzzing in the back of her head, in her fingertips, escalated.

Tension wound through her body.

It's coming. It's coming.

Lemongrass, ozone...

"Please, I need to leave."

Heating, bubbling up in her chest.

No, no no no, not now, just wait, just wait!

That smile, those icy eyes...

Adrenaline smashed through Kyla's body in time with her heartbeat. Had she thought it was cold in here a moment ago? It wasn't cold, it was boiling, sweat was practically drenching her, her hands swollen and hot in her gloves, and the gloves were too tight, her hands were suffocating, but she had to leave them on, couldn't take them off, had to get past this woman and get out, get out, get away—

"Sorry," she gasped, and threw herself past the woman—but the woman caught her arm as she lunged, jerked her to a stop, wrenching her shoulder. "Let *go*!" Kyla said. "Now!"

The pressure, building in her head, her hands, gloves so tight they were going to crush her hands, she had to take them off, she couldn't breathe.

Lights, glimmering, glittering, the air like liquid neon, thunder cracking overhead and making the shelves of glass jump—or had the glass shattered, was that the noise?

Kyla bit back on a scream. Twisted around in the woman's bruisingly strong grasp, ripped the glove off her free hand.

It was like the storm clouds entered the shop; the light dimmed and the scent of ozone filled the air.

Energy, black and strong, coiled around her, squeezing, squeezing, the pressure in her head building—

Snap.

Something did shatter this time, something glass exploding, and Kyla's face and neck and the v of her chest exposed between the lapels of her shirt were peppered with tiny shards.

The woman let go of Kyla's arm, folded her own…

She wasn't dead.

She wasn't *dead*.

Kyla's heart pounded not only at her chest, but through her temples, her neck.

The woman's mouth curled cat-like around a smile; she ran the fine silver chain around her neck between forefinger and thumb, the clasp where the glass leaf had hung twizzling madly as she did.

Kyla stumbled. Clutched at a shelf for support. Raised her hand instinctively to her own just-made protective pendant —which was perfectly fine.

Of course it hadn't shattered; she had been the one releasing the energy, so the energy couldn't come after her, wouldn't be absorbed by her own pendant. It was just that the woman's pendant had shattered all over her. She brushed fragments gingerly from her shirtfront.

Drinking glasses tumbled to the floor as Kyla released the shelf she'd been clutching. One bounced. The others cracked.

"I'm sorry," the woman said in a voice that wasn't sorry at all, with eyes that danced and a smile that evoked a predator licking its lips. "I admit, I wanted to see what you could do."

The calm that came after a full and complete discharge blanketed Kyla; the lingering disorientation of an uncontrolled, unexpected flash shed from her like an old skin and she drew herself up to her full height. She had at least two inches on the woman and she used every one of them. "That," Kyla said, "was incredibly reckless."

She glared at the woman, tension coiling in her chest as the woman's predatory expression held.

The woman shrugged, giving her silver necklace one last twirl before releasing it. "I was in no danger."

"It's not your safety I was concerned about." If the energy hadn't been absorbed by the pendant, if a store assistant had come to investigate at the wrong moment... Anger, hot and sour, rose from Kyla's stomach up into the back of her throat.

She gave the woman one last daggered glare and left, striding back down the aisle—just a perfectly ordinary aisle full of perfectly ordinary glass gleaming under fluorescent lighting—with her chin held high.

It was only after she'd let the shop's door clang shut behind her, the cool, salt-scented wind bearing the storm front that had finally obscured the dying sun gusting at her face and tugging her hair from its ponytail, that Kyla shoved her hands—one gloved, one bare—into her shorts pockets.

Her first thought was a thrill of adrenaline at the fact that she'd left a glove behind.

Her second was a brief frown of curiosity at the cool, hard object in her left-side pocket—which quickly turned to a second spurt of sour adrenaline as she pulled the object out and stared at the perfect, six-pointed crystal snowflake, about an inch across—and with an aura that gleamed in all the colours of the pastel rainbow in the darkness behind Kyla's eyelids.

12

I

T TURNED OUT THE STORM HAD BEEN MORE BARK THAN BITE, A grumbling but ultimately harmless visitor swept briskly out to sea by a strong wind that had picked up as evening had fallen. Clouds still obscured most of the rapidly dimming sky, but the salty wind drove them along, leaving the sky an uncomfortable, haphazard patchwork of silver and bone, hot orange and blood red.

Another fifteen minutes, thirty at most, and the walking paths around the wetland near the Yee girls' house would empty out, and Kyla and Lyssa would have the privacy they needed to continue training.

For now, Kyla stared with arms tightly folded across the small murky pond, three ducks dragging ripples behind them that reflected the fires of the sunset, the smell of fresh water at odds with the saltwater blowing in on the wind strong enough to bring the ocean scent all the way up here from the coast.

Kyla picked hair out of her mouth and twisted to face into the wind, tucking her hand back tightly into her armpit. Somewhere in the scrub, a flock of corellas were settling in to roost, screeching and screaming and arguing; another bird of some sort gave a haunting, echoing cry as if telling the bickering neighbours to hush.

Kyla wished her nerves would hush.

She ran her fingertips lightly over the mysterious crystal snowflake in her pocket, its edges angled and sharp, though not enough to do any damage.

Tane hadn't let her touch the snowflake he'd found, had said it would be dangerous for her.

Her Touch had seemed not to work at his house—the house where he was staying—around the snowflake.

It *couldn't* be the Touchstone, because if *one* Touchstone was a fable, two was patently absurd.

So why did she have an apparently dangerous snowflake in her pocket? Well, presumably the creepy woman in the glass store had put it there, unless the things were known for spontaneous manifestation—which, Kyla wasn't ruling that out, to be fair—but if someone had deliberately given her one, and Tane had said it was dangerous...

Well. Either Tane was wrong or the someone—the woman—ill-intentioned.

Kyla snagged her nail gently on the tip of one of the snowflake's points. She wanted to pull it out again, look at it with eyes mostly closed, lose herself in the gentle swirl of pastel colours... The feeling that it induced—almost the calm after a discharge of energy but not quite, a little heavier, slower, hazier—she could see that becoming addictive. Fast.

Best if no one else saw she had a snowflake. You never knew when the wrong person might see. And maybe Tane was right; maybe the snowflakes were dangerous and she just hadn't figured out why yet. She'd hunted enough arte-facts to know they rarely revealed all their secrets the moment you met them.

The crunch-crunch-crunch of footsteps through leaf litter; Kyla glanced sharply behind her, hair tangling around her face again. It was Lyssa and Eirene—which didn't actually do much to settle Kyla's pulse—the former looking significantly less like a wild animal and more like a human being, with her dark hair more-or-less tamed in a ponytail, her face no longer covered in dust that had washed out her deep olive skin, and a light blue brand-name hoodie hanging its sleeves down over her hands so only the very tips of her fingers showed.

Bare fingertips still, Kyla noted. Hmm.

She squeezed her own bare left hand briefly into a fist. "You made it."

Eirene darted a glance up at Lyssa through hair the wind was raking its fingers through, the overprotective parent searching the face of their chronically ill child for signs of remission.

"I'm fine," Lyssa said—but Kyla noted the tension in her jaw, the way her fingers twitched when she said it—and the pulsing web of darkness behind her eyes.

Fine Lyssa might be, but she was teetering toward full charge again, or at least toward the murky zone where control became precarious.

"Let's get started." Kyla rubbed her hands together, which felt strange with one glove on and one glove off—and she couldn't bring herself to deglove fully, not now, not yet, not after what had happened in the store—so she stopped and let her hands hang awkwardly by her sides. "Over here." Striding down to the pond's edge was as good a way to shed the awkwardness as any.

The two girls followed.

She stopped right at the edge by a patch of thick reeds; water seeped into her right sneaker and she edged back. The wind nipped at her sleeves; her bare left hand felt electric, every air current magnified. How long had it been since she'd had a bare hand in public like this?

A thrill of something ran through her chest. Excitement? Fear?

Whatever. Lyssa was the focus right now, not her shockingly bare hand.

"Okay," she said as Lyssa settled in beside her with her chin held high against the wind and her ponytail ruffling. "Just like with the bugs, except this time you can let a little more power through."

A little was the key: it wasn't possible to use a black Touch to do anything other than kill. A little death was still death. But with practice—something Kyla had had plenty of—and rigorous control—something Lyssa had developed perforce —instead of letting the full volume of your Touch energies escape at once, the way they naturally wanted to, you could learn to open the floodgates just a tiny fraction.

This morning, she'd taught Lyssa to let out just enough energy to zap a bug. Now, she was asking for something harder: a wider flow of energy, enough to zap a fish. The wider the flow, the easier it was to lose control; the wider the flow, the *stronger* the flow, and the more likely you were to be swept away by the rush of energy clamouring to get out, to flash, to earth.

There weren't many people around now as night began to settle over the bushland in earnest—but there were enough if something went really wrong, with the occasional shout of people playing out on the huge green oval carrying in on the wind.

Kyla *really* did not want to be responsible for a homicide tonight.

Unfortunately, if she did nothing, a homicide would be practically guaranteed.

So she watched as Lyssa raised her ungloved hands, shook back the over-long sleeves of her over-sized hoodie, and relinquished just a fraction of her control on her energies. The scent of lemongrass filled the air, strong enough to taste.

Kyla inhaled sharply. "Have you stopped practising at *all*?"

Lyssa shook her head, a fierce pride in her eyes—but Kyla didn't need the confirmation. Lemongrass scent that strong? Lyssa must hardly have paused to draw breath. Kyla had never imagined it *possible* to go from so unpractised the lemongrass scent was barely evoked to such intense smell—and taste—in just a single afternoon.

"There!" Eirene flung up an arm, and the three of them squinted in the last of the twilight.

Ripples broke the surface of the pond near the far edge.

"It's a fish!"

Eirene was right: the silvery scales of a small fish caught the last glint of light from the sky, bobbing in the manner of dead fish everywhere.

Lyssa grinned.

Kyla... Well, she grinned back and even completed Lyssa's high five, smacking hands with her loudly. But unease stirred queasily in her stomach. Lyssa was so strong. And she'd developed serious control so quickly. There were people who...

Kyla swallowed and forced away the memories of the requests that had begun to trickle her way when she'd come back to civilisation, had started up a business where it hadn't hurt for people to know of her Touch, even though using it made her feel sick.

She'd talk to Lyssa about that another time. When the salt wind wasn't whipping against her face and bare hand and driving her to distraction, when she wasn't carrying a rainbow-auraed crystal snowflake in her pocket, when her father's life wasn't on the line if she didn't track down a mythical object by Friday...

Eirene cheered as another fish joined the first one, floating belly-up.

They should have gone to the beach, Kyla thought wryly. At least then they could have eaten their catch.

She inhaled deeply and shrugged a couple of times, determined to dispel her unease. It was fine. She'd put feelers out about the Touchstone today, she was due to meet with Blood soon; something would come of it, and look, here was Lyssa being able to go out in public without killing anyone, when just half a day ago she'd been practically delirious with that same power, tied to a tree for everyone's safety, including hers.

It was fine.

Everything was fine.

Kyla breathed deeply again, the salt wind and the pond water and the air full of lemongrass.

Strange, bluish light flashed from somewhere to her left, illuminating the reeds and the rippling water for an instant.

The three of them whipped around. The wind tangled Kyla's hair in her face again, and she dragged it aside, searching the bushland. Shrubs now skulked in the dark, and gum trees cast dark silhouettes against only slightly-less-dark clouds—except for one slice of sky where the clouds had torn apart, exposing stars that seemed to gleam too brightly over the trees.

Another flash of aqua-blue light, at the far end of the pond.

"Stay here," she muttered, and paced quickly toward the light.

Lyssa followed right behind.

"I told you to stay," Kyla said.

Lyssa shrugged, her hoodie rustling in the night. "I'm the most dangerous thing out here."

Kyla sniffed. Most dangerous, sure. But 'most dangerous' wasn't always warranted; sometimes it didn't pay to use a tank to conquer an ant hill. But they were at the end of the pond now, and Eirene had sprinted to catch up, and the aqua light had gone.

"It was right here, I think," Lyssa said, gesturing to where the pond narrowed to a small stream, only a pace or so across, the water trickling away into the bush.

Obligingly, the aqua light flashed again—and this time, it didn't disappear. It seemed to come from deep within the pond, farther away than Kyla had thought the bottom to be, and it lit up the water from underneath, making it glow and casting light upward on all their faces.

Was there something down there, causing it?

Kyla frowned and peered into the depths that shouldn't have been that deep.

There, maybe, something at the bottom, a slight movement?

She leaned a little closer. Just a little more…

Something shot through the surface of the water and snatched at her forearm, clamping around the wrist of her bare hand.

A child, a boy made of ice, transparent, glowing in the strange light.

Eirene screamed.

Kyla thrashed madly, trying to shake his grip, her gloved hand scrunched in Lyssa's hoodie, trying equally to hold her back. Her heart hammered wildly.

A second child burst through the surface of the water, a girl with pigtails and teeth like needles.

Kyla let go of Lyssa, caught her glove in her teeth, tried frantically to rip it off.

The boy tugged harder; she overbalanced.

Lemongrass and darkness filled the air.

The ice children screamed, a wailing, haunted shriek.

The boy's grip on Kyla's arm slackened—a little, a fraction, enough. Kyla wrenched her arm free as Lyssa pressed both hands against the children's faces, Touch energy coiling around and around and around.

So much.

It wasn't going to be enough.

Kyla ripped her glove off, ducked under Lyssa's arm and fought to grab hold of the boy's shoulder; *slippery, so cold, can't get a grip, hold him,* hold *him.*

So little energy left after the glass store earlier.

Wasn't going to be enough.

She let all of her energy flood out of her, her whole body clenched as though she could force just a little more energy through.

The children screamed again—

—and vanished.

Kyla stumbled forward, catching herself just before she tumbled into the water.

Lyssa wasn't so lucky; she'd been pushing with all her strength against the ice children, and she landed face-down in the pond, drenched with icy water.

The blue glow faded as Kyla scrambled to help Lyssa, Eirene racing to Lyssa's other side to prop her up.

"Lyssa, Lyssa! Are you okay?" Eirene ran her hand over her sister's face, pushing back wet hair, fumbling for reassurance.

"I'm fine," Lyssa gasped, flinging her head to shift her ponytail, a spray of water droplets arcing through the air.

The lemongrass scent faded.

Lyssa's legs crumpled. Eirene squeaked, clutching frantically to hold her sister.

Kyla steadied Lyssa from the other side until she was sure Lyssa could stay upright. "Take her home," she told Eirene. "I don't care what you have to do, go home and stay there until I tell you otherwise."

"But her Touch—"

"Lyssa," Kyla said, tilting her head to demand eye contact. Lyssa's eyes were wide and a little spacey, but she held Kyla's gaze. "You can siphon the energy off into bugs and birds now, right?"

Lyssa nodded.

"Good." *So much power.* Kyla suppressed a shiver. "If you're consistent with it, you should be able to last a day or two at least, okay?" *Assuming you don't run out of small innocent fauna.*

"But what if—"

Kyla interrupted Eirene with a gentle push. "Go! I'll contact you as soon as I can. But in the meantime..." She glanced back at the pond, the aqua-blue light entirely extinguished. Goosebumps prickled her arms. "She's in just as much danger out here as at home," she said in a low voice.

Some of Eirene's desperation flattened from her face. She nodded. "Okay." Her grip on Lyssa's arm tightened. "Okay. I'll keep her safe."

The knot of tension in Kyla's chest didn't ease as the two girls hurried away through the shadows toward the paved paths. Instead, her bare left fingers sought out the snowflake in her pocket, digging hard against the almost-sharp points.

Her phone rang.

She snatched it out—but no, it wasn't ringing. It was her alarm. Time to go meet Blood.

Sighing deeply, Kyla shoved the phone back into her pocket.

What have *I gotten myself into?*

KYLA DISEMBARKED THE TRAM AT THE STOP NEAR THE museum, the smell of hot steel and the tram's brakes apparent even in the gusty night wind—though at least here, a little closer to the coast and broken by the skyscrapers of the city just a couple of blocks down, the wind wasn't quite so fierce, and held a little coolness from the ocean.

She'd texted Blood to say she was running late. He hadn't replied, but that wasn't entirely unusual. He'd still be there. He had to be.

Kyla looked both ways down the night-lit street, tongue touching the corner of her mouth in response to the salty air.

The tram set off again with the high-pitched whine of metal-on-metal, silvering away down the main road.

Kyla crossed to the park side, away from the row of double-storey grey-bricked buildings with their decorative ironwork that haunted the corners like the work of monstrously large spiders in the night.

Blood had chosen the park as their meeting place as a compromise: public enough to keep himself safe, private enough that Kyla wouldn't complain about the number of people around. But even so, the dark, grassy space, dotted with the tall pillars of some sort of coastal conifers, bristled with far more people than Kyla would have preferred.

What were they all doing in there, anyway? Apart from scattered lights down the main paths, the entire block was dark, the grass an interplay of shadow except way over near the museum, where bright spotlights created stark highlights.

An audience was the last thing Kyla wanted—and Blood didn't want one either, not really, so they had planned to meet in the middle of the darkness at the end furthermost from the museum—but as Kyla hiked across lawns that squelched slightly underfoot, the scent of it rising around her, she spotted a cluster of people gathered in the night at the meeting spot.

A jet roared overhead, light pulsing like a heartbeat in the sky between the torn strips of cloud. Back on the main road, a siren wailed.

Kyla's pulse skipped; she took a heavy, slow breath to calm it and hitched at her backpack. Sweaty. Her hands were hot and sweaty even without gloves and she wriggled her fingers as she held onto her backpack.

Was that cluster of people really *right* where she was supposed to be meeting Blood? They milled and shifted, a loose circle buzzing quietly in the night, their voices muffled by the wind shaking at the sparse tree canopy far above, lit sporadically by any number of torchlights shining from their phones.

She trudged closer. There was no way that Blood would be there, not with so many witnesses. And if he was, he wouldn't want to have a lengthy conversation with her about anything Touch-related, that was certain.

She stopped ten paces or so away from the crowd. Pulled out her phone. Hopefully he'd still be somewhere nearby.

The crowd was milling around something on the ground —multiple torchlights swept over it briefly—her phone was silent for a moment as it connected, dialling Blood's number.

Quietly, it began to trill against her ear.

The crowd startled at something, shifting in Kyla's peripheral vision. She glanced over—

—and frowned. Somewhere close, a phone was ringing.

Close...

Slowly, she pivoted, her own phone still pressed tight against her ear.

A parting in the crowd, a confluence of torchlights: it was a man, lying in a puddle on the ground.

Kyla walked forward, heart pounding.

The torchlights converged on a silver phone, gripped in the man's out-flung arm.

A silver phone that was ringing.

She stepped through the circle of people and, with glacial slowness, let her own phone drop from by her ear. Hit the red button to end the call.

On the spotlit grass, the silver phone went dead.

A light passed over the man's face, but she didn't need it; it was Bloodhound, real name Jason Makris, lying on the grass with limbs akimbo and a hole burrowing through his t-shirt in the soft inner part between chest and shoulder, and he was dead, lying in a puddle that likely had been frost in the recent past.

The sirens had gotten louder and abruptly Kyla realised an ambulance was practically on top of them, jolting to a stop and spitting out paramedics—for one heart-stopping second the blonde woman looked familiar, but it was fine, it was okay, it wasn't Pippa, just someone with similar hair in the dark—who immediately knelt at Blood's side and began their work.

It wouldn't matter.

Kyla watched numbly as they loaded Blood's body onto a stretcher—*I suppose they have to*—how had she never thought about her sister loading a corpse onto an ambulance trolley before, lips pressed tight as she performed the various mechanics of her trade that necessity—and decency—demanded, all the while knowing—*knowing*—they were futile…?

A man was standing by the trolley as the paramedics prepared to load it into the ambulance, tall, broad, familiar.

Kyla's jaw locked as Tane swept a hand over Blood's chest, a casual gesture to the casual—or emotionally distraught—observer.

Kyla, however, with eyes narrowed, recognised it for what it was: the palming of a small object from Blood's chest—or, more accurately, from the hole in Blood's chest.

Something which, if she closed her eyes and concentrated, auraed pastel rainbow.

Fury clenched a fist around her heart.

The paramedics loaded the body that had once been Blood, closed the doors—the crowd ebbed and shifted—and Kyla stalked after Tane, pushing a woman aside with a little skip-hop and jogging a few steps to catch up as he strode purposefully away into the shadows.

"Hey," she said as their footsteps scrunched through the night-dark grass. "Hey!"

Tane turned, his face a dapple of shadow in the night. "Kyla?"

She stumbled to a halt, discombobulated. The snowflake—Should she mention it? Should she not?—Blood. Blood was dead, and he'd been going to help her find the stone.

Her father would die.

More people would die.

Her heart twisted.

The frost children had attacked her in the middle of nowhere.

Lyssa had no one else to turn to.

Pippa was going to hate her even worse.

Tane touched her arm and she stiffened, her cheeks suddenly cold in the wind—they were wet. She was crying?

Tane let his hand drop. "Are you okay?"

"Why did you take the snowflake?"

He frowned, his face all creases and wrinkles in the night. "The other night? When you were hiding in the shadows?"

Kyla smeared her palms over her cheeks. "Tonight," she said. "From Blood."

His frown deepened. "Blood?"

"The boy," Kyla said, tossing her head impatiently. "Man. The one just now, who was"—her gut twisted—"dead. His name was—he went by the pseudonym Bloodhound. Or he used to. When I used to know him."

She forced the words to stop, made herself focus on drawing in a deep, long breath that hit the bottom of her lungs.

"There was no snowflake."

Kyla froze for the barest instant, searching his face for signs of truth or lie. Too dark. She stepped closer, almost toe-to-toe, and tilted her chin up just a little so they were eye to eye, reflections from the lights back by the museum glinting off his. "Maybe someone else got there first then."

A curt shake of his head. "No. There'd be a second dead body nearby if that was the case."

Kyla resisted the temptation to tuck her hand into her pocket, to feel the crystalline snowflake resting there right now. Her heart hammered. If she concentrated, she could shift past the close awareness of his deodorant, something fresh and oceany, and just catch the lingering swirl of pastel Touch energy emitted by the snowflake in the front pocket of his jeans. Surely he had some way of tracking them down— he found them unerringly enough—and he'd sense hers, and then what would she say?

She rolled the side of her mouth in, ran her tongue along her lips inside her mouth, breathed deeply. "*You* touched the snowflake. Last night."

His gaze was focused, unwavering, and something less anxious thrilled through her chest. "*I know what I'm doing.*"

She let an answering smile curl lazily across her face and cocked a hip. "*Do* you just."

Was she imagining things, or did he lean a little closer, shift his weight her way just a little? She leaned a little closer in response, watching his gaze that never left her face.

"Two bodies, same mark, same probable cause of death. You said you find people. Are you hunting a serial killer, Tane?"

A hesitation. A slow nod.

A car backfired out on the road.

Kyla jumped, overbalanced, and clutched awkwardly at Tane for support, one hand on his shoulder, the other at his hip, hooked around the rim of his jeans.

He waited a moment while she steadied her balance, then took the hand from his shoulder, holding it gently for a moment as though they were dancing. "You're jumpy," he said. "I'm sorry about your friend."

"It's not just that," Kyla said, shaking her head as he let her hand go, shoving her hands deep in her pockets and hitching her shoulders. "I..." She searched his face again. *What do you know, Tane? Tracking serial killers, hiding snowflakes...* "I was attacked this evening," she said. "Twice, I think." Had the woman in the glass store meant it as an attack? Kyla had no idea—but it certainly hadn't been an innocent encounter.

Tane's reaction made his focused gaze a moment ago seem like a casual glance; at rigid attention, he locked eyes with her as though it was the only way for them to stay alive. "Explain."

Kyla shifted, uncomfortable with the intensity of his attention, unable to look away. Still, she sketched the two encounters out succinctly—leaving out any mention of Lyssa.

As she concluded, Tane swore, cutting his gaze with her, hands fisting at his sides.

"You think the second attack is related to your serial killer?"

"The dead bodies are covered in frost and marked with a snowflake, and now two kids made of ice tried to kill you? Hell of a coincidence if they're not connected." He folded his arms and squared off with her. "Look. I know you don't want to hear this, but you *have* to be careful, okay? Really, *really* careful."

Kyla shrugged. "Tane, it's not that I'm not touched and all"—ha ha—"but honestly, I'm one of the most dangerous things around." Her stomach squirmed, remembering how Lyssa had said almost the same thing—and how she, Kyla, had almost been dragged into the pond by the ice boy, all because she couldn't get her glove off in time.

She shuddered.

"You caught her off guard, Kyla. It won't be so straight forward next time."

Her? Caught who? "Wait..." Kyla's brows knit tightly together. "*She's* the serial killer?!"

A hesitation—and he nodded. "Freja Sne," he said with an exhale that sounded suspiciously like defeat.

"The *model*?"

Tane nodded again.

So *that's* why the woman in the store had looked vaguely familiar; Kyla knew her face from the posters, from TV, from everywhere—she was just used to seeing it fully made up. "What—But—*Really*?"

"Really."

"So why is she swanning around town doing whatever she's doing then?! Why aren't the police hunting her? Tane! What? What!" She scowled as his broad shoulders shook with laughter. "Tane, stop laughing at me this instant or so help me, I will hurt you!"

He didn't.

Kyla whirled away.

"Wait, stop." Tane put a hand on her arm, retreating immediately as she glared at it. "I'm sorry," he said, doing a fair impersonation of contrite. "But seriously. The police? Kyla. If you decided to go on a rampage, what exactly could the police do about it?"

Words died in her throat as she cast back to the train the night before. Maybe the police could stop *her* if she decided to rampage, but Lyssa? With a Touch that built up again that quickly, it was a wonder she hadn't put a more serious dent in Melbourne's population already.

Kyla sighed. "So what, she's just... getting away with it?"

"For now."

Kyla's eyebrows rose. "And I'm supposed to, what? 'Be careful'?" She sketched air quotes around the words.

Tane opened his mouth... and shut it again. "Yes," he muttered. "Be careful. And *call me* next time if you get into trouble."

"Why, Tane? Because there's a *serial killer* hunting me?"

He shook his head. Scrunched up his face. Sighed. "No." He walked away, heading toward the museum for a few steps before turning and walking backward. "But if you attract her attention again, there might be."

He turned, and Kyla rolled her eyes at his back as he left. *I didn't do anything to 'attract her attention'.*

When she was sure he was far enough away that he wouldn't see even if he did look back—and he hadn't, not once, not that she'd been watching, ha—she pursed her lips and reached into the pocket of her shorts, drawing out not one, but two of the gleaming glass snowflakes: the one Freja had deposited on her (for what purpose?), and the one she'd picked just now from Tane's pocket. She stared at them, identical twins that seemed to draw in what little light there was, glittering more than they should have underneath the patchy starlight and the shivering trees.

Kyla wrapped her fist closed around them and set her jaw.

Alethea's store wasn't too far from here. 'Unless it's an emergency' be damned; either this counted as an emergency, or it didn't. Regardless, it was time to get some answers.

Proper answers.

14

KYLA HAD SPENT THE TRAM RIDE TO ALETHEA'S SHOP debating whether to try the front door or the back door when she got there. She'd settled on the front door; this was technically a business call after all, and it was, Kyla felt, a little more polite, giving Alethea the opportunity to keep it strictly business. She might have allowed Kyla in for tea the other night, but Kyla was definitely not going to make assumptions. Not where Alethea was concerned.

Besides. If she pretended it was a monumental decision—which door to go to—it kept her mind off other things, like how Blood's face had looked so hollow under the flashing lights of the ambulance as they'd loaded him in on the trolley.

Kyla's jaw clenched as the tram ricketed to a stop, and she slammed the door on that line of thinking.

Alethea. The snowflakes with their odd knot of Touch energy, and Tane and the fact that he was hunting a serial killer, and how she was going to find the Touchstone in time now without any solid leads.

Tane would have to talk. She'd have to make him.

Somehow.

She clambered off the tram, the night air gusting steel and brakes and petrol from the main road against her face, and headed back down the street. At this late hour it was mostly empty, with only the occasional vehicle and just a knot or two of people leaving the last of the restaurants closing for the night—and many hadn't even been open, being a Tuesday night. Still, the scent of various cuisines mingled and twined around her like the comforting arch of a cat against her leg, savoury and complex and delicious.

Her stomach rumbled, even though she'd had a fairly substantial dinner earlier. ...Way earlier, it felt like now— before seeing Lyssa and Eirene for the second time. If it wasn't already eleven, she'd have planned to come back and grab something to eat after seeing Alethea: something that— she inhaled deeply—tasted like browned meat and chilli-soy and light, delicious spices.

Comfort food. Goodness knew she deserved a little comfort tonight, after all.

But of course, the restaurants were closing, so there was no comfort to be had there. How appropriate.

Kyla stretched her hands as she walked, the air brushing past her skin with unfamiliar intimacy. How long had it been since she'd walked around town ungloved? Her stomach flip-flopped. A long time, anyway, so long it felt somewhere between thrillingly risqué and just plain risky.

Blood would have been proud. He'd never worn gloves.

Not that his Touch got people killed.

Well, not *directly*, anyway. Kyla was sure some of the people he had hunted down over the years hadn't exactly come to a happy ending, but that was... a few steps removed.

Not immediately his fault, or the fault of his Touch. A consequence of his choices, rather than who he was.

Her jaw clenched again and she sidestepped a couple fussing over a pram in the golden doorway of a Thai restaurant. (Brave decisions had obviously been made there, huh.)

Across the road in front of a dark shop window, a knot of four people strode easily along, bunching loosely. One of them had an orange Touch—Kyla couldn't quite pick which one. She smiled a little, though; an orange Touch meant a seeker, someone who could attract objects to themselves, or hunt objects down easily—or people, like Blood did. She would have liked an orange Touch in her line of work; probably would choose one, if she could make a choice other than black.

Onward, closing restaurants giving way to long-closed cafes and bakeries and a plethora of other stores, until finally the yarn store, soft woollens huddling in the darkened display under the dim security lights, and then the door that led into Alethea's short alleyway.

Kyla reached for the handle—and froze.

It was the same poster as yesterday, the blonde B-grade celebrity from Pippa's TV, but tonight it hit her like a punch in the stomach.

Freja Sne, Danish model, hair coiffed in an elegant up-do, bright makeup highlighting ice-blue eyes that matched her strapless, slinky gown... It was an advert for an upcoming gala at the museum, some sort of charity event—and according to what Tane had told her, one of the event's top sponsors was a serial killer.

Had Tane seen this? Did he know what Freja was up to?

What *did* he know?

He was hunting a magical serial killer... She revisited their conversation from the previous night, when she'd talked about needing the Touchstone for her father. He absolutely knew something about the stone, and maybe the snowflakes were relevant—she squeezed the pair in her pocket through the fabric of her shorts—and maybe they weren't, but damn it all, that was it. As soon as she was done here, she was phoning him, and this time, she *would* get answers.

She entered the alleyway, climbed up the bricked steps to Alethea's second-floor door and knocked, some of the flaking teal paint coming away on her knuckles. She stared at it in the alley's fluorescent lighting for a second before brushing it away. What was the last time she'd knocked on a door bare-knuckled?

She shook her head—and the door unbolted.

Alethea cracked the door open, her shotgun highly visible where she clutched it to her chest. "No."

Kyla blinked. "Alethea, I—"

"*No.* Not this time. Not again. I won't be part of it."

"Part of *what*, Alethea?" If Kyla's voice sounded tired, it wasn't only because of the lateness of the hour. A jet rumbled overhead, and Kyla tried once again to sort through in her head what it was Alethea believed about her.

For someone who was supposed to be able to magically sense the truth about all things, Alethea had certainly managed to get hold of the wrong end of the stick about the last time Kyla had been in town. Alethea was utterly convinced it was Kyla's fault that Melina had been killed, but—

"Bigger things are afoot than you know, Kyla. I can't tell you. I can't risk that again."

Kyla frowned—again? She skimmed over the events of ten years ago, but couldn't match anything to what Alethea was saying. She blinked.

Big things.

Right.

"I know," Kyla said. Let Alethea take that how she would. She pulled the twin snowflakes from her pocket and held them up at Alethea, glinting in the fluorescent lighting.

Alethea hissed sharply through her teeth and withdrew, not quite closing the door fully, though it was close. "Get those away from here."

"Alethea, please, I just need—"

"No. Do not bring those in here."

The door snicked shut.

Kyla wrapped her fist around the snowflakes—their sharp points bit into her hand—she closed her eyes, bowed her head.

Just *one* useful answer. Just one.

She hadn't even seen her dad yet.

Sighing heavily of damp alley air, Kyla gave the snowflakes one last squeeze. She bent down, dropping one snowflake onto Alethea's doorstep with an audible *clink*, pocketing the other.

Grinding her teeth, Kyla stomped down the brick steps and threw her backpack on the concrete floor of the alleyway. She rummaged around for her wallet, then fished in that for the business card Tane had given her. Angling it to catch the light, she dialled the number, the brrrrg brrrrg of the dial tone in her ear as she slung her backpack over her shoulder and left the short alleyway, slamming the door behind her with a vicious clang.

"Hello?"

"It's Kyla."

His voice sharpened immediately: "Where are you?"

"Not important."

He swore. "Kyla, don't play games with me, I know you took the snowflake."

Kyla marched down the street, chest tight, cheeks flushed. "What snowflake? You said you didn't have a snowflake."

"Kyla!" He drew in a deep breath.

She kicked at a crushed lemonade can someone had dropped right next to a bin.

"I need—I told you to be careful."

Careful. Heh. Right. Too late for that. Kyla forced a smile, her voice saccharine and bright. "Sure, Tane. You know how I can be careful?"

"How?"

She shifted her grip on the phone as the tram rattled past. "I can stay at your house again tonight."

"You—Wait, what?"

"I'll stay at your house," she said, reaching the side street that led down to the school—and Tane's rental, "and you can babysit me, if that would make you feel better. On one condition."

She glanced both ways for traffic out of habit, but apart from the tram the streets were empty, only the cooling breeze rustling the scrappy eucalypts down the street and another jet going past overhead, red light blinking between swelling clouds.

"What condition?"

"I need information. Real information this time." In the distance, past Tane's place, a train rumbled, hurrying along to wherever. "If I really *am* in danger, I need more information. You said to call you." She hadn't meant for that last part to sound accusing.

It was late.

Someone she might have called a friend was dead.

Alethea wouldn't help and more people were going to die, and—

"You didn't call me when you were attacked."

"I was supposed to call you if I needed any help finding the Touchstone," she snapped, striding over the crossing by the school, "not because you neglected to tell me that you were hunting a serial killer! You say she's not hunting me, but you're also insisting I'm in danger. So which is it, Tane?" *And what the hell do you know about the Touchstone that you aren't sharing?* Her footsteps slapped the pavement, echoing in the quiet, lonely night, frustration bleeding out of her.

If he didn't agree, what was her next move?

Blood—literal dead end.

Alethea also, if less literally.

Damon—had given her all the help he could.

Maybe she could go back to the glass shop, where—she shuddered—where Freja had found her. Maybe her sixth sense had been sirening because Freja had been there, but— Kyla shrugged awkwardly, something itching and prickling at the back of her neck. There had been *something* about the store, something more than just Freja and her creepiness.

"Fine. Fine!"

Kyla jumped; Tane had been silent for so long, she'd half forgotten she still had her phone pressed to her ear, growing sweaty in the hot night.

"Come and we'll talk. Make sure you bring the snowflake."

Kyla squeezed it tightly in her pocket. "I will," she said. "And..." Clouds drifted past, stars flicking in and out of view. "Thank you," she whispered. "I'll be there soon."

15

KYLA REACHED TANE'S FRONT DOOR NOT A MOMENT TOO soon: rain began to spit fitfully in the night, shockingly cold against her still-bare hands. She ducked under the verandah roof, a shiver shaking her. Wet dirt, green things in people's yards—and warm toast.

She frowned, blinked the confusion away, and knocked.

Tane opened the door almost immediately—and sure enough, the scent of fresh toast curled out the door to meet her.

Abruptly, tears prickled the corners of her eyes.

Tane narrowed his own eyes at her in the dim porch light. "Yeah. You're not okay. I figured as much."

He ushered her through to the kitchen, directed her to the same barstool she'd sat in last night, and flung two pieces of apparently burning-hot toast from the toaster onto a white plate in front of her. "What do you want on them?"

Kyla shook her head mutely, fighting the drowning sensation in her chest.

"You don't want it?"

Still shaking her head, Kyla snatched at the plate.

"You *do* want it." The lines of tension that had been tracing his shoulders, his mouth, his eyes, softened away. "Here." He conjured a jar of lumpy red jam from a cupboard somewhere and set it in front of her with a butter knife.

She unscrewed the lid and set the jar back on the bench with a plunk she hoped would cover her sniffling.

Was this what it was like? To have someone on your side? To come home after a long, hard day to warm toast and someone who relaxed when they saw you were okay?

Damn.

It.

All.

Tane passed her a green tissue box and she mopped up her tears with a soft eucalyptus-scented square, inhaled shakily, and finished spreading the strawberry jam on her toast.

"Sorry about the lumps," Tane said, watching her try to spread it right to the corners of her toast.

She glanced up at him. "They're my favourite part."

His eyebrows rose. "Really? I hate them."

"Clearly, we are extremely jam compatible then," Kyla said, and took a bite far too huge to be polite. "No arguing over the lumps," she added around a mouthful of half-chewed jammy toast.

Tane let out a burst of laughter that seemed to surprise him.

It was charming enough that Kyla felt tension fade a little from her shoulders—and her stomach grumbled. She devoured the second slice of toast in record time, brushed the crumbs from her fingers—and sighed. "Thanks."

"No worries." He swept the plate into the sink and leaned over, resting his chin in his hand, elbow propped on the bench—effectively pinning her in place with the intensity of his gaze. "You have something of mine."

Admit? Deny? Excuse?

Kyla forced down the tension that was rising in her shoulders, dug the snowflake out of her pocket, and placed it audibly on the bench, covered by her fingers.

Her pulse skipped. She forced herself to move her hand—and the snowflake glinted in the kitchen lights, throwing out tiny rainbows.

She swallowed. Toast crumbs stuck in her throat, or something; she swallowed again, trying to shift the dry, scratchy feeling.

Apart from Tane, the last person to touch that had been Blood.

Well, assuming that one was his, and not the one Freja had deposited into her pocket.

Tane reached for the snowflake.

There was a tiny rainbow just to the left of it on the bench. "I thought you said they were dangerous."

Tane's dark eyes may have been focused on her, but they were unreadable as Kyla searched them.

"They are."

"*I'm* fine."

"So far."

"*Explain*, Tane. If I'm in danger," she added softly, "I deserve to know what I'm facing."

It wasn't a full rainbow, cast by the light through the snowflake. Just a smear of pink-red-orange. *Come on, Tane. Please?*

He unfroze with a sigh, and the quiet scrape of the snowflake across the bench. "I told you she's a serial killer."

Kyla nodded, pulse skipping. Was it time? Was she actually going to get some answers? She licked the inside of her cheek, the taste of strawberry jam still lingering in the corners of her mouth, toast crumbs stuck between two of her teeth.

"She uses the snowflakes to mark her intended victims."

Kyla recoiled physically, leaning back to put space between herself and the glinting glass snowflake, now cupped in Tane's hand.

He sniffed quietly. "I told you." His fingers curled around the charm and he squeezed it tight for a moment before shoving it into the pocket of his shorts.

Kyla swallowed. "How long does it take her to find them?" How *does she find them? Why plant a marker at all—if she has the chance to plant the marker, why not just make the kill?* "Wait, is that why those"—Kyla shuddered—"those ice children attacked me?" She slouched forward, pressing her forehead into her hand. Then, "And why are *you* safe from them?"

She narrowed her eyes through her fingers at the man who was, for all intents and purposes, claiming to be an ally. "If she's a serial killer and she tracks marks down using those, and honestly you've had at least one on you since the moment I first saw you, why aren't you dead yet?"

Tane's jaw worked.

Kyla straightened on the stool, the curve of its back digging across her spine. "Tell me!"

"I told you last night that I had something that protects me, even from someone like you." His gaze searched her face.

Kyla frowned back. "Yeah?"

"It... cancels out the tracking on the snowflakes. Deflects it. Like a pendant."

Kyla narrowed her eyes at him again. "Tane Rangi, so help me, if you have the Touchstone and you're not telling me, I will seriously consider murdering you in your sleep."

His lips twitched. "It's not... I don't have the Touchstone to give you, Kyla, even if I wanted to. And I do." He leaned forward over the bench, dark eyes holding hers with an intensity that took her breath away. "Please trust me when I say, I really do want to help you."

His tone was clear and guileless, but something in his careful, slightly odd choice of phrasing... *I don't have the Touchstone to give you.*

Kyla exhaled slowly. *Maybe* it was enough. Maybe.

...Hold on.

Hold on.

"Tane," she said carefully, glancing down at the pocket where he'd tucked the snowflake, "do they only work if she planted them, or is anyone who comes across one in danger?" Her heart pounded at her chest, liquid fire rolling through her body like a wave.

Only if she plants them. Surely it's only if she plants them...

Tane frowned. "I'm pretty sure anyone who's near them is in danger, usually, at least if they have a strong Touch—"

Kyla leapt off the bar stool, sprinting for the front door.

"Kyla? Kyla! What's wrong?"

How long had it been? Fifteen, twenty minutes?

Too long.

At the front door, she whirled back to Tane, clutching the door's cold metal handle, pulling the door to her like a shield. "I had a second snowflake," she said. Her stomach clenched. She opened her mouth—and shook her head.

No time.

Kyla sprinted out into the fine rain—and the door didn't close behind her, not for a moment, not until Tane had pulled hasty shoes on and sprinted out to join her. Then the door slammed—hard—and Tane was at her side before she'd reached the footpath by the road.

She glanced over at him, saved her breath to run.

Gratitude cut through a little of the panic knotting her stomach nonetheless.

They ran down the street, Tane a half pace behind, sweat building rapidly in the clammy humidity of the rain.

Out to the main road, a right turn past shops sleeping in blissful ignorance in the dark.

Kyla dodged a cafe chair that had been left out, lying haphazardly on its side.

The wool store.

The alleyway with its aluminium door plastered in posters.

Kyla snatched it open, baring her teeth briefly at Freja's poster.

At the top of the brick stairs, Alethea's shop door was open.

Kyla flung herself toward it, chest aching, throat tight. "Alethea," she rasped. "Alethea!"

Kyla tripped in the doorway, caught herself on the frame, paused to reorient in the dark as Tane stepped up behind her. Over the sound of her gasping breaths, the shop was quiet.

Adrenaline.

She was too late.

"Kyla?"

Relief. Alethea's voice was strong and clear, carrying from the back of the shop in the silence.

"I'm here." Kyla strode into the herb-scented shop, still catching her breath, sweat slicking her face, heating under her arms, soaking her tank top. Tane followed as she headed down the aisle, past the counter, through the door under the loudly ticking clocks to Alethea's apartment, where every light had been turned on as though expecting ample company.

Alethea bent over an open wheeled suitcase that faced them from one of the rose-printed armchairs.

Relief, pure like the gushing of a river; Kyla's knees wobbled as she stopped.

Something glinted in the light.

Kyla froze: Alethea held the snowflake up between thumb and forefinger, twisting it slightly so it caught rainbows.

"I told you not to leave this here," Alethea said.

"I'm sorry, I—"

"Here is what is true." Alethea raised her gaze from the snowflake to Kyla—and past her, to Tane. Alethea gave a small, sharp intake of breath—and her eyes creased into a ghost of a smile. "Oh," she said softly. "Oh, I see." A firm, decisive nod as though suddenly she understood all the secrets of the universe—and who knew? With Alethea, perhaps she did—and she settled her gaze firmly back on Kyla. "Here is what is true," she began again. "Now that she knows I exist"—she gave the snowflake a little twirl—"there is no power on the planet that will save me from her. No," she said at Tane's aborted word, "not even you."

"Alethea, surely there's something—"

"Which is why I am leaving town immediately, and will not be back. Here is what else is true," Alethea continued firmly. "You have time for one question only. Then *you*"—she nodded at Tane—"will make sure *she*"—a nod at Kyla—"leaves immediately. There is absolutely no sense in either of you getting caught up with her tonight as well. I don't need any kind of Touch to tell me how poorly *that* would end."

"Yes ma'am," Tane murmured.

"One question, Kyla."

Kyla squeezed her hands at her sides, pulse thundering. She'd left her breath back out there on the road somewhere, and her chest was tight, and this room had always been tiny but now it was absolutely *too* tiny, and...

And she had one question.

Now.

Immediately.

Come on, Kyla. What do you need to know?

...Oh.

She exhaled. "One question."

Alethea nodded, making a 'hurry up' motion with her free hand before giving up on waiting and resuming her packing.

"What is the most important thing for me to know right now?" It was tempting to add 'to save my father' on the end of that, but then equally she could have added 'to stop the serial killer', or 'to stay alive' or any number of priorities, and trying to choose between them made her stomach queasy. This way... This way left less room for bias, for error, on her part.

And Alethea smiled brilliantly. "Oh, well done, Kyla. What is the most important thing for you to know right now?" She cocked her head—and sagged, deflating at whatever truth it was she heard. She set her mouth grimly. "That something here will be your undoing. She is murdering people to steal their Touches."

Kyla's heart fairly exploded. "She's *what*?"

Beside her, Tane had gone rigid. A quick glance showed his face mirroring the shock that Kyla felt on hers.

"If I had more time, I could listen and tell you how. Alas." Alethea spread her hands wide and shrugged, the snowflake still poised between thumb and fingertip. "You promised to make her leave," she reminded Tane.

In a moment he was grounded back in the room, whirling to Kyla, all purpose and grim-lined efficiency, his mouth and eyebrows set in equally straight lines. "We need to go."

"But—"

"You heard her, Kyla. We need to go."

"Surely there's something we can do, something *you* can do." She was backing away as he advanced into her space, doing a little hop and a skip as she tried to peer around his broad frame for a glimpse—not the last, never the last, it couldn't be the last—of Alethea, folding her hands neatly in her lap and leaning back in the rose-printed armchair. "You said yourself the police can't handle her but you can. Tane!"

He caught her wrist in midair and her cheeks flushed as she realised she'd been swinging to punch his chest. "We need to go," he said gently. Carefully, he spun her around, pointed her toward the front door of Alethea's shop, gave her a nudge in the small of her back to get her started.

It was hard to see in the dim emergency lighting of the store—and the blur of tears. Kyla snatched at the doorframe as she exited, turned for one last bleary-eyed view of the store with its nine neat rows of shelving and the dried flowers and leaves and grasses nesting in the rafters, the crystals glittering under the exit sign to the right and the knives—

The knives.

Kyla ducked under Tane's outstretched arm and lunged at the nearest knife rack, snatching up a one with a pearl-inlaid handle that felt soft as butter—and a blade that glimmered obsidian black in the dim lighting.

"Kyla, you can't fight her," Tane said.

"Get *out*," Alethea called. "I... I'll be okay. If I leave now. If *you* leave now. Remember what I said and *keep your allies close*."

Kyla dodged Tane's grasping hand—and beat him out the front door. "I wasn't planning to fight," she muttered. But that strange sixth sense that she often had when hunting artefacts down, the one that made her so successful in her chosen career path? Something had suggested *very strongly* that a knife would come in handy—and she wasn't going to argue.

Halfway down the brick steps in the alleyway, Kyla froze.

What had she heard? Something over the noise they were making...

Tane tried to hurry her down, but she shushed him and held up a hand.

Knocking.

Someone was knocking at Alethea's back door.

Tane's face went tight. He widened his eyes pointedly at her and tilted his head to the street.

Kyla nodded, shoving down the sensation of her thundering heart, swallowing back the tightness in her throat.

Clutching her new knife like it might just save her life, Kyla padded quietly to the alleyway's door and eased it open.

Tane passed through, held the door for her while she followed, latched it almost silently behind them.

Kyla shifted the knife against her palm.

Stealing people's Touches? How was such a thing even possible?

She forced herself to sink into the disorienting bewilderment, forced herself to ignore the sound of Alethea's back door bursting open; focused on the sound of her own footsteps slapping at the concrete instead of that one shout of pain, firing from behind her.

She stumbled.

Tane stretched out his hand.

Bare-fingered, she reached back and took it.

WEDNESDAY 7 DECEMBER

THE WINDOW SCREECHED OPEN IN THE DARK, VERTICAL blinds rattling and flapping in the sudden breeze.

Kyla opened her eyes. The streetlight shone in, illuminating the bare room, nothing but herself, the bed, and shadows.

The rain must have cleared up in the night; stars sprinkled the black sky, burningly bright despite the streetlights. Bright—and cold.

She shivered.

Peeled the covers back, and stood at the window, staring out.

There was parkland, dark and cold, shapes indecipherable except as some form of trees or bushes clumping across the foreground, the mid-ground.

Behind them, a mountain of ice, climbing high against the horizon, gleaming in the dark.

She shivered.

Stepped forward through the window. Was under one of the trees, a gum tree, the scent of eucalyptus winding around her.

Somewhere beyond her, something rustled.

Her heart leapt wildly.

Something was out here.

Did it know she was here?

She pressed her back against the smooth tree trunk.

Whatever it was, she couldn't let it find her, see her. Dread clamped down on her, nauseating her stomach, shallowing her breaths, tightening her chest.

Her heart raced.

Something was out there in the dark—which, suddenly, she could see through; it was like inhabiting a world painted black on a cloudy day, everything still dim and shadowed—just… visible.

If she could see through it, probably so could… whatever it was.

She pressed harder against the tree trunk, a cold pillar of strength behind her.

Cold. So cold.

She shivered again, goosebumps prickling her arms and legs so quickly they hurt. Kyla rubbed at them with hands that were gloved—bare—gloved.

Snow began to fall, huge, exaggerated snowflakes the size of coins, each one burningly white in the dark. She lifted up her face, made to open her mouth, to catch one on her tongue—and one landed on her shoulder.

She screamed at the burn.

Cold.

Pain.

So cold.

Someone was out there.

A pair of ice-blue eyes, staring at her through the gloom.

Kyla's pulse shrieked.

She pressed hard against the tree. It dissolved, and she fell backward, landing—

Kyla sat upright wildly, gasping, bed covers knotted in her fists.

It was early. The sun was still low enough to gleam its way in through the narrow crack between blind and window frame, casting a thin slice of gold up the far wall and over the otherwise white face of the cheap clock on the cheap desk, ticking out increments of time.

She inhaled deeply, shakily... let herself fall back limply onto the bed.

Phew.

She hadn't had a nightmare that intense for... well, a while, anyway. So vivid, too. Usually her dreams dissipated almost instantly upon waking, but this one...

Kyla shuddered as a crystal-clear view of the dark parkland with the mountain made entirely of ice in the background reappeared, fear knotting in her throat.

Deep breaths. Just a dream.

She dragged a bleary hand over her face and indulged for a moment in wistful thoughts of rolling over and going back to sleep; sleep had been hard to catch last night, after everything that had happened, and she couldn't have had more than what, three? maybe four? hours of sleep.

When she'd finally drifted off, it had been to the sound of a storm going over, thunder cracking the sky and rattling the windows.

Apparently, the weather had decided to offer up a glimmering fresh morning as compensation.

Regret twisted in Kyla's chest.

Some things couldn't be compensated for.

Without drawing up the blind, she scrambled into the same denim shorts she'd worn yesterday, pulled a thin navy-blue hoodie on over the tank top she'd slept in, gathered up her backpack, and headed out to the kitchen. Maybe she'd rummage around in the cupboards, find the bread, make herself a quiet piece of toast and just sit and think for a bit by herself.

A quiet scuff in the kitchen had her peering around the doorframe ahead though; Tane was already up, rinsing last night's dishes in the sink.

She should have known, really.

Kyla slid onto the black pleather barstool she was coming to think of as 'her spot', and slouched over the bench.

"Morning," Tane said as he set the last plate down and reached for a sage-green tea towel.

"Yeah."

"You a sweet-breakfast or a savoury-breakfast person?" he said, nodding at the two large paper bags on the wooden table behind her.

"Oh, sweet please," Kyla said, pivoting the chair around to follow his movement as he grabbed the bags from the table.

He passed one of the bags to her, emblazoned with an ice-cream shaped logo, presumably of a local cafe.

Warm air greeted her as she opened the bag. Her stomach rumbled and, mouth watering, she lifted the package out to discover two waffles swimming in some sort of maple-coloured syrup and topped with lemon curd, strawberries, and what was probably a raspberry puree.

Tane slid a metal fork across the bench and sat beside her. "I skipped the ice cream. Figured it'd melt. Hope that's okay."

"Are you kidding?" She snatched up the fork and dug in. "This is incredible." Her words were *mostly* intelligible around the mixed mouthful of waffle and syrup and lemon curd and that was going to have to be good enough, because this was *delicious* and she was going to *inhale* it.

The bagel he took out of his own bag didn't look nearly so appetising as a breakfast food, though at lunch she might change her mind; roasted red peppers and spinach and cream cheese and other things that were, at the right time of day, delicious, but which in Kyla's opinion constituted far too much vegetable matter for the first meal of the day.

The air conditioning had been switched off at some point overnight, and halfway through her waffles Kyla paused to shimmy out of her hoodie, the morning air already growing warm and humid.

She piled up her fork with more raspberry-laden waffle and curd, glistening red and yellow on the silver metal. "You don't have to keep feeding me, you know." It wasn't like it wasn't nice, obviously, and it was doing wonders for her travel budget, but... the last time Kyla had had someone organise so many meals for her, she'd been in the hospital, watching over Melina—

She scraped the stool back suddenly and stood, eyes prickling.

"You okay?"

"Bathroom," she said, and tried to leave the room at a normal sort of pace.

She locked the bathroom door and leaned against it, forehead pressing against the cold surface of the white-painted door. The room was cooler than the kitchen, and it smelled damp and soapy.

There was water on the shower door. Tane must have showered.

Something fidgeted in Kyla's stomach and she forcefully steered her thoughts away from any hint of Tane-plus-nudity.

Blood had died.

Alethea had died. Maybe. Kyla clutched at that straw, thin though it was.

No, scratch that, neither of them had *died*, if Alethea had; they'd both been *murdered*.

And she was going to distract herself thinking about Tane in the shower?

Kyla turned her back on the offending apparatus—and met her own gaze in the mirror.

The tears that had sent her scurrying from the kitchen leaked over the rims of her eyelids and slithered down her cheeks.

Setting her jaw, Kyla scrubbed them away.

Breathe. Idiot. Crying won't bring them back.

She inhaled deeply through her mouth, exhaled, and took stock: her hair could use a wash—it was looking limp and oily—and dark shadows stood out like bruises under her eyes, but she'd be fine. She'd survived worse than this. *Done worse than this.*

Another tear spilled over.

Kyla made an impatient hissing sound and swiped at it.

If you don't get a hold of yourself, she told her reflection sternly, *more people are going to die. Including Dad.*

There.

The prickling in her eyes settled, condensing instead into something hardened and fierce in her chest.

Kyla reached over, flushed the old porcelain toilet for pretences, and washed first her hands then her face in the icy water.

She returned to the kitchen—scraping her hair into some sort of ponytail as she walked—flashed Tane a tight smile, and sat down to make her way through the rest of her waffles. "Thanks," she said again around a mouthful of crummy sweetness.

Tane nodded and shoved a loaded forkful of vegetables into his mouth.

Kyla stared at the pantry cupboard, letting her mind wander back through the events of the last few days. "The thing is," she mused, tapping her fork against the rim of her plate, "how *do* you steal someone else's Touch?"

Tane shifted, angling a little more toward her. "Million dollar question, right?"

"Did you know that's what she was doing?"

He shook his head. "I figured she was after targets with significant Touches. I thought she was... eliminating competition, or something."

Kyla licked a drip of sweet raspberry puree from her fingertip. "So, what? She finds high-powered targets, drops a snowflake on them which she uses to track them down later when the time is right, then she appears and murders the victim, and… steals their Touch?"

Tane shrugged, his knife scraping on his plate as he sliced off another bite of bagel. "Apparently."

Kyla sniffed. "You must have *some* ideas. Tell me what you were planning to do about her at least."

Another shrug.

Kyla speared a strawberry half with her fork.

"I can track her," he said, staring intently at the black marbled bench, his own fork momentarily forgotten in his hand. "I'm starting to get a good feel for who she's likely to target. I was… hoping that I'd be able to start getting to her victims before she did, eventually set a trap for her. I was *this close* with both the man the other night and your Bloodhound."

"Even closer with Alethea." She leaned back a little so as to better stare him down. "You could have saved her, if you were going to save anyone."

"She's—was—is, a red Touch, Kyla."

"So?"

"So if she said the only way this ends was for me to prioritise keeping *you* safe last night, then that's what was true." He stabbed viciously at a slice of charred red pepper.

Guilt tugged at Kyla's chest, a tight squeeze around her heart, a tiny trill of adrenaline. She kicked back from the bench and stood, hands fisted. "You should have saved *her*."

He pivoted on the chair. "I'm sorry," he said quietly. "I know she was your friend. And to be fair, we don't *know* she's dead. She did say she would be able to leave. Red Touch, remember?"

Kyla threw her hands up in the air with a wordless cry. Friend? No. Maybe once. But since Melina… Still, she'd let Kyla in two nights ago, had confirmed her quest for the Touchstone wasn't vain; had died so that Kyla could live.

Maybe.

Kyla ground her teeth.

If there'd been something handy to punch, she would have.

Instead, she squeezed her non fork hand as tight as she could, her nails biting into the palm of her hand.

Her phone rang.

She snatched it out of her pocket. Pippa. Right. She'd left a message for her to call. ...Urgh. "Hey, Pippa," she said so Tane would know who was calling.

Blood, Alethea, Dad... Urgh.

"You said to call when I got off."

"Yeah, I did."

"Well? This is me calling?"

Okay. Deep breath. Okay. Kyla squeezed her eyes shut. "The lead I had for finding the Touchstone is gone."

"So find a new lead!"

Kyla's grip on the phone tightened. "He's dead, Pip," she said softly. "The lead I had is dead." And at one point, he had definitely qualified as a friend.

Kyla clenched her jaw as hard as her grip on the phone to stop the prickling tears.

There were too many puzzle pieces and not enough pictures of the damn box.

I need a pen, and some paper, and to write them all out and spread the on the bench and—

"So what now?"

Kyla returned to the conversation with a double blink. She hadn't heard Pippa sound soft like that in... forever. "I... I don't know. I need..." She took a deep breath. "I need time, damn it, which I don't have. I don't know, Pip. I need... I need to talk it all out, try to make sense of it. I know we haven't had the best of relationships but do you think—"

"Yeah." Pippa cut her off, but not sharply. "Yeah I know. We can talk."

Tane wriggled in Kyla's peripheral vision. "If you need to plan, plan here," he murmured at her as he finished up his meal and laid the fork down on the messy plate. "At least then you'll be safe while you do."

Kyla searched his dark eyes while the phone line vibrated quietly with the noise of Pippa's car—at some point, she was going to sit Tane down and make him explain exactly what it was he had here that he thought was so special it could protect them all—her stomach clenched; *did* he have the Touchstone?—but for now... She exhaled. "Will you come here?" she asked Pippa.

"Where's here?"

Kyla gave her the address.

"Do I have time to sleep first?"

Maybe that wasn't softness in Pippa's voice; maybe it was just exhaustion.

Kyla exhaled slowly. "Yeah. Yeah, go home and sleep. Meet me here around midday?"

"Thanks," Pippa said, and this time it was definitely exhaustion in her voice. "I'll call Theo, tell him to come too."

"Good idea," Kyla said, and then, "You don't need to eat first okay?"

Since when was this a thing Kyla did, offering to care for Pippa's physical needs? Tane's hospitality must be catching.

"Are you... Are you offering me lunch?"

Apparently the situation was as weird for Pippa as it was for Kyla.

Kyla cleared her throat. "Uh, yeah. I guess I am."

Road noise through the phone.

Tane raised an eyebrow at her, which Kyla ignored, rearranging her grip on the phone.

"Sure," Pippa exhaled. "Sure okay. I'll call Theo, and I'll, uh, see you there for, um, lunch and... and talking. Around twelve. Okay?"

Kyla nodded, remembered she was on a phone call, and croaked out a farewell.

The call ended.

Kyla stared at her phone.

Maybe aliens really had interfered with the phone line.

"You okay?"

Kyla gave herself a shake and glanced up at Tane. "What? Oh, ah, yeah, I'm… I'm okay." Dumb. There was so much to be un-okay about.

Whatever.

More pressing matters.

She shook her head again, set her shoulders. "Okay, around midday, my sister and her boy—husband are going to be here for lunch. And to… talk." She let that sit in the air for a bit while she munched down the last few mouthfuls of sweet, sticky waffle, licked sour lemon curd from the rim of the fork, tried to settle her racing brain.

"The people who threatened your father," Tane said, interrupting her stream-of-consciousness.

She straightened. "What about them?"

He picked at the fork on his plate, changing its angle slightly. "Your father's still alive, right?"

"Yes…"

"But they, what did you say? He's in hospital?"

"They poisoned him," she said, words clipped. "They'll give me the antidote if I bring them the Touchstone by Friday." She shoved the final strawberry into her mouth and chewed. Compared to the others, it tasted a little sour.

"Did they say anything else?"

She raised her eyebrows. "No. Why would they?"

Tane pushed his plate across the bench impatiently. "Somewhere to meet them, a specific time, anything. What did they *sound* like?"

"Scratchy. They were using some sort of filter." Kyla leaned back against the back of the barstool, its hard upper ridge digging across her spine. "Are you trying to help me find them?" He'd said he found people, after all, and she couldn't deny the tiny seed of hope taking root in her chest at the thought of *not* having to face all this alone.

"No. Maybe. No." He avoided eye contact, studiously re-arranging the fork yet again.

She eyed him. "You know something about the Touchstone."

His hesitation was confirmation enough.

"Tell me! Please." Kyla leaned forward, elbows on the bench, head low, trying to force him to meet her eye. "Tane, it's my dad."

He looked up, dark eyes sad and full of pity. "Not the Touchstone."

"Then what? You meet a random stranger on the street who's being mugged, you take them in, you feed them and make sure they're okay, sure, I'll buy that, I guess." Her fork clinked as she set it carefully down on the bench and folded her arms. "But offering to help said stranger track down someone threatening to murder their parent? Tane, that's not just a random act of kindness. *What do you know?*"

His gaze flicked over her and away again. "Nothing. Nothing helpful. Nothing."

"Tane."

"I told you. Call me."

"Oh, sure, next time someone tries to jump me or attack me or murder me, I'll just whip out my phone and be all, 'Hey Tane, wanna come rescue me again?'" She rolled her eyes. "Brilliant." The last person who'd found out she was a black thumb and subsequently offered their phone number and 'help' had been trying to frame her for murder. They'd nearly succeeded.

Kyla shoved her plate across the bench next to Tane's. "Thanks for breakfast," she said as she stood, the barstool's legs protesting against the floor. "I think we're done here. Trust me, I won't call you again unless I'm dying, Tane Rangi. Forget lunch. I'll find somewhere else for everyone to meet. See you around. Or not." She headed for the hallway.

"Kyla, wait. I—"

"Either you have something to tell me or not, Tane." Kyla cocked an eyebrow at him—but he closed his mouth, and his eyes, frowning. "Yeah I thought so. Thanks for... I don't even know. Whatever. I have a Touchstone to find."

And I'll find it alone, just like everything else in my life.

Alethea's words reverberated in her head, but she swatted them away as she stalked to her room and snatched up her backpack.

Alethea was dead. What did she know anyway?

L ACKING ANY BETTER LEADS TO FOLLOW, KYLA MADE HER WAY back to strange glass store she'd visited the evening before, trying not to fume too hard about Tane's lack of forthcoming information.

They barely knew each other.

He was clearly involved in something dangerous.

There were good reasons for him to be circumspect.

...And Kyla didn't care about any of that, not if he knew something that would help her save her dad.

She pushed the door to the glass shop open rather more firmly than she'd planned. It flung inward, bounced against the front window, and came back for her face.

Kyla rocked as she caught at it just in time to prevent it smacking her nose, rolled her eyes, and entered the cool air conditioning of the store.

In the morning light with the city skyscrapers blocking any direct sunlight from the storefront, the place seemed perfectly normal. Not a trace of the otherworldliness she'd experienced yesterday remained: it was just a long, skinny shop that sold an extensive variety of glassware.

Kyla gave a small exhale and headed deeper into the store, letting her fingers skim along the front of the shelf at waist level. Vases large and small, tumblers in sets or odd pairs, flatware, bowls, decorative pieces: all of it glass, mostly crystal-clear and uncoloured—and most of it, to her Touch sense, irrelevant.

Halfway down the aisle, a mirror hung up on the wall above the highest shelf. Kyla paused to glare briefly at herself. She swiped a strand of dark hair from her forehead, now dry of sweat thanks to the fierce air con of the shop.

Her phone rang.

Unknown number. "Hello?"

Her pulse skipped before she knew why.

"Him being dead doesn't change anything."

Her grip tightened convulsively on the phone. "Who?" *Dad can't be dead. It's not Friday. They said I had till Friday.*

A cleared throat. "You knew him as the Bloodhound. He was one of us. His death changes nothing."

Kyla pressed her free hand against the shelf to steady herself, the brickwork cold under her bare fingers. *Blood??*

"For *you*, anyway." The phone line went dead.

Kyla pulled the phone from her ear. Stared at it until the screen went dark.

Blood had been one of... them? Them *who*? The ones who'd threatened her, obviously. But he'd been trying to *help* her, he'd been going to give her information...

The thought she'd had that night boarding the train from Pippa's house collided with the present moment:

Why wouldn't they just hire me to find the stone?

Because I would have said no.

She drew in a long, shaky inhale, rubbed the heel of her hand over one side of her face, and tucked her phone back into her pocket.

Light glimmered off the edge of a round glass platter, the sparkle bright and eye-catching. If she tilted her head—not in defeat, never in defeat—there was a tiny rainbow visible on the shelf below because of it.

She sighed.

Okay. Well. As they said: Blood's death changed nothing, at least as it impacted finding the Touchstone and saving her dad. Which meant continuing to search.

She took another step down the shop aisle, dry, sterile, air-conditioned air wafting against her face.

Something on the shelf to her left caught at her, at tiny tug of intuition that she'd seen something important without realising it. She scanned the shelfs: glass mugs, a stack of bowls, an owl statuette... Ah, there.

Kyla picked up the bee with its wings folded back to make an almost circular paperweight, edges smooth and gentle. The bee that was identical to the one Damon had shown her yesterday. Hmm.

She let out the tiniest spark of her Touch energy, and once again the black energy slid through the bee, visible to her Touch sense—until suddenly it wasn't.

There was no price tag on the bottom of the bee.

Hefting it gently, Kyla pivoted, scanning over top of the centre shelving for the checkout. It was the next aisle over, halfway toward the front of the shop, and she quickly made her way there and dinged the little bell for attention.

Her toes tapped out a rhythm on the floor and she worked her tongue against teeth that still held traces of minty toothpaste as she waited a short eternity for a dark-haired woman to appear from the storeroom that jutted into the store halfway back, smoothing a hand down her white blouse and plastering a customer-service smile on her face.

"Hello. Find something you like?"

Kyla showed her the bee and tried out her own smile. It felt rusted, but the woman either didn't notice or didn't care.

She took the bee from Kyla, noted the lack of price sticker, and began tippity-tapping on the register.

A frown deepened on her face. "I can't find this in the system. Where was it?"

Kyla pointed to the shelving. "Near that owl."

The woman's frown continued another moment, and then, "I'm just going to put it through as one of the owls, okay?"

"How much?"

"Uh, twenty-four ninety-nine."

Kyla paid, interrupted the woman before she could wrap the bee in purple tissue paper, and slipped both the satisfyingly round glass weight and the receipt into her pocket as she headed to the front of the store. She'd take the bee to Damon when she next went and they could compare them, see if they could figure out more about what they did and how they worked. It wasn't the Touchstone, but maybe, when this was over... Maybe next week the bee would prove a worthwhile find as an intriguing artefact in its own right. It might even be worth something, to the right collector.

Before she could linger over that thought, however, her phone rang again.

Eirene.

Kyla answered. "Hello?"

Sobbing greeted her, words choked out by ugly crying.

"Eirene, Eirene take a breath," Kyla said, brows drawing down tight. "I can't understand you. What's wrong?"

A ragged, soggy breath. "The ice boy," Eirene forced out. "We were practising in the wetland again. He grabbed Lyssa."

Adrenaline shot through Kyla's body. She clutched the phone. "Did he take her?"

"No, I"—another snotty, soggy inhale—"I dragged her away. But she's hurt, I think. Please come. Please, I need your help, I can't do this on my own."

Around her, the glass store glittered and glimmered. Kyla squeezed her hand around the glass bee tucked in her pocket. Likely she had all she was going to get from the store, and if her father still needed her to find the Touchstone, well, Lyssa needed her more right at this moment.

"Sure," she said to Eirene. "Yes. I'll be on a train in few minutes. Hold on until I get there."

18

I T HAD TAKEN KYLA FORTY MINUTES TO CATCH A TRAIN UP TO the station near the girls' house and then walk—hurriedly—to find them. Eirene had called to say she'd managed to move Lyssa from the bit of scrubby wetland where they'd been attacked back to their house, and Kyla let herself in through the back again, up onto the verandah, through into the hallway that split the house in two with the side table and its missing urn.

As yesterday, the hall was cool and dim, though the formal lounge was bright with slivers of late morning sunshine splitting through the blinds. Incense still scented the air, fresher than yesterday.

"In here," Eirene called, and Kyla turned left into a room she hadn't seen yesterday, opposite the formal lounge.

It was the kitchen/living area, and Eirene had Lyssa lying on a peridot-green couch, a damp towel over her forehead and a pile of towels underneath her. Someone was cooking toast in a white toaster that gleamed in the cool dimness of the dark-wood kitchen area.

Kyla strode over to the girls, lips pursed, trying to ignore the way her heart pulsed. "Is she okay?"

"I'm fine," Lyssa grumped, though she lay still enough.

"Now, maybe, but you were out cold for a few moments there, so don't you dare insinuate that I'm being over-protective. You're lucky Dad isn't here to send you to the hospital."

Lyssa's jaw did not enjoy that thought, twitching wildly.

"What happened?" Kyla said in an attempt to defuse the growing tension. She rubbed at the back of her neck, habit rather than any particular sensation from her Touch, which had been quiet since flashing yesterday.

"We were practising," Eirene said. "Like you showed us. Lyssa was standing near the pond—so was I—and..." She shuddered.

"It's okay, I—"

"She screamed," Eirene continued, chin lifted, anger chilling her gaze. "By the time I turned around, the ice boy had already dragged her halfway in."

In the kitchen, toast popped out of the toaster, filling the room with the smell.

"Did it seem like the child was specifically after Lyssa?" Kyla said with a frown as Eirene got up and headed into the kitchen.

Eirene shrugged, snagged the toast out onto a waiting black plate. "It could just as easily have taken me, I was right there. Either it was coincidence and Lyssa was a just a little closer, or it was specifically after her. How can we tell?" she finished as she snagged a butter dish and began buttering the toast, the knife scraping over it.

"It was after me," Lyssa muttered darkly from the couch. "Right as I was blacking out, I heard a woman's voice saying,

'Yes, that one.'"

Eirene frowned, pausing in the act of toast-buttering. "You didn't tell me that."

"I only just remembered," Lyssa said, readjusting the damp towel so it covered her eyes.

Kyla exhaled forcefully through her nose. "We need to get you a cloaking charm," she said.

"We had one," Lyssa muttered.

"We discussed that," Eirene said with an air of finality as she plunked the knife in the kitchen sink and headed for couch, bearing the plate of hot buttered toast. "It's not an option."

"Well not *now* it's not," Lyssa said.

"Much as I hate to intrude on this critical moment of sibling bonding, what am I missing?" said Kyla as Eirene perched on the edge of the couch.

Lyssa lay still, fingers curling into fists at her sides.

"Eat," said Eirene.

A moment more, and then Lyssa struggled upright and took the plate, the damp towel flopping to the floor with a quiet little smack. "We had a cloaking pendant," Lyssa said around a mouthful of toast.

Eirene's glare just about singed the toast to charcoal, but Lyssa glared right back and continued crunching. "She's trying to help us," she said around a mouthful of crumbs. "And it's gone now, anyway."

Kyla's eyebrows lifted. "Someone stole it with your mother's urn?"

"It *was* the urn," Eirene muttered, still glaring at Lyssa. Abruptly, she shifted on the edge of the couch and faced Kyla. "It's was Mum's urn. She... kept it with her, at times, to help dull the effects of her Touch. She... was a black thumb too."

Kyla's heart stuttered. "How did it dull the effects?" An urn wasn't a stone... "What was it made of?" ...but anything that interacted with Touches was of interest right now, more than ever.

"Obsidian," Lyssa said—Kyla's heart skipped a second time—and paused to pick up the small chunk of crust that had fallen to her plate when she'd spoken.

"We've no idea," Eirene said. "How it worked, I mean. But it did. It meant she didn't have to discharge as often."

"I thought you said it was for cloaking."

"Yeah, if she carried it with her it did," Lyssa said. "But she could discharge into it, too. I used it, obviously. To help with… you know."

Kyla did know. But what she didn't know was what to do with this new information. Another Touchstone candidate? Absolutely. But… stolen, location undetermined right now.

The fact that someone had considered it worth stealing was definitely a vote in favour of it being the stone.

…And Kyla would never feel completely safe to go look for it if she had to worry about being called back to help the girls any time the ice children reappeared.

"Why weren't you using it?"

"I was," Lyssa said, and despite the cloth over her forehead, Kyla heard the eyeroll. "My Touch is just *that strong*."

Okay, so maybe not the Touchstone after all? The Touchstone didn't have limits on how much power it could nullify… did it??

One person might know. The same person who could keep Lyssa safe from further attacks.

Grinding her teeth, Kyla dug her phone out of her pocket. "I'm going to make a call," she told the girls. "Regardless of anything else, you need to be somewhere safe, somewhere no one else can reach you right now."

Before either of them could protest, Kyla strode from the room, across the incense-scented hall, and into the formal lounge where the sun was just leaving the walls.

She hit dial on the number she'd sworn she wasn't going to use again, and scrunched up her face as the dial tone rang in her ear.

"You're dying after all?" Tane said mildly in answer, and Kyla sniffed.

"Hilarious. I'm not calling for me, I'm calling for Lyssa."

"Who?"

"The black thumb I've been helping?"

"Right, I forgot her name. What about her?"

"She's in danger," Kyla said. "The ice children came back again, attacked her in the bushland by her house where we were when they attacked us yesterday."

"Is she okay?"

"I don't know. Her energy is all... weird."

"Weird how?" Tane's voice was sharp, laser-focused.

"I don't know! I think..." Kyla heart hammered in her ears. She swallowed down her nerves and licked her dry lips. "You said things were... safer. Around you. That includes her, right? If she's with you, you can block Freja from finding her?"

The neighbour decided it was a great time to start their lawnmower, at which point Kyla had to start questioning their sanity, given it was eleven a.m. on a stinking hot summer weekday.

"Tane?"

A long exhale. "Yes. Fine. Yes. Bring her over. Or do you need me to pick you up?" he added. "Since you don't have a car."

Kyla shrugged, forgetting for an instant that he couldn't see her, wishing she had any other option in the world for keeping Lyssa safe. "We're a twenty minute walk away, tops. Are you home? Is there a key?"

"I'm home. If this place counts as home, anyway," he said. "See you in twenty?"

"Tane..." The noise of the lawnmower grumbled outside, and if she strained, she could hear the girls chatting in the other room. She sighed, air tasting of incense. "Thank you." The words were bitter in her throat, but she wasn't a monster. He *had* offered to help—it just wasn't the help she wanted.

He snorted. "Should I be expecting anyone else? Do I prepare catering? Turn this into a party, now you've decided to work with me?"

His words might have been sarcastic, but the tone was more exasperation than real malice, and Kyla's mouth tugged sideways into a wry-ish smile. "I'm an arse," she said. "I'm sorry." Her pulse pounded at that. "Can Pippa still come over for lunch?"

"Sure," Tane said, and Kyla could practically hear his eyes rolling. "Fine, call the sister, call everyone. I'll organise a picnic."

Again with the exasperation—and this time, Kyla thought that maybe she recognised a little of it, mirroring her own earlier frustrations: that of a competent person used to working alone, suddenly saddled with a team.

She exhaled softly, lips tugging again into that wry little sideways smile. "Thank you," she said. "I'll bring..." What did someone bring to a picnic? She'd been intending it jokingly, but given the propensity toward feeding her that Tane had exhibited so far, he probably *wasn't* joking. "Uh, what do you want me to bring? Dessert? Drinks?"

Another snort. "Kyla. Make your phone calls. Bring the girls. Let's just get everyone safe first, okay? I'll see you in twenty, thereabouts."

"Yeah," Kyla said. "Yeah okay, see you in twenty."

Tane hung up.

Kyla stared at her phone.

Some days, her life was incredibly confusing.

KYLA WAS ON THE GREY COUCH IN THE SUN AT TANE'S RENTAL, watching Eirene and Lyssa absolutely decimate a plate of waffles each over at the small dining table, when Pippa entered the room.

Tane had gotten the door; Pippa's husband Spy was sandwiched in the middle; and Pippa held them all up as she froze in the hall doorway, scanning the room with her mouth pressed in a firm line.

"You okay, Pip?" Spy muttered behind her, reaching forward to take her hand.

She squeezed it tightly, jaw set, still scanning the room, then let go to move into the room. She locked her gaze onto Kyla like a missile and strode for the other couch. "I'm here," she said. "Talk."

Kyla took a second to shove her irritation aside. Was Pippa being rude? Yes. Had she expected anything else? No. So there was no point engaging when this really was an excellent opportunity to get all the cards on the table.

All the cards.

"Hey, um, could everyone listen up for a second?" Kyla clenched her hands in her lap, shifting so she was perched right on the edge of the couch facing the kitchen.

Spy sat beside Pippa; Tane surveyed the room for a moment before pulling out Kyla's barstool at the bench—no, not Kyla's, none of them were hers, it was just the one on the end, closest to the couches—and the girls twisted around in their seats, still busily shoving forkfuls of sticky, sweet-scented waffles into their mouths.

Briefly, Kyla wondered when they'd eaten last.

Should she let Pippa and Spy get their food first?

Surely there were guidelines or something for how this was supposed to go.

...How a hunt for a mythical object and a serial killer should go? Kyla nearly giggled.

Oh wow, okay, she was a lot more discombobulated by all this than she'd realised. *Giggling*? Wow.

She took a deep breath. ...Was 'thank you all for being here' a ridiculous way to start? It sounded like a ridiculous way to start.

Pippa leaned forward, elbows on knees whose bony-ness was only highlighted by the loose, dark-blue uniform pants she wore. "Kyla Jewel, calm the hell down or so help me I will smack you. *What is going on?*"

Sometimes, Kyla really hated her sister.

Sometimes, she really appreciated her sister too.

She closed her eyes to block out all the faces staring at her, focused on the warmth of the sun on her skin, and began. "I'm going to start with the beginning of what I know, and lay it all out," she said. "Because while you all know some of it, none of you know all of it. And I... have a feeling"—the same feeling that had made her a nationally renowned artefact hunter—

"that all of you have something to contribute to this. Okay?" She peeked just long enough to see heads nodding.

And then she laid it out for them: the phone call about her father and the poisoners holding him for ransom, her visit to Alethea who'd confirmed that the Touchstone was in town, her meeting with Lyssa—though she did shoot a questioning look at her first, waiting for permission before divulging Lyssa's talents to the room, ignoring the way that Pippa squirmed as she did—the glass shop incident, the attacks by the frost children, Blood, the second phone call from the poisoners—and the facts of what Freja was hunting.

"And so," she concluded, "we have a serial killer on the loose who has good reason to target at least two of us in the room, and a quest for the Touchstone that's left me with a literal dead end—though Pippa," she said, turning to her sister, "you said Spy had found a lead on the phone call?"

Pippa scowled deeply at Kyla's name for him—it had always been a bone of contention between them that not only would Kyla not call him by his first name, she wouldn't even call him by his full last name either, though Theo Spyrou himself didn't seem to mind—but Spy shifted forward on the other couch and answered before Pippa could.

"Yeah," he said, his voice light and melodic, brown curls tumbling over hazel eyes like he was still nineteen—with fair, lightly-freckled skin clear enough to pass for that, if he cared to, even though he, like Pippa, had just turned thirty. "We tracked down the address that the phone belongs to, the one they used to call you."

Kyla nodded, adrenaline sparking in her chest. Now for the tricky bit. "Great. So, how much do you know about Touches, about the energy?"

Spy glanced sideways at Pippa, obviously not wanting to get too deeply into something they both knew was a trigger for her sister. "A little."

"Tane," Kyla said, and he lifted his head in response. "What exactly is it that Freja can do? Not the things we're speculating on, but, like, what specifically do you *know* she can do?"

Tane frowned, one arm wrapped around the back of the barstool. "Let's see. She can sense other people's Touches, possibly even despite a cloaking pendant. She's willing to murder, and it's probably via magical means rather than mundane, given none of the post mortems I've seen were able to identify a means of death beyond 'hole in side of chest'. I don't know that she's been identified as having a black Touch, though."

Kyla pursed her lips and shifted so the sun stopped burning the back of her forearm. "I didn't get any read off her yesterday, let alone a black one, so I've no idea what colour her Touch is."

"Hmm." Tane pursed his lips. "Another mystery. Clearly she can create artefacts, powerful ones, since the glass snowflakes seem to have a Touch aura of their own."

Oh, so he *could* see the rainbowness of the snowflakes then.

"She's powerful then, right?"

He nodded. "Extremely."

"And the police, do you think they are likely to be able to contain her?"

He snorted. "Hardly. I've seen them try with weaker Touches. Look, *maybe*," he said, shifting forward, "if someone was able to neutralise her first, cut her off from her Touch energies. I've seen no indication that she's physically violent or likely to put up a fight by regular means, but who knows? She hasn't been cornered yet."

Perfect, thank you. Kyla turned back to Spy. "You understand we have a magical serial killer on the loose?"

"Yeah." The corners of his mouth didn't look happy about it.

Kyla didn't blame them.

She leaned closer. "So do you agree that dangerous stuff is going on, this is beyond what the police can handle, and I'll go check out the address which you'll now give me?"

Words formed slowly in Spy's mouth. "No..."

Kyla's chest constricted.

"But... I suppose I could organise for you to come with. As a consultant."

"Theo!" Pippa glared at him.

"I'm trying to *help*," Kyla said, incredulous, as Spy held his hands up defensively and said, "What? She's right, Pip. If something goes wrong, what am I supposed to do about it?" ·

Pippa's jaw could have split granite. "Nothing's going to go wrong. Not for you."

The two locked eyes, and Kyla had the distinct impression she was being left out of a very detailed conversation.

Over at the table, Lyssa surreptitiously finished her waffles and tucked the empty plate back into its paper bag. She started guiltily as the bag crinkled.

Kyla let one side of her mouth soften into an almost-smile. *You're fine,* she hoped her expression said.

Spy was the first to crack. "Do you really want to do this now?" he said softly.

Pippa tried to maintain her glare, but her squirming hands spoiled the effect. "No! No. But..." She glanced around the room, opened her mouth to speak—and instead collapsed forward into her hands.

"Hey," Spy soothed. "Hey, it's okay. You don't have to do this now if you don't want to."

"Do *what*?" Kyla's eyebrows were drawn tightly together as she watched Spy rub Pippa's back, her blonde ponytail flopping forward and hiding her hands over her face.

Tane hadn't moved from the barstool, but his grip on the seat back was tighter, his attention rigidly focused.

"Pippa?" Kyla ventured. She hadn't even looked this unsettled when she'd told Kyla about their dad. What in the *world* was going on?

Pippa drew in a long, shuddering breath. "You remember how it happened?" she said, dropping her hands and peering wide- and sad-eyed at Spy.

He nodded, his own brows furrowing.

"This woman, Freja, is stealing people's Touches, right?" Pippa said to the room at large, gaze still fixed on Spy's face.

He reached out and took her hands.

She knotted her fingers tightly in his. "Maybe it will help."

Spy brushed her ponytail back from her face. "I'm here."

Pippa took a deep breath and turned to face Kyla, closing her eyes at the last moment. "I... I don't even know how to say this," she muttered. "Kyla, I have a Touch too."

The room spun. Kyla's stomach fell through the floor. "You hate the Touched."

You hate me.

You've always hated me, ever since it came, ever since—

Something moved beside her.

It was Tane, sitting down on the couch. Not close enough to touch her—she was grateful—and he wasn't looking at her anyway, he was on the edge of the seat staring fixedly at Pippa. "How did it happen?"

"And, wait," Kyla said, leaning forward to match Tane. "How did I not know about this? I mean, I should be able to *sense* it!"

Pippa fished a heavy gold chain out from under her dark green uniform shirt. It was longer than Kyla expected, and even though she knew what must be hanging from it, her stomach still flipped and her breath caught as Pippa pulled out a glass pendant easily twice the size of the one Kyla wore, a flat disc thick as her pinky, round as a tennis ball. Pippa let it drop over her shirt—and the moment it left contact with her hand, Kyla could see fine ribbons of a dark, desaturated mauve in the darkness behind her eyelids.

She inhaled sharply.

"What's purple again?" Eirene murmured from the kitchen table.

Kyla stared at her, mind blank, body numb.

"Fortune-telling," Tane said in the same hushed tones someone would use to describe a giant brick of gold that had spontaneously appeared in their house.

Pippa shook her head. "It's very limited, though. And I can't do it often."

"What *can* you do?" Tane wasn't the only one fixated on Pippa right now, but he was the one closest to Kyla, and his tension was palpable.

"I..." Pippa rubbed at her arms as though goosebumps had suddenly risen. "I can see how people will die," she said hollowly. "Not always. Just occasionally."

"That's because your colour is desaturated," Kyla said automatically. In her mind, however, she was reeling back to last night, watching the paramedics load the body into the ambulance, already knowing it was futile. She'd thought that might be bad enough—but knowing it was futile before the person had even died?

She shuddered.

"You stopped," Tane said. "When you first walked in here. What did you see?"

Pippa's mouth opened around silent syllables. She rubbed her arms again, twisting to stare out the window that was letting in the sun into the small, grassed square of the yard.

"*What did you see?*"

A fleeting glance back at Tane, and then, "It's not always clear. Sometimes it changes," she told the window. "But..."

"Which one of them?" Kyla said gently. It wasn't Pippa's fault that the deaths she saw occurred... but it might well feel like it if Pippa had tried everything she could to prevent them, and it had made no difference in the end.

"Which one?" Pippa's eyes were wide as she met Kyla's.

Kyla nodded. Pippa had ignored the two younger girls from the first moment she'd walked in, hadn't said hello, hadn't looked at them, hadn't acknowledged their presence in any way. It had to be one of them... Or, wait... "Both?"

A train rattled past out the front.

Oh Pip. Why didn't you tell me? Do you hate me that much?

Slowly, Pippa nodded. "It's... hazy, though. Which I think means it's a long way off. I..." She swallowed.

Spy shifted to wrap an arm around her, and she leaned against him.

"It still feels so new," she whispered hollowly. "I don't know how to interpret it all. I think... I think what I saw for them was a long way off though. Maybe the end of their lives. Well, I mean, obviously it was the end, but you know what I mean," she added in a rush, colour rising in her cheeks.

"How did it happen?" Tane said, locking his hands together into a fist over his knees.

For a moment, Kyla thought he meant the deaths Pippa had foreseen—but Pippa had obviously remembered his earlier question, even if Kyla hadn't.

"I was at work," she said hoarsely. "On a job. It was... messy. Awful. The person... They died. Right as they passed, I got an absolute killer of a headache. My partner grabbed me to steady me. I grabbed him back. Touched his hand." Her voice sounded rote, distant, like she was reciting lines she'd learned once, devoid of emotion. "I saw how he would die..."

Kyla flinched as Pippa met her eye again. The rawness, the horror... "It's okay, Pip," Kyla said. "I get it."

Tane leaned back in the couch, pressing the back of one crooked finger thoughtfully against his upper lip.

"There was a car crash right before Mum died."

As one, the room pivoted to stare at Lyssa.

She swallowed. Blinked a few times. "There was a car crash," she said more quietly. "It was when I... When I got my Touch. I was covered... I bet you were covered in blood too, weren't you Pippa. The day you got yours?"

Tense, Pippa nodded, still without turning to look at the younger girls.

"Me too," Lyssa whispered.

"So what," Kyla said, looking from the girls to her sister and back again. "You're saying Lyssa and Pippa both got their Touches from someone else via... their blood?"

"How did you get yours?" Tane said beside her.

Kyla twisted to him. "I..." She'd been going to say it had had nothing to do with blood, but... Her face went hot. "Same time as I got my first period," she said. "But that's not the same."

And it's also normal and a thing that half the population of the planet experience and I am not going to squirm.

Tane nodded thoughtfully—and his complete nonchalance allowed Kyla to breathe normally. "Maybe," he said.

"So what now?" Pippa asked.

"Right," Kyla said, standing so she could pace, because it was better than staying still. "Here's where we're at. Item one. Pippa has a Touch no one knew about. Creepy serial killer woman has a Touch no one's been able to identify yet. Could creepy serial killer woman have a disc like that too? Maybe.

"Item two. Creepy serial killer woman is stealing people's Touches. Touches can be transferred from person to person then. We don't know how, but maybe"—she glanced at Pippa, and at Lyssa—"maybe blood. And speaking of, we have Blood, who was apparently one of the poisoners but was also willing to help me search for the stone."

"I've been thinking about that," Tane said with a frown. "Why was he going to help you if he was one of the people threatening you? It's more likely last night was a trap and you just missed—"

"No. I thought it through. I wouldn't have said yes if he'd just asked me. I wouldn't," Kyla insisted at Tane's sceptical expression. "I guess..." Kyla shoved her hands as deep in her pockets as they would go. "I guess these people are desperate."

"I know how they feel," Pippa muttered.

Warmth rushed through Kyla's chest. She made a kind of frowny-smile, the smile that meant 'I hear you, this sucks' and didn't touch the eyes.

"There's the address, though," Spy said. "We have that."

Kyla nodded. "Right. So someone needs to go talk to Damon about pendants. Tane," she said, turning to him, heart pitter-pattering—she didn't think he'd mind her giving orders, but you never knew—"can you do that, please? I'd love for you to take him a snowflake, too, see if he can shed any light on what she's doing with them."

Tane pursed his lips. "I don't think—"

"Please," she said. "He makes the best pendants in the state. And he's a friend. He'll be discreet, and you said yourself you have a way to nullify the tracking on the snowflakes." *Which, just as soon as I have a moment, I am going to grill you about thoroughly.*

He scrunched up his face and muttered, "Please do not let me regret this. Fine," he added more loudly. "I'll go. But they"—he pointed at Eirene and Lyssa—"are not leaving my sight."

The girls straightened like roos under headlights.

"You're both too strong," he said. "I know we don't have proof, but I'm sure Freja's behind the ice children. If she finds you again, things will get ugly."

Lyssa paled, no doubt remembering her recent re-encounter.

"We'll investigate the Touch stealing at the same time," Eirene chipped in brightly, looking at Kyla but reaching out to place a hand on Lyssa's arm. "We'll call Dad. Ask him about..." She exhaled. "About the accident."

"Thank you," Kyla said. This whole having people to delegate things to was disorienting. It wasn't that she hadn't relied on other people for information before, of course, but being able to deliberately send someone out to investigate something?

Kyla's shoulders tensed briefly. Hopefully, she could trust them to investigate *right.*

"Which leaves you and me to go scout out this address," Spy said, slapping his thighs and standing. "I don't have a warrant to enter the place yet but we can at least drive past the street."

Kyla nodded. "Depending on who's in there, I might be able to get a read on them from the street anyway." *And if I can give you the slip, I can do whatever needs doing. You might not have a warrant, but I'm not a police officer.*

"What will I do?" said Pippa in a small voice.

Kyla hesitated.

Spy drew Pippa up to her feet. "Come with me, of course," he said, beaming at her.

"I'm exhausted," she said, and abruptly Kyla was aware of the dark circles under Pippa's eyes, the paleness of her skin, and the slump in her shoulders despite her jutted chin.

Going to Damon's would elicit more knowledge at this point than driving past a house she wasn't going to be allowed to examine anyway. "Go home," Kyla said. "Get some sleep first," she continued over Pippa's protests. "We can drive past the address this afternoon. Who knows." She glanced at Spy, ignoring the way Pippa's stare widened at her. "He might even have a warrant by then."

20

T HE COOL OF DAMON'S AIR-CONDITIONED SHOPFRONT WAS A welcome change to the sweltering heat outside, where the metallic scent of tram brakes fought with the taste of petrol and hot concrete for dominance.

The bell over the door tinkled as Kyla walked in, followed by Tane and the two Yee girls; she let the door fall shut with a gentle whumph and took a deep breath of the cool air, exhaling tension.

Inside the shop was quiet, light sparkling through the chandeliers and throwing gentle rainbows over everything, no loud noises, no loud smells—just the quiet hum of drily air-conditioned air, the huge glass angel still poised with saxophone in hand.

Kyla breathed it in deeply and flexed her hands, willing her heart to stop pounding, her nerves to stop jangling. "Hi," she said to the youngish man behind the counter, his mop of curly black hair dropping rakishly down one side of his forehead. "I'd be so touched if Damon could see me right now." She cocked her head and leaned on elbow on the glass counter, shooting him her best dazzling smile.

He stared blankly for a moment, then gave a jerky nod and vanished out the back in a flurry of warm air.

"I'm still not sure about this," Tane said, glancing around the store.

The Yee girls were currently examining a double-length strand of purple beads hanging amidst the many strands on the far wall, and Kyla had to admit the colour was good on them.

"Damon is the most trustworthy and discreet person I know," Kyla told Tane. "This is fine."

A moment later, Damon appeared, lined face already arranged in a smile. "Kyla," he said, then an eyebrow lifted. "And friends?"

Kyla nodded. "You know that, uh, object we were discussing yesterday?"

Damon squinted one eye at her. "Yeeees…"

She shoved her hands deeply into her pockets, elbows locking. "I have a sample for you."

His eyes immediately widened. "Please. Come out back. We will talk." He gestured for them to follow him, an all-encompassing wave that included the four of them.

Leading her little team—oh, now *there* was an interesting thought, since when was anybody 'her' team?—Kyla followed him behind the counter and into the hot workshop.

If the storefront had been intended to evoke something heavenly, with its rainbows and saxophone-playing angel, then the long, narrow workshop behind was the hell that powered it, the floor paved with bricks, the walls industrial, the multiple furnaces glowing and the entire place pervaded with the scent of things hot-but-not-quite-burning.

A work-a-day hell, though, with assistants who nodded politely and little evidence of actual torture, despite the racks of rods and irons and clamps that certainly looked appropriate.

And the heat.

Kyla swiped at the sweat that was already dripping at her hairline with the back of her wrist, breathing with relief as Damon led them into his office and the cool of air conditioning washed over her. She sat in a spindly little chair not designed for hard use, facing Damon across a white laminate desk that bore a computer monitor up on a stand, a keyboard and mouse, and swathes of hastily stacked papers with hand-drawn designs for glass objects varied and multifarious.

Tane sat on the similar chair beside her, while the girls lurked in the background.

"First of all," Kyla said, "don't kill me, but I need another protective pendant."

"Again?" Damon blinked. "Kyla Jewel, I made one for you *yesterday*. What in the whole wide world have you been up to?"

"Attracting trouble," she said wryly, just preventing her glance from slipping to Tane.

"Fine!" Damon said, hands up defensively. "I do not wish to know. But what about this other matter?"

Kyla gave Tane a nod, and reluctantly, with a somewhat huffy sigh, he withdrew a snowflake from his pocket and plunked it onto Damon's desk.

Damon blinked once, twice. Removed a handkerchief from a pocket somewhere and mopped at his brow. "Oy." He flicked a brief glance up at Kyla before returning his focus to the snowflake. "You were right, Black Jewel. You were right."

Kyla sniffed. "Obviously. So, here's what I'm thinking," she said, leaning forward over her knees. "This is clearly an object that can contain, or hold onto, Touch energy. A Touchstone would have to do the same for it to truly block out Touch energy, right? And these girls"—she waved a hand at the Yee sisters hovering behind her—"say their mum had an obsidian urn she used to use that also fully absorbed her Touch. She could discharge into it—she was a black thumb too—and pfft! That was it. No more need to flash the energy out into the world."

"Not quite," Lyssa murmured in the background, shifting her weight. "It didn't work like that for me."

"No," Kyla said, twisting to face her, "but it's proof of concept, right? Something can be made to take in Touch energy, to absorb it. It's just a matter of how much. What do you think, Damon?" she said, pivoting back to him.

He'd picked up the snowflake, was twirling it around under the lights. "If I use the... them to sandwich the energy like this," he muttered, mostly to himself, "and then twist it like the disc..." He frowned deeply, his face creasing into lines and folds of consternation. "What are you asking of me, Kyla Jewel?"

Her heart pounded. "A Touchstone," she said. "To save my father."

His lips pursed into the thinnest line as he spun the snowflake around and around and around, chin vibrating as he bounced his lips between his teeth.

"You say this is a matter of life and death for your father, no?"

Kyla nodded.

Damon sighed heavily. "In that case, I can do this thing."

Adrenaline spurted through her. "You can?"

"Yes," he said, "but *once. Once* I can do this thing. I will have to imbue the glass with a sliver from something very particular to achieve it, and..." He lapsed into muttering and Kyla wasn't sure if she couldn't understand him due to the volume, or if he was speaking his native tongue. "You do not understand the sacrifice you are asking me to make," he said. "No." He held up a hand to forestall her protests. "You do not, no matter what you may think, and that is not your choice but mine, for I have my secrets and I will keep them. But I am serious, Kyla Jewel, extremely: this is a thing I can do for you *once.*"

"Once will be enough," Kyla said, ignoring the chills that goosebumped and prickled at her arms.

Once has *to be enough.*

21

HOURS LATER, KYLA ENTERED TANE'S HOUSE AGAIN, watching with bemusement as he shepherded the two girls ahead of him, and her phone rang: it was Pippa, informing—not inviting—Kyla that she and Spy were going to drive past the address of the poisoners soon.

Kyla left the girls with Tane, who'd been increasingly quiet all afternoon—tired, probably, and as bewildered as the rest of them by this turn of fate—and got into the car with Pippa and Spy, feeling really quite positive about the whole situation.

The feeling lasted through about ten minutes of 'quality' time in the car with her sister and brother-in-law.

Kyla knotted her fingers around her seatbelt in the back seat and stared out at the suburbs, resolutely pretending she couldn't hear Act Two of Pippa's Sisterly Rant about why literally everything in Kyla's life was wrong, and what Kyla should do to fix it—a rant Pippa had apparently felt entitled to do once it became clear that she could no longer rant at Kyla about the threat to their father's life, since Kyla had obviously solved that problem in convincing Damon to make them a Touchstone.

The car's air conditioning was doing its level best to fight against the summer afternoon heat, but in the back seat, up against the window on the sunny side of the car, Kyla had to award the win to the heat. She shifted restlessly. If she leaned toward the middle of the car, she'd catch more of the cool air—and more of Pippa's ranting.

She reached up and gripped the grab handle above the window, fingertips blanching white.

The nausea in the pit of her stomach was probably just motion sickness. After this afternoon, she felt certain that everything was going to be just fabulous. They'd pick up the pendant tomorrow, arrange a meeting with the poisoners, get the antidote... Why, by tomorrow evening, she and Pippa would be driving to the hospital instead, bursting with relief at the thought of welcoming their father back to consciousness, and to health.

Her stomach still flip-flopped, though.

Kyla stared as rows of narrow-windowed brick-and-concrete houses flashed by—tried counting them, but that made the nausea worse.

Twenty-four hours.

So much could change in twenty-four hours.

Twenty-four hours ago, Alethea had still been around.

So had Blood.

She wrenched her mind away from memories of last night, watching them load Blood onto the ambulance—that last glimpse, his hand, his bare fingers so still...

He'd never worn gloves. Neither had Alethea.

Kyla realised her own fingers were hurting and relaxed her grip on the grab handle a little.

Her own fingers. Her own bare fingers. She wasn't clinging quite so tightly now, but little crescents at the tips of her nails still blushed white.

She hadn't thought to grab her gloves before she'd left for Damon's glass store this morning. Hadn't thought again to grab them in the rush to come out with Pippa.

It had been a long, long time since she'd forgotten something like that.

Pippa would hate it, when—if—*when* she noticed. Which she would, just as soon as she finished cataloguing everything *else* that was wrong with Kyla's life.

...Pippa wasn't wearing gloves. Admittedly her Touch's consequences weren't quite so fatal (though it must feel like it at times, Kyla was sure), but still.

A little trill squeezed Kyla's chest. She could just never wear gloves again...

She met Spy's eye in the rearview mirror.

"How about we put the radio on?" he said brightly as Pippa paused to draw breath.

Kyla let her eyes sink closed as Pippa nodded curtly and tapped the car's dash screen to wake the radio.

There were still so many questions.

Freja was using the snowflakes as trackers, hunting down people with strong Touches, presumably murdering them and probably stealing their Touches through their blood.

But did they *have* to die in order for her to take their Touch? Could she draw off their Touch energies *without* death as a catalyst?

And the ice children. They'd come from nowhere. How? How had Freja done that?

What *else* could she do with her Touch? Her Touches *plural*, which was a mind-blowing concept in and of itself. Or, instead, was it still just a Touch singular, with the colours mixing in some way and giving her whatever resulted?

Ice children.

From nowhere.

Cold hands.

A pendant blocking Kyla's Touch wouldn't help her if Freja came after her.

Someone clutching at her wrist...

Cold, ice cold.

The grip too tight, couldn't move, couldn't escape.

Couldn't get her gloves off...

Kyla jolted sharply as her head nodded.

"Wakey wakey," Spy said, glancing at her in the rear view again. "It's just around the corner."

Kyla blinked, disoriented. The trees outside were different, shorter gum trees with white trunks, and some other short, bushy trees that might turn out to be crepe myrtles when they flowered.

Urgh. Her neck had cricked.

She shrugged, rubbing at it, and leaned against the warm window to peer up at the upper storeys of the buildings as they passed. "This is where the call came from?"

"Yep," Spy said. "The row of houses just there." He pointed up a street that was really too narrow to host a tram and yet apparently was determined to do so, silver rails set into the road and wires running over head. "Number eleven," he said. "On the left."

Kyla examined the row of boxy townhouses that were trying to be cutting-edge design with their offset concrete-coloured upper-story rooms, their darkly bricked under-storeys, and the overall minimalist colour palette. Number 11 was barely discernible from its neighbours, three or four down from where Spy had pulled over against the curb. Its curtains were closed... and that was about all there was to set it apart from the others.

Kyla closed her eyes, focusing with that strange, slightly elusive part of her that sensed Touch energies. No scent of ozone, no taste or smell of lemongrass, just the air conditioning of the car... And no colour behind her eyelids except what she'd have expected to see there on a bright and sunny summer's day, a slowly shifting pattern of charcoal grey and orange.

"Anything?" Spy said.

Kyla swivelled around and saw him watching her. "Nothing." She blinked.

Wait, hold on...

She blinked again, longer this time—then closed her eyes entirely. "Wait. There is something there."

Cloth scuffed on leather as Pippa turned in her seat.

Aqua-blue light patterned the darkness of Kyla's closed eyes, intermingling with the orange caused by the sunlight.

"Blue," Kyla said. "But light, not dark. Like..." Like the colour of the frost children yesterday.

She clunked the curb-side door open.

"Kyla, what are you doing?"

"I'm just going to walk past," Kyla insisted. "Just down to that tree and back." She nodded at the huge plane tree sprouting from the pavement at the corner of the next street. "I'll be nonchalant."

"We don't have a warrant, Kyla!" Pippa cut in; Spy snapped his mouth closed in a prim little line.

Kyla shot Pippa a withering glare. "*He* doesn't have a warrant. *I* am a private citizen."

"Trespassing is still—"

"I get it! I'm not going in!" Kyla held her hands up, palms out not in surrender but a request for her sister to back the hell off. "Find a farm, will you," she muttered as she slid across the backseat and popped open the door.

"If I do, I'll bury you on it," Pippa shot back.

Kyla rolled her eyes at the irony of the person with the ability to see how people died threatening with death the person who could actually murder people.

Sisters.

Urgh.

She stifled a yawn as she stretched out of the car. A few more hours of sleep would probably go a long way toward cooling her temper, but sleep would have to wait until *after* she was sure no one else was going to die.

Her father included.

Damn Blood, and Freja, and the poisoners, whoever they were.

"What if they recognise—"

Kyla slammed the car door shut and got a jolt of satisfaction as Pippa squawked. Her heart skipped briefly as she considered the possibility of being recognised. But the house's curtains were drawn, and she was just going to do a quick amble past, no more than a minute, tops...

The sinking sun beat down and she shrugged her shoulders, angling her elbows out from her body for a moment to let some of the sweat evaporate. A tram trundled past, its noise temporarily blocking out everything else, dragging in its wake the smell of brake fluid and hot steel.

Kyla resettled her shoulders and strode away from the car, her footsteps slapping purposefully on the concrete path.

The street smelled faintly green, the leafy, growing things fighting hard against the hot concrete and car brakes and warm asphalt.

A woman with a small, curly-coated tan dog hurried past, gaze hidden behind her large sunglasses but from the deliberate angling of her chin, probably averted nonetheless.

Even the dog kept its distance as it passed, pink tongue lolling in the heat.

That was fine with Kyla; she had no desire to be noticed by anyone.

She drew level with the house. Risked an extra-long blink in the edge of the plane tree's shade—and without the interference of the sunlight, saw clearly the same shade of blue that the frost children had emanated from the pond.

Something at the back of her skull itched, her own Touch agitating in response to what she was sensing.

It might be the frost children, it might not.

Whatever it was though, it wasn't just a person with a Touch. The pattern wasn't right.

Kyla strode quickly back to the car and bent over by Pippa's window.

Grudgingly, making a great show over how much effort it was, Pippa let the window down.

The air con blasted against Kyla's face, raising brief goosebumps on her neck.

She rubbed them away inattentively. "There's something in there," she said, staring back over her shoulder at the house where nothing seemed to move except the shifting pattern of shadows where the leaves of the plane tree blocked the sun.

"Something like what kind of something?"

Her neck prickled. "I don't know. Something like strange. Maybe the frost children who attacked me last night. I don't know," she repeated, still idly rubbing at her arms. "I need to go in and see."

"What? No—" Pippa began as Spy said, "Kyla, seriously, you can't. You'll put the whole investigation at risk," he continued, leaning across Pippa toward her. "No. I don't care what you saw, I can't let you risk it."

Kyla grabbed onto the car's window sill so she had something to clench in her hands that wouldn't break. "And *I* can't risk letting whatever is in there right now get away. Do you want me to save Dad or not?" She raised an eyebrow at Pippa.

"You'll die if you go in."

It was a lie and Kyla knew it in her bones, but Pippa stared unflinchingly, chin raised, defying Kyla to ignore her.

And...

Pippa was lying.

She was.

She had to be.

Kyla had forgotten how many blues were in her sister's irises. Like the ocean, just as shifting and moody and unpredictable.

She gave the car one last white-knuckled squeeze and flung herself upright. "Argh! Fine!" She wrenched open the back door of the car, threw herself down onto the leather, and slammed the door shut after her. "For the record," she said, "I hate you both."

"You're welcome."

If Kyla had been just a *few* years younger, she'd have kicked the back of Pippa's seat for the amount of smugness she'd packed into those two words, dignity be damned.

She shifted huffily as she buckled her seatbelt, maybe accidentally-kind-of-sort-of shoving a knee into the small of Pippa's chair back as she did.

Unsatisfyingly, Pippa said nothing.

This is exactly *why I work alone*, Kyla thought as Spy pulled the car away from the curb.

That, and the fact that her Touch needed discharging far more than she'd be comfortable with if she had a team around her.

Hell, it discharged far more often than was comfortable with only regular passersby around.

Whatever.

Kyla rubbed hard at the knuckle of her left index finger. Tomorrow. Everything would be better tomorrow.

22

To Kyla's great surprise, Pippa and Spy had come in with her when they'd dropped her back to Tane's rental. Pippa had brought a bundle of dark blue fabric in with her and disappeared into the bathroom, only to emerge a few minutes later dressed in her paramedic uniform.

"Another night shift?" Kyla said as Pippa slid onto the stool next to her at the bench, where Kyla was busily watching Tane do something magical on the stove with a hot wok and vegetables.

"Yes," Pippa said, and although it was still stiff and formal around the edges, it at least didn't have the usual air of judgement.

Kyla let her chin sink into her hand.

Tane had left the wok sizzling and spitting up the delicious smell of caramelising onions, and was now industriously scooping and mixing ingredients into a small bowl for a sauce. Satay, probably, given the giant scoop of peanut butter he'd just added.

Kyla's stomach grumbled.

Hungry, sure; but mostly what she felt was tired, worn out. She'd cycled through too many different emotions in the past couple of days and they'd apparently hit their limit; there would be no more emoting, her frazzled brain insisted, until she'd had at least nine solid hours of sleep.

At the kitchen table behind her, Lyssa broke out in a fit of giggles.

Idly, Kyla twisted around to watch. Spy was grinning too, while Eirene's expression was somewhere between shock and impish disbelief.

"What's so funny?" Pippa voiced Kyla's idle thought, albeit in a slightly more abrupt tone.

"He said we should test out our theory on him," Eirene said, eyes wide and voice hushed.

"What theory?"

Lyssa pulled herself together and the giggles resolved into a grin. "The whole idea of Touches being conveyed through blood. We were wondering some more about whether, you know, the murder part of Freja's plan is strictly necessary, if all she's after is more Touch energy. Only then..." She dissolved into giggling again.

"All I said was that if it was all the same to them, I'd rather not try for Lyssa's black Touch, because it would make chasing down criminals pretty complicated."

"And then Lyssa said..." Eirene stopped to press her lips tightly together, eyes dancing.

"I only said I thought a black Touch would make catching criminals a whole lot *easier*!"

Kyla rolled her eyes good-naturedly. If Pippa had made the joke, Kyla might have been offended. But Lyssa knew enough about the complexities of a black Touch, knew it would never be as simple as that in real life.

Speaking of, however, Pippa was apparently the one who did not find anything about the situation amusing; she frowned sternly at the group around the table, deep creases between her eyebrows. "Theo." Her hand clenched around the backrest of the stool. "You were joking, right?"

He shrugged. "You can't say it wouldn't be good to know if she's murdering as part of her power grab, or just for lols and funsies."

Pippa sniffed. "You don't want a Touch. You hate the Touched."

Kyla stiffened, sitting a little more upright. That wasn't the read she'd ever had from Spy before...

"Pip," Spy said gently, "I complain a lot about how it makes my job harder. That doesn't mean I hate them."

"But you said—"

He shook his head. "*You* said." Abruptly, he rubbed at his hairline over his forehead and winced. "Maybe we should talk about this later."

Pippa stared at him, hand still gripping the backrest of the bar stool so tight her knuckles were blanching.

The sizzling from the wok suddenly increased, like someone had doubled the volume.

Oh, Tane had added the sauce, and steam was billowing up from the wok, carrying with it the delicious savoury-sweet flavour of satayed onions.

Kyla's stomach grumbled again, this time loud enough for everyone to hear.

Lyssa giggled again behind her hand.

The noise seemed to deflate whatever had been holding Pippa rigid; she sighed, stood up, and paced over to sit in the spare chair at the table next to Spy. "Fine," she said. "But it's my Touch you're getting."

He leaned away from her, hands up defensively. "Whoa, hey, hang on now, I'm not sure that seeing how people die is that much better than killing them myself, actually."

His tone was light and easy, but Pippa winced as though he'd shouted at her.

He flinched. "Pip, you know that's not what I meant."

She nodded, but stood up anyway, the chair legs scraping across the floor.

"Pip..."

She shrugged and left the room. A moment later, the front door banged shut, followed by another violent sizzle from the wok as Tane dumped in the vegetables.

"She'll come round," Spy said, staring at the hallway.

He sounded certain, but he was experienced at putting a good face on things and there was no real way to tell if he was really sure.

Still. Not actually Kyla's problem. She sighed, shook it off, and took the chair Pippa had just vacated. "I guess it's Eirene, then."

The girls looked at her, puzzled, and Spy said, "Sorry, what?"

"Her Touch. You don't want to risk a black Touch, you don't want Pippa's Touch, but you're the one who raised the whole idea, so you must be thinking of Eirene's Touch." Kyla leaned back in her chair. "I can see the appeal. Being able to read minds would be pretty handy in your line of work, if not admissible as legal evidence."

Spy had the good sense to look sheepish. "That wasn't the reason, though."

"Of course not." Kyla turned to Eirene. "What do you think? Are you willing to risk losing your Touch to Theo here? That's a hell of a risk."

Eirene's face tightened. "Um."

"Wait," Spy interrupted. "I don't want her to lose her Touch."

Kyla shrugged. "That's what you're risking though, isn't it." It wasn't her fault people didn't think through the implications of their actions.

"I..."

"I'll need to think about this," Eirene said quietly, and then she too stood and left.

Spy put his elbows on the table and made a small grunt of frustration.

"Hey, you can take my Touch any time," Lyssa said lightly. It didn't take careful observation to see the very real pain in her eyes as she said it.

"It's not worth the risk," Tane said, and Kyla twisted around, having forgotten he had stakes in this game as well.

Tane concentrated on ladling the satay out into bowls, eyes fixed on his work as though spilling a drop would have disastrous consequences.

He was right, though. Nice as it would be to get an answer about the how of what Freja was doing, the risk just wasn't worth it.

"Who knows," Kyla said in an attempt to break the tension, "if Damon succeeds in making a Touchstone pendant, the whole idea of Touches might become obsolete anyway."

Tane's face spasmed.

Great. Now she'd managed to stress *every*one out. Kyla sighed. "Let's just eat," she said. She got up, took bowls full of steaming hot veggies from the kitchen bench, and handed them to Lyssa and Spy at the table.

Tomorrow, she'd collect the pendant from Damon and then everything would be fine.

Of course, handing over a Touchstone to the poisoners in exchange for an antidote might cure her father—but it wouldn't stop Freja mid-rampage.

Kyla shoved the thought aside. Tomorrow. Everything would be better tomorrow.

23

THURSDAY 8 DECEMBER

PIPPA HAD REAPPEARED BEFORE TOO LONG, THOUGH SHE'D eaten her satay mostly in silence. She and Spy had left soon after, pleading the need for sleep—and Tane had disappeared shortly after that. And without him there to (notionally) protect the girls, they'd left first thing in the morning, leaving Kyla to breakfast alone, keyed up, and with no one to take her frustrations out on, sitting at the kitchen bench chewing furiously on dry toast, Touch energy prickling at her back of her neck.

Pippa rang.

She ignored it. The mood she was in, that was only going to be a disaster.

Instead, she shoved the still-buzzing phone in her pocket, slung her backpack over her shoulder and her crumby plate in the sink, and headed out to catch a tram down to Damon's workshop. She'd collect the Touchstone, contact the poisoners and deliver the damn thing, and wrap up the day with a visit to the hospital with the cure for her father and then the whole bloody incident would be over and life could go back to the way it had been.

She slapped at the back of her neck, jaw clenching as the Touch energy prickled and prodded.

The tram ground to a halt, brakes squealing with the high-pitched grind of metal-on-metal. Kyla jumped down onto the street-level platform the second the doors opened wide enough, hot-brake smell smothering her for the first few of her stalking, emphatic strides.

She hitched her thumbs under her backpack and strode down the street, a teenaged boy walking a Dalmatian taking one look at her and veering aside to give her space.

She hitched the backpack again. Good. Space was exactly what she needed.

What she wanted. What she always wanted. Getting close to people was dangerous, in every sense.

The noise of a passing passenger jet had her scowling at the sky, the jet ruling its white lines across the depth of the clear, blue expanse.

Her footsteps slapped out her irritation against the footpath.

Tane was definitely hiding something from her. Why had he vanished? Where had he vanished to?

Ahead, a very young child cried out in frustration as its mother snatched at its arm, yanking it back to safety, its bid for freedom straight into the oncoming traffic of the main road aborted.

Adrenaline twisted in Kyla's chest. Well. Nothing ventured, nothing gained. She took her phone out of her pocket and texted. *We need to talk.*

A clatter ahead drew her attention, a workman in paint-spattered black work pants setting up a ladder that looked to be... Yes. He was setting up the ladder over the doorway to Damon's shopfront.

Kyla hurried up, shoving her phone away. Had something happened? Was Damon shut for the day? Surely he'd have contact her if she couldn't come to collect the pendant...

As she approached, the door swung inward and none other than Damon himself appeared, peering down the street with frown lines creasing his face.

"What's happening?" Kyla said, her forehead mirroring his.

"This?" He glanced upward at the ladder over his head and lost himself in muttering for a moment.

Kyla reached him as the workman snapped open a yellow 'caution' sandwich-style sign.

"Won't take a minute," the man said. "But you'll have to keep the door closed."

"Come in, come in," Damon muttered, hurrying Kyla in before flipping over the closed sign on the door and twisting the lock.

"What happened?" Kyla said again.

"Robbery," Damon said curtly as he led the way behind the counter.

"Robbery?!"

The glint and glitter of the morning light through all the glass had barely registered until a beam hit her right in the eyes. Kyla winced as she rounded the counter.

"Attempted."

The light was bouncing off the small round mirror hanging on the wall, the dark one wound around with tiny leaves and flowers. Kyla narrowed her eyes at it as though it had spat light into her face out of spite and let the counter gate thump shut behind her. "Nothing was taken?"

"They did not get past the front door. Only caused a lot of mess with the security mechanisms, and now I will be paying out of my pocket for the mess for a month, confound the one that did it." He scowled over his shoulder at the locked front door as he held open the one to workroom.

Warm air and fiery smells wafted around Kyla as she stepped past him. She shifted her tongue at the bitter smoke catching in the back of her throat.

Tane hadn't texted her back yet.

It had only been ten minutes, a perfectly reasonable interval.

She ran her tongue along the inside of her teeth, trying to dispel the itchy feeling at the back of her neck that was part building Touch energy, and part the jittery feeling that something was about to go wrong.

She pulled her phone out and sent another message. *I just need to know you're okay. Did Freja snatch you?*

A wave of self-consciousness flooded over her and she added a wink on the end. Didn't want to appear too desperate or personal or...

She shook her head, switched the screen back off—and a notification pinged through.

Alive, the reply from Tane read. *Back soon.*

How soon is soon, she wanted to ask, but Damon had unlocked the three locks on the tiny back room and was waving her into the room full of glass cabinetry and blank pendants, and besides, she didn't want to give Tane the wrong impression.

She shoved the phone back in her pocket again with a grimace and let the workroom door fall shut behind her, latching with a loud *click*. Her Touch energies roused like a snake uncoiling and she stumbled, clutching tightly at it with whatever mental part of her it was that did the clutching.

"You are okay?"

Damon was peering narrow-eyed at her, lips pinched as his gaze flickered to the cloud of black energy he'd said he could see around her before finding her face again.

She nodded. "Fine." She rubbed at the back of her neck, tensed as she felt energy spark from her fingertips like an electric shock.

She'd only discharged two days ago, in the shop when she'd first met Freja; for it to build again so quickly was absurd, especially after laying quiet all day yesterday like it hadn't even existed.

"Mm," Damon said, turning away to rummage in the one cupboard whose door wasn't glass. "You should hope that your friend gets back quickly."

"I wasn't—" Kyla's face went hot. She *had* been texting Tane, just not... like that. Urgh. It was too much effort to correct Damon, and she wasn't obligated to explain herself anyway, but what a good thing then that she hadn't replied further to Tane; if Damon could get so easily confused, she had to be extra careful in her conversations with Tane.

Something intense and not unpleasant rolled through her, and she had a sudden flash of standing in his shower. No, in the shower in the house he was renting. Not his shower.

...Would it be so terrible...?

Kyla stamped on that line of thinking, her face now feeling like it was incandescent. "I assume the pendant—the Touchstone—is ready?"

Damon straightened, a small, paper-wrapped package in his hand. "But of course." He shook his head, marvelling as he slid the glass, snowflake-shaped pendant from its wrapping. "To make such a thing..." He offered it to Kyla, and she accepted it. "But of course, you must be careful. Such a thing is not made to last."

Kyla barely heard him; the glass snowflake in her hand was twice the size of Freja's ones, heftier but otherwise identical in style—only where Freja's snowflake had edges sharp enough to cut, Damon had softened the edges on the glass. Or—she lifted it right up close, peering intensely—no. He hadn't softened or rounded off anything; he'd made the entire thing piece by piece, each strand an individual thread, so that the snowflake was a single design formed by scores of individual strands rather than a single, solid piece formed in a mould as Kyla had expected. "It's beautiful," she breathed —and that was before she closed her eyes to examine the delicate interplay of Touch energies swirling up and down the arms of the snowflake.

It wasn't quite the pastel whirlpool of Freja's snowflakes, but it was close—and anyway, this was designed to do something else, something different, so there was no reason they ought to look the same.

This snowflake's colours were darker, less pastel and more saturated, and the colours were more distinct: a swirl of six specific, precise strands of colour, rather than a gentle, graduated blend.

Breathtaking, though.

She blinked, sighed deeply, and roused herself. "How do I test it?"

Damon shrugged. "Test it."

"What, here? Now? On you?"

He shrugged again.

Kyla stared. "You're that certain of your work?"

A third shrug, but this time with a hint of a gleam in his eye.

Fine.

It was this or test it out on someone random, anyway; it wasn't like she had anyone else she could pass it off to for testing—well, okay, she could call Pippa and get her to test it, that would probably be safer, but it would take Pippa ages to get here, assuming she wasn't at work—was she at work? She was at work by now, surely, and waiting until nightfall for her to be done, with their father's life hanging in the balance…

"Kyla." Damon's voice broke gently through her spiralling. "It is well. You may test it on me. Have some faith in my work." He folded his hand over top of hers, the snowflake closed in between them.

Kyla nodded slowly, adrenaline snaking in her chest. "Okay," she exhaled.

Her Touch prickled at the back of her neck, itched at her fingertips.

Just a little spark. Just like when she was discharging at

bugs.

Of course, if the pendant didn't work, a tiny discharge would kill Damon just as surely as a huge one—a tiny bit of death was still death, after all—but at least, if she could minimise the amount of energy, if things went wrong, it wouldn't bounce out around the building and catch any innocent bystanders in its way.

Kyla relaxed her hold on her Touch, the energy sighing through her, something like a wave of cold fluid rippling down inside her arm.

Her fingers flashed hot.

Energy sparked.

The snowflake in her hand went from room temperature to burning in an instant. She jerked her hand back, hissing— but Damon grabbed her tightly, prevented her from dropping the snowflake to shatter on the ground... and he was fine.

Kyla froze, awkwardly balanced with Damon still supporting her wrist—but something was raging fiercely in her chest, a hot, golden band of triumph surging through her. "You're alive," she said.

Damon smiled smugly.

"You're alive!" she said. "And the pendant..." Damon let her go so she could open her fingers, and the pendant sat in her palm, whole and unshattered. Her eyes couldn't get any wider if she tried.

He shook his head at her look. "It will not last forever. But it is better than the one-use pendants I have made before. And who knows?" A creaky shrug, chased by a grin. "Maybe now that I understand how the power is anchored, I can make a better one again than this. Maybe one day, I will make a permanent one."

The Touchstone. This was it. This made so much more sense than vague rumours of a single stone; of course it had to be something replicable, something iterable. The rumours made the Touchstone sound mythical, singular—but everyone knew that myths inflated their subjects, made them more than what they were, and a special type of pendant, the making of which had been lost, made so much more sense than one random, specific stone that just so happened to completely nullify Touch energy, because where would a single stone like that even come from? How could it possibly be singular?

This made so much more sense.

Kyla wrapped the snowflake back in its silver tissue-paper wrappings, a fierce grin fighting for control of her mouth.

It didn't matter what Tane was hiding. She'd deliver this Touchstone to the poisoners, and Damon could make another Touchstone—Touchsnowflake? Touchflake?—and another, and another: one for her and one to give to Tane so he could capture Freja and one for Lyssa.

She pressed her lips together to suppress the grin.

She hadn't even left the store before she'd hit dial on her phone: she would set up an exchange with the poisoners, then call Pippa. At least this time, Pippa would be happy to hear from her.

24

THEY PLANNED TO MEET IN THE GREEN STRETCH OF PARKLAND south of the Royal Exhibition Building where Blood had died. Not exactly, not to the metre; they were closer to the building, within earshot of the white fountains, close enough to smell the pond water... but close enough to where Blood had been killed that Kyla kept finding herself scanning the clipped grass, the concrete pathways, trying to triangulate where it had been in the dark.

Impossible to tell by daylight now, of course, with the sun blistering down and the trees—now recognisable as largely Moreton Bay figs, with a few towering gums and something that the back of her mind wanted to call a cedar—dotting the grassy area and casting jagged, sharp shadows.

Kyla shook her attention back to scanning for people instead, trying to ignore the waves of anxiety pouring off Pippa, who shifted restlessly on the park bench beside her, fighting to keep her gaze from the corner of the Exhibition Building where Spy waited with his team.

Hot grass and the occasional whiff of petrol fumes from the road filled the air, the heat heavy and burdensome. Kyla flapped her elbows, trying to dispel some of the warmth.

"What are you doing?" Pippa snapped.

Kyla stopped. "There," she said, tilting her head in the direction of two youngish men who'd appeared around the curve of the main fountain. The way they clustered together, eyes gawking in every direction—that would have been give-away enough even without the wave of electric blue Touch energy that billowed in their wake.

Pippa went rigid, jaw clenched, eyes narrowing.

Kyla exhaled noisily. "Don't piss them off," she muttered.

"I can see their Touch as well as you can," Pippa shot back—but at a similarly muttered volume.

Good. She'd be careful then.

Pippa inhaled sharply.

"What?"

Pippa pressed her lips into a thin line.

"What?"

"One..." Pippa roll her shoulders. "One of them is going to die. Soon."

Kyla's eyebrows rose. "How?"

"Touch."

It was Kyla's turn to shrug deeply at the itch between her shoulder blades, the unpleasant response crawling there like a bug.

She breathed deeply.

The two men—boys? Either way there was barely any change in it—drew closer, then one dropped behind, taking up a position by the nearest bench some twenty or thirty metres away. Some of the Touch energy flared, ripping away from the rest to stay with him.

Despite the cloudless sky, the scent of ozone rose all around.

Kyla shifted one leg. Sit still. Stay still. Hold it together.

Was that a hint of lemongrass in the air, too, borne toward her on a momentary hot breeze?

She shivered.

Well-practised. The one who'd lingered behind would have no trouble reaching her from where he stood, if something went wrong—and with a blue Touch that intense, Kyla might not even have time to realise it if he did.

The other one stopped out of arm's reach. His expression was calm, his body language still—too calm, and too still. Kyla certainly wasn't any kind of blue Touch, but it didn't take a genius to spot that underneath his facade, the young man was packing it.

"Did you bring it?" he said, and sure enough, his words were clipped and tight.

Pippa tensed up beside her, but Kyla leaned back on the bench, lifting her chin lazily and smiling in her best shark-like manner. "Did you?"

He fumbled at his messenger bag, plunging one hand in and withdrawing a small, medical-looking plastic bottle; Kyla had seem similar as a child on the rare occasion she'd had to take medicine for a cough or an infection. "It's here," he said. "This will cure him."

Pippa jerked; oh, she'd very nearly leapt up, and even now seemed to be clutching at the front rim of the bench in order to prevent herself from snatching the antidote from the boy's hand, every line of her body straining for control.

Kyla pulled her backpack up from the ground onto her lap and unzipped it with a little zzzzz sound.

In the distance, a pair of children shrieked—with distress or laughter it was impossible to say.

Adrenaline sped through her chest.

Not yet. Just be cool. Not yet.

She dug through the tangle of clothing in her backpack, burying her hand deep into the coolness of the cloth... and drew out the pendant that Damon had made: the Touchstone.

Kyla unwrapped the silver tissue paper with a crinkle and held the pendant up in the light, sunshine glinting off it, Touch energy vining around it in thin primary-rainbow strands that fought to be seen in the full light of day.

The poisoner tensed.

"How do we do this?" Kyla said.

"You're sure it works?"

He was only just out of arm's reach. It barely took anything for Kyla to scootch to the edge of the bench and stretch out, grabbing him firmly by the wrist and letting her Touch discharge.

He yelped and snatched his wrist back, even as Kyla's black energy dissipated smokily into the air.

He clutched his wrist to him, eyes wide. "You could have killed me."

She shrugged. "You wanted to know it worked."

Pippa threw herself upright with a noisy exhalation. "There. You've seen it works. Hand over the antidote."

The young man moved to the side of the path as a family of bike-riders whizzed past, a lolloping Golden Retriever throwing air kisses as it passed.

"Now," Pippa said, hands on hips.

A brief moment of hesitation, then he thrust the plastic bottle at her, and Kyla let the pendant fall into his other outstretched hand. He shoved it hastily into the pocket of his jeans.

Kyla eyed the bump it made, one side of her mouth lifted in a non-smile. "What's to stop me making another one of these?" The answer, of course, was nothing, but she was curious to see their response.

He shot her a puzzled glance. "You can't make a Touchstone. It's not possible."

Something flip-flopped in Kyla's chest. They didn't know. They didn't know!

"If you could, though," he said, "I'd tell you to do it. You're safe enough from—for now," he said, abruptly changing what he'd been going to say, "but at the rate—well, you won't be forever. And this Touchstone can't be everywhere." He was already moving away, nearing the one Kyla was thinking of as Backup Boy.

And out of nowhere, it seemed, Spy and his team of police officers melted into view, having casually surrounded the two young men, who tensed, thought for a moment about rabbiting, and then sagged as they realised any chance of escape was cut off.

The one who'd handed over the antidote shot a scathing glare at Kyla. "You have no idea what you've just done."

The other boy was struggling against an officer who was trying to cuff him. "No, you can't! She'll kill us! You can't take us in, we'll die!"

Kyla's chest twisted; Spy had insisted on this part of the plan point blank, and Kyla couldn't exactly deny him, not when Pippa was his wife, not when Pippa insisted on being at the handover—but she didn't disagree with the young man's assessment of the situation, and the terror in his voice stabbed like a knife.

"Spy had better set those guards he promised," she muttered.

Footsteps sounded on the concrete path in response—Pippa was already striding away in the opposite direction.

"Wait!" Kyla ran the few steps to catch up.

"This had better work," Pippa muttered, the medicine bottle clutched firmly in her hand.

Adrenaline cascaded down Kyla's body. She hoped it did too. If it didn't...

She took a deep breath.

It would.

It had to.

That was all there was to it.

KYLA HADN'T EXPECTED THE HOSPITAL HALLWAYS TO BE SO busy, though if she'd stopped to think about it, she wasn't really sure when she thought they *should* be busy. Probably, she reflected, dodging an oncoming trolley laden with squishy-looking hospital lunches that smelled vaguely savoury and vaguely like the inside of an old fridge, she should have realised lunchtime was kind of a peak.

Of course, she hadn't really been expecting the backstage tour; as a paramedic, Pippa had just waltzed the two of them through the staff door into the emergency department, and with a few brisk waves and greetings kept them moving smoothly around corners and down corridors until Kyla was both hopelessly lost and, despite herself, a little impressed.

Nurses at a workstation—grey blue like the floor, the walls, the doors—chatted loudly in jargon that flew right over Kyla's head; machines beeped, wheels clattered—and there were people. Everywhere. Around every corner, down every passage, in every room...

Kyla took a long, steadying breath and tried to dispel the tension between her shoulder blades.

So many people. Quite a few of them with Touches, mostly pale, pastel colours with no smell or taste to them.

No black.

No one like her.

No one like her would be stupid enough to visit a hospital, not just full of people but full of *vulnerable* people.

It felt like a massacre waiting to happen—and she was the one holding the gun.

They stopped at a door where a swipe-lock and intercom barred their way.

"Just a second," Pippa muttered, and Kyla took half a step back, though it wasn't like Pippa needed room.

Breath shallow, shoulders tight, Kyla stayed back anyway.

A brief negotiation over the intercom and the door swung open.

The sign on the door had the visiting hours posted in big red letters. Kyla snuck a glance at her phone; they were about an hour too early.

But the door was opening anyway, and Pippa was leading the way, winding past blue-curtained cubicles all containing people whose vulnerability Kyla could practically taste.

She knotted her hands into fists; folded them into her armpits. Why hadn't she put her gloves back on for this? Stupid. Stupid, stupid.

The beeping of the machines here in the ICU seemed even more insistent, more urgent; Kyla couldn't ignore the fact that she was literally hearing the *life* of the people around her, measured out in increments by machines created for the sole purpose of keeping them alive.

Her throat tightened.

It's okay. This won't take long. You don't have to hang around.

Her nails bit into her palms, warm under her arms.

Goosebumps popped up over her shoulders. Was it actually colder in here, or was she really just that uncomfortable?

Pippa shot a glance back over her shoulder. "You okay?"

Kyla nodded, fully aware that every muscle in her body was taut.

Pippa pursed her lips, stopping by a blue curtain that seemed indistinguishable from all the others. "Ready?"

Another nod, just as taut.

Ready? Ha. No. Never. The last time she'd seen her father was ten years ago, and he'd been trying not to cry as she left.

Kyla's own eyes stung with unshed tears. But Pippa was sweeping back the curtain, the movement stirring the antiseptic air, and there, there was Dad, lying pale and drawn under a white hospital blanket, hooked up to his own array of beeping, bleeping machinery.

"Have you got it?" Kyla asked in a low voice. The nurses were occupied elsewhere, no one paying them any attention, thank God for Pippa—not a sentiment Kyla uttered often— but her heart still kicked, her neck prickling like someone was watching.

"Obviously," Pippa said, pulling the bottle from the deep pockets of her navy-blue work pants. "Shut the curtain."

Kyla did.

Pippa uncapped the plastic medicine bottle, squeezing the lid tight.

Even from a few steps away, the chemical scent of the antidote set Kyla's nose twitching—and she inhaled sharply. "Can you see that?"

Pippa had been more focused on Dad. She glanced down at the antidote—and gasped too. "What the hell?"

"I didn't know that was possible," Kyla admitted as the subtle flickering of Touch energies unfurled from the bottle, scent made visible, at least to those with Touches.

More shades of green than she'd known existed, with the odd spark of yellow or cyan.

"What is it?" she murmured.

Pippa narrowed her eyes. "I was going to ask you."

Kyla's eyebrows flickered up and down. "I told you. I didn't know that was possible."

There were a lot of things she didn't know were possible colliding this week.

Coincidence?

Hmm.

She pursed her lips.

"Do... Do you think it's safe to give it to him?" Pippa's blue eyes had widened, and something about that with the way one lock of her blonde hair curled down her cheek reminded Kyla of how she'd looked as a kid, back when Kyla had thought she was the most beautiful person in the world and had wanted nothing more than to be just like her big, beautiful sister.

"Yeah," she said softly. "Can't be worse than this, can it?" She gestured at their dad, eyes closed, cheeks hollow, his breathing labouring on with the aid of an oxygen mask. "Can... Is he still... You know. Dying?"

Obviously he was dying; a child could see that by looking. But Pippa knew what Kyla meant. "Nothing's changed," she said. "Yet." She looked down at the antidote, drew in a heavy breath, and held the swirling, twirling liquid to Dad's mouth.

How did you get an unconscious person to swallow? Kyla had no idea, had never thought it through before—but Pippa seemed to know what she was doing and once again, gratitude surged through Kyla's chest.

Wild.

The liquid—Kyla squinted—probably white, but the greenness of the Touch overwhelmed it to her senses—disappeared into Dad's mouth...

And... nothing.

Kyla clenched her hands again. Shouldn't there be some sort of visible sign? A change in the cadence of the machines?

Something? "How long do you think it takes to work?" she said.

Pippa frowned. "It worked."

"What? Then..." Kyla studied the crease between Pippa's eyebrows. "What's wrong?"

Pippa shook her head, a dismissal of thought rather than a negative. "I don't know. His... It's changed. But not all the way." She breathed a long, slow exhale. "We'll see."

Kyla's own brow creased. "If it's the antidote though, and we gave it to him in the right timeframe, shouldn't that be it? He won't die now? He'll be okay?"

"I don't *know*," Pippa snapped. "And besides, they never said he'd be *okay*, just that he wouldn't *die*."

Kyla's stomach turned. Shoot. She hadn't thought of that.

"You never do," Pippa muttered, capping the bottle viciously.

Kyla shot her a look.

"I know what you were thinking," she said, "and you don't." Her tone implied crossed arms, even though her hands were gripping the bottle tightly. "There's a reason you haven't gone insane with that Touch of yours."

Kyla's face took on a life of its own, flickering through a cascade of emotions Kyla couldn't catch, let alone name or identify. *Gone insane?*

Pippa sighed dramatically, just shy of rolling her eyes, and shoved the antidote bottle back into her pants pocket. "I've seen it, you know," she said. "People driven insane by their Touch. Usually black, or a dark colour near it. Kills them, sometimes." She glanced at Kyla for just an instant, her expression strangely softer than Kyla might have expected. "You haven't. You won't. Or you won't die from going insane from it, anyway."

A hook lurched in Kyla's stomach, her inner world destabilising. *I won't...* She shook her head.

No. That way madness *did* lie. She had no interest in knowing how she would die, had never stopped to think about what Pippa's Touch might mean in that regard—and realising that now made not one difference at all.

"No, you don't want to know," Pippa said, still staring at Kyla with that inscrutable expression. "Trust me. No one really wants to know."

Dad lay without moving, though it seemed possible that he was breathing a little more easily than he had been before.

Kyla exhaled, forcing her shoulders to soften. "Thank you," she said, and she wasn't really sure what she meant, or even who she was addressing—but Pippa moved shoulder-to-shoulder with her, and the warmth of her arm even through her uniform shirt felt like a shield against the ferocious air conditioning.

AND SO IT HAPPENED THAT KYLA HAD AN AFTERNOON ALONE: Pippa and Spy were working, the girls were doing whatever it was they did on an average day, and Tane was still MIA.

So Kyla did what any sensible person would do in her situation: with the poisoners firmly out of the way in the holding cells of Spy's station, she caught a tram out to the poisoners' house and strolled nonchalantly up the concrete path to its front door. It was tempting to hesitate, but the bright afternoon sunlight beat down, illuminating her for anyone to see, and hesitation would just draw suspicion. So she walked to the door with confidence and paused in the shade of the portico as though she had every right to be there. The tram she'd disembarked rattled off on its way, followed by a rush of traffic whose progress down the street had been temporarily blocked.

A jet flew overhead, the noise clear as the sky.

No clouds this afternoon. Not so humid as it had been. It was unlikely there'd be a storm tonight.

Kyla breathed deeply of the warm afternoon air—and realised she had absolutely no idea what to do next.

She closed her eyes. The odd aqua luminescence she'd sensed last time still marked the house as something worth investigation, and she rubbed absently at the back of her neck where her Touch energy was tingling.

The front door was locked, of course, and as it was a townhouse, neighbours sharing walls with it to either side, there was no access to the backyard. She could either stand here as long as possible, trying to glean what information she could—or what? Break in to the house? Absurd.

...She was going to break in to the house.

Squaring her shoulders, rolling her neck to dispel some of the agitation at the base of her skull, glancing up and down the street again—plenty of cars whizzing past but no foot traffic, thank goodness—Kyla set her jaw.

She stepped off the concrete path onto the garden bed, pushing past the bushes underplanting the front window, house bricks scraping her thighs, twigs prickling her bare calves. Her heart flip-flopped, adrenaline pulsing as she paused with one hand on the window frame.

Cars trundled past. None of them paid her any heed.

There was still no foot traffic.

Kyla peered closely at the edge of the window frame through the screen. It was an up-down window, not a side-to-side one, but—she squinted, tilting her head—it was possible that it wasn't fully latched.

A car door slammed.

Kyla jumped, whirled around—but it was further down the street, out of sight. She rubbed the tips of her bare fingertips against her palms. Energy crackled faintly.

It was possible the window wasn't latched shut, which meant if she could just get through the screen, she might be able to pry it open.

But she had to get through the screen.

Abruptly, Kyla remembered the knife she'd taken from Alethea's store. Jaw twitching, she slipped her backpack to the ground behind the bushes and rummaged. The knife was bigger than she remembered, not something delicate she could hide in her palm; if anyone bothered to look at her right now, they'd call the police in an instant.

Okay. That just meant she had to be fast—and lucky.

Gripping the mother-of-pearl handle tightly, Kyla drew the obsidian blade across the bottom of the window screen. She wriggled her hand into the gap, searching along the edge of the window frame for purchase... There. There *was* a gap between the sliding window panel and its frame, not enough to get her fingers into, but...

She jammed the knife into the gap and twisted slowly, testing to find the balance between pressure enough to open the window and not so much pressure it caused the knife to snap.

A scuffled groan: the window slid open a fraction.

She twisted the knife some more; another quiet scuff from the window.

That should do it.

She dug her fingers into the window gap.

Footsteps echoed in the street behind her.

Kyla whipped downward, crouching between the small-leafed bushes (probably a box hedge), cradling the sweaty back of her neck in her hands; the shifting shadows of the plane tree ripped over her; if she stayed still enough, surely no one would see her.

The smell of dirt and fertiliser clouded around her.

A dark-haired woman walked past with a tri-coloured Beagle, who twisted its head to stare at Kyla and her cloud of earthy scents for just a second before being distracted by something more immediate to sniff at in the street.

Kyla let go of her breath as the pair moved out of sight. With the back of her wrist, she wiped sweat away from her hairline. Phew.

She stood, changing her grip on the knife, and slashed the screen open wider along its lower edge. Tucked the knife back into her backpack. Dug her fingers into the window's gap and pulled until the gap was wide enough for her to fit.

Touch energy crawled along the back of her neck and her shoulders—it was always like this when she was amped up, didn't mean it was going to discharge, it had only been two days since it had last discharged and it had been quiet all night, so there was no reason to assume—

Thud.

She landed awkwardly on the carpet in the lounge room, one leg up on a low table that skulked against the window, the gauzy sheer curtain covering her like a veil.

So long as it wasn't a funeral veil. Kyla sniffed and dropped her backpack to the floor.

A pair of armchairs squatted on either side of the window, a dark couch lay against the side wall, and opposite that a large TV was mounted on the wall, gleaming dully as it reflected the light from outside. Something beside the TV sparkled in the light, too—a mirror, perhaps, or a picture in a frame, glass glinting—something round and approximately face-sized, anyway, whether home for a painted face or somewhere to reflect one.

Kyla strained her ears. Only the usual ticks and creaks of a house warming in the late afternoon.

Seemed like it really was empty.

She pursed her lips. Passersby notwithstanding, that had been almost too easy.

Outside, under the portico at the front door, a blue light began to flash, slicing at the sheer curtain with the same aqua blue that had drawn her here.

Urgh. Speaking of things being too easy.

An alarm, of course; it had to be. Kyla scrambled to her feet, knocking her shin soundly on the low table—she hissed

—and raced to the front door.

Control panel, control panel... Ah, there.

She flung open the little panel mounted on the wall, stared blankly for a second in shock—no control panel, just a simple on-off switch—and hurriedly recollected herself. She flicked the switch.

The light outside the front door still flashed, sending waves of aqua blue light through the frosted glass panel by the door.

Kyla whirled around, neck prickling. She'd have to leave. There was no other—

There was another control panel, on the other side of the entryway.

She snapped that open—yes, the alarm panel—how in the world was she going to guess the code?

She jabbed in 1234—no way that would work, she'd have to leave—

—and the flashing light outside the house subsided.

Kyla slumped against the wall and tried to remember how to breathe.

Her mouth was dry. She swallowed, tapped her fingers against the wall, dragged herself upright with a shaky inhale.

Well. That was fun.

She gave a slow, deliberate blink.

Huh. The aqua light was gone—not just the flashing one out the front, but the Touch-energy glow she'd come to investigate.

The box on the other side of the wall, the one with the on-off switch that hadn't been the alarm, tugged at her senses. Something she'd missed...

She crossed the hall in two steps and, without giving herself time to second guess, flicked the switch in the box back to the 'on' position.

The aqua Touch energy reappeared in the darkness behind her eyelids.

Breath catching, she flicked the switch off... and the light vanished.

On. Aqua light.

Off. No aqua light.

Off, and her Touch prickled watchfully at the back of her neck and in her fingertips.

On, and her Touch… disappeared.

What the heck? Not just an object, but an entire *system* that could influence Touch energy?

The hairs on her arms rose and the back of her neck prickled.

Who *were* these people?

A muffled thump came from the lounge room where Kyla had entered.

She stiffened. Nowhere to hide in the entryway. Surely no one had been in the lounge, though, when she'd come in through the window? She hadn't seen anyone, and if anyone had been there—

—Someone had to have followed her lead, entering in through the now easy-access window.

Kyla scrunched up her face and cursed her carelessness.

"So, you decided to let me in at last."

The light, feminine voice was familiar.

Kyla's chest twisted.

Freja.

Well. There was no hiding then, was there.

With a deep, steadying breath and a determination to keep her expression unruffled, Kyla stepped into the door-way that led to the lounge.

The woman standing in the middle of the room with one hand in the pocket of a dark blue trench coat far too hot for the weather tilted her head, her hair pulled back into a perfect blonde bun, flawless makeup tinting her eyelids ice blue to highlight the natural blue of her eyes. "*You* are not supposed to be here," she said, and withdrew her hand from her pocket. The statement was factual, an observation about the weather, or the inevitability of death.

Kyla gave Freja a slow nod, determinedly keeping her face relaxed and the lines of her body fluid. What had Freja just pocketed, hmm? She could see the outline of it against Freja's thigh. "Neither are you."

A smile ghosted across Freja's mouth. "I wasn't trying to hurt you, you know."

"Oh?" Kyla folded her arms and leaned casually against the door frame. "Unlike everyone else you've approached since coming to town?"

The smile dissolved. "I needed something different from them." She shrugged, nonchalant. "And, they were bad people."

Despite herself, Kyla scoffed. "They were bad people? Last I saw, they weren't the ones running around murdering people. Blood was my friend. So was Alethea."

A long, searching look from eyes that had Kyla shifting and resettling, despite her determination to appear calm. Something about them seemed haunting, familiar, beyond the familiarity Kyla had from seeing Freja's face on posters and TV.

"No," Freja said. "He might have been, once. But I've been watching you. You have standards. He? The others?" She shook her head. "They were bad people, Kyla. I'm just trying to make the world a safer place."

The nonchalant shrug, the innocent micro-tilt of the head... She was good, Kyla had to give her that. Even as she analysed Freja's body language, her tone, the way she was leading Kyla down a carefully scripted path... Even then, Kyla could feel her resolve softening. She shook her head briskly, trying to dislodge the clouded thoughts. Her Touch energy buzzed. *Good. Focus on that.* "No. *Tane* is trying to make the world a safer place."

Freja laughed, the same gentle, inviting sound reminiscent of fairies in the woods that Kyla had heard before in TV interviews—only, in real life, it was even more enchanting. "Don't you think you were given your gift for a reason, Kyla? Don't you think you deserve to stop masking who you are?"

"And who is that?" Her heart hammered.

Freja laughed again. "I understand," she said. "Truly, I do. You want the Touchstone so you can be free of the burden that comes with your gift, so you can be the one in control of the energy instead of the energy in control of you. To choose how and when you release your power…" She shook her head sadly. "Kyla, that's all I want as well."

"Then why are you stealing people's Touches?"

"Who told you that?"

"Alethea. The truth-teller. You killed her, too." A rush of grief welled in Kyla's chest, expanding until there was no space left to breathe. "She wasn't a bad person."

The head tilt again, less micro this time. "No? Do you think it was only products and artefacts she sold in her store? Do you think there weren't people, big people, powerful people, bad people, who would pay whatever it took, do whatever it took, to obtain the kind of information she could provide?" Freja had stepped forward with each assertion and stood now within hugging distance—no, within hitting distance; why had Kyla thought hugging?

Kyla shook her head.

"People like that," Freja whispered, "are too dangerous to let live. People like that"—she reached out and swept a wisp of hair from Kyla's cheek as though Kyla were a child Freja was indulging by sharing a grown-up secret—"will always live at the mercy of those most willing to threaten them."

"People like that…" Kyla closed her eyes tight. "People like me."

"Yes," Freja breathed. "People like you. They have blackmailed you, have they not? Told that if you hand over the Touchstone to them, they will save your ailing father?"

Kyla swallowed, nodding, eyes still closed as though that might guard her against the whirlpool of thoughts clamouring to drown her.

Freja tsked. "And yet, what motive do they have to keep their word? What is it they want the Touchstone for?"

"They… I…" But the answer could only be similar to her own—to Freja's own, if she could be believed—questionable—but the only possible motive was to nullify a Touch they didn't want to have.

And if her father weren't being held ransom... What difference would it make, whether they had the Touchstone to nullify their powers, or she had it to nullify hers?

And the poisoners hadn't exactly proven trustworthy.

Besides. Damon could always make another.

Kyla opened her eyes, snatching at the question to keep herself anchored. "Why haven't you made one?"

Freja's eyes widened a fraction.

"You make the snowflakes, surely if you can make those you know how to make a Touchstone."

Freja blinked once, twice—and laughed.

After the quiet tone of the conversation, the full-volume noise was jarring, and Kyla jerked back a step, jaw and shoulders knotting, fingers twitching.

"Oh, precious child, you really do not know. All this time, I thought you were engaging in an elegant deception, and yet..." She shook her head, an indulgent smile spread across her pink-lipsticked mouth. She leaned in, making up the distance Kyla had gained, and Kyla's hands tightened into instinctive balls. "*Ask your hunter friend*," Freja said in a hoarse stage whisper, eyes dancing. She straightened. "The handsome one. Tane?" She gave a decisive nod. "And when you don't like his answer, use one of the snowflakes. My children will fetch you to me—and I will give you the answers you *deserve*."

Freja vanished.

Kyla jolted. But Freja had really and truly vanished, not out the window, not behind some furniture, just... gone.

Was manifestation a Touch power now too? Or was that a side effect of Freja having meshed so many Touches?

Kyla groaned and rubbed at her neck. Had Freja directly avoided Kyla's comment about stealing Touches, or had it just gotten lost in the thread of the conversation?

Ask your hunter friend.

Kyla set her jaw. First, she was going to examine the poisoners' security system to figure out how it worked—and how it had been able to keep Freja at bay—and then she was going to call Tane, and keep calling until he answered. Whatever he was hiding, it had gone on long enough.

27

KYLA CHEWED ANGRILY ON A HOT CHIP, THE CRUNCH AND SALT of it all a convenient foil for her anger as she strode down the dinnertime street, crowded with evening shoppers and dinner take-awayers, all of them—presumably—as dripping with sweat as Kyla was, though most of them weren't dumb enough to be carrying a tub of hot food around to make themselves even hotter. Ha.

A tram rumbled past down the middle of the relatively narrow road, all squeaks and metallic screeks, and overhead a jet streaked a contrail through the scattered-cloud sky.

The scent of spicy-sweet samosas and lemongrass curries and deep-fried deliciousness filled the hot air, overpowering the usual city smells of petrol and oil and hot concrete, and the smell of brake fluid from the passing tram.

People muttered and mumbled and chattered, an ebbing, flowing human tide of dinnerers and shoppers and dog walkers, bumping Kyla's bare arms as they wove around her, or brushing her backpack as they squeezed past in the throng.

The back of Kyla's neck itched, and she scowled. Her Touch had been steadily demanding more and more of her attention since yesterday evening, but now it was itching up a fit, and her fingers tingled.

Add that to the list of things she wanted to ask Tane about.

Things she would ask just as soon as he stopped avoiding her calls.

True to her resolution, she'd examined the poisoners' security system and determined that the aqua light was some sort of interference field; if she stood on the perimeter (at the front door, for example, by the control panel) and it was on, it deflected her Touch—but unlike pendants, which deflected other people's Touches away from the one wearing the pendant, the system deflected Kyla's own Touch away from her so it was inaccessible, unreachable.

Though it was the same concept, really, just as though the house was wearing a pendant that deflected Kyla's energy from reaching it.

In practice, it meant that along that perimeter, Touches didn't work—which, Kyla assumed, was enough to prevent Freja from waltzing into their house.

Why they wanted to keep her out was another matter—assuming it was Freja they were warding against, of course. But given she'd killed Blood, it seemed likely that she was after them all; perhaps that's what they wanted the Touchstone for in the first place, though with a security system able to exclude Freja and keep them safe, Kyla wasn't quite sure how the stone fit into all of that.

She ground another chip between her teeth and dodged a woman walking some sort of bulldog down the footpath, her footsteps practically stomping holes in the concrete.

Briefly, Kyla crushed her eyes closed despite the human throng around her. Her chest constricted: her father, lying pale and wan in the hospital bed, the moment of adrenaline-fuelled excitement when she'd thought the antidote would work…

She forced the memory aside.

Anyway, she was here now, striding past the wool store to the poster-plastered metal door that led to Alethea's shop, the one place she could think of that might provide any sort of lead to guide her search.

Overhead, a narrow slice of sky separated the two, cerulean in the late sunny evening.

Adrenaline zinged through Kyla's stomach as she reached, bare-handed, for the metal doorknob: that poster was still hanging on the door, the one from the Melbourne Museum advertising the gala this coming weekend—the one sponsored by Freja.

Kyla's jaw clenched. She tore the poster from the door, folded it deftly, and tucked it into the back pocket of her shorts.

Another hot chip—now a lukewarm chip, despite the ambient temperature—went into her mouth, crunch crunch, salt and starch to take away the sting of her anger.

He knows more than he has told you.

Well of course he does, Freja, hence my entire frustration with him in the first place. Kyla twisted the cool metal doorknob, shoved the door open, and ducked into the small, short alleyway.

Of *course* Tane knew more than he was letting on. That wasn't news. Kyla had known *that* since the moment she'd first talked to him, which, inconceivably, was only a couple of days ago, and very near this spot in fact.

She shut the door behind her with a clang and took a deep breath—and immediately wished she hadn't. Alethea hadn't emptied the bins before she'd left, or perhaps the storekeepers to either side were using this area now she was gone, because the skip bin was full and the smell *wasn't* that of old cardboard, Kyla could assure anyone willing to listen.

Wrinkling her nose against the stink of overripe fruit and rotting leftovers, next to the skip bin Kyla climbed the worn brick steps, the handrail cold against her bare fingers, backpack weighing against her shoulders.

The alleyway was, at least, a little cooler than out on the street.

At the top, the door that had once been teal and now showed silvered splinters waited.

It was easy enough to pick the lock: it was old-fashioned and hardly worth the brass it was made from. Alethea relied on her Touch to keep the store safe more than any mundane means.

The door swung inward with a creak.

Kyla had a feeling that whatever she was here looking for—and she had no idea what that might be, not really, nothing beyond her reliable intuition that here was a good place to look—it wouldn't be out in the main displays, so she strode into the store that seemed frozen in time: bundles of dried flowers and herbs still festooning rafters, wire racks of the kind of miscellany sold and pawned by people drifting through life still clinging to the walls.

As she stepped through the doorway, something frissioned down her spine; she glanced left and right—and realised, for the first time, that a matching pair of glass statues sat on small shelves bookending the doorway, emanating red Touch auras so faint that, even in the darkness of the closed store, it was barely visible, easily missed.

Breath catching, Kyla reached out to the one on her right —it was a glass dolphin, with sleekly patterned red-and-blue sides and a pleasingly curled dorsal fin—and let some of her energy spark into it.

Black smoke swirled inside the dolphin for a moment, then flashed red and was gone.

Exactly like the bees.

She chewed on the inside of her lower lip. The dolphin sparkled in the fluorescent light slanting in from the alleyway.

On the wall behind it was a switch Kyla would have previously assumed to be nothing more than a light switch.

She flicked it.

Fed a sliver of energy into the dolphin—or tried to, and failed as the energy parted and slid over the dolphin like water.

She flicked the switch again, and now the glass dolphin absorbed her energy again, the blackness swirling through it like smoke and flashing red before it vanished.

She'd always assumed that Alethea knew who was at her front door because of her Touch; she'd certainly used her Touch when Kyla had come to the back door the other day, and Kyla didn't remember seeing any statuettes near that door.

But the dolphins switched on and off like the poisoners' security system, and took in her energy like the bees that she and Damon had variously found.

So the bees... were a security system?

Red was truth-telling. So the dolphins were... a fancy version of a bell over the door, alerting Alethea not only was someone entering the store, but also providing some sort of... identity check?

Freja was using the snowflakes as beacons, planting them so she could find her marks later, presumably when the moment was right to kill them. But how did she find her marks in the first place?

There had been a bee in that glass store, where Freja had found Kyla and planted the snowflake on her.

The bees might belong to someone else... But it was a heck of a coincidence if so.

Kyla sighed and made a note on her phone to call Damon at some point and get him to examine the bees, see if they had any sort of Touch aura to them like the red dolphins of Alethea's or the aqua blue of the poisoners' security system.

(...And Freja's ice children, also aqua blue; how did they fit in?)

Kyla shook her head, dispelling the thought. Enough questions. More than enough questions. She was here for answers, not more questions, although possibly, if her guesses were right, here was at least something of an answer regarding the bees.

She sighed again.

At the far end of the store over the counter the pair of clocks sliced time away in dissonant ticks, and Kyla ducked under them, through the doorway to Alethea's personal quarters.

The air was warmer in here, and the faint scent of toast lingered in it, though that was just as likely a scent recalled from her imagination and memory than any real odour. The floral wallpaper was still clean and neat and slightly worn, the chintzy armchairs still huddled around the small Queen Anne coffee table, and abruptly Kyla's chest constricted; it was like she might turn at any moment and find Alethea still there, her long grey hair bundled up atop her head, deeply lined face creasing into a smile as she offered Kyla tea and biscuits.

It was only that Kyla had seen Alethea so recently, she reasoned. Before that, it had been years—more than a decade—since she'd seen Alethea last, and she'd never gotten emotional about it then.

Of course, she'd had no reason then to think that Alethea might be dead, too.

Sniffing softly, Kyla moved through the tiny kitchen space with its gleaming silver sink and old, squat refrigerator, wound past the armchairs and climbed the narrow staircase that led up to the loft where Alethea both slept and kept her business records.

Again, Kyla had no real idea of what it was she was hoping to find, but she hadn't made a name for herself as one of the most formidable artefact hunters in the country for nothing, so up the creaky stairs she went, until she saw the towering four-drawer filing cabinet and knew that was her best bet for finding something.

Something, anything, it didn't matter: anything that would lend clarity to this mess and help her know who to believe. Freja was... unhinged, absolutely, but her comments about Tane...

Kyla's jaw twitched. She so badly wanted to believe Tane was the good guy in all of this. But he was holding information back, she knew it. And he'd disappeared.

She winced at the screech made by the filing cabinet's top drawer as she pulled it open, but no one would hear it unless they were already in the shop, and if someone was already in the shop, Kyla was already in trouble.

She took a deep, steadying breath, licked salt from the corner of her mouth, and flicked her fingers over the files at chin height in the top drawer.

At first there seemed to be no order to the files at all, the labels on each folder neither alphabetically organised nor categorically organised nor anything else that Kyla could detect.

But slowly, as the minutes ticked on and she browsed drawer after drawer and folder after folder, Kyla began to get a sense of things.

Prophecies—well, not exactly, that implied something slightly less certain and more future-oriented than Alethea's complete and absolute knowledge of the present, but to Kyla they *felt* like prophecies—about people were in the top drawer. Places went in the second drawer, with events in the third. The bottom drawer was half prophecies that seemed to be ideological in nature, and half general correspondence that Alethea had seen fit to hold onto for whatever reason.

Kyla was about to give up on that section and head back to the top to more thoroughly investigate people, hoping for something on Tane, or Freja, or *any*thing, when a familiar name caught her eye.

It was an email from Tane, printed out, dated six weeks prior.

It was an email from Tane to Alethea, who he'd claimed he didn't know—well, Kyla frowned, wrinkling her brow, he never *said* that, but he definitely let it be heavily implied—enquiring about...

Kyla's stomach dropped like the hot chips had decided to do a barrel roll.

Enquiring about *her*.

Okay, okay, it hadn't started out that way. Skimming down the chain of previous emails that had been printed below the most recent response from Tane, Kyla quickly surmised that he'd written to Alethea with a general enquiry about people in the area with strong Touches.

Alethea had responded with a shortlist—Kyla's finger skimmed back up the page as she read the emails in chronological order—Tane had asked for more details on a few of them, including—Kyla's heart skipped again—herself, and gradually they'd narrowed their conversation down to discussing four people in the greater Melbourne district other than Alethea, all with—Kyla swallowed—Touches sufficiently strong enough to interest a serial killer.

Jason Makris. Kyla knew him better as Blood, short for Bloodhound, and he was already dead.

So was, she presumed, one Adam Katsaros. He must be the body she'd found the first night.

Which left two names on the list of powerful people Freja might try to target: Kyla Jewel, and...

Kyla's jaw clenched so tight it hurt. The printed-out email crushed in her grip as she pressed her fist to her forehead.

Because the last name on the list was Lyssa Yee.

28

BY THE TIME KYLA HAD FINISHED IN ALETHEA'S SHOP—WELL, in the filing cabinet, though she had stopped to grab a few choice artefacts on her way out, justifiable payback to bloody Alethea and her bloody secrets—the sun had disappeared under the horizon and stars were twinkling overhead. But the lack of sun didn't matter; Kyla was angry enough to burn on her own.

Tane had promised to share anything he knew with her. Anything he could. And yes, okay, he'd gotten around to telling her eventually that Freja was maybe possibly targeting her, but dammit all, wouldn't you think that was the kind of information he should have *led* with?

Kyla stalked down the footpath, past the tall fence of the primary school a block behind Alethea's shop, feet smacking the pavement hard enough to jar her teeth.

As if she cared.

She was tired.

Tane had vanished.

Alethea had left town.

Pippa was mad at her, and the girls were too young and too untrained to be any real help at all.

Kyla kicked at a rock in the path, and the sound of it skittering into the gutter should have been satisfying.

Instead, it fanned the flames of her outrage.

But besides being pissed off at both Tane and Alethea for their secrets—secrets which they *apparently* had decided were more *important* than, you know, helping Kyla save her father's life—Kyla was tired.

Dinner sounded impossible.

Hot chips counted as dinner, right?

Right.

So, fuming, she stalked the couple of blocks west toward the train line, the blinking lights of a jet roaring past overhead and the occasional late evening car whooshing past on the road beside her, until she Tane's house—because where else was she going to go? Pippa might have begrudgingly worked with her this week, but Kyla wasn't foolish enough to assume that would extend to an offer of accommodation.

She unlocked the door to the dark cottage with the spare key she'd somehow ended up with, padded into the kitchen-living area, and flicked on the lights before dumping her backpack on a dining chair.

A hot shower and a mug of tea later—English breakfast tea, despite the time of day, since the rental's options were sorely limited—and she was curled up on one of the grey couches in the living area, some free-to-air movie with spies and explosions playing in the background as she sipped the slightly bitter tea contemplating her options, no longer quite so fuming but not exactly... Well, she'd been thinking that she wasn't feeling ready to forgive Tane or Alethea yet, but that was a given. Bastards.

Anyway.

Kyla pressed the warm mug against her forehead and closed her eyes, sighing. The bitter-rich scent of the tea wound around her, the steam misting her hair, which was wafting slightly in the air conditioning.

There was a knock at the front door.

Kyla's brow furrowed.

Pippa hadn't messaged or called to say she was dropping by, and even if it was one of the girls, they'd have messaged or called first too. Surely.

She set her mug down on the black laminate bench in the kitchen as she passed and wandered out to the hallway.

Tane had a key, though if he knew what was good for him, knew she was home and furious at him, knocking might be more sensible, ha.

Freja wouldn't track her down like this, would she? Or at least if she did, she wouldn't knock.

Kyla flicked the entryway light on as a shiver crawled down her back. Turned on the front porch light too, to be on the safe side.

Opened the old-fashioned front door with a frown, because the silhouette showing through the stained glass panels in the wood didn't seem familiar.

It was a man, broad and tall, dark hair cropped close to his skull, t-shirt close-fitting above black work-style pants where —Kyla's pulse thrummed—the hilt of some sort of knife was visible in his right thigh pocket.

He noticed her noticing, lips stretching broadly into something that wasn't a smile. "I'm here for the Touchstone."

Kyla blinked. "The... Touchstone?"

"Don't play games," he said, his mouth changing instantly to a deep scowl. "You know. The pendant."

Kyla's heart double-kicked in her chest. But... "I don't have it," she said, which was true. Fat lot of good it had done her, but it was true.

"Bull. They said you had it. I'm here for it, the easy way or the hard way."

Kyla nearly rolled her eyes. Instead, she folded her arms and draped herself against one of the doorposts. "Oh really." Her Touch energy was itching at her anyway, prickling in her fingers and the back of her neck, and she wasn't wearing her gloves—nerves tugged at her stomach for a brief moment before she pushed them aside.

She let a thin strand of Touch energy spool out into her hands. She didn't think this man was Touched, but sometimes a Touch was so faint you couldn't sense it. If he was, regardless, he'd be able to see *her* Touch, see how the energy gathered in her fingertips, and even though her cloaking pendant would make it seem grey to him, not black, that was usually more than enough to scare anyone who could see it away.

The man loomed closer. "I'm not leaving without it."

"I *don't have it*," Kyla ground out, sighing internally. Of course it would have been too easy for him to see her energy and just... go away.

She concentrated for a second, working to rein the energy back in again... and it didn't respond.

Kyla frowned. Since when was her energy that strong after only two days, strong enough that she had to fight it a bit to get it to settle, to drain it away from her fingers where it could do harm?

The man stepped toward Kyla, pressing his advantage as her fight with her own Touch energy distracted her.

Unthinking, she stepped back. *Come on, settle down,* she snapped at the energy even now pooling in her hands. *I don't* actually *want to kill him.* It had been years since she'd done that; usually posturing was all it took.

The door shut with a click.

Shoot. She'd let him inside, and he'd closed the door, that not-a-smile stretching his mouth again until the teeth showed.

"Where are you hiding it, pet?" he said.

"I'm not your pet," she said through a jaw that kept twitching and clenching, "and I told you: I don't. Have. The

Touchstone. I already offloaded it, earlier today."

"Oh?" He cracked his knuckles. "To who?"

"Not you." She sniffed. "Get out of my house." Well, not her house, but whatever.

Energy crackled in her fingertips.

What the hell? The last time her energy had been this feisty, she hadn't discharged it at all in over a week. But she'd fully emptied herself two days ago, done some minor discharges since then...

Gritting her teeth, Kyla fought to reel back the energy before it exploded and killed the man in front of her. She had a whole swathe of options before death.

(*Alethea*—the name was sarcastic, even in her head— would be so proud.)

But the man stepped forward, inexorable, and then suddenly, he leapt.

Snatched at her hand, caught her wrist.

Her Touch energy flared.

Nauseated, she fought it back.

She screamed wordlessly at the man—*Let go of me, I don't want to kill you!*

Itchiness at the back of her neck. Ozone and lemongrass bursting through the air.

She wrenched her arm away, pivoting and ducking down to throw her opposite shoulder into his solar plexus.

He tensed in expectation. She might as well have hit the wall, though he did grunt before reaching over her to grab her upper arm, his knee rising to smack her in the face.

She twisted at the last moment and it hit her chest instead. Oof.

Breath vanished from her lungs. She gasped, gaped.

He spun her around, pinning her arms behind her on an angle that practically tore them out of her shoulder sockets.

Kyla threw her head back.

Blinding pain as she smacked into his nose, his teeth tearing her scalp.

His fingernails raked her upper arms.

She twisted again, one arm flying free from the torsion.

The man bellowed, lashed out, grabbing for her flailing hand.

His wrist flashed past Kyla's face and instinctively, she snapped, tearing at him with her teeth.

Blood flowed from the side of his hand.

She spat the metallic gunk from her mouth, eyes wild.

Itchiness at the back of her neck. The smell of ozone and lemongrass, hanging thick in the air.

Kyla squirmed—and his wounded hand brushed her upper arm, where he'd scratched her skin open. Blood from his hand touched hers.

Orange energy flared.

Kyla's eyes widened, her breath catching.

The man gasped too, a horrified noise of confusion.

Orange?

But...

No...

What?

Black energy coursed down Kyla's arms in a tidal wave. She wrenched her attention away from the fact that her attacker was suddenly showing a Touch he hadn't had a moment ago, trying to control her own Touch.

She ground her teeth. Strained, with every ephemeral part of her, even as his arm thwacked across her back, bruising her spine.

It was too much.

Couldn't stop it, couldn't restrain it.

The black energy burned more than the man's vice-like grip on the back of her neck.

It exploded.

Darkness snaked and swooped around the hallway, constrained by the walls, too big for the space, too much, too powerful...

The man's heart stopped.

His grip on Kyla's neck slackened.

The man thudded to the floor.

Kyla dropped to her knees likewise, her throat raw as she gasped for breath.

No.

No, I didn't want...

No! I only discharged two days ago! It shouldn't have been strong enough for this...

A thunderous knocking at the front door interrupted her.

She scrambled to her feet.

"Hello? Hello, is everything alright in there?"

No, she thought. *Everything is not alright.*

She stepped over the man she'd just killed, stalked to the doorway, and forced a placid expression to her face.

Alethea's words rang in her ears:

"Keep your allies close, Kyla. You weren't meant to do everything alone. You know what happens when you do."

29

IN THE NIGHT AROUND HER, INSECTS CHIRPED AND CLICKED. SHE stalked alone through bushland scented with eucalyptus and fresh pond water, anger still fuelling her as late evening gave way to night.

The man at the front door—the second man, that was—had been easy enough to persuade to leave. He'd heard a scream as he'd been walking past, lived in the area, didn't love that the cottage was a short-stay rental, wanted to make sure everything was okay, had to keep the area safe, didn't you know.

Kyla assured him that she did in fact know, and was doing her level best to aid him in his quest for suburban security, and thank you *very* much for stopping by, so neighbourly of you, do call again if you feel like, thanks for coming, bye.

She let out a tight breath. The eucalypt and acacia—gums and wattles—about her rattled and rustled, and her footsteps crunched through the litter of dry leaves and bark and twigs—no way to be quiet here, not in the dark. She couldn't walk quietly here even in the daytime. But it didn't matter; she wasn't trying to avoid attention, was she—so long as no person interfered, and why would they, a scant hour or so before midnight in the middle of forsaken bushland?

Kyla snorted softly.

And stumbled as a thin branch clawed at her shoulder and face. Oops. Maybe...

She slipped her phone from her pocket and turned the torchlight on. Probably should have thought of that before, but Alethea—and the man Kyla had killed—and Freja... Kyla hadn't killed someone in oh-so-long, hadn't let her near-perfect control slip in a decade, and her chest was tight, and her throat hurt, and it didn't matter because he'd been trying to attack her, it was self-defence, and Alethea couldn't possibly be right, Kyla wasn't a murderer like Freja, it was just that Tane wasn't being any *help*, and her dad was going to *die* if she didn't get the real Touchstone for the blackmailers, and maybe so was she, and Lyssa...

Kyla took a deep, controlled breath, slowing her breathing back down again, fighting for control of her heartbeat as it raced.

There. The pool was ahead, the water glinting in the phone light.

She'd be careful.

She'd get the answers she needed from Freja, and she'd be careful.

Alethea was wrong. She wasn't going to end up like Freja, even if she had no one around to help her.

...Now what?

Kyla drifted in a slow circle, shining the torchlight through dark-trunked gnarled acacias and willowy grey-and-white gums... but she was definitely alone.

A rustling scuffle made her jump—

But it was just a brush-tailed possum, grey and adorable, scurrying away from her over the other side of the small pond and up a tree, where it disappeared.

Kyla pressed the back of her hand to her chest.

Shut up, she told her pulse. *We're fine.*

Dammit. Freja had said to use a snowflake to get her attention, but Tane had them all, or else he'd hidden them well before he'd disappeared.

Get Freja's attention. Okay. Freja had found her because she'd been near one of the bees the first time, and near the poisoners' security system the second time. Presumably, her Touch had passively triggered them, just like it did the dolphins in Alethea's store. There was no way of knowing how sensitive Freja's bee network was—*if* that was indeed what it was—but perhaps something big and loud might be enough to set them off and get Freja to look this way.

She didn't know who else to turn to for answers.

Kyla cast around in the darkened bush, but a) there was nothing around anyway except presumably a few more possums, and b) the problem with big and loud was that her Touch was good for one thing and one thing only: it was black, and that meant death. She'd done enough killing for one night, even if she *could* summon enough energy to make it fully discharge again.

Kyla rubbed at the back of her neck where her Touch energy prickled when it was at full charge. Right now, nothing.

On the other hand...

On the other hand, right before the man had... okay, right before she'd *killed* the man, he'd suddenly developed an *orange* Touch. Did that mean...

Kyla frowned, forehead furrowing. If there was some sort of orange base to her Touch, how could she *access* it? As far as she knew, as long as she'd been dealing with her Touch (nearly twenty years, ever since she'd turned fourteen and had to confess to her parents that not only did she have a boy in her bedroom, he was a dead boy), there wasn't any such thing as a little bit of death: black Touch was black Touch, and when she discharged her energy, something died.

Death was death. Black was black.

An *orange* Touch?

Orange was for finding things, tracking things down.

...It was literally her job to hunt things down. After all, wasn't that why the poisoners had presumably picked her to blackmail into finding the Touchstone in the first place?

Far out.

Kyla needed to scream, or collapse on the grass, or cry, or do something dramatic enough to signify the total shifting of identity that was occurring, but everything seemed trite— and useless.

Okay.

So maybe the base of her Touch was orange. She'd figure out why it had always appeared black later; right now she needed to know how to access that orange part of it, because she had a sense she could do more with that right now, running on virtually empty, than she could with her black Touch energy—which was strong, powerful, and recharged often, but with which she could do basically nothing unless it *was* near full charge.

Her pulse pounded.

She licked her lips.

Despite the warm breeze, her hands were cold.

Her hands were cold, and she didn't even know where her gloves were anymore, and she couldn't remember when she'd worn them last.

...And maybe, right now, that was a good thing.

She put her phone back in her pocket. Her mind's eye filled with the poisoners, striding down the path near the Museum, Touch energies billowing out behind them, a cloud of intensity.

Kyla inhaled deeply, warm, bushland air hitting the bottom of her lungs like satisfaction. She held her hands up in front of her, dark silhouettes—and let her Touch energy flow.

Even running at near empty, it wasn't like she had nothing to let flow: the sense of her Touch energy was always there, something a part of her was constantly aware of, a container constantly in need of supervision. The container might be more or less densely full, but like a gas, the energy expanded to fill the space she allowed it. It had never occurred to her before to let the energy billow out of her like this, letting the 'container' stretch and stretch at the behest of the energy itself.

Adrenaline shot through her chest.

Yes. Letting her energy billow like this would never have occurred to her if she hadn't seen the blackmailers do it... and if it had, she'd have been too afraid to try it.

Power thrummed through her until her fingers vibrated in the night.

Black. All of it was black, and death, and none of it was going to help her, but the orange she'd given the man had to have come from somewhere...

Out and out and out she let her Touch energy spool, the sense of it swallowing the stars, and she gaped; how had she had this much energy within her all this time? She was running on empty, and yet here it was, still billowing—thinly, sparse and not useable yet, but immense nevertheless. Was this why it always felt so hard to hold on to?

And still it kept coming, until the cloud of it reached higher than the trees.

And there, right at the end in the tiny thread that kept her power tethered to her instead of flashing away out into the world: a flicker of orange.

Satisfaction settled in Kyla's chest, salty and warm. Working instinctively, she tugged at the tiny thread of sunset orange, teasing it out from the cloud of blackness around it.

Just a tiny thread, fine as a hair.

The most infinitesimal fraction of power compared to what she usually used.

Slowly, she let it scan the bushland around her, an unfamiliar landscape of light and dark that didn't match up with any visual map she had of the area. Instead, light seemed to flare randomly—a flicker here, a flash and sparkle there.

Kyla frowned. What was she seeing? How could this help?

The energy began to dim, and she stumbled; letting her Touch energy out was often tiring, but not like this. Usually it was a sense of depletion, an expulsion of anxiety that left her still and calm.

This? This was like extreme fatigue, the brain fog that came after concentrating hard on something challenging for an extended period of time.

But she'd only been letting the energy out for what, a couple of minutes?

She fought past the sense of light and dark fed to her by her Touch, swimming back to her physical senses.

The stars had moved.

She didn't know them well enough to guess exactly how long that meant, but that one bright star there, flickering and twinkling, it had been quite a bit further to the right.

Okay.

So she'd been here a while then. No wonder she was tiring.

But there was no sign of Freja.

Maybe she just wasn't charged enough, regardless of how large she let the energy she did have billow out.

A flicker of aquamarine lit up at the far edge of her Touch's range—right in the middle of the pool on the other side of the small clearing.

Hmm.

Something about it seemed familiar...

But she couldn't walk toward it, not and hold her energy like she currently was.

She shut off the flow of Touch energy that had been seeping orangely out into the world—

—and time slammed back into focus. Leaves rustled at a normal speed, the shadows snapped back into clarity... Kyla hadn't realised how *blurred* the world had appeared through the softening lens of her Touch.

The aquamarine glow was at the edge of the pond, where it narrowed into the trickling stream that ran away from it.

Oh.

Something flipped in Kyla's stomach.

She strode over tussock grass, her footsteps crunch-crunch-crunching. A momentary change in the wind intensified the smell of fresh water, and brought the gentle trickling sound of the creek that fed the pond.

Kyla stopped beside it. The surface rippled gently in the dim light, and if Kyla didn't think about it, she might have assumed it was just the warm night wind.

The wind wouldn't make each ripple glow like that, pale aquamarine in the dark.

The wind wouldn't mimic precisely the way the pond had lit up the other night with the Yee girls, when the ice children had hidden in it.

She bit the inside of her lip. Reached into the cool water toward the glow—and withdrew from the pond a glass bee, smooth and rounded, identical to the others she and Damon had found.

Satisfaction might have nestled in her chest had not all the room been taken up by thunderous adrenaline.

So. Freja had found her after all.

...Kyla could put the bee down, could run before the ice children (or Freja herself!) appeared...

But she wanted answers, didn't she?

She crouched down. Leaned over the pond. Her reflection rippled back at her, the odd star visible between the ripples.

The sandy bottom of the pond glimmered pale beneath the water, only a foot or so deep even in the middle—except it wasn't, right there where it seemed bottomless, deep, dark...

The ripples quietened.

Kyla's pulse thundered in her ears.

She reached out to the water, still glowing in the night, the bee slick and cool in her other hand.

Closer, closer...

Fingertips an inch away from the surface, she paused. Drew in a sharp breath.

What was she doing? What if Freja killed her next?

She'd been on that list, seen her name right there for herself.

Tane thought Freja was going to kill her. Alethea probably thought so too.

Her jaw twitched.

...What was she doing? Whatever she had to. There was nothing else left to try.

Her fingers broke the surface of the water—

And nothing happened.

Tension eased from her shoulders.

She took a long, slow breath, exhaling loudly as her body relaxed.

Fine. She'd just have to do it the long way, track Freja down in person.

Something exploded from the surface of the water.

Kyla screamed.

A vice-like grip around her wrist, a burning cold that seared the back of Kyla's throat.

Her chest ached.

Limbs thrashed in the water.

Pale blue eyes, staring at her from only inches away.

Kyla inhaled to scream again—and the ice child tugged her forward.

She toppled into the now-freezing pond, and if her lungs hadn't already been full of air, she'd have sucked in water just trying to survive.

But there was no point trying to fight: this was what she wanted.

30

S HIVERING AND DRIPPING ONTO THE CONCRETE FLOOR OF A room that felt and smelled like a small warehouse hadn't exactly been in Kyla's plans when she'd determined to go looking for Freja, but, on the other hand, she hadn't had a plan beyond 'loudly attract Freja's attention and demand some answers,' so.

The room was wide and dark. Shadows lingered in the corners in a way that seemed to eat at the yellow lamplight, and Kyla couldn't quite tell if they were just normal shadows, or if something Touch-related writhed within. The whole place smelled of dust and disuse, the silence overwhelming and unnatural.

Kyla pulled her arms tighter around her ribs, fingertips digging at them through her tank top.

A drop of melting ice broke free of Kyla's hairline and slid down her cheek. The shivers turned to a violent shudder for a moment, her teeth chattering. She wriggled her toes in squelchy sneakers.

The floor was completely bare. No furniture visible in the polygon of light created by the four lamps, not a stray box or magazine or chunk of dust bunny. In fact, the whole place seemed meticulously clean, not even a cobweb apparently in the exposed aluminium rafters. Would sitting convey the right kind of nonchalance, or would it just make her seem vulnerable?

Kyla's jaw tightened.

Another violent shudder ripped through her—and it took an instant for her brain to move beyond *cold* and recognise that someone with an incredibly immense Touch had just entered the building.

There. Somewhere not far in front. She squinted against the lamplight, straining to catch movement, colour, anything. *Something* had registered, if only for a second, but now she could almost swear there was no one there.

Another shiver.

Damn if it wasn't cold in here. No sound of refrigeration, and there was a narrow highlight window to her left letting in a sharp sliver of starlight, so the room couldn't be that insulated from the sultry summer night outside.

There, a movement: someone beyond the furthermost light in front. No trace of a Touch, though.

Kyla's neck prickled. The scent of lemongrass and ozone filled the air.

The temperature dropped.

Kyla wriggled her hands up under her armpits, the shivering now constant as she tried not to clench her teeth—her jaw would ache something stupendous tomorrow. Her wet tank top felt like a magnet for the cold, and her sodden shorts weren't much better. Great. Someone with a Touch that was clearly both strong and well used, but which was nevertheless almost completely cloaked. Freja, obviously (or else

she was in even bigger trouble than she'd imagined, if someone *else* with that much power was also running around
town).

Why had she thought this was a good idea again?

Oh, right: because she was out of other options.

Shadows behind, shadows to the side, shadows in front,
all of them practically vibrating now with a prickly, electric
sense of being watched.

The police wouldn't stand a chance against energy like
this. Neither would anyone else.

At least this way Kyla wasn't risking any more lives.

Footsteps.

The lamplight lit the woman from the ground up, ice-blue
pointy-toed heels, matching light blue slacks, a simple shawl-
collared blouse in a slate grey that glimmered silkenly.

Freja. She paused just to the left of the light so it lit her
head-to-toe without silhouetting her, weight to one side, one
elbow cradled in her other hand, fingers pressed thoughtfully
against pearl-pale lips. "Well," she said, and her voice was
rich and musical. "Were you unsatisfied with the answers he
gave, just as I said?"

Kyla blinked. Answers?

Oh.

Tane.

Freja had told her to ask Tane for answers, to use a snowflake to visit again if she didn't like the answers Tane offered.

"No," Kyla said, fighting the word out through chattering
teeth. "He was... not particularly chatty." An understatement,
since he was still ignoring her calls and texts.

Another shudder. How long could she survive being this
cold? Not long. Definitely not long. Even her tongue felt
numb.

Freja laughed. "And yet, you have been busy since then,
finding answers of your own to questions you didn't know
you had, yes?"

Did Freja know about Kyla's visit to Alethea's store, or
was she referring to the new way Kyla had used her Touch to

set off Freja's little bee system? Probably the latter. Hopefully the latter. "Yes."

"Good girl." Freja stretched out her arm.

In the middle of the room, Kyla recoiled from the sudden warmth that caressed her cheek. *Breathe*, she told herself. A fraction at a time, she forced herself to unclench, to accept the warmth slowly defrosting her face, her neck, her shoulders, until she stood on a damp patch of concrete, mostly dry except in the creases, no longer shivering like she'd die any second of hyperthermia.

Freja stepped in front of the light, her long shadow reaching to Kyla's feet. Honestly, the hypothermia might have been less dangerous.

"So," Freja said as she approached, "you have been experimenting, no?" She paused, taking a half step to the side so her silhouette no longer blocked the lamplight.

Kyla winced at the sudden influx of bright light against her retinas.

"How did it feel?"

Kyla narrowed her eyes just a fraction. Freja was standing motionless, poised in the same way an eagle did before it launched into flight with claws outstretched—watching, waiting. For whatever reason, her answer mattered to Freja.

And she could spend time trying to guess what the reason was, whether truth or lies would serve her better...

But how many Touches had Freja collected now? Any one of them might be red, like Alethea's. She might *have* Alethea's.

...No, surely not. If she already knew everything...

Kyla swallowed. If Freja had that kind of red Touch, if she already knew everything that Kyla and her—she hesitated to say her team, given how they'd all abandoned her, but damn it all, they'd been her team, at least for a moment there—if Freja knew what everyone had been up to, she wouldn't be standing here questioning Kyla. Surely. Even a cat didn't play that hard with their food.

...If Freja didn't have Alethea's Touch, it meant Alethea was still alive.

Something uncoiled just a fraction in Kyla's chest.

Alethea was alive.

Kyla inhaled, tucking in her chin. She didn't need to tell Freja the truth, but of course, she also didn't need to lie outright...

How did it feel?

Kyla licked her lips. "Incredible," she said hoarsely.

Freja's mouth curled around a smile.

And it wasn't a lie: the way her energy had burst out of her and into the man, blood to blood, awakening a Touch in him... If she ignored the death that had followed, she couldn't deny it had felt... sacred. Intimate. Orgasmic. Akin to the way a full discharge of her Touch left her empty and satisfied, only this time with the knowledge that she'd shared that feeling *with* someone.

...There hadn't been time in the moment to really understand the feeling, and she'd been too busy focusing on her anger and her need for answers since to process it, but hot *damn*...

And the fine spooling out of her energy, letting the black billow away so she could access only the orange, the expansiveness of trusting her energy to inflate like that—the direct connection with the orange base of her Touch that, surely, was the reason she'd always been so good at finding artefacts in the first place?

Kyla shivered. This time it wasn't from cold.

"Yes," Freja said softly. "Yes it is, isn't it. Imagine if you could do that all the time, instead of fretting away, buried beneath a cloud of black. Imagine not having to *fear* the release of your power, but instead being able to *control* it."

Kyla inhaled sharply. Could Freja read her thoughts?

Freja's mouth twitched. "No," she said. "I cannot read your thoughts, but they are simple enough to guess at right now." She shrugged delicately. "Especially when they so closely mimic my own when I had a similar experience."

Kyla's eye twitched. Alethea was not right; she and Freja were nothing alike, no matter what Freja might say.

"So, will you aid me now? Ironically, of course, the one thing that will give us both complete power is the stone that allows us to switch our power off. The real stone, I mean," she said, her smile turning sardonic, "not some fancy party trick."

Kyla's pulse quickened. A party trick? What did Freja know?

Freja's irises matched the ice-blue of her slacks almost perfectly, the grey ring around their outer edge identical to the slate of her blouse. Deliberate? Undoubtedly. Touch-augmented? Kyla couldn't see what kind of Touch could help with such a thing, but with the kind of power Freja must have...

Kyla was suddenly conscious of the way her hands knotted in her armpits, her arms still wrapped around her ribs as though she was cold—as though she was vulnerable. She let her arms drop and buried her hand self-consciously in the pockets of her shorts. "You want me to trust you," she said. "You tell me I should have the Touchstone. But I don't want it for myself. I need it to... to save my father."

That steel in her spine reasserted itself, and Kyla cocked a hip, arms folding assertively, an almost-mirror of Freja's entrance pose. "You want me to trust you. You've murdered people, people I loved. My father's life is on the line. I'm going to need more than your say so if you want me on your side."

Freja's lips pursed, and around the edges of the room, the shadows writhed.

Oh. Oh, the shadows weren't just shadows, they were some sort of security system, like the one the blackmailers had had. Kyla hadn't thought to try her Touch before Freja had appeared, and wouldn't now in front of her—far too risky, especially if Freja decided Kyla was trying to kill her— but it wouldn't surprise Kyla in the slightest to discover that her Touch wouldn't work within the boundary of the shadows.

"The truth, then," Freja said abruptly, and Kyla jumped, disrupted from her thoughts. "Come." Freja spun and marched away, heels tap-tap-tapping on the concrete floor as she headed back to the lamp she'd first appeared behind.

Kyla's eyebrows settled to their rightful place, and she squelched after Freja, arms swinging in a space many degrees warmer than when she'd first arrived.

Beyond the lamp, the darkness led to a door, which led to a room that felt and sounded small in the dark—probably the usual entrance to the also-small warehouse.

A switch clicked, and fluorescent lighting flooded the room.

It *was* small—and it was also lined with shelves full of glass objects enough to rival even Damon's shop. Was the warehouse another glass store—or was this a personal collection of Freja's?

Kyla blinked to stop herself from staring.

Freja, with a little knowing twist to her mouth, crossed the room and lifted a large jar off a shelf, dipping her hand into the contents with a soft clink. As she returned, Kyla's heart stuttered: the jar was half full of glass snowflakes, each about the size of a large coin, each glowing to Kyla's Touch senses with a pastel-rainbow energy.

Was this how many people Freja had already murdered? ...Or how many she was preparing to?

"The truth is uncomfortable, no?" Freja's smile was wan, a tightness about her eyes saying she understood exactly the weight of the jar that she was carrying. "But tell me, Kyla," she said softly, hefting the jar between them with one hand still swirling the glass snowflakes inside, a gentle maelstrom of pastel-rainbow energy. "How many have *you* killed? What would your jar look like, if you kept one?"

Adrenaline spiked in Kyla's chest. "I only discharge my Touch on insects," she said, jaw jutting in response to Freja's stare. "Or small animals." An inaudible 'these days' appended itself to her sentence.

"Life is life, no?"

The hollow hopelessness hidden deep in Freja's gaze sent a shudder down Kyla's spine far worse than the cold had.

"No," Kyla said.

But... it was, really, wasn't it. When all was said and done. She'd read somewhere that dogs remembered their birth families their whole lives, and plants screamed supersonically when caterpillars ate them, and it was all death, wasn't it? It was all just death, other people, other creatures dying to keep someone alive.

She fought the urge to bury her face in her hands, clenching her fingers instead and shoving them inside her pockets again.

Her deep, steadying breath smelled of concrete.

"It's all just death," Freja whispered, as though she'd heard Kyla's thoughts again.

Kyla's heart skipped.

"And it begs the question," Freja continued, taking a half step closer amid the glitter of the glass-lined shelves, "if all death is equal, and fate has decreed by giving you your Touch that you must kill in order to survive..." She shrugged, and a rainbow of reflected light bobbed over her face. "But we *all* must kill to survive, mustn't we. You know that. You've thought it before, in the earliest hours of the morning while you lay awake after your latest kill, wondering what the difference really is between you, and everyone else. *Everyone* requires death to survive. You, they would lock up and throw away the key. But you?" Freja drew a single snowflake from the jar and held it between them, interrupting their line of sight.

The snowflake glimmered, sparkling both in the fluorescent lights and to Kyla's Touch sense.

"You are no different than they, Kyla. We *all* must kill to survive. It is simply that some of us are blessed with having the pretence stripped away. We know the *truth*, Kyla, the truth of what it means to *live*—that for our lives to continue, other lives must end. And *you* know," Freja said, offering the snowflake to Kyla, "that the truth has set us free."

"I WILL GIVE YOU THE ANTIDOTE, ON FAITH," FREJA HAD SAID, rummaging in a small cupboard and drawing out a glass bottle stoppered with a cork, something the size and shape of an old-fashioned Coke bottle. "Here," Freja had said, handing it to Kyla. "Take it. Give it to your father. He will be well within the hour."

Kyla had taken the bottle, cold against her palm.

"And I will tell you the truth," Freja had continued, adopting the same pose she'd entered the warehouse with, one elbow cradled in her hand, her other fingers pressing lightly against her jaw like a picture frame.

A quiet thrill in Kyla's stomach. She'd clenched the bottle. *The truth.*

"Tane has the Touchstone," Freja had said.

Cold anger had bubbled up into Kyla's chest and her fingers had clenched into knots. *I don't have the Touchstone to give you, Kyla.* She'd known at the time the phrasing was too careful to be accidental.

She'd spat her rage onto the concrete floor.

This. This was what came from trusting people.

"I can help you get it from him."

Kyla had tensed, but Freja's expression remained calm, placid. "Why?" Kyla had said. "Why would you help me?"

Freja had inhaled, seeming to measure her words for a moment. "Let us simply say I am motivated to ensure that the Touchstone stays in the hands of someone I can trust. Someone who will allow me the freedom"—a tightly flashed smile—"to continue to do my work. I cannot have it on me, of course," she'd said, turning away, "or it would inhibit me. But to have someone close, an ally I could trust, who would be there, ready to step in when required?" She'd shaken her head as Kyla had opened her mouth. "No. Do not answer now. It is an utterly unreasonable hour and we have both done far too much this night. You, I suspect, have more to do, as I very much doubt you will hold onto that bottle until morning."

Right. Yes. The antidote. Kyla had lifted it a little, the pale pink opaque liquid rolling inside like honey. "Uh. Thank you?" she'd said, heat rising in her cheeks. Thanking a murderer for helping her save her father from other potential murderers. This wasn't what she'd gone there for.

But on the other hand, she'd gone because—as Pippa had so kindly pointed out—something needed to be done still to save their father.

This would save their father.

Impulsively, Kyla had unstoppered the bottle and inhaled. False strawberries, something floral and sweet.

Freja had laughed. "It will do you no good at all, Kyla. Go. Give it to him, and when you have seen that I am a woman who keeps my word, come back, and we will talk."

"You're quiet," Pippa said, interrupting Kyla's memory of the night before.

Kyla blinked back to awareness of her surroundings: fluorescent lights still flickered overhead, but this time the ceiling they lit up was covered in square office tiles, the walls covered in blue-grey lino to match the floor, and the beep, beep, beep of the hospital machinery filled the air.

"Yeah," Kyla said.

Dad looked peaceful, now, all traces of lingering pain and tension gone. He slept easily, oxygen no longer taped under his nose, face no longer pale and drawn.

A rush of warmth hit Kyla's chest. She gripped the cold foot-rail of the bed tightly, inhaling a deep breath full of antiseptic.

"Thank you," Pippa said, twitching in Kyla's peripheral vision like maybe she wanted to move closer. "What... What-ever it was you had to do, thank you."

A second pang of warmth.

Dad slept peacefully on.

"It's not what you think," Kyla said, because she knew her sister assumed it had involved her Touch.

Pippa shrugged. "Still," she said. "Thank you."

Kyla twisted her hands around the bed's cold foot-rail.

Maybe it was exactly what Pippa thought. She might not have used her Touch on anyone last night, but she was seriously considering going back to Freja, wasn't she, now that Freja's antidote had proven good, now that it had been revealed that Freja was the one who kept her word, and Tane... Tane was the one who lied.

All lives are equal in the end.

There was a fault in Freja's logic... but it was like a Gordian knot, a tangled ball she couldn't find the right string to pull.

People die either way.

And there was absolutely no doubt whatsoever that some Touches made their bearers magnets for others who wanted to use them. Wasn't that why she, Kyla, had kept her own Touch so hidden for so long? Why the poisoners' blackmail wasn't so much a lightning bolt from a clear sky as a figure plucked from her nightmares and given flesh?

Kyla shuddered and closed eyes gritty from lack of sleep.

"Let's go get breakfast," Pippa said, staring at her intently, blue eyes searching.

Kyla sighed, shrugged away from the foot-rail, swung upright. "Yeah," she said. "Let's. Your shout, of course," she said, aiming for an injection of light-hearted humour.

But the sombreness of Pippa's reply said she'd widely missed the mark. "Of course. I... Of course."

She hadn't meant it like that. The last thing she needed was for Pippa to feel like she owed Kyla.

She'd never wanted Pippa's enmity, but she didn't need twelve years of guilt weighing down their relationship now either.

Shoving the irritation deep down, Kyla bent to kiss Dad on the cheek. "Love you," she said. "We'll be back when you wake up."

Which could be any time today, the medical staff had said, astounded by their patient's sudden improvement. They hadn't wanted to commit, hadn't wanted to actually voice that he was better just in case he wasn't—the recovery seemed so miraculous, so spontaneous to them after all—but Kyla had already known: within minutes of giving Dad the antidote from Freja, Pippa had nodded decisively. "He's clear," she'd said. "He'll be fine."

And Kyla had marvelled again at the fact of a paramedic having the ability to tell how and when her patients would die, and what might come from that.

Not the kind of Touch Freja was trying to eliminate, at least.

Their footsteps echoed down the antiseptic hospital hallway as Kyla followed Pippa along the twisting, turning route toward the exit.

Or was it the kind of Touch Freja might one day feel a threat? Surely not. Kyla turned Pippa's Touch over and over in her mind, this way and that, a slide puzzle as she tried to force something negative to resolve.

By the time they reached the exit, though, she was satisfied that of all the Touches that ought to be prohibited, Pippa's wasn't one of them.

Maybe—*maybe*—if people knew of it they might pay to have some sense of certainty around the ending of their lives, but beyond that, what could Pippa be bribed to do?

No. Pippa, surely, had to be safe.

The automatic doors to the outside world shushed open. Cool morning air rushed against Kyla's face, petrol and salt air and damp, humid greenery. It was sunrise. Between her visit to Alethea's, the thug at her doorstep, her visit with Freja and now this trip to the hospital, Kyla hadn't slept at all over night—hadn't slept, in fact, in about twenty-four hours.

Her jaw cracked open in a yawn, and she rubbed at sore, gritty eyes as Pippa waved at someone in their paramedic uniform entering the hospital across the ambulance bay.

What now?

The sudden sense of purposelessness was disorienting. Kyla had come to town because Dad was sick. She'd been tasked with finding the Touchstone so the people who'd poisoned her Dad would give her the cure. But...

Dad was cured.

Did it matter that the task wasn't complete, that she'd neither found the Touchstone nor aided the poisoners in whatever it was they wanted?

A shadow flashed across her face.

She started.

Something grey squawked up on the gutters.

Right. Only a bird, a native noisy miner screeking its displeasure.

Pippa opened her mouth, inhaled, closed it again.

Kyla couldn't even begin to guess what Pippa might have been going to say. Did it even matter? Did any of it?

Her ringtone split the silence. She scrabbled at it—Tane? She'd sent him two more messages overnight, asking where he was, if he was coming back, hinting that she had information she could share...—and answered Spy's call.

FRIDAY 9 DECEMBER

"WHY ARE YOU CALLING ME?" KYLA SAID. WAS SHE confused because she was tired, or was it genuinely confusing that Spy should be calling her and not Pippa? She had no idea, couldn't tell.

"Who is it?" Pippa mouthed, brushing strands of blonde hair that had fallen from her hasty ponytail out of her face.

"Spy," Kyla said, eyebrows pulled tight.

"I'm sorry," Spy said, and his voice was thick and heavy. "You were right."

"I was?"

An early tram trundled past, all squeaks and squeals, mostly empty in the pastel morning light.

"About what?"

"Freja... She..."

Kyla's chest ratcheted tight and she reached out to grip Pippa's shoulder.

Spy cleared his breath. "One of them didn't make it."

Kyla clutched at the phone, moved it from her ear to press against her forehead while she struggled for control of her crumbling face.

Cockatoos screeched overhead in the dawning sky.

I told you.

I told you you couldn't handle her.

Another one dead, hell.

What do we do?

What do we do?

"I... I don't know where to stash him, Kyla, the one who survived. What do we do with him?" His voice was high and plaintive, the words so nearly an echo of her thoughts as she scrunched her fingers in the fabric of Pippa's shirt and fought for breath.

Pippa gripped her wrist, not trying to detangle her, but anchoring her, eyes tight, brows knitted.

"I..." Kyla put the phone back to her ear and cleared her throat. "I'll be right over. Pippa's here with me, she can drive me." Kyla caught her sister's gaze questioningly, but Pippa nodded without hesitation. "See you in twenty."

She hung up.

"Where are we going?" said Pippa.

"Police station," she said. "Freja got one of the black-mailers."

Colour drained from Pippa's face, but she gave a tight nod.

Spy met them in the waiting room of the police station, striding over the grey lino floor with a beleaguered expression. It was early enough that the plastic chairs fixed to the walls were empty, and a slant of morning sun cut through the window over a tall, green, broad-leafed plant that Kyla realised on second glance was fake.

"Thanks for coming," Spy said as Kyla fought not to wrinkle her nose in response to a faint stagnant odour.

"Yeah," she said shortly.

His jaw twitched at her glare. "Come sign in."

They did, then Spy led them through the gated entrance that led to the holding cells. Here the air stank of stale sweat and body odour, and in one place the grey lino was sticky under Kyla's sneaker. She blinked eyes gritty with tiredness and stifled a yawn.

Down on the right-hand side, a familiar-looking young man sat with his face in his hands on the bench against the back wall of his cell.

Kyla cleared her voice. "I'm, uh, I'm sorry for your loss," she said.

He startled upright, glaring at her over tear-tracked cheeks, and his hands tightened to fists. "You." It was the shorter one who'd survived, the one who'd actually taken the pendant from her. He scrubbed an arm over his cheeks, dark eyes afire. "How did you do it? It worked when you showed it to me, how did you know it would fail after that?"

Kyla's chest constricted. "I didn't," she said quietly—but of course, he wouldn't believe her. She wouldn't, in his place.

Pippa laid gentle fingertips on her shoulder, and Spy stood at her other side.

Kyla's own jaw twitched, once, twice, and anger cooled in her chest. "I told you not to do this," she muttered at him, fighting to keep the fury from her voice. "I told you."

"I know," he said, despair thick enough in his tone that Kyla glanced sideways. His face was contorted into something like a snarl, only directed inward, not at her.

"Tell me what happened."

He gestured with his head, and led them to an interview room, empty but for a rectangular table and two plastic chairs, the naked fluorescent lightbulb overhead flickering despondently.

"Hold on," he muttered. "I'll get another chair."

He brought a third chair in, its feet scraping against the floor, and let the door fall shut with a thud behind him.

"It was about four this morning," he said as he sank down into the chair he'd brought in, closing his eyes and tilting back his head. "She just waltzed in the front door. Stood by the door to the back here making a fuss until Leon went out to subdue her, and as soon as he opened the door, she threw something—one of those glass snowflakes. It must have been enchanted, the way it flew through the air like that; Leon says he never saw anything like it. Curved right through the bars of the holding cell, got Thomas, the taller blackmailer, clean in the shoulder. I wouldn't have thought a wound like that'd be fatal, but the security footage shows him dropping like a stone, covered in ice.

"By the time Leon bundled Freja up and threw her outside, Alex was shouting the place down from inside the cell. I came out to see what the fuss was, and…" He shrugged, a deep, unsettled gestured, and swung the chair back on its rear legs. "The ice was already starting to melt. By the time Leon came back in and we figured out who'd done it and what had happened, she was long gone." He sighed heavily. "You were right, Kyla, and I've no doubt she'll come back for Alex, and I haven't the faintest clue how to keep him protected."

Kyla couldn't tell if the queasiness in her stomach was over what had happened, or because she was so exhausted. Of course, it could be both.

The front legs of Spy's chair touched down again with a tap. "Alex's been asking to go home since it happened, says at least he'd be safe there, offering to be under house arrest or something instead. I'm not against the idea but that kind of thing takes paperwork, and who knows how soon Freja will be back."

"Of course," Kyla murmured. "Their security system."

She'd been thinking of Tane, of how he'd insisted that the girls stay near him, of how he'd been unafraid of Kyla's black

Touch—but even if he had still been around, what could he have done? Hung out at the station indefinitely?

The blackmailers' security system, on the other hand…

Kyla stood, her own chair legs screeping against the floor. "I need to talk to … Alex, that's his name?"

"Yeah, Alex Zhang. You have an idea?" Spy's eyebrows followed her upward.

"Maybe. Let me talk to him, we'll see."

Spy led them back to the holding cells again, Pippa trudging silently along behind, yawning when she thought no one was watching.

Kyla wasn't the only one who'd had no sleep last night. She clenched her jaw and for a short moment, her nails dug into the palms of her hands.

Security first, she told herself. *Then we can sleep.*

Alex sat on the bench, face in his hands again.

"Alex?"

He ignored her.

"Your security system," she said. "Can it be moved?"

Nothing.

Kyla sighed. *I'm too tired for this.* "Look, the police aren't going to let you out, not after what you did to me, but—"

"*You?*" His hands dropped into his lap like lead. "After what we did to *you*? We were just trying to stay *alive,* Kyla. We weren't going to let your father die, but you? You were perfectly happy to sit back and watch her pick us off one by one. I thought Jason was your *friend.*"

The force of the vitriol in his voice nearly rocked her back on her feet. Her eyes stung, and she blinked rapidly lest the sting become tears that spilled over and betrayed her.

"I wasn't sitting back watching," she said. *I wasn't.* Resolve stiffened her spine and she flexed her fingers again, voice firming. "And if you won't talk to me about the security system, you can guarantee that you'll be next, because the police have no way of protecting you, as you know full well. I thought that maybe I could take the security system you have at home, the one keeping Freja out, and bring it here, set it up around the station so she can't get in."

Alex was scowling deeply. "So it wasn't enough to watch us all die, you had to break into our home, too."

Kyla inhaled, setting her shoulders. "I can pretend I'm sorry about that, if you like, or I can go get the system and bring it here. *If* it can be moved."

He stared daggers at her, motionless, and Pippa shifted uneasily at her side.

Somewhere in the station, a clock was ticking.

Spy opened his mouth to speak.

"Yes," Alex said, then swallowed, the tension in his back and shoulders deflating. "Yes, it can be moved. They"—he nodded at Spy—"have the key to the front door. Once you're in..."

Briefly, he outlined to Kyla what needed to be done to safely dismantle the system and pack it down. "But if you do that, you *must* bring the mirror that hangs in the lounge room as well, okay? She can't be allowed to have it."

Kyla nodded. "Mirror, got it. Thank you. I know you don't believe me, but I really don't want you to die."

Alex snorted, turned his face away to stare blindly at the wall.

"I want Freja gone as much as you do," she said softly. "We all do." And abruptly, she realised it was true: Dad was healed, the antidote Freja had given her had worked, and technically she could walk away from this all right now, go hide somewhere Freja couldn't find her, take a holiday with her family for a bit and ride it out. It was no longer her problem.

But Freja had said some Touches were too dangerous to be allowed to survive.

What did that make Freja, then, the one collecting them all?

Kyla shivered as her body finally reacted to the station's air conditioning. Or maybe someone walked over her future grave; Pippa might know.

She snorted at that.

"Come on," she muttered to Pippa, to Spy.

"I'll get the paperwork for the key," Spy replied.

Kyla's phone binged in her pocket. She took it out.

A text message, from Tane. *Meet me at the doughnut place at 9?*

Kyla forced her grip on her phone to relax. *Yeah*, she texted back. *See you then.*

33

PIPPA HAD DRIVEN KYLA OUT TO THE POISONERS' HOUSE. Getting in had been much easier this time and it had only taken ten minutes or so to dismantle the security system there, though the wall in the lounge room had been bare of mirrors.

Kyla had had a sudden moment of insight, standing there in dim morning light: this was where Freja had appeared in the house, and when Kyla had seen her, she'd been putting something in her pocket.

"What's wrong?" Pippa had said.

"The mirror Alex wanted. I think Freja already has it." *Because of me*, she didn't add.

Pippa had sighed. "Nothing we can do about it now."

They'd brought the security system back to the station.

"And the mirror?" Alex had asked.

"Missing," Pippa told him shortly.

He'd blanched. "Don't even bother, then," he said as he watched the set the security system up. "You can't stop her now."

Alex's fatalism aside, Kyla and Pippa had finished setting the system up, then Pippa had dropped Kyla at the bakery to meet Tane before heading home to sleep.

Tane had not been at the bakery when Kyla had arrived, not at one of the mostly empty square tables out front, nor in the padded beige booths inside, and neither had he answered her increasingly pointed—and then, if she was being honest, a little frantic—text messages.

His phone went straight to voicemail.

Multiple times.

But—Kyla closed her eyes, uncaring what passersby would think, inhaled deeply of air that tasted like doughnuts and smelled of sugar, gripped tightly the wireframe back of an outdoor café chair, and spooled out just the tiniest thread of her Touch—he *had* been here.

He had been here, and now he was not, and he was no longer answering her texts.

Again.

What the hell was going on?

Kyla ground her teeth, trying to hold on to the anger that had surged through her when she'd first realised he wasn't coming, when she'd rung the first time and gotten his curt voicemail.

The anger was better than fear.

She exhaled loudly through her nose, jaw still clenched tight.

A young woman passing by, her navy slacks and blouse out of place on the hot, midmorning street, shied away from Kyla's stony glare.

Kyla tried to soften her expression, gave a little nod of apology... There was nothing for it but to see if she could follow him.

A bracing inhale. She could do this. It was no different than what she'd always done, letting her Touch energies float and guide her. She was just doing it deliberately now, was all, instead of feeling like she was just wandering at the whims of fate and chance.

And so she let the energy of her Touch thread out, and followed as it unspooled across the city, and it followed Tane's path—and the place Kyla followed to shouldn't have been as shocking to her as it was: a smallish warehouse on a street steaming hot in the now mid-morning sun, the air thick with hot dust and hot concrete and the baking red bricks of the warehouse.

Kyla worked her tongue against the dust.

So Freja had him.

Well. She hadn't wanted this, not exactly, but she had told Tane she'd be getting answers this time.

Jaw set, eyes squinting against the bright sunlight, sweat dripping indelicately, Kyla stepped into the shadow of the warehouse. Leadlight windows interrupted the wall at regular intervals, but they'd been papered over from inside.

No sounds, either.

Kyla realised her whole body had gone rigid and fought to unclench herself, shoulders, hands, jaw… She rolled her neck.

Have to go in. Nothing else for it.

She did tell me to come back.

Unlikely that Freja would kill her, maim her, injure her for doing what she herself had suggested… But it was always a risk.

She was delaying again.

Another steely inhale. Kyla strode down the concrete of the drive that led up the side of the warehouse to a regular-sized door.

She raised her hand to knock—and gave her head a quick shake. No sense relinquishing the element of surprise.

So instead, she grabbed the metal knob, cool even in the heat of the day, and cracked the door gently open. Kyla stepped into the antechamber to the warehouse, a kind of reception with a single high-fronted desk and chair, a dusty, faded plastic fern in the corner by the window.

Kyla shut the door behind her, and the heat of the day and the smell of baking stone and dust and dirt disappeared.

The antechamber was air conditioned—naturally, hopefully—Kyla shivered, recalling the cold Freja had conjured last night—and the air sterile, if still dustier than an actual office in use might be.

She angled herself so the desk was against her left hip, a comforting reassurance that at least that side was covered.

Ahead, the door into the room where Freja had showed her the jar of snowflakes. Right, a door that led directly into the warehouse, its small square window papered over like the leadlight windows of the warehouse itself.

Nothing that her Touch could sense. For all she knew right now, the entire warehouse was empty, a feeling made all the more disconcerting when footsteps tap-tap-tapped from within the warehouse, heading toward her...

Kyla exhaled, her shoulders untensing just a little as Freja—it had to be Freja—entered the storeroom instead of the antechamber.

Pulse pounding against her chest, Kyla decided. Three paces to the right across dingy, corporate-blue carpet, and she cracked open the heavy whitewashed door to the warehouse.

Kyla peeked through the warehouse over at the door into the storeroom, the mirror of the antechamber door.

Shut.

No sign of Freja.

No assurances how long that would last. Freja could come back into the warehouse space any second.

Kyla licked dry lips.

Best to scout as quickly as she could, then feign nonchalance when Freja did inevitably reappear.

She slipped into the warehouse, easing her sneakered feet down quietly on the polished concrete floor, easing the antechamber door shut behind her, the similarly white-washed door to the storeroom unmoving, its knob unturned.

Her heart hammered.

She licked her lips again. Backed slowly away from the pair of doors.

Her neck prickled.

Just her Touch, no doubt, slowly building...

Kyla's brow furrowed. No, not her Touch, her Touch was... quiet. Quiet like it was before at Tane's house, when—

She turned.

Her stomach lurched.

On a wooden chair in the middle of the white-painted warehouse, in a pool of light cast softly by one of the fluorescent downlights set into the silvered ceiling insulation...

Tane.

Tied, bound to the chair, gagged.

Jaw twitching, Kyla hurried to him, ignored the frantic gesturing of his eyes, and tugged the gag from his mouth.

"*Bitch*," Tane said loudly, gesturing very pointedly with his eyes now at the back of the warehouse.

Kyla quashed the anger that flared, glanced under her arm—Freja, emerging from the storeroom.

Kyla straightened, pulse now galloping as though she might have a heart attack.

Freja's face curled into a languid smile. "So," she said, the same ice-blue heels as last night—this morning—tapping out a staccato on the concrete floor. "You have discovered my little prize."

Play along. Sell it. "Yes," Kyla said, drawing herself up, staring haughtily down her nose at Tane as though he were pure filth.

Honestly, she barely had to act.

She could always give him a good, solid kick. That would help her sell things better, and it might even make her feel better.

"I see your opinions of him as a companion are perhaps

not as high as they once were," Freja said, amused.

What? Oh, yes, Kyla had indeed been staring at him like he was something noxious, someone who she'd trusted for a hot moment there to help, someone who'd had her back, until suddenly he hadn't.

Someone who'd lied to her.

Kyla turned her back on him, ignoring his wide eyes that were clearly trying to convey a message she hadn't the faintest idea—or inclination—how to decipher. "No," she said curtly. "Has he given you anything yet?"

Freja shrugged. "We shall see." She angled herself toward Tane, straight and imposing, with the poise of an ice statue. "You have it on you," she said—and Kyla started.

Of *course*. Of *course* he did, that's why her Touch had calmed, why she felt that vast sense of quiet opening up in the back of her skull again like she had when she'd been around him before.

All this time.

All. This. Time.

"Give it to me," Freja said, "or I will take it from you."

Tane smiled broadly, rolling his head back to stare up at her from half-lidded eyes. "Really? You can't use your Touch. Your Touch*es*."

Kyla's pulse skipped. No denial of the fact that he had the Touchstone.

He'd lied. He'd lied outright to her about having the stone, even as he'd sat there, feeding her and imploring her to believe him, that he'd do anything he could to help.

The impulse to spit at his feet was strong.

He had the Touchstone. And what had he done with it? Hidden in the shadows, ineffectually flailing as he tried to hunt down just one person, all the while holding onto a stone that should have been the greatest weapon in the world against those whose Touches were too strong.

...She wasn't saying Freja was *right*, of course.

Just that she'd really like to *slap* Tane. Repeatedly. Maybe until a modicum of sense made it into his thick skull.

"Hm." Freja made a little noise of ironic agreement. She leaned down slowly, not quite nose-to-nose—he could have slammed said thick skull against hers all too easily—but close enough, and, lips quirking, she whispered, "I do not need Touches to undress you."

And, Kyla had to give it to her, she absolutely did not. Despite the fact that Tane was tied firmly to the chair, despite the fact that he was at least half a foot taller than Freja and weighed probably double what she did, Freja peeled his clothes away from him piece by piece, carefully doubling then adjusting and strategically removing his bonds one at a time so there was never any danger of him escaping.

Not that he seemed to be trying too hard; he barely strained against his restraints as Freja worked, stripping back his shirt to reveal a chest that sent adrenaline singing through Kyla's own body in response.

She slapped the ill-timed feelings away.

He lied to you. Liar, liar, liar.

Freja reached into the pocket of her slacks, pulled out something small, narrow, metallic... A pocket knife—maybe a switchblade, if that was the appropriate term for a pocket knife on steroids.

Kyla's eyes widened; if Freja tortured him, what would Kyla do? She resented him, maybe even hated him, for sure. But... torture? Could she stop it?

Would she?

But Freja gripped the thick cotton of his tan shorts firmly and sliced down the seams, left side, right side, removing them as easily as if she were deftly skinning a rabbit.

She shook the shorts, felt around in the pockets—threw them to one side with a hiss of disgust.

Nothing, obviously.

"Well," Kyla said, stepping closer as though her heart wasn't hammering in her throat, as though his presence wasn't still soothing away the restlessness of her own Touch like a silken caress, like she wasn't totally rattled by her own body's reaction to seeing him there, strapped to a chair in his underwear. *Traitor.* She cleared her throat. "Unless he's hiding it in his underwear, I'd say he doesn't have it on him."

Freja made a noise of frustration. "He must do. I can feel it. *You* can feel it. Use your Touch on him."

Her pulse sped up, which was probably not healthy.

Kyla shrugged it away.

Besides. It wasn't like she hadn't used her Touch on him before. It hadn't hurt him then—and if it happened to this time... Well, the downside would be that she wouldn't get the answers she wanted quite so easily.

Whatever.

Kyla ground her teeth. Reached for Tane's shoulder, ignoring the wounded puppy look he was trying to pierce her with.

Let her Touch discharge, forcing it out with a bit of effort against the calming reassurance that was, presumably, the Touchstone.

Nothing happened.

Something in the back of her shoulders released tension. Disappointment, probably, that it hadn't worked.

Kyla scowled. "Nothing."

"See?" Freja leaned right down to Tane again, grey eyes flashing with fury. "I know you have it, you horrible little man," she hissed. "And before I am done with you, you will wish that you had given it to me willingly. I will carve you to *pieces* if that is what it takes."

Abruptly she straightened, spat at him as Kyla had been sorely tempted to do, and stormed from the warehouse, heels clacking furiously on the floor.

The white-painted door of the storeroom slammed behind her.

Dust fell gently down from the rafters.

Kyla sneezed.

"Kyla."

She ignored him, shoulders tensing once again.

Sure, Dad was fine now, but also... The white door was

still, its papered-over window revealing nothing of the secrets hidden within.

Freja hadn't really given the antidote to her for free.

Maybe Freja was right about there being Touches that caused too much trouble in the world—and maybe she wasn't.

And maybe, right now, that didn't matter, because Kyla was indebted to her regardless, and if Tane had given her the Touchstone to begin with, this wouldn't have had to happen.

"I would have stolen it back for you," she said quietly.

The storeroom door's handle glinted softly in the filtered light from the papered-over windows.

"After I'd traded it for the antidote. I would have found a way to get it back for you." Her chest constricted. *Past*-her would have. She would have done anything she could to get the stone back, to help Tane in *his* quest to bring Freja down...

She blinked furiously against hot, threatening tears.

"Kyla." His voice was urgent but soft, a liquid caramel, far gentler than he had any right to be.

She whirled around, swung...

—and stopped herself, the back of her hand a foot away from his cheek. She curled her flat hand into a fist that she withdrew and let hang uselessly at her side. "Don't talk to me," she hissed with narrowed eyes.

"Kyla," he said, dismissing her anger, his tone low and urgent, "I told you I couldn't give you the Touchstone."

"I know," she whispered back furiously, folding her arms tight. "You lied." She turned and stalked away.

"I didn't lie," he said, still quiet, but pitched to carry to her. "I can't give you the stone. I *am* the stone. Kyla. Kyla stop, look at me: I *am* the Touchstone."

She was less than ten steps from him, she'd covered less than a third of the distance between him and the storeroom, but something shifted, telescoping her vision so he seemed lightyears away as she slowly turned and looked back at him.

The *Touchstone*?

He *was* the Touchstone?

But how...

What...

She shook her head, fighting to catch a breath in the torrential flood threatening to overtake her. "I'm sorry, *what*?"

Tane gestured her closer with a slightly frantic nod and a glance at the storeroom.

Kyla exhaled, so deeply it took almost all trace of tension with her, leaving her tired—just tired.

She tracked back to stand in front of him.

"I'm the Touchstone," he said. "It's... well, not genetic, but inherited. Sort of. A mantle. Only one person in my family has it at once. Look." He glanced at the storeroom again. "Can we talk about this later?"

"How can a person be a Touchstone? No," Kyla interrupted, shaking her head. "Don't answer that. I just..." She squeezed at her forehead. What the hell. What the *hell*?

Tane was the Touchstone? What the *hell* was she supposed to do with that?

"I don't suppose you'll agree to be a 'person she trusts' and work for her in order to make this easy, will you?" She'd respect him less, probably, but then, what did it matter whether she respected him or not if it got them both out alive?

"Kyla." Tane's soft tone drew her attention back to the way his eyes, deep and dark, searched hers. "She has me now, there's no reason for her to keep you alive a minute longer. Go. Get out of here."

"Go? She'll kill you," Kyla said blankly.

"She can't. I'm the Touchstone, remember?"

Kyla scowled, arms crossing tight over her chest. "Cancelling out Touch energy won't stop a knife, Tane." *Idiot*, she politely didn't say.

There were a lot of things she was politely not saying right now.

Tane shrugged as best as he could. "She doesn't have it in her to commit murder with her hands. I know her type."

Kyla arched an eyebrow. "You're willing to bet your life on that?"

A long look, while the metal roof ticked in the rising heat, the temperature slowly building in the warehouse, dust and concrete thick in the air. "I have to."

Kyla's eyes narrowed immediately. "No. You don't. And *I'm* not willing to bet your life on that. See?" She huffed, swinging her arms down and crouching to examine the cords that bound him to the chair. "This is exactly why I don't work with a partner," she muttered.

"I'm not asking you to work with me," Tane said, twisting his neck around to follow her progress as she circled his chair in a waddling crouch. "I'm asking you to run."

The knots were tight, too tight to unpick. "Shut up." His dark eyes stared down at her, tight, his mouth drawn. "Partner."

Tane's lips quirked. He leaned back, following her movement as she stood, stretching his neck back in a manner far too leisurely for their actual situation. "You only want me because I'm the Touchstone."

The man was dumb as a brick or arrogant as hell or some ungodly combination of the two, and Kyla ground her teeth, because he had no right to be sitting there in nothing but his just-teal-of-navy boyleg undies, sweat glistening off pecs she could bounce a coin—or a snowflake—off, eyes half lidded and sultry, while she was literally trying to figure out how to save his butt.

Save it, so she could kick it.

She ground her teeth. "Because I have an ounce of dignity," she said—the warehouse was empty apart from the chair, not even a pile of random assorted concrete in a corner, definitely not a knife or anything sharp—"I won't smack you for that."

Besides—a chill shook her for the briefest instant—she couldn't exactly promise he was wrong.

34

"**O**KAY," KYLA SAID. SHOCKINGLY, THE WAREHOUSE remained empty, devoid of anything useful— just dust and concrete and more dust. "Okay. I think I have a plan."

"Kyla, you need to leave," Tane said earnestly. "I can take care of myself."

Kyla sniffed, raising a pointed eyebrow at the man in front of her, stripped almost naked and tied tightly to a wooden chair. "Sure you can, big boy." She backed away, light on her feet. "Give me a second. I have something."

She turned, strode purposefully toward the storeroom.

Purposefully, purposefully, that was the key. People rarely questioned you when you looked like you knew what you were doing.

The key, of course, would be to avoid doing anything to trigger suspicion that might prompt Freja to use any of her ill-gotten Touches to find out what Kyla was up to.

The white-painted door to the storeroom opened easily, the silvered knob cool underneath her hand—and cool air wafted against her face, her arms, her legs as Kyla left the heat of the warehouse behind and entered the storeroom, six or so paces square with rusted racks lining the walls, the one to the left of the door stacked haphazardly with paperwork too new and white to have come with the warehouse.

In the middle, by something that was either a tiny chipboard desk or else a cheap, tall coffee table, the pocketknife sitting atop it, Freja sat cross-legged on a round grey rug, eyes closed, lips moving in some kind of mediation, or chant. Touch energy billowed around her like it had around the poisoners in the park—only this cloud was both significantly smaller, and much more brightly coloured.

Adrenaline tugged at Kyla's stomach.

Much more brightly coloured: almost every colour of Touch was represented in the seething, roiling mass of energy that was thick enough to obscure Kyla's view of Freja entirely if she let whatever sense it was that saw Touch energy overtake her eyes.

Kyla rolled her shoulders against a shudder, arms, body, legs tense against discovery. *I can't believe he betrayed me. I'm going to* murder *him. Don't worry, Freja, I'll get you the Touchstone, no matter what the cost.* The litany of defences rolled through her mind as ceaselessly as the soundless words on Freja's lips.

Freja shifted, eyes still closed. Something sparkled under the fluorescent lights.

Kyla inhaled sharply. A mirror. *The* mirror, Damon's mirror. Or one identical to it, anyway.

What was Freja doing? Was she... making a pendant?

Kyla smoothed the wrinkles from her brow and crept toward table, keeping it between her and Freja. Never mind.

Whatever Freja was up to, it could wait—and hopefully keep her occupied for long enough.

Slowly, Kyla reached for the knife.

No. Too slow. If Freja saw her, it would look suspicious.

She set her jaw and swiped it up, palmed it, stuck it in her pocket. Nothing to see here, everything perfectly ordinary.

A shatter.

Kyla jumped wildly, defences ready...

But Freja didn't even seem to have registered Kyla's presence. (Impossible, surely she would see Kyla's Touch, but hey, if she was going to choose to pretend Kyla wasn't here, fantastic, Kyla wasn't about to argue.)

Glittering shards of mirror covered Freja's ice-blue slacks, the grey rug around her—and her hands.

Eyes closed, she swept her hand down her slacks, gathering a handful of razor-sharp shards.

Clenched her fist.

Blood dripped from her hand, so red Kyla imagined she could smell it, taste the metallic flavour of a bitten cheek.

And the Touch energy around Freja flared, a hooded cobra, a whirling snowstorm.

Freja opened her hand.

Shards of colourless glass fell to her lap—colourless except for the blood, but glass now, not reflective, not mirrored.

What in the...

Kyla blinked. *Get moving while you can.*

She hurried toward the warehouse door. Slipped through; Freja still sat with perfect poise, sweeping mirrored shards up in her hand and crushing them, her Touch responding by billowing, growing, massing like thunderclouds about to storm.

Kyla let the door shut with a quiet click. Hurried back across the concrete floor, footsteps slapping, to a waiting Tane.

He glared. "I told you to leave, Kyla."

Kyla pulled out the knife. "Freja's up to something," she muttered.

She glanced up; Tane's derision was thick enough to grow legs and walk away.

"Really," he said dryly. "What gave you that impression?"

Kyla sniffed, slicing the knife through the cords at Tane's wrist. "More than usual, I mean." She sketched out what she'd just witnessed, moving clockwise around Tane, slicing cord after cord.

He massaged his wrists as she talked, then shook out his arms, rubbed feeling back into his legs.

Kyla scooped up his clothing from behind the chair and tossed it at him. As he struggled into it, she turned away. The white storeroom door was still closed, but for how long? Even through all the warding Freja had placed around the warehouse, Kyla could feel pressure building; not recognisable as the Touch energy she'd seen whirling around Freja, but it had to be that—what else would cause it?

Goosebumps prickled her arms.

She smoothed them away.

Shattering mirrors. Blood dripping from a fist squeezed tight around shards of glass.

Power, massing.

Kyla shivered again. "Hurry," she muttered at Tane, who'd given up on his shredded shorts and was struggling his t-shirt over his head.

"I'm trying."

The storeroom door burst open. It should have ricocheted off the wall and slammed back again, but something—power—pinned it open.

Kyla winced away from the sound—and adrenaline spurted at the sight of Freja, straight and imposing, Touch energies whirling around her in a cloud too big for the doorway, colours flashing in and out like giant koi in a stormy pond.

"Oh Kyla," Freja crooned, positioning herself by the storeroom doorway.

Kyla ought to move, should run…

"What have you done?"

Tane pressed against her back.

Kyla's hands knotted at her sides, pulse pounding. "I—" *I what? I'm only trying to help you? I set him free so I could torture him some more? I... I what?*

Freja stretched out her hand.

For a heartbeat Kyla knew nothing would happen, because Tane was there and he was the Touchstone—

But Freja knew that, and was carefully keeping to the perimeter, as far away from Tane as she could, twenty or thirty metres at least, and as she stretched out her other hand in an echo of the first, shadows pooled around them.

Kyla's stomach flooded with adrenaline.

The shadows billowed and lengthened, obscuring the paper-covered windows, unreal, invisible to the eye but not the Touch, clouding, blurring, darkening...

Power surged.

Tane shouldered Kyla aside, gripping her upper arm to keep her mostly upright. "Run!"

Touch energy shot into Tane, pouring into his chest, filling him like an electrical surge.

It should hurt. That much power surging through him, it had to be painful, had to burn.

His back arced, but his gaze remained focused on Freja.

She couldn't run. It didn't matter that he was the Touchstone, that the Touch energy couldn't kill him. Whatever it was Freja had done with the mirror, it had grown her Touch energies twofold and the pressure of it filled the warehouse to breaking, and concrete scraped at Kyla's knees and the smell of lemongrass and ozone burned through her nose, and her knees were on fire and shadows writhed all around her unless she blinked the Touchsight away, only she couldn't, because there was too much of it.

Freja wouldn't kill him. He'd said she wouldn't, not with her bare hands, and if she'd wanted Kyla dead, why hadn't she done it before?

Because Kyla hadn't betrayed her before.

Sour, bitter bile in her throat.

The Touch energy streaming into Tane winked out, leaving only the seething cloud behind, colours flashing.

Tane was there, lifting her, pulling her to her feet—

—and Touch energy blazed from Freja again, consuming Kyla's senses, aiming directly for her.

Tane snatched at her wrist. Shoved her ahead. "Move!" he shouted, even though the noise wasn't real, the dull roar filling Kyla's head was Touch energy only and nothing more, it wasn't real, none of it was real, there was no real reason why she couldn't hear silence or see the light filtering in through the papered-over windows, only she *couldn't* see, couldn't hear, and Tane was shoving at her.

Fumblingly, she made her feet keep moving. Out. The exit. A double door with a push-bar handle. She leaned against it.

Something thunked into the door beside her ear.

A half brick crashed to the floor near her feet.

Kyla turned, wide-eyed. Pulse in her temples. Blood in her mouth, on her tongue. Tane shoving at her to *move*.

Freja's arm, flung toward her.

A small, glassy object, glittering in the light.

It streaked toward her on an arc of pastel rainbow light.

Ice crusted around it, thin like frost, thick like frozen rain, impenetrable like a bullet of ice, aiming at her heart.

Tane shoved.

Kyla stumbled out the door.

A soft thud.

Tane grunted.

Then he shoved her again.

In the sunshine, Kyla's head immediately cleared. Empty cul-de-sac, bright sky overhead, the regular city noises of distant traffic, an overhead jet—

—and back in the warehouse, Freja screamed.

Tane snatched at her wrist again, one hand pressed to his shoulder. "Run."

This time, she did, pelting away from the warehouse with its miasmic cloud of swirling Touch energy as fast as her lungs would allow.

35

T ANE HAD BEEN SHOT, AND THAT WAS THE SUM OF IT. NOT BY a bullet, of course, but by a pellet of ice that had crystallised around a very familiar-looking snow-flake, right in the soft, fleshy part between shoulder and chest.

In the back seat of Pippa's car, Kyla gripped the grab handle with a white-knuckled hand, mouth locked tight.

Beside her, Tane was wan, one hand keeping pressure on the seeping wound, the other knotted in his seatbelt, bracing as the car bumped and jolted its way across town.

You didn't realise how bumpy even a modern car was until you had reason for it to be smooth.

Kyla met Pippa's eyes in the rearview. For once, they weren't narrowed in disapproval.

The wound wasn't fatal, Pippa had said. She didn't love the idea of not taking Tane for proper medical attention and had argued for taking him to the hospital instead of her house—but on the other hand, in Kyla's opinion, Pippa *was* proper medical attention, so the house won out in the end.

Tane groaned. "Much... further?" he gasped out.

Kyla's jaw clenched tighter.

"Couple of minutes," Pippa said. "Nearly there."

The snowflake was still in his shoulder.

Bile surged in Kyla's throat at the thought of that, of a foreign body lodged in Tane, a weapon, a trackable, traceable taint created by Freja, and Pippa had said the wound wasn't fatal but it shouldn't have been fatal for any of the others, either, and she could have at least taken out the snowflake and it was sickening, sickening, sickening.

They jolted into the driveway. Tane groaned again.

Pippa put the car into park, unclipped her belt, leapt out.

The door slammed.

Tane shifted his weight, just a fraction, hands still pressing, clenching, bracing.

Wind buffeted the car.

Pippa yanked open Tane's door. "Come on," she said. "Let's get you inside so we can get that thing out." She eased him from the back seat, an inch at a time, slammed the door shut with her hip, guided Tane up the drive to the house.

They vanished around the corner of the garage.

The silver birch tossed in the wind.

The car ticked, engine cooling even as the interior began to heat up now the air conditioning was off, now the morning sun was baking Kyla like bread in an oven.

She let out a gasp of air, her jaw cracking as she unclenched. Forced herself to relax her hold on the grab handle so she could open the door.

Clunk.

Hot air rushed in.

Step out into the sun. Blink in the bright light. Thunk the door shut again with one hip.

Sunlight sparkled off the car's silver trim. Spots danced in her after-vision.

"Kyla!"

Pippa's shout cut through the haze, and Kyla whipped toward the house. Strode up the pathway between garage and front yard, into the cool shade of the house.

From the half-open front door, Pippa motioned at Kyla to hurry up.

She did, pushing aside the tension in her forehead, between her eyes, in her shoulders.

Tane lay on the floor in the hallway, his feet and legs in the bathroom.

"Only flat space big enough to work on him without risking a mess," Pippa said by way of explanation, kneeling at Tane's side and gesturing for Kyla to do the same.

A mess was the least they were risking.

Kyla sank to the white-tiled floor, wincing as scraped and bloodied and bruised knees hit the hard surface, crossing her legs, the tiles cold against the bareness of her thighs below her shorts. "What do you need me to do?"

"Clean up the blood," Pippa said, throwing a white hand towel at her.

Kyla hesitated. So white. The blood…

"Just do it, La-La."

The childhood nickname cut through Kyla's haze—and Pippa stared determinedly back, like she had known it would.

Right. Clean up. I can do that.

Kyla mopped at the blood seeping from the wound, dripping down the side of Tane's chest.

He moaned, shifting in something that wasn't quite a wince.

"Ignore him," Pippa said. "You can't damage him worse than he is. It'll hurt, but dying will hurt worse."

Dying. Sickened adrenaline pooled in Kyla's stomach—then she frowned. "You said he won't die?"

Pippa pursed her lips, strands of her blonde hair sticking to her sweaty forehead as they escaped their braid. "No," she said curtly. "But that doesn't mean he can't lose the use of his arm." Deep blue eyes, serious, efficient—just like her deft movements as she peeled back Tane's shirt, pointed for Kyla to wipe, crouched over the wound.

She pulled long, silver forceps out of a pocket somewhere—no, a bag, she had her first-aid kit propped open beside her, dark green with a red cross on it.

Kyla tensed as Pippa stuck the forceps into the wound and fished around.

Tane moaned again.

Transfixed by the silver forceps, still mopping trickling blood with the now-stained towel, Kyla used her free hand to push Tane's neck gently back down. "Stay still," she murmured, nausea swirling in her gut.

Wouldn't look away though. She owed him that much.

She swallowed heavily as Pippa withdrew the forceps, a glittering glass snowflake smeared with dark blood in their grasp.

She'd seen corpses plenty of times. Caused them too often, too. But this? Watching someone fish around in another living being?

Kyla pressed the back of her forearm against her mouth. The smell of it was too fresh, too strong, too—much.

But it was done, and Pippa had dropped the snowflake onto another towel—ruined, now, like the one Kyla was still mopping ineffectually with—and then there was nothing else to do but dab occasionally as Pippa swabbed the wound with disinfectant and stitched it up, Tane groaning, taut, but doing his level best not to move too much.

"There." Pippa rocked back on her heels and swiped her sweaty forehead with her arm. "It's not the prettiest job, sorry. A hospital could have done it neater, though you'd have a scar regardless I guess."

"Thank you." Tane's voice was as washed out as his face, but some of the tension went out of his body.

"I assume that"—Pippa's gaze travelled pointedly to the bloody snowflake—"is safe enough?"

"As long as it's near me," Tane said, eyes tightly closed.

Pippa nodded curtly. "Right. I'm going to bring a clean cloth to wash you down, since I assume you're not feeling particularly up to a shower, and then you're going to go lie down until I tell you otherwise, okay?" She stood without waiting for an answer, and reappeared from the bathroom a moment later with another towel, damp this time, which she threw at Kyla. "Wash him. I'm going to get cleaned up." She gestured with bloodstained hands, then vanished once again.

Kyla watched the empty doorway for a second.

The cool, wet towel began to warm in her hands.

With a blink and a shake of her head, Kyla refocused on Tane, lying half naked on the floor in front of her.

Right. Clean him up.

She swallowed—because of the nerves, the nausea, the trauma of it all, of course, and not because she was about to start rubbing a towel over his exceptionally well-sculpted chest.

Which she did.

Gently, of course, because he was in pain, and not because the thought of towelling him off with any force turned her thoughts to other reasons she could be towelling him off, other situations where he might be lying like this in front of her.

Her cheeks heated, even though he hadn't said anything, even though his eyes were closed and Pippa was still in the bathroom.

The towel shifted as she wiped. Her fingers met his skin, in the soft hollow between shoulder and chest—the side that wasn't wounded.

Her breath caught.

Why was she even washing there? There was no blood, nothing but smooth, dark-olive skin...

Kyla swallowed hard.

He was the Touchstone.

He'd lied to her.

But... Well. He'd said he didn't have the stone to *give* her, which was true.

Lies by omission, then.

A quiet sigh. A *lot* of omission.

"Where did you go?" she whispered. "Why did you leave?"

And, more to the point... why did you come back?

Tane rolled his head on the white tiles so he was facing her, even though his eyes stayed closed. "I couldn't stand watching you... and not being allowed to help."

Her pulse jittered. "Not allowed?"

"My... family. The guardians of the Touchstone. I was in... in so much trouble... as it was."

Oh.

And then...

"Why did you come back?" The words slipped from her mouth like an accident, like a four-leaf clover fluttering to the ground, like a breath of foggy air.

To finish what he'd started with Freja, obviously.

To catch the murderer he'd been chasing.

"Because I couldn't stand"—he shifted on the floor—"not watching either."

Kyla's pulse danced. What... What did that *mean*? She opened her mouth—

Pippa rustled back into the hallway, wiping her hands on yet another of her seemingly endless supply of identical white towels.

Well.

Kyla eyed the small pile of bloodied towels slumped against the doorframe.

Not all of them were identical now.

"Help me move him," Pippa said, putting paid to any further questions.

Probably for the best. Kyla could always reopen the conversation later. Once she'd had time to consider what she really wanted to know.

TANE WAS SETTLED IN THE BACK GUEST ROOM WITH A BIT OF lifting assistance from Spy, who'd returned home from his night shift and been filled in on everything that had happened in the interim.

"My mind's too busy to sleep," Spy had said a good forty or so minutes later, and had led the way to the kitchen. "Let's do a cooked lunch."

And so Kyla had accepted a wooden chopping board and a sharp, expensive-looking knife with a nice weight to it, and found herself pyramiding finely chopped onion on it, waiting for a glug of olive oil to heat in the frypan.

The oil began to shimmer, and she scraped the onions in, leaning back a little as they sizzled ferociously and she lost herself in the simple motions of food preparation.

It wasn't like she wanted to do this *every* night—cooking for one had its advantages, and most of them were called 'leftovers'—but also, having someone else on hand to chop the veggies and hand them to her right as the onion was sizzling just so, translucent and sweet, someone to take the used utensils back and start the next stage of prep while all Kyla had to do was stand there, staring at the oil that spat and slurped happily, veggies gradually softening, their savoury scent billowing up with the steam from the pan...

It wasn't terrible.

Abruptly, a tiny piece of carrot got the fidgets and leapt sizzling from the pan.

Kyla scooped it up and wiped it back on the edge of the frypan—and frowned. A little orange spark, zapping through the air.

Why, when her blood had mingled with the thief's, had he suddenly shown an orange Touch? Why not black? And why did she have an orange Touch under the black at all?

"Spy," she said slowly, "I just realised I have something I should probably confess." She squeezed her eyes tightly shut for a moment, contemplated leaving town and not coming back...

She sighed heavily. Freja was still out there. And it wasn't like she wouldn't be connected to the body the minute it was discovered by someone else, so it was better that Spy hear it from her.

"What's that?" he said as he added some liquid to the pan.

Steam flashed up and he switched on the stove's exhaust fan.

Kyla's jaw twitched. "There's, uh, a, um, a body"—she winced—"back at Tane's house, and I, um, might know exactly what happened to him."

Spy's gaze bored into the side of her face, and her shoulder blades itched as though they could feel Pippa's gaze on her as well.

"Was it plausibly self-defence?" Spy said, his voice strained.

"Incredibly so," Kyla said, turning to him with the wooden spoon hovering over the frypan. "He forced his way into the house and assaulted me. I tried to keep a lid on my energy, but..."

The itching in her fingertips, the pressure mounting, the flash of it rolling down her arms as the energy snapped unbidden.

She squeezed her eyes closed again.

"I'm sorry," Pippa said in a small voice from a barstool at the kitchen bench.

Spy exhaled loudly. "Any witnesses?"

"No, just a neighbour who stopped by afterward to investigate the noise."

"Did they see anything?"

"No." Was Spy asking because he was hoping for an eyewitness, or hoping to avoid one? Kyla couldn't tell.

More liquid sloshed into the pan with another loud sizzle.

"You know I have to call it in," Spy said, and Kyla nodded —"but I'll do it after lunch, and hopefully forensics can corroborate your story. That from him?" he added, nodding at the deep scratches on her arm.

She nodded back. "Yeah."

He snorted. "Right. Fine. Might even be able to get some DNA from it or something. Can you cover your arm, make sure it doesn't get wet until you can go back down to the station for a swab?"

"I'll get you a shirt," Pippa said, and left the room.

Kyla tapped the wooden spoon on the pan so it wouldn't drip, set it in the spoon holder on the bench, and wrapped her arms around her ribs while she waited.

An orange Touch.

"I, uh, accidentally gave him a Touch," she said to the white floor tiles. "Before my Touch, you know. Flashed."

Spy was staring at her intently, hazel eyes focused.

"It was orange, not black."

His eyebrows lifted.

Pippa returned with a sheer white blouse and passed it to Kyla. "Let me stir the curry, I don't want you getting sauce on the shirt." She swapped into Kyla's place by the stove as Kyla pulled the shirt on over her tank top and buttoned it up. "You gave the guy an orange Touch? Because your blood met?"

Kyla nodded and moved around to perch on the barstool. "Yeah, his hand was bleeding, and he grabbed my arm"—she shrugged the one with the scratches—"and then bam, he had an orange Touch. And then afterward, when I would have said I had no Touch left, or not enough left to do anything with anyway, I went to the bush and let my control go and… and there was a bit of orange there, right at the end of my energy."

Spy set the knife down in the sink with a clink. "Okay that's it, we need to just do this and get it done so we can figure out what Freja's game is."

"Do what?" Pippa said, blinking.

"Give him a Touch," Kyla said as he folded his arms, jaw set, eyes determined.

He jerked a nod.

Pippa's expression turned sour. "It's too risky. What if he ends up with black?"

"I deal with risky every day," Spy said. "We need to do this. We need to know how it works."

"But Dad—"

"This isn't just about your dad anymore. You know that."

Pippa adjusted the stove so the curry wouldn't boil over. "I want it to be," she mumbled.

Kyla's eyebrows flickered at the unexpected vulnerability, and she said, "I don't know that the risk is as high as you think, though." She held up a hand to forestall Pippa's complaint. "Yesterday, I would have agree with you. Really. I *did* agree with you, remember?" She waited for Pippa's reluctant nod. "But today… After this morning…" She arched her shoulders against a shiver, remembering the way the Touch energy had leapt out of her.

"That's it," Spy said, jaw setting in emphasis. "We're doing this." He plucked the knife back up from the sink, soaped it, and washed it off under the tap.

Humid, spicy air from the stove curled around Kyla; her stomach rumbled in anticipation.

Spy went to grab the blade with his hand—

"Stop!" Kyla snatched at his free hand, leaning forward over the bench.

"Kyla, get off," he said, trying to shrug her aside. "I said I'm doing this."

"She just means not like that." Pippa closed her hands over the knife's handle. "Don't cut your hand, that's stupid."

"More nerves there than almost anywhere else," Kyla agreed. "And you'll need your hand."

Spy blinked first at Kyla, then at Pippa. "I am either very concerned or very impressed that you've both put this much thought into this."

"Both, probably," Kyla said mildly. "Do it on your shoulder, or your upper arm or something instead."

"Should we maybe do this after dinner's ready?" Pippa said, eyeing the steaming, bubbling pan with its murky, delicious liquid.

"Why?" Kyla asked. "If something goes wrong either he's going to be dead, or he's going to have the power to make other people dead."

"He could at least..." Pippa pursed her lips. Scrutinised Spy for a moment. Exhaled. "Fine. Whatever. Upper arm, like she said. Use the point, don't slash. Pretend you're giving yourself a needle."

With a precision Kyla hadn't expected, Spy drew just the very point of the knife over the skin of his upper arm. He winced, and blood beaded. "Your turn," he said, pinching at the tiny wound.

Kyla, lips pressed thinly together, picked the scab off one of the scratches on her arm, wincing too. She squeezed until blood welled, wiped up a large drop on her fingertip, and reached for Spy.

The tiny bead of blood on his upper arm glistened in the light.

Breathe stuck in her chest. What were they doing?

"Get it over with," Pippa snapped, although she probably didn't mean to.

Kyla stretched the final distance, touched her bloodied fingertip to the nick on Spy's arm.

...Nothing happened.

Kyla scowled.

"Maybe it can only happen periodically?" Spy said, doing an admirable job of hiding his disappointment.

"Or maybe she just imagined it," Pippa snapped.

"Maybe," Kyla said, anger rising in her chest, "you just—"

Touch energy flashed out of her, channelling through her fingertips.

Abruptly, Spy began to glow orange in the darkness behind Kyla's blinks.

Pippa's mouth dropped open. So did Spy's, though his was tempered with a gleaming kind of delight in his eyes as he held his hands out in front of him, fingers wriggling experimentally.

Kyla set her jaw, pulling her hand away and pressing firmly on the scratch on her arm with a tissue plucked from the box on the bench. "Well," she said. "That answers that: if I can give you a Touch, presumably Freja can indeed steal other people's Touches when she kills them."

Pippa was staring at Spy with a kind of horrified fascination. "Why is it orange, though? Your Touch has always been black."

"I know," Kyla muttered, eyes closed as she examined the faint interplay of glowing orange—it was a very saturated orange, so Spy would be able to use his new Touch fairly often, but it was also a very pure, bright orange, no hint of darkness, which meant it likely wouldn't be that strong.

Which made sense, given that it was only the tiniest fraction of Kyla's own Touch.

And also...

Kyla gasped. "I think I've got something," she said. "You know how the more saturated the colour is, the more often the Touch energy builds up?"

Pippa nodded, though Spy simply lifted his eyebrows.

"And how the darker it gets, the stronger it is?"

Another nod from Pippa, an intense look of concentration from Spy that drew his eyebrows down tightly.

"What if... What if once it reaches a certain strength, a certain intensity, it flips over into being a death Touch? Like, the darker orange becomes, the blacker it becomes," she said, speaking quickly now. "Orange, darker orange, darkest orange, and then bam, black." She illustrated the spectrum with her hands, moving from high to low.

Something Eirene had said when they met popped into mind: "Eirene even noted that her Touch wasn't only uncon-sciousness, because she *wasn't that grey*. Her blue is dark, dark enough to cause, what, like, a little bit of death? Uncon-sciousness, right? But it's not so dark that it's black and the death overwhelms the mind powers of her blue base!"

A loud sizzle from the stove interrupted them; the curry was boiling over. Spy leapt to turn down the element, lifting the pan from the heat.

"That makes a lot of sense," Tane's voice came from behind Kyla.

She whirled on the barstool; he was standing in the doorway to the guest room, expression thoughtful.

"Shouldn't you still be in bed?"

He smirked at Kyla's comment, strode through the lounge room—if a little gingerly—and sat on the second barstool beside her. "I'm fine," he said.

Kyla's right eyebrow rose sceptically.

He laughed, and pulled down on the neck of his t-shirt until the soft hollow between chest and shoulder was exposed.

The skin wasn't *smooth*, but the edges of the wound had definitely sealed, and the blue stitches looked out of place, redundant.

Kyla blinked.

She'd seen Pippa stitch it up, not two hours ago. "How...?"

"Touchstone," he said, and although his mouth wasn't grinning, his eyes definitely were.

"Indeed." Kyla let her eyebrows drift back to their usual position, trying to quash the part of her still imagining the soft skin of Tane's inner shoulder.

"So what now then?" Pippa asked, setting bowls out on the bench with little clinking thuds as Spy gave the sauce a last swirl in the frypan and switched off both heat and exhaust fan.

The sudden lack of mechanical noise made Pippa's question seem even weightier.

"We need to talk to Alex," Kyla said, frowning. "About the mirror, if nothing else. We need to know what she was doing with it."

Pippa served rice into the four white bowls, and Spy followed, ladling in the curry that filled the air with sweet, spicy deliciousness.

"He doesn't seem the chatty type," Spy said.

"He's the only lead we have right now," Tane countered.

"Yes," Kyla chimed in, heartbeat suddenly spiking in anticipation of what she was about to say: "and it must have been the mirror she was after all along, since none of the blackmailers except Blood were on your list of people Freja might be after"—she pointedly did not look at Tane, even though the comment was clearly aimed at him—"and she got to Blood first. So why keep after the others?"

She could feel Tane scrutinising her, his gaze laser focused. She reached for a bowl with as much nonchalance as she could muster, wincing at the heat as she lifted it toward herself.

Pippa passed her a fork.

Tane exhaled quietly, just loud enough for Kyla to hear. "I'm sorry," he murmured.

Kyla shovelled a large forkful of rice and curry into her mouth and, pretending her eyes weren't watering at the sudden heat, gave him a bright, false smile.

He shook his head a little, then: "Thanks," he said as Pippa pushed a bowl over in front of him. "But you're forgetting something, Kyla. If she took the mirror yesterday, as you say, then why kill the other blackmailer overnight?"

Kyla paused mid-mouthful. Tane had a point.

Pippa sighed. "I need more sleep for this," she said. "Spy needs sleep. Kyla, I know you don't want to hear it, but you need sleep too. Can we all go nap and then talk to Alex again this evening?"

Spy shook his head, curls bouncing. "We can only hold him without charges for another couple of hours."

"So charge him with something," Pippa said tiredly.

"If we want to talk to him while he's still at the station," Spy said, "we'll have to go now."

Tane swallowed down his mouthful and nodded over the bench. "You guys sleep if you need to. I'll go down to the station. It's not like we all have to be there."

"I'm coming with you," Kyla said.

Spy shrugged. "I have to be there, unless you want to let one of the other officers in on all of this right away."

Pippa's spine stiffened. "Well I'm not staying behind if you're all going."

"Seriously," Kyla said, "we can handle this. Sleep, Pippa."

She shook her head. "This impacts us all. I'm coming." Her eyes flickered to Kyla's for a breath. "And, what if... I mean..." She shifted her weight restlessly. "What if we took Eirene. You know. With us. To talk to him."

Spy narrowed his eyes.

"Is that legal?" Kyla watched as his eyes narrowed even further.

He let out a breath. "It's not *technically il*legal but I can't say I'm comfortable with it."

"Fair," Tane said.

"Never mind then." Pippa shook her head again. "We'll manage. But let's eat first. Please. If I can't have sleep, at least I can have hot food."

Kyla shovelled in a forkful of rice and curry, munched it down, swallowed while avoiding everyone's faces.

Maybe it wasn't just the curry warming her insides.

Maybe this was what it felt like to have people watching your back.

37

KYLA STOOD TO ONE SIDE OF THE HOLDING CELL AS SPY unlocked the gate, stale sweat permeating the air. "Come on, now," Spy said to Alex, who lay staring at the wall. "Up you get."

Alex complied vacantly, staring sightlessly at the wall while Spy cuffed him and escorted him out, down the hall to the cool of an interview room—a nicer one than they'd used earlier, with a white cloth over the table and a cheap print of some blue flowers in a white vase on the wall.

Not what Kyla usually expected of an interview room, but perhaps it was done to make interviewees more comfortable—and more likely to answer questions.

The smell wasn't any better than the other room, though; although the room looked clean, the same stagnant smell of the waiting room out front hung in the air.

Spy sat Alex in the interview seat and took the plastic chair opposite.

Kyla sat at his side, and behind the one-way mirror to her left, Pippa and Tane were presumably watching on.

"None of it matters," Alex said, gaze flickering over them for a moment before returning to the grainy pattern of the tablecloth.

"Yeah you said that," Kyla said, hoping Spy wasn't going to arc up if she took the lead for a minute. "Why? Because she has the mirror?"

Alex shrugged, still staring sightlessly at the tabletop.

"What does she want with the mirror? Do you know?"

He shrugged again.

Kyla exhaled loudly. "Okay, I get it. You're scared, you're grieving. But the security system from your house is protecting this building so she can't get you here, and if you don't tell us what she's planning, we can't stop her."

He met her eye briefly. "You can't stop her anyway. *You* could have done, before she got the mirror, but not now she has it."

"Me? Why me?" *Tane was the one hunting her,* she didn't add.

Alex's eyebrows rose. "Your shard?" he said in a tone that implied 'obviously'.

Kyla wrinkled her brow. "What's a shard?"

Alex blinked, one slow movement of astonishment. "You don't know?" He turned to Spy and repeated in a dry tone, "She doesn't know." He threw his hands up in the air, cuffs rattling, and swore. "How is it possible you've gotten this far and you don't even know what shards are? You, who are apparently blundering around in utter ignorance, get to live, and he, who actually knew what he was doing, died. Tell me how that's fair." His jaw twitched, and Kyla turned away from the intensity of his stare.

"I can't," she said. "It's not."

Alex snorted. Tried to fold his arms, and realised he couldn't with the cuffs on. Knotted his hands in his lap instead, leaning back and throwing out his legs, crossed at the ankles. "Shards are what cause your Touch," he said, and Kyla stiffened. She sensed more than saw the similar sharpening in Spy's attention beside her.

"They're in your bloodstream, as far as we can tell, and it's possible for them to shift around from person to person under the right circumstances."

Kyla nodded; that was pretty much what they had confirmed when she'd given Spy some of her Touch.

"Usually the larger your shard, the stronger your Touch, but it's not quite a one-to-one relationship. Freja's targeting people with large shards because she's trying to steal them, but she has to be careful: if she tries to siphon off a shard that's larger than hers, she risks having hers taken away instead."

Kyla inhaled sharply. "And how are the shards related to that mirror of yours?" she asked with narrowed eyes.

"It's not a normal mirror," Alex said, his head shaking. "It's not glass. It's... well, it's whatever the shards are made of. When they're, um, distilled out from a person, they kind of... congeal... into a dark mirror. From what we've seen, they're kind of, like, magnetised to each other, or something?"

Kyla's pulse was skipping. "She's using the mirror to increase the size of her shard." All of a sudden the bloodied mirror fragments in Freja's lap, the way they seemed to absorb into her... it all made sense.

Alex nodded dully. "Yours is large enough that she probably didn't dare attack you earlier," he said, "but if she has the mirror, if she's absorbed that amount of shard material, she'll be stronger than anyone alive. We can only hope she doesn't figure out how to use it."

Kyla's lips thinned, and she shifted on the plastic chair that, despite the air conditioning, was sticking to her thighs. "She knows," she said, and quickly sketched out for Alex what she'd seen in the warehouse overnight. "And not only that," she said, shoulders slumping as she leaned back in the chair, "it's likely she has the mirror from Damon's shop, too." She explained that to Alex, hoping he'd contradict her, tell her she was worrying needlessly and that it couldn't possibly be more of the same mirror.

But as she finished, he slumped back in his own chair. "You see? There's no use then. Nothing can stop her now."

Kyla glanced at the one-way mirror, looking up over the head of her reflection to where she imagined Tane's eye level might be. "She didn't attack me, though. This morning, when I... escaped. Maybe it's not as bad as you think." Was Freja simply more keen to have anything that could dampen her powers out of the way, assuming she'd be able to get to Kyla later?

Or... Kyla swallowed, remembering the half brick thunking to the floor beside her, the whine of the snowflake flying through the air—and the way Tane had pushed her at the last minute.

Maybe the snowflake *had* been meant for her.

Alex shrugged despondently again. "Regardless, she'll come for you sooner or later. You're too much of a threat, and she wants your Touch."

Wait, that was another complicating question. "Okay hold on, about that. I, uh, figured out that I can give a Touch to someone else, only my Touch is black and when I give it to someone else, it's orange." And there was no logical reason why her cheeks were flushing hot at that, even if the thought of basically asking advice from the person who was responsible for her father's "illness" was, well, weird at the very, very least. "We're working on the theory that once a Touch becomes strong enough, it presents as black,"—Alex nodded like either he knew and was confirming she was right, or else he agreed it was a plausible theory—"so why doesn't Freja's show black if her, her *shard* is so, uh, large?" Kyla frowned. "For that matter, do we even know what colour her Touch *is*?"

"Nah, she has a cloaking pendant," Alex said. "A strong one. We were never able to get a fix on what colour she is. Your theory about a strong Touch presenting as black makes a lot of sense on the surface, but if that's the case then her shard is absolutely big enough that is could only result in a black Touch, so what's the point of collecting other people's Touches?"

Kyla exchanged glances with Spy. "Eliminating the competition? You did say her shard had to be larger than the one she was trying to steal. Maybe she's just going for size so she can, I don't know, eliminate the possibility of anyone else having a larger shard and stealing hers?"

"If she's eliminating competition," Spy said thoughtfully, "then competition for what?"

Hmm. That was a good question too.

Kyla shifted on the plastic chair, wincing slightly as her thighs stuck to it again. "Okay," she said, "new question: tell me more about the mirrors. Are they, like, physically, actually made of the same thing as... shards? Where do they come from?"

Despite his apparent reluctance, Alex leaned forward in his chair a little, some of the sourness in his expression clearing. "They're not just *made* of the same stuff, they *are* the same stuff. And they're not mirrors plural. As far as we can tell, it's all part of the same mirror. Or at least, the fragments are, like, magnetised to each other in some way, so if they're near each other they want to form a single mirror. That's why she can absorb the mirror fragments into her; they want to get to the shards in her bloodstream."

Kyla shook her head; she could practically feel her paramedic sister vibrating through the one-way mirror. "If these things are in people's blood, how come no one's found them before now? Why haven't they shown up in scans, especially if some of them are large? Freja absorbed that whole entire mirror of yours; you're telling me she has a shard of glass the size of a basketball floating around in her bloodstream somehow?"

Alex grinned. "You're willing to believe that a bit of glass dust in someone's blood gives them the ability to tell the future, track people down, read people's minds, or *kill them*, and you want to worry about how the glass fits?" He leaned back, splaying his hands wide. "Magic," he said. "Obviously."

Kyla rolled her eyes. *Should have seen that one coming, I suppose.* "So where did the mirror come from, then? And can we get it back out of her blood once it's in there?"

Alex shrugged. "There are rumours," he said. "Some references in some of the lesser-known Greek philosophers."

"Mnason," Kyla said suddenly, and in her mind she was back on a train, forehead pressed against cool glass while the nightlights of the city flashed passed, humid, sweat-soaked air around her.

Alex's eyebrows rose as his eyes widened. "Yeah," he said, "that's one of the key references. Who... Oh." His brows lowered, knitting together. "I guess Jason told you that."

Kyla nodded, swallowing down the tightness in her throat.

"What did he tell you?"

"Nothing. I..." She shrugged. "He was launching into lecture mode, so I cut him off." Grief tugged at her chest; she'd never be able to hear his lecture mode again, never hear what it was he'd been planning to tell her.

"Yeah," Alex said softly. "That was Jason." He drew in a stabilising breath and exhaled loudly. "Anyway. Mnason mostly concerns himself with the Touchstone, which I assume"—he shot Kyla a dark look—"you've decided you're no longer looking for."

Kyla's stomach twisted, but she wasn't about to tell Alex what she'd uncovered in that regard; she hadn't even told Pippa yet. Hadn't needed to, since Freja had provided the poison's antidote. She worked her tongue in her suddenly dry mouth, shifted again in the cool, conditioned air of the interview room.

"Anyway, if you put the references together, it seems like maybe the shards were all part of a singular mirror sometime way in the past—like, the ancient past even for the Ancient Greeks. But it was shattered, ground to dust, and the dust cast out into the atmosphere."

"So why are we only just starting to see Touches now?" Spy said from beside Kyla—saving her the trouble of asking the question.

"Took that long for the dust to accumulate into shards big enough to create an effect, we guess," Alex said with a shrug.

It made sense, especially paired with what he'd said about the various sizes of people's shards. Hmm.

"Okay, but that still doesn't tell us how these particular mirrors formed in the first place. Were they parts of the original mirror that didn't shatter? Or is there really some way to extract the shards from someone's blood and reform them into the mirror?" Kyla said.

Alex nodded. "There's no outright confirmation, but yeah, there are enough references in the texts to someone's shards coming 'undone' that we assume it must be possible. And the mirror itself was definitely fully ground to dust. These mirrors must have reformed since then somehow."

Kyla frowned. "You'd need something capable of draining and holding onto Touch energy." Not the snowflakes; though they obviously helped Freja absorb people's Touches, Kyla had the feeling that was more a substitute for the little flash of willpower it had taken to move some of her shard over to Spy. The snowflakes were… magnets, or conduits, that was a better word: conduits allowing Freja to access the power of other people's shards.

"Anyway, one thing's certain," Alex said, interrupting her line of thinking. "Freja was afraid we were close to figuring it all out. She certainly wasn't after all of us for our shards, and you said she got the mirror already before… You know. Last night. Which"—he shifted uneasily, glance darting around the room—"you sure seem like you're trying to keep me alive and I appreciate that, but I'd feel a lot better if you'd let me make sure you set up the security system properly."

Kyla's phone rang in her pocket. "Sorry," she muttered, pulling it out with every expectation of silencing it.

It was Eirene.

"I guess we can let you view it," Spy was saying.

Kyla scraped her chair back and stood. "Excuse me for a second."

She hit answer as she slipped out of the interview room into the oppressive heat of the unconditioned hallway. "Hello?"

"She's found us," Eirene said breathlessly. "She's attacking the house. Help."

Kyla's pulse skyrocketed, her grip on the phone tightening like a vice. "We'll be there as soon as we can. Hold on."

38

F ROM THE FRONT, THE YEES' HOUSE LOOKED TRANQUIL AND sleepy in the hot afternoon sun that streamed into their front yard through the bright leaves of a street oak. Jasmine scented the air with warm spice, and a dreamy sort of daze lay over the neighbourhood.

Kyla wasn't fooled.

She leapt from Pippa's car at a run and pounded up the path to the front door, Tane and Spy hot on her heels while Pippa parked the car.

Kyla thundered on the white wooden door and, without waiting for an answer, tried the brass knob.

Locked, of course.

She hammered at the door again.

"They might not be able to come if Freja's got them pinned down," Spy said over her shoulder. "Is there another way in?"

"Around the back," Kyla bit off, already whirling to run back down the front path to the road.

"I'll cover this door," Spy said.

Wordlessly, Tane sprinted down to follow Kyla, practically spinning Pippa on the spot as she stepped up off the road.

"Stay with Spy," Kyla told her, then ran. Her long legs ate up the length of the footpath, past three houses similar to the Yees', front gardens spilling an array of flowers that perfumed the hot, humid air, down to the turn at the corner of the block where the air tasted more of concrete than of jasmine as Kyla breathed heavily.

Sweat dripped from Kyla's hairline.

"Let me try to get close enough to nullify her powers," Tane said with only the slightest trace of exertion in his voice.

Kyla nodded.

The footpath terminated at the cobblestones that covered the narrow lane behind the Yees' house, and Kyla was forced to slow to avoid twisting her ankle. To the left, gum trees and tea tree scrub overhung the laneway, held back by a wooden railed fence. The scent of them hung thick in the air—but not thick enough to hide the smell of lemongrass that grew stronger and stronger the closer they got to the Yees' backyard.

A cry echoed down the laneway.

Kyla pushed herself to run faster until, just moments later, she swung around the Yees' back fence and—gasping—took in the situation.

Freja stood at the back door in the shade of the verandah, somehow taller than should have been possible, her ice-blue blouse drawing in light and sending it out again in shattered rays that stabbed painfully at Kyla's eyes.

She winced, flinching away.

Tane overtook her, threw himself at the back steps as Freja drew herself up.

Blinking rapidly, Kyla spotted Lyssa curled on the ground in a patch of frost, half in the house and half out, with a dark figure that was probably Eirene standing over her.

Kyla started forward again, over the square of lush, shadowed grass. Tane might be able to prevent Freja from using her Touch, but that hadn't prevented her from hurling a snowflake at him earlier—hell, had that only been this morning?

Kyla shoved the ensuing wave of tiredness aside. She could be exhausted later.

A shout came from inside the house, and suddenly footsteps thundered on floorboards and Spy and Pippa appeared over Lyssa's prone form.

Tane lunged for Freja, but she was already moving, dodging away from Spy's outstretched baton as her access to her Touch powers vanished.

Pippa dragged Lyssa inside, Eirene helping.

Kyla made the back steps, leapt up them, leapt toward Freja—to do what, she had no idea, she was running on instinct, on adrenaline, and the only coherent thought she had was to protect Lyssa, to prevent Freja from discharging her power.

Tane threw himself at Freja's legs but again, she was already moving, dodging Spy a second time.

Kyla lunged at her, only to be knocked aside, landing awkwardly on the gravel path at the foot of the steps as Freja, with apparently superhuman strength, fought free of the verandah and leapt down onto the grass.

Before any of them could do more than right themselves, she was gone, out the back gate and away.

Spy sprinted to the gate, out onto the cobbles—but it was no good, Kyla knew it was no good: the scent of lemongrass was already fading away.

Eirene was crying.

In the dimness of the back hall, Pippa and Eirene knelt on either side of a fully prone Lyssa, Eirene already sponging at her face with a damp cloth.

Tane stood himself up from the back verandah and brushed himself down.

"She's gone," Spy said, re-entering the yard. "Vanished as soon as she hit the lane."

"I'd love to know how she does that," Tane muttered.

Kyla sniffed. "Wouldn't we all." She stretched as she stood up off the gravel path, rubbing at a shoulder that now bore a fairly impressive graze, wincing as rocks and pebbles pattered to the ground. She peered around at said shoulder; it was going to need a good clean at the very least.

She sighed heavily. "Now what?"

There was a thud in the hallway inside: Eirene, twisted on the floor by her sister.

"Spy!" Pippa hollered.

Kyla followed him into the cool interior of the house, the air stripped of the humid smells of tea tree and jasmine.

But before Pippa could even get Eirene's limbs straightened out, Eirene blinked groggily and came around.

"Are you okay?" Pippa said, pressing her wrist against Eirene's forehead, then pulling gently at her lower eyelid.

"Tired," Eirene mumbled.

"She held Freja off almost the whole time it took for us to get here," Pippa explained.

Dark blue. Eirene's dark blue Touch meant mental powers, and Kyla never had checked in with her about what specifically she could do. Too busy trying to keep Lyssa safe.

Kyla tilted her head consideringly as Eirene gripped Pippa's forearm and struggled up until she was sitting by Lyssa's side. "You held her off that whole time?"

Eirene nodded.

"Nice work." Her Touch was so dark it was almost black; that had to mean it was strong, but her name hadn't been on Freja's hit list, so her shard couldn't be big enough to warrant Freja's attention. Kyla pursed her lips. Too many unknowns.

"So what now?" Spy said, echoing Kyla's question from outside.

"I have to stop her," Tane said with a shrug. "That hasn't changed."

"No," Kyla said, and Tane tilted his head quizzically, deep brown eyes warm and confused. "*We* have to stop her. This is way too big for one person to handle; the only way we do this is by working as a team."

39

"**A**LRIGHT," Kyla said, stalking back and forth in the cool dimness of the Yees' kitchen-living space. Grey tiles were pleasantly cool underfoot, and the air conditioning unit on the wall wafted cold air over her every time she passed it. "What have we got?"

Pippa was leaning her elbows on the white kitchen bench, highlighted by the square of light filtering down from the skylight; Spy stood next to her, arms folded, freckled face as stern and unamused as was possible for someone so boyish.

On the dark green velveteen couch where Lyssa had lain after the ice children's attack, she now sat with her legs curled up underneath her, cradling a tall glass of orange juice while Eirene sat practically on top of her, still the picture of big-sisterly concern.

Tane was in the matching armchair, hands gripping the squishy arms tight.

"I saw your potential hit list," Kyla told him, working to keep her tone light. "She's either killed or attacked everyone on it. Any idea what her long game is, or what she'll try next?"

"No," he said. "I left to try to figure that out, but I'm no further ahead now than I was." His voice was tight, and although she'd only known him a few days—something that kind of broke her brain to realise—Kyla thought she detected a faint trace of panic.

"I don't suppose you'll tell us about that, will you?"

He set his mouth in a grim line. "I can't."

Of course not. Kyla sighed to herself and shoved her hands deep into the back pockets of her shorts, disturbing folded paper in one of them. She paused in front of the air conditioner, cold air streaming over her bare arms, fingers curling around the crumpled page.

"I don't even understand what list you mean," Eirene was saying from the couch, forehead creased by a frown.

Tane shook his head and covered his face with his hand. "It was Alethea's best guess as to who Freja was here to target," he mumbled. "Beyond that, I've no idea what she wants, or where to find her."

Kyla smoothed the wrinkled, worn poster she'd pulled from her pocket. "Uh, actually," she said, "I think we know exactly where to find her." She held up the poster that had been stuck to the door to Alethea's alleyway, the one promoting the gala at the Museum—the one with Freja's face.

Lyssa's eyes widened. "That's the Transparent Charity Gala."

"What does that mean?" Kyla said. Freja's heavily made-up face stared up at her, pristine ice-blue make-up highlighting her blue-grey eyes, dark hair twisted into an elegant up-do.

"Are we sure that's part of her, like, 'evil plot'?" Pippa said from the kitchen, sketching air quotes around the word, her voice laden with scepticism. "Couldn't it just be part of her job as a celebrity?"

Eirene shook her head, dark hair swinging. "The Transparent Charity? It's a hot new thing, for victims of... of..." She faltered, then cleared her throat a little. "Touch-related crime."

People like that are too dangerous to let live.

Was that it, then? Did Freja really just fancy herself as some sort of vigilante, protecting the world from Touches she thought were dangerous?

"How have you not heard of this?" Lyssa said, shaking her head before taking a swig of her juice.

Kyla shifted, the air conditioning raising goosebumps on her skin. "Is that what she was on TV for?" she asked Pippa, who straightened thoughtfully.

"I don't know, I wasn't really paying that much attention, but yeah, it might have been the charity."

"I've heard of them," Spy said grimly. "They're not exactly on our watch list, but we keep track of their events. One too many of them have ended in a rabble."

"Interesting." From the gala promotion, Freja stared up at Kyla. "The gala is this Saturday. Like, tomorrow. What do we think?"—Pippa and Spy in the kitchen, Lyssa and Eirene on the couch, Tane in the armchair: they all watched on thoughtfully—"Is this a coincidence, or I guess a convenience, or is the gala part of her end game somehow?"

Eirene thumbed open her phone and tippy tapped away.

"What time's the gala?" Tane asked.

"Eight p.m.," Kyla read from the poster.

"Huh," said Eirene, eyes on her phone. "The primary exhibition in the museum right now is Kerry Williams."

"Who's she?" Pippa said before Kyla could.

Eirene's eyebrows rose. "Like, the most famous glass artist in the world?"

"Glass?" Tane leaned forward in the armchair. "That sounds promising. What else do we know?"

"Glass can be used to cloak Touches or deflect them," Kyla counted off on her fingers, "and apparently to hold Touch energy, if you know what you're doing." Freja's large jar of glass snowflakes, each one gleaming with pastel rainbow light. "But you need someone who knows how to do that, and doesn't the glass need to be, like, primed or something? Like, you can't just pick up a random piece of glass and expect it to cloak you, so why would Freja benefit from a glass exhibition?"

Eirene was shaking her head. "Kerry Williams is Touched. Her art isn't just glass; it's an open secret that she influences it with her Touch, though I'm not sure how, she's pretty cagey about the details."

Kyla frowned. "It's not like it's made of mirror shards though, so she can't use it to boost her own power. What else have we got?"

"Actually, Alex's comments about the original mirror got me thinking," Tane said. "My family..." He sighed deeply, and then in a pained voice continued, "I'm not sure if we all are aware, but, um, I'm the Touchstone."

The Yee girls rocked back a little on the couch. "How does that work?" Lyssa asked.

Tane shrugged. "It's a family role. Kind of genetic, but it's like a mantle; only one of us has it at a time. And there are... stories in our family histories about mirrors. A lot of family stories about mirrors being bad luck, about needing to break mirrors, about large mirrors being evil, that sort of thing."

"You think your family was involved in breaking the original one?" Kyla lifted an eyebrow.

Tane shrugged again. "We're talking thousands of years of history, here. How would I know? I'm just saying, my family has a lot of legends about how dangerous and bad mirrors are, and I literally cancel out Touch energy, which we've learned comes from the mirror shards, so it's not wildly implausible, yeah."

"Mirrors?" Eirene frowned.

Quickly, Kyla filled them in on what Alex had said down at the police station.

"What do you think?" Lyssa said quietly when Kyla had finished, facing her sister on the couch. "Mum's urn?"

Eirene nodded. "It's possible."

"Mind sharing with the group?" Pippa said drily from the kitchen, the skylight gilding her blonde hair as she leaned over to prop her elbows on the bench again.

"Mum's urn acted kind of like a limited Touchstone," Eirene said. "It was made of obsidian, and she could discharge her Touch into it. It wasn't... It's like it didn't have enough space for her to do it often—it didn't help Lyssa much because her Touch built up too quickly—but it definitely took some of the energy away."

"What are you thinking?" Tane said, his expression implying that he was having lots of thoughts of his own.

"I don't know, exactly," Eirene said, shrugging. "But it clearly interacts with the shards somehow, right? Saps away some of their power? Maybe it draws some of the power *out*. You weren't old enough to see it"—she glanced at Lyssa— "but I always felt like Mum's power had gotten weaker before she died. Almost like... like the urn was actually siphoning part of it away for good each time." She turned wide eyes on the room. "Could it be possible that the urn was drawing out some of her shard?"

"But you couldn't always rely on it to take on your Touch, could you?" Kyla said to Lyssa.

She shook her head. "No. It had a pretty concrete limit."

"But it was made of obsidian."

"Yeah."

Hmm. The urn was obsidian.

Blood had speculated that the Touchstone might be obsidian.

There was another obsidian object Kyla had acquired recently, guided by that sixth sense that she now knew was the orange component of her Touch to pick up: the knife from Alethea's store.

"I think I know something we can try," she said, and explained the knife she'd taken from Alethea's shop. "Blood told me he thought the Touchstone might be obsidian instead of glass," she added. "It's worth a shot."

"We still don't know what Freja's end game is," Spy said. He lifted the black kettle off the bench and gestured to the Yee girls. "Have you got coffee to go with this?"

Eirene nodded and unfolded herself off the couch. "I'll get it."

"Freja is collecting the shards of people with strong Touches," Kyla said. The seam where the dark green couch met the floor had a little shadow darkening the tiles. "I know Alethea IDed the people with strong Touches who live in Melbourne"—Tane dipped his chin in a fractional nod—"but what about people visiting? Who's attending this gala? Maybe that could give us an idea of what she's planning to do."

"Are the guest lists for things like this usually publicised?" Tane said with a frown.

"I could maybe get a warrant to ask for the records from the organisers..." Spy suggested as he filled the kettle with tap water and set it on its cradle to boil.

Lyssa downed the last of her juice in one long scull and waved her phone in the air. "Give me five minutes," she said.

The kettle rumbled and vibrated, smothering conversation while it boiled. Lyssa tapped away at her phone while Eirene ground coffee in the grinder, the scent of it filling the air.

Kyla's stomach rumbled and she drew her brows down, trying to remember when she'd last eaten. Right, curry at Pippa's house for lunch, that wasn't that long ago. She rubbed her fingers up and down the middle of her forehead. It was sleep she really needed.

"I'm in," Lyssa said as the noise of the kettle clicked off. "It's like a who's who of people with strong Touches."

Pippa furrowed her brow as she accepted a white mug

from Eirene. "But why would people with strong Touches be attending a gala for an anti-Touch charity?"

"Ah, but you see, Transparent Charity isn't anti-Touch," Eirene said, pouring the hot water into Pippa and Spy's mugs, "it's anti the *fallout* of Touches. The attendees all want to be seen to be on the side of the victims. They want to be seen as harmless, or at the very least concerned with protecting society from harm."

Kyla blinked. "That's... clever of you to deduce." Ordinarily, she might have gotten there before Eirene, but right now her eyes were feeling gritty and her brain couldn't seem to connect things as easily as it usually could. She cast around the room, but there was nowhere to sit apart from the already occupied couches. She leaned herself against the wall as a compromise, folding her hands in behind the small of her back, the air conditioning breezing away on her left shoulder. "Okay. So an exhibition of glassworks, possibly Touched; a bunch of people with potentially large shards; and a woman known for murdering people for their shards. No matter how you slice that, it doesn't look good."

"How are we going to get in, though?" Lyssa said, still focused on her phone.

"What do you mean?"

Lyssa's dark eyes met Kyla's "It's like five hundred bucks a ticket."

Kyla's stomach flip-flopped.

"I can fund it," Tane said quietly.

Kyla's eyebrows practically found orbit. "For how many of us?"

Tane shrugged and released his grip on the arms of the armchair to fold his arms defensively. "All of us, if that's what's needed."

Kyla stared.

Then stared some more.

"Nope, it's no good, my brain's short-circuited." She blinked rapidly and gave her head a little shake.

"I'll see if I can even get last-minute tickets," Lyssa said.

She unfolded from the couch and drifted over to perch on the arm of Tane's chair.

Kyla considered the now-empty couch... But, glass, glass that needed to be charged to interact with Touch energy, glass that could hold Touch energy...

At the very least they'd need something to disguise themselves, or Freja would know they were there the minute they stepped through the door.

She sighed. No rest for the wicked.

She pushed off from the wall and pulled her phone out from her pocket. "Okay," she said, inhaling deeply the warm, rich smell of coffee as it drifted from the kitchen. "You look that up and see if you can get us last-minute tickets. I have an idea about something else we'll need, and I'm going to go fetch my backpack and the knife. Can I borrow your car?"

Pippa nodded and dug out the keys.

Kyla took them and strode out into the incense-scented hallway, the hall rug soft under her socked feet.

She unlocked her phone and scrolled through her contacts to the one she was looking for, then hit dial.

"Hi," she said as the call connected and she slid her feet into her sneakers. "Damon, I have some questions for you."

40

ON THE DRIVE BACK TO TANE'S RENTAL, KYLA HAD TALKED Damon through the specifics of what they needed: something that would cloak each of them, and hopefully something that could also provide some measure of protection.

With only one of his pair of mirrors remaining, Damon had at first declared any Touch-related creation impossible, but Kyla had explained what the mirrors actually were, and given he couldn't do anything with only one mirror anyway, she'd eventually persuaded him to try cracking the one he had in half—very carefully.

She'd fetched her backpack with the knife from Tane's, holding her breath against the awful smell and trying to avoid looking at the corpse still sprawled in the hallway—

she'd have to remind Spy of that, it had been nearly twenty-four hours—and been back in the car when Damon had called her back.

"I can do it," he'd said, voice alight with passion—and gratitude.

He'd assured her he'd have something ready for them by tomorrow afternoon, more than prepared to work through the night if that's what it took to get revenge on the woman who'd stolen his mirror—and he'd do it all for free.

Kyla had smiled to herself as she'd hung up. A team wasn't so bad.

She parked Pippa's car back out the front of the Yees' house and climbed out, back into the hot, jasmine-scented air. The half-high front gate creaked as she passed through it, her sneakers thumping on the paved walkway up to the house.

Eirene had answered when Kyla rang the doorbell, and they'd gone back through the cool, dim, incense-scented hall-way to the kitchen/living space, the aroma of coffee still lingering in the air even though Kyla had been gone nearly an hour.

"You can probably phone that body in now, Spy," Kyla said as she crossed the room to the kitchen bench.

Both Spy and Pippa stood in the kitchen near the sink, apparently having just finished washing up some mugs.

"Oh, yeah, right," he said, and drew his phone out of his pocket. "You'll need to come down to the station for a swab."

Kyla nodded. "I've got one thing to try first, then I'm yours for the evening."

She plonked her grey-and-black backpack onto the bar-stool at the white bench and zipped it open. She fished down through cool layers of clothing to the very bottom, where the cold handle of the obsidian knife met her questing fingers. Drawing it out, Kyla untangled it from the sock she'd had it sheathed in and held it up for the room. "I got this from Alethea's shop," she said. "On instinct, mostly, but instinct—I mean, my orange Touch—hasn't led me astray yet."

"What do you think it does?" Eirene said, sliding onto the neighbouring barstool.

Kyla drew in a deep breath. "I think it has the ability to draw out a person's shard and turn them back into the mirror."

Tane stood from the armchair on the far side of the room and made his way over. "That's a big claim. What makes you think it?"

"Right before I picked it up, Alethea did a seeing for me. She told me..." Kyla hesitated, shifting her grip on the knife's hilt. She cleared her throat. "Amongst other things," Kyla said, her thoughts ringing with what Alethea had said on that first night: *someone's looking for you, someone good for you*, "she told me that something here would be my undoing. You were there," she added, nodding at Tane who was now leaning on the bench with his elbows.

He frowned. "I remember her saying Freja was stealing people's Touches."

Kyla nodded. "That was all I remembered too until the girls started talking about their mother's obsidian urn. Then I remembered picking up the knife, and what Alex said at the station—and what Alethea had said right before I picked up the knife. 'Something here will be your undoing.' I thought she meant 'here' like here in Melbourne generally, but what if she meant *here*, like, her store, specifically?"

Tane was still frowning, his unfixed gaze staring through the bench.

"Alex said what, that there were references to people's shards coming undone?" Pippa said.

"You think we can slice someone with their knife and draw out their shard?" Spy said, his brow furrowing to match Tane's. "How is that different to what Freja is doing with the snowflakes, or what their"—he nodded at Eirene—"mother's urn does?"

Abruptly, Kyla's pulse sped up. She inhaled to speak, paused, let the breath out, and tried again. "I think it does more than that. I think... I think it might not only draw out the shard, I think it might reform it into the mirror. Look," she added, and turned the knife around to show them all the little hollow in the butt of the hilt. A tiny hole was just visible in the deepest point of the hollow, leading up through the hilt of the knife, and along the spine of the blade was a very narrow but comparatively deep channel.

"So how do we do this? How do we confirm what it can or can't do?" Pippa said, grey eyes searching Kyla's face.

Kyla inhaled again, her pulse slowing to normal speed.

Eirene shifted on her stool, and Tane straightened.

"Surely we have to test it on someone," Spy said, eyes fixed on the blade.

"Yeah," Kyla said, thoughts spinning with images of wandering the street trying to find a random Touched person willing to let them test it, because this wasn't the kind of thing she was going to be comfortable testing without consent. Briefly she considered asking Spy if he'd be the guinea pig, since he'd only had his Touch literally since this morning — but the joy in his eyes when his Touch had flared...

No. She couldn't ask that of him.

"I'll do it." Lyssa stood up from the dark green couch.

Kyla blinked; Lyssa had been so still and quiet, hidden where she'd been sitting on the couch, that Kyla had mostly forgotten she was there.

Everyone was staring at her now, though.

Lyssa's hands fisted at her sides, and her face had paled.

"Lyssa, are you sure?" Eirene said, her voice hesitant, fragile—but nonetheless containing a thread of hope.

Lyssa nodded, her jaw tight, black hair falling over her face for a moment until she tossed her head. "Yes," she said. "I'm sure. Kyla has her Touch under control, and of all of us, mine is the most out of control, the most dangerous. The most useless," she added quietly.

Eirene got up from the barstool at once and rounded the couch to her sister, sweeping her into a tight hug.

Lyssa refused to soften into the hug, holding herself stiff and straight. "Do it now," she said, eyes boring into Kyla.

Kyla pursed her lips, swallowed—and nodded. "Yeah," she said. "Yeah okay." If it worked, it might be a solution to all Lyssa's problems. If it didn't... well, nothing would change.

If it worked...

Kyla exhaled heavily as she walked over to meet Lyssa, trying hard not to lose herself in a tangle of imaginings: what she would do if she could really, truly get rid of her Touch forever; what it would feel like for Lyssa to be bereft of something that dominated so much of her identity.

Lyssa was already holding out her arm, Eirene refusing to let her go and instead holding onto her from behind, arms wrapped around Lyssa's waist, face pressed against her taller sister's shoulder blade.

"Not the hand," Kyla murmured, her stomach tugging sharply as she flashed back to Pippa's kitchen this morning, where she'd said almost the identical thing to Spy.

Only that was the opposite situation, wasn't it, where she was going in trying to share her Touch and the risk was that she'd accidentally birth another human condemned to eternal responsibility for murder.

This time, maybe she could alleviate that responsibility, just a little bit.

If it worked.

She gripped Lyssa's left forearm in her own left hand to steady it, and with her right hand, pressed the point of the obsidian blade against Lyssa's upper arm, midway up below the cuff of her t-shirt.

The blade was sharper than it looked, and blood welled instantly.

"Now what?" Lyssa said, craning her head to stare at the bead of red.

"I think I need to... pull," Kyla said. "It would help," she added, glancing up to meet Lyssa's dark-eyed gaze, "if you pushed a little at the same time, I think."

Lyssa nodded.

Kyla pulled

Lyssa, presumably, pushed.

Touch energy flashed into the knife and for a moment, startled, Kyla nearly dropped it—the energy flash wasn't subtle, wasn't small: this was the entirely of Lyssa's power drawing out of her, draining, and Kyla had to fight to hold the knife steady as power raced along the channel in the blade's spine, wanting to billow and stretch and unfurl far faster than the channel could accommodate. "Don't push so hard," Kyla muttered, and gritted her teeth, holding the knife now with two hands and pushing back a little herself to slow the flow.

The handle of the blade turned ice cold. It burned Kyla's hands a little, and cautiously, she swapped her grip, giving her left hand a turn in immediate contact with the hilt.

At the butt, something began to bead: a tiny pinhead of silver, then a sesame seed, then a bead.

Abruptly, the flow of energy vanished.

The silvery bead dropped to the floor with a tiny sound like *tack*.

Kyla stooped, picked it up—and straightened immediately in horror as Lyssa let out a sob. "Are you okay?"

Eirene's grip on Lyssa turned white-knuckled.

Tears flowed rapidly down Lyssa's cheeks below closed eyes, and she pressed the knuckles of her left hand to her mouth.

Oh no. Oh no oh no oh no.

Pain twisted Kyla's chest, regret, and she reached out for Lyssa—*What have I done?*—but Lyssa raised her eyelids, and her eyes were bright, and shining.

From the tears, of course—but also from relief.

"It's so light," she whispered. "I feel so light." She broke down entirely, sobs wracking her body, and as she turned and leaned into her sister's hug, her head bowed down on Eirene's shoulder, Kyla drew back, knife clutched tightly in one hand, the tiny, bead-sized mirror that represented Lyssa's Touch folded in the other.

"Well," she said softly and held the bead up for the others in the kitchen to see, even as her gaze remained focused on Lyssa's bowed head, "I guess we know it works."

SATURDAY 10 DECEMBER

THE HUGE CONCRETE PLAZA THAT LED TO THE MAIN entrance of the museum buzzed with people in the hour before sunset. Magnolias in giant wooden crates towered over the crowd, a busker provided a saxophonic soundtrack, and the skateboarders who appreciated the wide open concreted space darted in amongst the throng of gala-goers, reluctant to cede ground. The smell of cut grass permeated the air, the sound of a ride-on lawn mower just audible above the chatter of the crowd.

Kyla cast a longing glance at the lush grass carpeting the grounds, the towering figs and gums dappling the ground with a shade that was bound to be cooler than the huge concrete pad of the Museum itself. Self-consciously, she ran a hand over her hip, the silky fabric of her hired cocktail dress smooth and soft. The sunset-orange was quite pretty, really, even if it was nothing like she'd ever worn before—but she did miss having pockets.

Ahead in the crowd she spotted Pippa, blonde hair twisted into a sleek updo (her own dark hair was hanging loose over her shoulders, tickling her bare skin instead of being bound up in its usual ponytail), dress a frilly white concoction that could have looked like a poorly prepared meringue, and yet somehow, on Pippa, didn't.

Somewhere nearby, Spy would be lingering with a full contingent of police officers, ready to swoop in the moment they got a signal from one of the team—and Tane was here somewhere in a suit, and Eirene in a dark, shimmering pant-suit that matched her Touch; they'd only been able to procure four tickets at such short notice, and now that Lyssa was Touch-less, it had been an easy decision to let her wait this one out with Spy.

Kyla had spent a restless night tossing and turning as she'd considered the implications of the knife. It was everything she'd ever wanted: a chance to rid herself of her Touch for good.

And by 'for good', she'd meant both 'permanently' and also 'for the better'.

Only...

Her Touch wasn't just black. There was also the orange to consider.

In the end, it had been too easy to put off that particular decision anyway in favour of preparing for the gala, with dresses to find and plans to make and contingencies for what might happen.

As Kyla filed toward the Museum doors with the crowd, a whiff of potting soil from one of the big magnolias in its huge wood-slatted pot tugged at her attention. It was gone within a step though, and then she was walking through the first set of automatic glass doors into cooler air, her fancy, strappy flats tick-tacking on the ridged floor. She exhaled heavily and set her shoulders. *Focus*.

The second set of doors opened and the air was fully air conditioned, the cold slithering over her bare shoulders, stirring around her toes—and curling over her the scent of something savoury and rich, a complex, gravy sort of smell that had her mouth watering.

To the immediate left and right the floor vanished about twenty paces to either side forming a mezzanine, escalators —currently motionless—heading down to the basement level. Immediately overhead hung an old biplane, tiny as aeroplanes went but large enough as a sculpture.

In front, the concrete floor opened out into a vast entry foyer, which had been cleared of its usual ticket counters and was now peppered with round tables, their white tablecloths skimming the ground. Over the foyer, a glass-walled walk-way clove the room in two at the height of the second storey, demarcating the high-ceilinged front of the foyer from the slightly more intimate back half; wominjeka, it said in huge white letters, *welcome* in the local Aboriginal tongue.

Deep behind, at the far end of the foyer, a fern forest provided a backdrop of greenery, long fronds catching the last of the evening sunlight.

The Museum shop walled the right side of the foyer in aesthetic black cladding, and the left... Well, it was black too, but largely obscured by the real highlight of the room: across the whole foyer ceiling in front of that upper walkway, dripping down to cover the left-side wall, twisted glass objects hung. Some were only as big as Kyla's arm, some as large as the round twelve-seater tables.

At the right, the twisting, branching, octopusing sculp-tures were black and dark blue; as they crossed the ceiling they faded into greens—forest and teal and ocean and hunter —before becoming lime, and then lemon, then gold. At that point they left the ceiling, branches twisting and twining down the wall through orange and sunset into blood, crim-son, vermillion, before finally landing on the floor in a swathe of glittering magenta, roped off from wandering hands by thick black ropes.

The setting sun didn't reach into the void directly, but the ambient light gave the glass ornaments an otherworldly kind of glow that stopped Kyla's breath in her chest—and her feet in their tracks.

"Sorry," she murmured as someone bumped into her from behind.

Absently, she moved forward in the queue that had formed, pulled out her phone for a museum attendant to scan her ticket.

The savoury smell intensified, drifting up from the lower level.

She moved out of the main flow of people who milled and congregated, most standing in clusters in the front third of the huge foyer, some moving further in to check out the seating arrangements, draping suit coats over the backs of chairs or leaving beaded or sequined clutches above plate settings.

Kyla leaned her hip against the glass that fenced off the void of the basement floor and scanned the ground for the Eirene and Tane. Down below, potted plants waved fronds of greenery, black ropes delineated the space into a snaking queue, now empty for the day, and white-coated waiters scurried about as they prepared for the evening.

In the foyer, the tables bore centrepieces of twisted glass lit by softly gleaming fairy lights, and each place setting was headed by a glass sculpture no larger than a wineglass in tones that matched the larger pieces overhead, a gentle hint of rainbow washing over the tables from one side of the room to the other.

The crowds at the Museum doors began to ebb. There: Eirene in a navy blue pantsuit, her black hair pulled back into an aesthetic mess of small braids, and not far behind, Tane in his rented tux.

Kyla pushed off the railing with her hip, took a deep breath of delicious air, and headed toward the big board propped up on a wooden easel that instructed people where to sit. She took advantage of the small crowd gathered around it, using the cover as an excuse to press her inner elbow tightly against the side of her strapless bra, checking for the reassuring pressure of the cloaking ward: not her old one, which had muted her visible Touch from black to grey, but a flat disc the size of a golf ball that had glittered gold when Damon had revealed it to her with a flourish, a proper cloak that blocked her Touch from others' senses entirely, would deflect any casual Touch energies aimed at her—and that swirled with pastel rainbow light when Kyla had closed her eyes.

Her lips quirked now into the ghost of a smile, both at the reassurance the disc was still in place, and at the memory of Damon's pride as he handed over not one, but three of the items, and a few other goodies besides.

"You may repay me yet for all the work you cause me," he'd said with a shake of his balding head, but his eyes had twinkled nearly as brightly as his creations.

Kyla skimmed the seating chart that was decorated in the four corners with illustrations of the glass sculptures that hung from the roof.

Table nine, a green table.

Their tickets had been so last minute that getting seats together had never been going to happen. So a little bubble of delight—or was that also reassurance?—buoyed in her chest as she saw Tane's name on the table neighbouring hers; they were seated practically back-to-back.

Tossing her hair back over her shoulder with a flick of her head, Kyla headed toward table number nine, with its array of little green sculptures. Wait staff were circling now amid the guests, long-nosed gas lighters at the ready as they checked to ensure no candles had extinguished, that guests were finding their seats, that cloth napkins were laid just so over patrons' laps.

Kyla set her lipstick-pink clutch above her plate and allowed herself to be seated. The scent of burning candles swirled in the air, and Kyla blinked in surprise at the little tug of nostalgia it evoked. "Thank you," she said as a napkin was laid in her lap, and pushed aside memories of candlelit dinners with her family before her Touch had appeared.

A woman in a dark wine taffeta gown sat to her right, and a dark-haired man in a crisp tuxedo took the seat to her left.

Kyla nodded politely to each of them and took another deep breath to still her nerves. Freja would be here some-where—she was sponsoring the gala after all—and Kyla reminded herself that the plan was not to jump on Freja the second she appeared anyway.

She twisted around in her seat on the pretence of stret-ching, and away behind her, against the far wall where the glass display swept from blood-red at the ceiling down to magenta at the floor, Pippa was being seated: the glass sculpture in the centre of her table was deep, dark pink. Pippa nodded at the blond waiter who'd seated her, her own blonde hair wisping its aesthetic tendrils around her face, then caught Kyla's eye. She dipped her chin, a slow nod of acknowledgement that somehow seemed to convey confi-dence—in Kyla, in the situation, in Pippa herself, Kyla had no idea, but regardless, it helped to soothe away some of her nerves.

Somewhere to her left, toward the front of the room where the little rainforest soaked in the last rays of dusk, was Eirene, ready to break out her mental Touch again and try to hold Freja at bay if the worst came to the worst.

Kyla hoped fervently that it wouldn't.

Then, suddenly, the crowd hushed, and someone with dark hair in an ice-blue ballgown was approaching the micro-phone on its stand on the small platform at the front of the room, backdropped by the tall ferns and tangling vines of the rainforest through the glass behind her.

Anger, fear, loathing—they all bundled together and fris-sioned down Kyla's spine as Freja took the stage, a twisted glass tiara glittering on her head.

It was a generic preamble, a thanks for coming and supporting this wonderful charity, isn't it lovely that someone is doing this, and that so many of the Touched are here among us tonight to show their support, etc etc. Kyla was too far away to see the find details of Freja's expression, but she had the impression of a dark shadow passing over it as she mentioned the number of Touched here tonight.

Nervously, Kyla pressed her inner elbow against her cloaking pendant again.

But Freja finished her welcome speech without anything untoward occurring, and waiters began serving out the entrees on the other side of the room.

Pippa was at one of the first tables and, glancing over her shoulder, Kyla saw Pippa politely nod to the waiter who deposited a small white plate of something green and red in front of her. As soon as the waiter moved on, though, Pippa took the napkin from her lap and tucked it under the edge of the plate, then stood without touching it.

Kyla's lips pursed, brow furrowing just a little as Pippa wound her way between the tables in that white, frilly dress that made her seem ethereal.

"I need a moment," Pippa said in a low voice as she passed, squeezing Kyla's bare shoulder and nodding toward the Museum shop. She continued without pause, and after a brief moment, Kyla nodded to the wine-taffetaed woman in the next seat and stood. The chair barely made a sound as its felted feet slid across the polished concrete floor—amazing how a layer of polish and care could delineate this concrete floor from the undressed, industrial one at Freja's warehouse —and Kyla quickly wound her own way through the round tables toward the shop.

Pippa stood around the corner on the far side of the Museum shop's folding glass doors, out of sight of most of the tables, tucked behind one of the large black posts that had to be decorative elements in the narrower hallway along this side of the mezzanine.

"What's up?" said Kyla, her voice low as she glanced around for any sign of people paying too close attention.

"At least three of the people at my table are going to die tonight."

No wonder her grey eyes looked strained and her fingers were curling to fists as she folded her arms tightly over her ribs.

Kyla found herself chewing on the inside of her lower lip and stopped. "Can you see how?"

Pippa shook her head, a brief, tense movement. "It's messy. There's blood."

"Are they Touched?" Kyla said, eyebrows rising.

"Yes."

"Shoot. She's planning to collect their Touches." Kyla exhaled, then—"Are *we* still okay?"

Pippa gave her a piercing kind of glance before nodding tightly. "You're the same as you've always been."

Kyla's eyebrows quirked a little at that turn of phrase, but she nodded back. "Okay. Let's see if Eirene can uncover anything." She turned and headed back toward the tables, the heels of her flat, strappy sandals tapping on the concrete floor.

Pippa's footsteps sounded behind her, but instead of following Pippa made her way back to her own table on the far side of the room.

Kyla headed right, past the black-clad side wall of the Museum shop, past the decorative window showing shelves of Museum knickknacks, toward the front of the gala set-up.

Eirene was seated at a table where the glass sculptures were dark navy blue trending toward black—an exact match for Eirene's Touch, Kyla realised with a blink.

She drew near, and Eirene looked up, catching her eye before quickly excusing herself and coming to meet Kyla by the wall where the shop ended and a long, wide hallway led off to the exhibits on either side of the rainforest courtyard. "What's wrong?"

"People are going to die. Tonight. Messily. Pippa reckons at least three people at her table."

"Can we stop it?" Eirene said, eyes widening.

"I'm not sure how Pippa's Touch works, but we're definitely going to try. Do you reckon you can somehow get close enough to Freja to figure out what her play is here? We're flying blind right now, and unless we can get some sort of edge on her, she could kill everyone in the room before we can act to stop it."

Eirene nodded, lips pressed thinly together. "Leave it with me."

Kyla stopped her with a hand on her forearm. "Don't let her recognise you."

"Yeah."

Kyla sighed heavily as Eirene moved away. This was the worst part of any job, the leap of faith that you were trusting to the right information and the right conclusions—but the stakes weren't usually so high. Usually, all Kyla had to risk was her own skin, and even that risk wasn't usually fatal.

She bounced the inside of her cheek between her teeth, exhaled loudly through her nose, and returned to her seat.

"Everything alright?" Tane murmured as she drew out her seat.

"Give Eirene some space to work," she murmured back without turning toward him. She smiled brightly at the taffetaed woman beside her and laid her napkin back over her lap.

Behind her, the quiet sound of Tane's chair shushed across the floor and she felt rather than saw him move away.

Her entree was served moments later, and she was midway through the half spatchcock delicately arranged on a bed of barbecued mushrooms, the piquant garlic sauce dripping from her fork, when her phone buzzed in her clutch purse on the table above her plate. She set her fork on the side of her plate and dug out her phone.

It was a text message from Eirene.

Can't get too close or dig too deep. Best I can make out is an obsessive loop about glass, possibly the stuff overhead. Want me to try for more?

Trying for more meant seriously risking exposure, and that seemed counterproductive—if Freja recognised one of them, she was just as likely to launch right into her plan as she was to reveal more information. And that was assuming she didn't have something protecting her thoughts from deeper examination, which was frankly an absurd assumption at this point.

No, Kyla texted back. *Sit tight.*

Eirene's getting something about the glass in the roof, Kyla sent Pippa. *Does that match your impressions at all?*

Could be, the reply came quickly. *Lots of blood.*

"Yours looks good," the dark-haired man to Kyla's left said.

"Hmm? Oh, yes. Delicious." Kyla stretched on a smile, put her phone face down on the table, and took up her fork again. The meat *was* juicy and tender, a genteel savoury background to the sharp sauce and the deep, savoury notes of the assorted mushrooms.

The man said something else and Kyla nodded on auto-pilot. Above them, the glass fronds twisted and twined, even more ethereal and otherworldly now the sun had set outside and dusk was dimming, the Museum's artfully applied spot lighting making the display seem to almost pulse and glow.

Kyla squinted, something tightening in her chest.

No.

It wasn't seeming to pulse and glow; it *was* pulsing. It was faint, hard to distinguish through the vibrant coloration of the rainbowed glass, but... the artist was known for her Touch-related glass working too, Eirene had said so.

Anyone else getting a read off the glass over our heads? Kyla sent to the group chat.

Down the front, Eirene glanced upward speculatively. *Matches the read I was getting from her thoughts,* she sent back.

Tane, how similar is the energy in the stuff above us to the energy in the snowflakes? Pippa asked.

Kyla's heartbeat spiked as she realised what Pippa was thinking.

Similar enough.

Think she's gonna bring it down? Kyla sent, imagining the tentacles and tendrils that twisted artfully above them suddenly falling, a shower of razor-sharp shards that would cause everyone in the room to bleed, allowing Freja to easily drain everybody's Touches.

Kyla fought the urge to hunch her shoulders protectively.

The man next to her said something again.

"Hmm?" Kyla raised her eyebrows at him, lowering her phone to the table, images of shattered glass filling her mind's eye.

He repeated his comment, but once again, Kyla missed it: she was too busy having her stomach flip-flop as she noticed for the first time that he was Touched. Cloaked, probably, since the sense she was getting was faint but the colour seemed saturated—a deep green, like jade, or emerald grass.

The guest list read like a who's who of Touched. The roof was covered in Touched glass. And Freja had been stealing Touches.

"I'm sorry, excuse me." She pushed her chair back, snatched her phone, and hurried away from the table with horror knifing her chest.

She glanced at her phone as she wove between tables, heading back toward the Museum shop and the mezzanine over the lower floors where she'd spoken earlier with Pippa—where Tane had gone.

The chat had reached the same conclusion as her twisting stomach: Freja was going to bring the roof down—literally—and once everyone was bleeding, she'd draw all the Touches into herself. Somehow.

Kyla frowned as she reached the front of the Museum shop. How was Freja going to manage drawing in all the Touches?

Tane appeared in front of her, stepping out from behind the same black post beyond the shop doors that Pippa had stood behind as he saw her approach.

"What, she's going to make everyone bleed and then just… swan around collecting everyone's Touches one by one? That will take too long. Someone will stop her, surely she's got to have thought of that," Kyla said without preamble.

Tane opened his mouth to reply, and the group chat pinged again.

It was Eirene.

I know how she'll collect the Touches, she sent. *She's got Mum's urn.*

Kyla's grip on the phone tightened.

"What is it?" Tane said rather than checking his own phone, dark eyes widening a little.

Kyla showed him her phone screen and he huddled close to read it. "What are we going to do?" Kyla's own eyes were wide too, and her heartbeat was running at double time—though of course, she noted, pressed against Tane in his tux in a private-ish corner, his hands warm on her bare upper arms, her heartbeat would likely have been elevated even if Freja wasn't about to try to kill everyone.

She gave a little sniff of self-derision. *Focus.*

Her phone buzzed again.

I think she saw me, Eirene had sent to the group chat. *She acted like she didn't but I caught something in her surface thoughts.*

Get out, Kyla sent back immediately. *You need to stay safe.*

You mean like everyone else here? The emoji combination that followed managed to artfully convey scepticism and rebellion.

"She's seen Eirene," Kyla relayed to Tane since he hadn't checked his own phone.

He nodded. "We need to act fast, then. It would be stupid of her not to assume that the rest of us are around some-where if Eirene is here."

"What are we going to do?" Kyla said again as Tane let go of her arms and pulled her back into the walkway, one hand trailing down her arm to find her hand. He laced his fingers through hers and held tight. "Honestly?" he said as they hurried back toward the tables. "I've no idea."

42

T HE SEA OF TABLES OPENED OUT BEFORE KYLA AND TANE AND the savoury scent of the entrees wound around them, the massive display of twisting, twining glass above —black and blue at this side, like a bruise.

"This is going to be so messy," Kyla muttered with a shake of her head, imagining it all shattering to the ground. "Did someone tell Spy to have the paramedics on standby?"

"Far side of the room, by the ferns," Tane muttered and Kyla glanced over, half expecting to see a half-hidden gaggle of paramedics.

Her heart stuttered.

Freja stood there in front of the now night-dark rainforest, her ice-blue gown shimmering, the twisted glass tiara atop her dark updo glinting in the light. She was staring at them—or at least it seemed that way across the sea of tables.

Tane tensed beside her. "She's trying to lure us over there."

"I figured," Kyla said. "But surely we're better off trying to overpower her out of the way of the crowd anyway? We have you, that has to give us the advantage."

"She knows her power doesn't work around me, even if she doesn't know why. She'll have something planned." His hand was growing sweaty in hers, though Kyla wasn't about to let go for anything.

"Do we wait then?" Kyla said softly, adrenaline pulsing in her stomach. Waiting would give Freja more time to make her play, would get more people killed. But they were doing this as a team. Kyla wasn't going to run off this time unless everyone agreed.

Tane exhaled loudly, drawing a look from the nearest seated gala guest, their fork midway to their mouth. "Let's go see if we can convince her to be reasonable."

As he strode forward, Kyla's first thought was that there was very little Freja had done so far that suggested she'd be willing to be reasonable—but on the other hand, she did seem to enjoy power monologuing at times, so Kyla supposed it was worth a shot.

Regardless, she made sure to swerve past the table where she'd been seated and grab her lipstick-pink clutch from where it sat above her unfinished entree—the clutch containing a tube of raspberry lip balm, a spare key to Tane's rental, and the obsidian knife she'd nicked from Alethea's shop.

In the air, the sharpness of the garlic sauce merged with the savoury spatchcock and the lightly spiced scent of the baked red capsicum entree; Kyla pressed a hand against her stomach, but it wasn't hunger that had it twisting. She clenched her jaw.

By the time they'd wound through the tables to the front corner of the room, Freja had vanished around the corner—

and, rounding it, Kyla was greeted by a huge, long skeleton on a pale sea-green plinth in the centre of the wide hallway.

Oh, it was a whale, strategically speared through by upright silver poles to hold it hovering a couple of feet above the platform—but Tane was pulling her forward, and in the wide walkway on the near side of the whale, Freja stood waiting, a cat-with-the-cream smile playing about her mouth, one elbow cupped in her hand as her long fingers toyed with her smile—the pose she seemed to love so much.

Kyla's pulse sped up. Freja was waiting for them, she had to know they'd come to stop her, she'd have tricks up her sleeves and the fact of Tane being the Touchstone might not foil them all.

The whale's flipper was tucked against its body, the bones so very hand-like. Freja stood a few paces beyond it.

A blur of movement from Kyla's right; something pale threw itself up from under the whale's ribcage.

Tane grunted as whatever it was hit him. Kyla whirled, ready to back him up as he cried out in pained surprise—and vanished.

Water pooled on the floor, and on the whale's plinth, and along the nearest ribs of the whale frost glittered in the overhead lights.

"Whoops," Freja said lightly, then shrugged. "He did seem *so* determined to hold on to the Touchstone. He could have stayed if he'd just let it go, it was only programmed to go after the stone."

The ice children. It had been one of her ice children...

...Programmed?

Kyla blinked, squeezed her fist as though clutching at Tane to bring him back—but all she caught was air.

How had the ice child overcome Tane's Touchstone abilities?

Things were happening too fast, she wasn't supposed to be facing Freja alone again—she must have known she'd need something to combat the Touchstone, the ice children must not need Touch energy to act—

Freja laughed, a tinkling, silvered sound that made Kyla want to stab something. She settled for grinding her teeth, hands curling into fists, one of them knotted around her clutch—which still held the knife.

"And what are *they* going to do, precisely?" Freja said, inclining her head to something over Kyla's shoulder. "The little one fought admirably enough the other day, but I have *grown*"—she spread her arms wide, hands delicately poised like a ballerina, displaying her shoulders, her dress, her self—"since then."

Colours rippled over her skin, and Kyla wasn't sure if she was seeing them only with her Touch sense, or if they were so strong they were actually visible to her eyes. She turned away; Pippa and Eirene stood at the mouth of the hallway fifteen, twenty paces back—they were hurrying forward, dark blue energy curling and twining around Eirene's legs like a cat, a herd of cats, a... a pack of smoke-coloured, shape-shifting, mind-entrancing felines, eyes glinting, claws flashing as they stole all of Kyla's vision, all her attention, capturing her senses, ensnaring her mind as the scent of lemon-grass filled the air, along with the taste of ozone...

Freja laughed again.

Kyla's vision telescoped out from the smoke-cats.

Freja's head went back when she laughed, exposing her throat, Kyla noted dreamily. Didn't she know the cats would be on her in a moment, tearing into that soft skin that was somehow taking up all of Kyla's vision until Freja's neck was all she could see...

Coloured light, a multi-hued aura, pulsed from Freja, doming outwards, rippling past Kyla toward the cats, the others.

Abruptly, the smoke cats vanished.

Kyla stumbled, wobbling as though her sandals had grown six-inch stilettos; her fingers found the cold concrete of the floor, her head gave a single cushiony pulse of pain— and her vision returned to normal.

She shook her head with her fingertips pressing against the floor, clenched her jaw as the after-effects of Eirene's mind control drained away, leaving behind only the smell of lemongrass in the air.

Freja laughed again, and this time there was nothing noteworthy about her throat except that it was there. "You'd have been better off bringing the other black thumb. At least her Touch might prove a threat."

Kyla's hands balled, one still gripping the satiny pink pouch.

"You could still join me, you know," Freja said, considering Kyla crouched on the floor.

Kyla pushed herself upright, rubbing her fingers together where they'd been pressed against the cold concrete, and snorted. "The deaths will happen regardless, right?"

Freja's lips pressed together thinly. "I do not lie to you."

"No," Kyla said, reaching into her clutch, "but unlike you, I'd like for the deaths that occur to keep me alive to mean more than just a power grab."

That same cat-with-the-cream smile curled Freja's lips again. "Not a worry," she said, her energy coiling tightly like a spring, "I'd rather have your shard anyway."

Touch energy burst from her, multi-hued and headed by something coin-sized that glittered in the light.

Kyla ducked.

Dark blue energy lanced past her from behind, spearing into Freja.

Freja's energy bolt veered off course, smashing into the ceiling, pink and red glass shattering.

Crimson and magenta light coruscated over the hallway.

Back in the foyer, people screamed.

Kyla lunged at Freja, the handle of the knife smooth in her hand as she tried to whip it out of her pink clutch.

It stuck; Freja snatched at Kyla's wrist.

Kyla cried out as something slashed at her bare shoulder; there was red blood, there was a black... something... in Freja's hand, pressing cold against Kyla's skin.

"You'll have to thank your little friends for me," Freja said, all tooth and shining grey eyes. "This particular tool has made my work ever so much easier."

It was the urn, Kyla realised; the Lee girls' urn, and somehow Freja was using it as a cup or a goblet, and Kyla's Touch energy was draining from the wound in her arm, blackness gathering in the urn.

"They didn't know how it worked, I assume, or they'd have been using it properly. *I do.*"

The urn began to hum, and energy seeped through it into Freja's grip, her hand shadowed by the energy, Kyla's energy, as the urn channelled it through, and through, and through.

Someone screamed behind her.

It was Eirene; and it was Pippa, fending off the second ice child, who ducked and skidded across the hallway, blocking them, blocking their blows, blocking their Touch energy.

Energy streamed from Kyla, spooling out and out and out. With the part of her mind that controlled her Touch, she grabbed after it. *No, no, no!*

She fought to wrestle her arm away from Freja, but Freja's grip was too tight, or else there was some magical enhancement to it—she had so many Touches now, so many shards, was there even a limit on what she could do?

The black spooled away until all that was left was a fine trickle, then a thread.

Eirene shouted again; there was a loud clang, then a shattering of ice.

Freja flinched, visibly pained as behind Kyla, her sister and friend fought the remaining ice child.

Kyla dragged her arm away from Freja, landed a solid kick to her chest that jarred her ankle—strappy sandals, even without heels, were definitely not ideal combat footwear.

Freja snatched after her and missed, still dazed from the blow to the ice child; the child was missing an arm and ice shards littered the floor as it dodged between Pippa and Eirene.

Kyla leapt up onto the sea-green platform with the whale skeleton, ducked behind a rib, clutching the smooth bone as the smell of lemongrass drowned out everything else, her feet slipping a little on the smooth, glass surface of the platform.

Pippa kicked a chunk of ice and it skittered across the floor, joining the thousands of pink and red shards of glass glinting like tiny knives; the foyer was in uproar.

Kyla's heart pounded and the back of her throat tasted tinny. She stumbled, caught at another rib with her other hand for balance.

No energy. Freja had drained her completely and she was swaying on her feet...

Wait.

Orange.

The tiniest, faintest bit of orange.

Hope buoyed Kyla's chest.

Orange was for finding things, and usually that meant hunting them down, but...

She closed her eyes even though Freja was lunging toward Pippa and Eirene with her arm outstretched and flash of pastel light in her hand.

Tane, she thought. *Where are you?*

Orange.

She held onto the thread like her life depending on it—and, she thought wryly, it probably did—let it billow up, nothing so large and grand as when she'd let her black energy out, this was just a small cloud over each hand, something maybe the size of a small melon, orange and glimmering.

She let it billow.

Tane. We need you. I need you.

Her mouth tasted like blood.

She swayed again and tightened her grip on the whale bones, the only thing preventing her from sinking onto the platform and fading into unconsciousness.

"Kyla!" Pippa screamed.

Tane, please. I need you.

Something thumped into her leg.

She let go of the whale's ribs in shock, slumped to the platform—only there was something angular in her way.

Legs. It was someone's legs.

She forced her eyes open, worked her tongue against the taste of blood. Lemongrass filled the air.

"Tane," she gasped.

He blinked up at her, bewildered—and nearby, Freja *screamed*.

She whirled around in the hallway, ballgown flaring, tiara knocked askew, eyes wide and wild.

There was a shattering as Pippa kicked the second ice child into the wall and chunks of ice flew everywhere.

And Freja saw Tane, untangling his limbs from Kyla's, pulling himself to as much of a stand as he could manage perched inside the skeleton of a blue whale.

And she shrieked.

She flung her arm at Tane—Kyla's breath caught—and nothing happened.

She shrieked again.

This time, there were no ice children left to ambush him for her.

Kyla's heart remembered how to beat. She swiped the back of her hand across her forehead, took Tane's hand as he helped her up to her feet. She wobbled, but didn't fall.

Tane wriggled through the ribs of the whale and dropped down to the concrete floor of the hallway.

Lemongrass.

Blood.

Freja's glanced darted left and right. She leaped.

Tane was too quick for her, grabbing her arms and pinning them behind her back. "Quick," he called to Kyla. "The knife."

It lay on the floor at the foot of the whale's plinth.

Kyla extricated herself from the skeleton, wobbled as her feet hit the concrete floor, bent to grab the knife with her head whirling.

Gasping, she staggered toward Freja.

Freja struggled, slamming her head backward.

Tane dodged his head out of the way and she missed, slamming only into his shoulder.

Her long, creamy throat was exposed.

Kyla shifted her grip on the obsidian knife. One swipe, that's all it would take, and after all, a life was a life, wasn't that Freja's own argument? How would it be any different from what Kyla had done all her life with her Touch?

One swipe and Freja would be gone, no one's problem any longer.

Kyla had killed plenty before. She had a right to do this if anyone did.

"Kyla?" Tane's brown eyes were wide, the veins pulsing in his neck as he fought to maintain his grip on the ice queen.

Kyla lunged forward, leading with the knife.

She slashed, and red blood flowed from Freja's upper arm and part of her chest.

Power spiralled.

The air around them seemed to thicken, to tighten until it was hard to breathe; Kyla's eyeballs felt like they might pop.

Lemongrass hung like a tangible fog in the air; colours whirled, a shimmering, swirling, writhing vortex as the knife sucked the Touch energy, the power, the shards from Freja's blood and absorbed them all.

Kyla gasped, an attempt to catch air but also wonder, amazement. It worked. The knife really worked.

Her knees weakened again, but the pressure in the air held her upright, the swirling vortex of power still going, Touch energy still flooding from Freja.

How much power did she *have*?

She must have killed *dozens* of people to have acquired this much energy, and it was flooding, rippling, writhing from her, and the handle of the knife grew first cold like it had with Lyssa, then hot.

Pressure built behind Kyla's eyes.

The knife grew hotter, hotter, burning—

Kyla dropped it.

The air pressure snapped and vanished.

Kyla fell to the ground—and so did Freja, alive, but now a husk of a woman in an ice-blue pool of satin that looked like nothing so much as a puddle of ice slowly melting around a corpse.

Sirens were sounding, Kyla realised; the klaxon-like alarm of the Museum itself, and outside the discordant harmony of emergency vehicles.

And Spy was there, checking on Pippa, who slumped against the pale-wood veneer of the hallway's wall, her white dress torn, her hair mussed, before checking on Eirene, who sat with her elbows on her knees beside Pippa. And then he was hurrying forward, handcuffs glinting in his hand, and he was pulling a conscious but non-responsive Freja upright as a second officer hurried up to assist.

Kyla panted, her hands splayed on the cold concrete floor, the lemongrass smell slowly fading. She spat out a mouthful of saliva striated with blood, worked her tongue against the taste of it.

"You didn't kill her," Tane said as he crouched on the floor beside her, a small, dark mirror the size of large coin glinting between thumb and forefinger.

Annoyance flickered through Kyla's chest. "I thought I wasn't supposed to." The mirror was at least an order of magnitude bigger than the one the knife had drained from Lyssa. So much power.

Kyla scowled and pushed herself to a more upright sitting position, tugging the neckline of her sunset dress straighter, then dragging a hand over her mouth.

It came away bloodied, and finding no better alternative, she wiped it on the thigh of her dress. It was too damaged to get the rental bond back anyway.

"Here," Tane said, pulling a handkerchief from the pocket of his tux. He took her hand and began gently to clean it. "No," he said, staring hard at her fingers. The rhythmic movement of the handkerchief, a little too firm to be stroking, a little too gentle to be scrubbing, soothed Kyla's pulse. "You weren't supposed to kill her." His gaze flickered to hers and then back down again. "But for a moment, I thought you would."

Kyla's jaw tightened. "For a moment I thought I would too."

He cleaned the last of her fingers, squeezed her hand, and let it drop, fussing about for a moment with folding up the handkerchief so the blood was inside before tucking it back into his pocket.

Sirens screamed.

The sound of distressed chatter filled the spaces in between.

Something shattered; Kyla whipped around, but it was just a fireman, using a pole to knock a precariously hanging tentacle of pink glass loose from the wall.

"You did well," Tane said quietly.

Kyla turned back to him.

His eyes were so deep, so serious—and so approving.

Something other than irritation fluttered in Kyla's chest.

She smiled—just a small, one-sided thing, almost wry. "Yeah, well," she said. "It turns out, when there's a Touchstone around, I don't actually have to kill anyone. I think I like that."

Instantly, her cheeks flamed.

Flustered, she pushed herself up off the ground, waiting a second with her fingertips still in contact with the cold floor before standing upright.

Heart pounding again, she made her way over to Pippa.

Behind her, Tane chuckled. "I think I do too."

Was she supposed to have heard that? She didn't think so. But her cheeks warmed again, this time for a happier reason, and the smile that played about her lips was less wry, more hopeful.

Pippa pushed herself off the wall and reached for Kyla, wrapping her tightly in a hug that said everything words couldn't.

Kyla's brow furrowed deeply—her jaw tightened, twitched—and then her eyes were wet, and she wrapped her arms around Pippa in return, and buried her face in her sister's neck. "Thank you," she said. "For everything."

"No," said Pippa, stroking down Kyla's hair. "You saved Dad. You saved all of us. Thank *you*."

EPILOGUE

SOMETIME IN WINTER

Kyla leaned back in her chair and yawned wide enough for her jaw to crack. The computer screen in front of her blurred for a moment as her eyes watered, and she glanced past the screen and out the upper-storey office window, where the early-evening view was mostly the two-storey buildings on the opposite side of the street, just as scruffy about the edges as the one she was in, their muted green and purple and grey render chipped at the edges, exposing bricks far older than Kyla. In the dying, wintry light they seemed even duller than ever, and the long-fingered shadows of naked deciduous trees rippled over them.

Behind them, some sort of broad-leafed tree was convinced it was still autumn, holding onto leaves that were somewhere between orange and brown—a similar colour, in fact, to Kyla's Touch these days.

She'd assumed at first that what Freja had drained from her was lost for good; that she'd been left with only that fine trickling thread of orange, and that was it.

But in the kerfuffle of rounding Freja up and dealing with all the damage, Eirene had picked up her mother's urn—and some of the Touch energy Freja had taken from Kyla had been in there still, a residue intangible to her hand but somehow tacky to her Touch sense when Eirene had passed the urn to Kyla, a hopeful light sparkling in her dark eyes.

It hadn't been enough to bring back Kyla's black Touch— they were right about that, it seemed: any Touch sufficiently strong enough became black—but it was more than the tiny thread of bright orange she'd had: something dark orange, something brownish, something more than strong enough to let her continue in her previous line of work as a finder of artefacts.

And not just continue, but flourish, because now she knew she was working with orange, Kyla had put her Touch through its paces to find out what it could do.

Calling Tane back into the whale skeleton in the Museum?

An orange Touch wasn't a just finding Touch after all, or at least not for Kyla; for Kyla, it was a conjuring Touch. It might lead her to the thing she needed—or, if she knew the thing well, it might bring the thing to her.

The scent of coffee curled into the room as behind her, Tane opened the door from the tiny kitchen-slash-breakout room as though conjured by Kyla's musings on the ways she'd been able to develop her use of her Touch the last eight months.

She spun on her chair to face him, grinning, and he paused in the doorway, hip leaning against the frame, green coffee mug emblazoned with their agency's logo steaming.

"Did Andrea call back yet?" he asked.

"Not yet," Kyla said, smothering another yawn. Of course, she didn't have to use her orange Touch to conjure Tane these days; working together in the same tiny office made that entirely unnecessary. "I guess she'll call in the morning now."

Tane did that little thing with his mouth that was the facial equivalent of a shrug. "Maybe she's decided she wants to keep her Touch after all."

Kyla was quiet for a moment, recalling the red-haired woman with freckles to rival Spy's as she'd sat with slumped shoulders in the third room that made up Kyla and Tane's little office headquarters. Andrea had a dark teal Touch, and she'd come tearfully to see Kyla and Tane because she'd reached her breaking point: a highly empathetic person had enough to deal with, subconsciously sensing other people's emotions; add in a teal-coloured Touch, and Andrea was practically drowning in emotion on a minute-by-minute basis, feeling the emotions of everyone around her as clearly and sharply as her own, unable to work, unable to function.

"No," Kyla said, remembering the way exhaustion and hope had warred in Andrea's eyes as they'd spoken about the options. "She'll call. She'll choose the knife."

Tane made a noncommittal noise and sipped at his coffee.

The knife, of course, meant a permanent removal of someone's Touch, and every month there were one or two clients who opted for that. Most of them, though, were happy enough to book regular sessions with Tane, allowing them to discharge their Touches safely before they became a danger —or a burden.

Regular sessions with Tane suited Kyla just fine too, even though she no longer had a Touch that needed discharging. She smirked.

"What?" Tane said, eyebrows lifting.

"Nothing," Kyla said, shaking her head. A buzz of her phone made her pick it up, and she blinked when she saw the time. "Tane, we have to go! Why didn't you say!"

"I have time to finish my coffee," he protested.

Kyla stood and stretched out her lower back, wincing. "As soon as the Crawford payment comes in, I am buying a better chair. Come on." She tucked her phone into her pocket, grabbed her handbag from the bottom drawer of her desk, turned off the computer monitor and switched the heating onto away mode. "We don't want to be late."

Tane slurped at his coffee. "Seriously, I have a few minutes to finish this, don't rush me."

"I know something else you can do in a few minutes, if you're looking for reasons to be late." Kyla winked and followed it up with a grin.

"That takes more than a few minutes," Tane said, smirking back. "But if *you* want to be late, no worries."

Kyla laughed and turned off the light switch. "Tempting," she said as she brushed past Tane into the kitchenette. "But Eirene will kill us if we're late for Lyssa's party."

"We're going to be the only old people there, you know that right," Tane said before draining the last of his coffee.

"Nonsense," Kyla said. She scootched one of the three chairs back under the tiny chipboard table with its fellows. "Pippa and Spy will be there too."

"Great," Tane muttered, crossing the room in five steps to wash his mug in the sink in a rush of water. "So there'll be four adults in a room full of teenagers."

"I think it's amazing that she's made so many friends already," Kyla said, staring absently at Tane's back muscles rippling beneath his business shirt as he dried the mug.

He set the mug away in the cupboard, folded the towel neatly in half and hung it on a cupboard handle, and turned to face her. "I do too," he said. "Come here." He drew her in for a hug and Kyla went willingly, pressing her face down against his shoulder, breathing in the smell of coffee and his nutty, herbal cologne. "I love you," he said, and it was so soft it was like a breath of wind in her hair.

Kyla froze.

"Sorry," he said at once, tensing. "I shouldn't have said that."

She let her handbag slide to the ground and reached up to wrap her hands around the back of his neck. "No," she breathed against the warmth of his cheek. "It's okay. I..." She swallowed.

Eight months. Eight months they'd been together, the idea for their agency birthing naturally from the incident with Freja: a place for the Touched to come for solace, for assistance—and sometimes for permanent relief from their abilities. They'd worked together side by side all that time, and they'd visited Pippa and Spy often enough that they now thought of them as friends—something Kyla would never have dreamed possible in a million years—and they'd all stayed in touch with Eirene and Lyssa, as friends, as mentors... Kyla had a life, and a stable job—and family.

Friends.

Support.

Her nostrils quivered; tears blurred her eyes, and not, this time, because she was tired and yawning.

"I love you too," she whispered.

The clock on the microwave read five nineteen, and the last place she'd have expected to find herself at this time of evening in the middle of a Melbourne winter was in the breakroom of her very own company, in the arms of a man who loved her, with family and friends waiting on her for a birthday party.

But nevertheless, here she was. It turned out having a team wasn't so bad after all.

ABOUT THE AUTHOR

AMY LAURENS is an Australian author of fantasy fiction for all ages. Her story *Bones Of The Sea*, about creepy carnivorous mist and bone curses, won the 2021 Aurealis Award for Best Fantasy Novella.

Amy has also written the award-winning portal-fantasy *Sanctuary* series about Edge, a 13-year-old girl forced to move to a small country town because of witness protection (the first book is *Where Shadows Rise*), the humorous fantasy *Kaditeos* series, following newly graduated Evil Overlord Mercury as she attempts to acquire a castle, the young adult series *Storm Foxes*, about love and magic and family in small town Australia, and a whole host of non-fiction.

Head to www.AmyLaurens.com to find out more!

ALSO BY AMY LAURENS:

HOW NOT TO ACQUIRE A CASTLE
Kaditeos: Mercury #1

Forget graduating in first place; Mercury just found something *better* to want.

Available from all major online retailers
in print and ebook.

www.amylaurens.com

HOW NOT TO ACQUIRE
A CASTLE

IT BEGAN, AS A GOOD MANY FANTASY STORIES DO, IN A FOREST, THIS one populated with black-trunked ironbarks so as to be suitably broody and foreboding. (Ironbarks, in case you have never seen them, are a type of eucalyptus tree; their bark is rough, and black, and split by deep fissures that hint at the red-coloured wood underneath, much as a tear in your skin hints at the redness of the flesh underneath.)

I suppose it might have begun in a palatial or castellan room, probably with someone Important dying—a wife, perhaps, slain unknowingly by the protagonist's hand; a mother, that her infant may be marked indelibly as the Chosen One (as though parents are all that stand between us and greatness); or perhaps an old man, slain for deserting his post.

Alack, nobody died to make this story, and the births of both protagonists were perfectly average. Thus, we must make do with the ironbark forest.

When the rain began in the forest of ironbarks, just south and east of the great Eye-city of Tumul Tuos, it was ordinary —which did not bode well for a story. But before too long, the water took on a lilac glow that was definitely not—which did.

The oddly coloured drops splattered on the sparsely leafed trees, rolling down the branches and streeeeeee-eeetching all the way to the ground.

Normal raindrops, in case you have momentarily forgotten, do not stretch.

These stretching drops reached the red-dirted ground, where puddles began to puddle. The oddly coloured puddles glowed, and a faint hum began to resonate throughout the forest.

More stretching drops. More dropping drips. More puddling puddles.

The electric-purple puddles thickened like curd, soupy and opaque, until—abruptly—they were a solid instead of a liquid, some sort of leftovers from an experiment gone wrong. And out of the solid, soupy puddles rose purple shapes, parodies of humans and animals, twisted as though a cruel fire had warped their limbs and faces.

The demons stood, and the demons walked, in the forest of the ironbarks—and somewhere, in the distance, someone laughed.

⚷

On a hard plastic chair in the front row of the Great Hall in the world's fifth-best Evil Overlording Academy, with its red-wooden parquetry floor that spoke of wealth and the beige, square panels of soundboards speaking of conservatism on the walls, Mercury sat, pointedly not sweating.

Partly, this was because the Academy Administrators had deigned to turn on the air conditioning earlier in the day, in recognition of the fact that the hall would be packed out with approximately six hundred bodies, all here to celebrate the graduation of about a third of that crowd.

But mostly, Mercury was pointedly not sweating because she made it a point never to sweat, sweat being an indication that she was working hard, and hard work being antithetical to her way of life.

However. If she *had* been sweating right now, it would not have been due to the uncomfortable warmth of six hundred packed bodies that even the air-conditioning system couldn't completely shift, or, in fact, from over-exertion. Instead, it would have been caused by an even more unfamiliar concept in Mercury's emotional vocabulary: nervousness.

Mercury did not *get* nervous. Mercury got things *done*.

So the fact that she was sitting here, in the front row of the Great Hall, about to graduate from Evil Overlording Academy (with distinction), and was feeling *nervous*... She crumpled the black paper program in her pale fists. It made her furious, that's what it did. Abjectly furious, that snooty-tooty Deviran with his stupid morals and his stupid I-don't-want-to-be-here and his stupid Overlords-are-empty-figureheads and his stupid face sitting ten people over, looking implacable with his deep brown skin and barely there, precision-groomed beard, as though he knew it gave him a stupid air of alluringly stupid mystery...

Mercury scowled and searched for the train of thought that had been derailed, yet again, by Deviran's stupidity.

Ah. Yes. She was angry because she was nervous because she wasn't absolutely entirely one hundred and fifty percent sure that she'd beaten Deviran in their final exams, and 1) being anything less than a hundred and fifty percent certain of anything made her cranky, and 2) being beaten by Deviran for dux of the year would be utterly unbearable. She flicked away a piece of fluff that had become snagged under her immaculately magenta-painted nails and smoothed out the black paper program.

In the front corner of the hall, the starkly attired string quartet with their traditional black instruments began playing the March of the Oncoming Doom. The screechy scrapes of hundreds of chairs on the hall's wooden floor sounded as the crowd climbed to its collective feet.

Mercury sat with her arms firmly folded for a few moments longer, until her best friend Sparky kicked her in the ankle.

"Get up, idiot," Sparky hissed, hints of real flame flickering through her flame-coloured pixie cut.

"No," Mercury said, flouncing to her feet and tossing her own glossy brown hair back over her shoulders. Four years she'd been playing by the Academy's rules in order to get what she wanted, and she'd had just about enough. Other people's rules should only be applied to plebs too stupid to invent their own.

Sparky rolled her eyes somewhere over Mercury's head before focusing on the stage, where the ceremonial party had begun entering.

Mercury clenched her jaw and narrowed her own eyes as the teachers of the Evil Overlording Academy filed onto the stage, dressed in their formal finery. Each teacher had their own distinctive look that matched their personality and their Overlording style, from severe charcoal suits to jet-black leathers, pastel ballgowns and gem-toned lingerie and eye-blinding spandex, and even on one tiny old woman at the back, worn jeans and a grey flannel shirt. She was the one to watch out for, of course; Mercury could respect an Overlord who was confident enough in their abilities that they didn't need to telegraph them. It wasn't a look *she* would consider, of course, but still. She could respect it.

The band's march finished and, after a moderately awkward pause, the crowd sat. The Principal, pale skin and dark hair matching his suspiciously vampiric red-and-black suit, took the podium, and Mercury narrowed her eyes. He was doing a superb job of hiding his emotions—he was a premier Evil Overlord, after all—but she was Mercury, and unlike anyone else, she had the benefit of being able to rummage through people's consciousnesses. She was better at adding things *into* people's minds than taking information out, but he was telegraphing fear loudly enough that she could sense it without trying overly much.

Mercury pursed her lips. Hmm.

The Principal cleared his throat at the blackened-wood podium, and the fear made it into his usually unreadable eyes. "Before we begin," he said, and Mercury's stomach did a peculiar kind of flip-flop. "I have a pressing announcement to make regarding the safety of our students and their families." He cleared his throat again and took out a sheet of paper from his pocket, unfolding it carefully and smoothing out the creases before beginning again. "The Council"—quiet booing echoed around the hall, and Mercury tsked impatiently—"have asked me to recommend that students from Tumul Tuos seriously consider postponing their return to town for a few days. The city is dealing with a *situation* at present which may present a danger to our students' health and safety."

Mercury's hands fisted at her sides and she forced herself to remain seated. What was wrong with her city? What had the Council mucked up now? A risk to the students' safety? There had to be more he wasn't telling them. Gently, Mercury tugged on his consciousness, implanting the suggestion that it might be better to share the news than to keep it secret. After all, how could they fight an enemy they didn't know?

"There are, ah..." He trailed off, glancing side to side as though wondering why his mouth had decided to continue.

Mercury didn't snicker, but she did press her lips together in satisfaction.

The Principal took a deep, steadying breath and seemed to change tack. "There has been one death already. The family have already been notified, so it is with much regret that I must inform you that Woovermyer will no longer be with us at the Evil Overlording Academy."

Murmurs broke out around the room, not all of them sad—to be expected in a school devoted to raising the next generation of dictators (ish) and despots (of sorts).

Mercury, however, crushed her program in her left hand, fist so tight her nails bit her palm.

"You okay?" Sparky murmured, leaning toward her.

Mercury gave a single, tense shake of her head and stared at the podium. Dead. Livie Woovermyer was dead in *her city*. And the Council hadn't done anything to stop it. Couldn't do anything to stop it, probably, given they'd warned the students to stay away. Livie hadn't been the strongest candidate in the year level, but she was no lightweight, either. It would take a lot of power to kill a Seven.

Enough was enough. A good thing Mercury was about to graduate at the top of the class, giving her the right to knock the lowest ranking current Overlord off their perch. Tumul Tuos would be hers in a matter of hours. And then there'd be no more of these wasteful deaths. Her city would be safe at last.

Madame Pompadour was up the front now, elbow gloves the same glimmery silver colour as her elaborate, piled-curls wig, eyelids gleaming with matching silver eye shadow, and abruptly Mercury realised Madame was there to make the announcement that would change her life forever. She leaned forward in her seat, ready to stand when her name was called.

"And now the announcement you've all been dying for," the Political Alliances teacher trilled, the frills on her evening gown fluttering as she moved. "The dux of this year's cohort!"

Sweat slicked Mercury's palms. Irritated, she reached over and wiped them on Sparky's thigh.

Sparky pushed Mercury's hands back into her own personal space bubble and Mercury, nervous to the edge of distraction, let her.

"Will you please join me in welcoming to the stage, our wonderful dux for this year, Deviran Goodsmith!"

Mercury froze halfway to standing. "Did she just say Deviran?" she whispered furiously to Sparky.

Sparky hauled her forcibly back down into her seat. "Yes," she hissed back. "Sit down, you're making a fool of yourself."

Mercury's spine snapped upright as she sat, and she arranged the folds of her long black skirt demurely. "No I'm not." She closed her eyes. "Deviran's going up to the stage, isn't he?" Even at a whisper, the misery in her voice was clear, but this time, she didn't care.

Sparky reached over and squeezed her hand.

Mercury squeezed back, lacing her fingers through Sparky's, and held tight as all her plans and dreams vanished in front of her.

A stone had landed in her chest. That must be it. Some strange sort of magic that made her chest contract and sink, and made the world distort for just a moment, long enough to trick her into thinking Deviran had beaten her so that someone could jump in front of her and yell SURPRISE!

Any moment now.

Any moment.

She refused to open her eyes and watch Deviran parading across the stupid stage like some stupid stupid-person, receiving his stupid medal and stupid symbolic crest pin.

It was that last exam question. She'd known Deviran would pull out his ridiculous 'Evil Overlords are merely figureheads, the Business Guild is where the power really lies' rant that everyone had heard a million times back when he was younger and angrier, and she'd tried to counter it, she really had. She'd argued for the importance of the Overlording position, for the power of having a symbolic figure to unite the population in their hatred, for having a person able to make all the difficult, necessary decisions the Council was too weak and spineless to make... But it hadn't been enough. Everything she'd worked for, everything she'd set out to prove—and it wasn't enough.

There were words, there were names, and then forever later, once she'd died twice already, Sparky elbowed her in the ribs. "Come on," Sparky muttered. "We're up next."

And sure enough, there was a shuffling of presenters as the last of the Powers Behind The Throne graduates departed the stage, and the next speaker announced in threatening, funereal tones, "The Overlording cohort."

Mercury blinked furiously and followed Sparky to the end of the line at the right side of the stage. The other candidates proceeded one at a time across the stage, two girls and then stupid Deviran, and then a handful more and then Sparky, and then the speaker was calling her name.

Hands fisted, Mercury tossed her head high, climbed the four steps, and marched across the stage. She wouldn't look at them, the stupid faculty who'd denied her the city she rightfully deserved, and she wouldn't look the other way either, at the classmates and crowd undoubtedly sniggering at her failure.

She shook hands with the presenter, and while he pinned the tiny crossed-swords badge on her collar, her eyes betrayed her and slid toward the audience. Her stomach flipped as she saw the crowd of parents and friends behind the rows of students, all the way to the back of the hall, twenty rows at least, illuminated by the late afternoon light streaming in through the ceiling-high windows to the right. Everyone had someone here to watch them graduate. Everyone except Weird Al—and her.

The presenter finished with her pin, muttered something to her, and offered his hand again. Mercury coldly ignored it and strode from the stage. It didn't matter. None of it mattered. Tumul Tuos was her city anyway, and no one could change that. She'd think of something. She'd take a day or two out, make some plans...

And she could always hope that Deviran would choose some other Overlording territory. He'd be stupid to, but then again, he was stupid, so. Mercury could hope.

All at once, mid-way down the steps off the stage, Mercury came to rigid attention, scanning the room. Somewhere out there in the crowd, an exchange of power had just taken place, and it felt... unusual.

But the final few students were backing up behind her and muttering, so Mercury headed back toward her seat, craning her head all the while and searching for some sign of whatever it was that had just discharged a dizzyingly quiet amount of power into the room.

She sat, and Sparky leaned over. "Okay?"

"Mm," said Mercury. "Did you feel..." She accidentally caught the eye of the student behind her and twisted back to face the front.

"Feel what?"

Mercury turned it over in her mind. It had felt like a large shot of power discharged very quietly—but perhaps it hadn't been. Perhaps it had only been a small discharge after all, something most people wouldn't have noticed.

But still, something about it had tugged on her. It very nearly felt like something she'd felt before, only she *knew* she'd never sensed that kind of discharge.

She shook her head. "Never mind. Don't worry."

Sparky sighed and straightened. "It's fine, Mercury," she said, drily exasperated. "I know you didn't win, but I promise, you'll live through it."

Mercury waved a hand for silence.

The power had just discharged again, and it had come from somewhere in the back corner, far away from the windows and light.

Impatiently, Mercury waited for the formalities to conclude. The crowd stood while the quartet played the exit march, and the stage party left, Mercury tapping her foot all the while.

The moment the last notes of the march died away, Mercury turned and headed to the back corner, weaving in and out of the students and parents who had seemed to explode slowly but inexorably out from the neat rows of seating, ignoring Sparky's calls behind her. Power, something that tugged in a way that was strange and familiar, all at once. She pushed her way through a family posing for pictures—and halted.

In the shadows of the back corner, Deviran stood with his family, with his stupid, smug little smile, looking as tall and dark and stupidly alluring as ever. Prat.

His mother, short but sleek, and his father—tall, and utterly terrifying in a way not at all diminished by his gleaming smile—gushed over him, patting his back and hugging him tight. Within moments the Principal was there, glibly shaking hands and congratulating them on the success of their son. Something flickered across his consciousness, and also Deviran's father's—some moment of recognition in response to what they were saying. But Mercury brushed it aside just as the mother brushed melodramatic tears from her cheeks and handed Deviran a silver-wrapped package about as long as her hand but half the width.

That. That was the source of the strange, magical feeling. Mercury watched hawk-eyed as Deviran unwrapped the gift. A glimpse of gold set her pulse racing—What was it? What did it do? Could she steal it?—and then the paper fell away to the floor, and Deviran stood staring wordlessly at the object in his hands, and Mercury did too.

Wide-eyed, Deviran raised his gaze to his parents, and even from where she stood Mercury could hear the reverence in his voice as he thanked them.

But Mercury had eyes only for the object. No wonder she'd felt it discharge, and no wonder it had felt both strange and familiar. In Deviran's hands lay a glorious, sunshine-gold key, large and strong—and with a handle in the shape of a stylised fish, long, flowing fins curving to make the grip.

A Key. They'd given him a Key. And not just any Key, but *the* Key, *her* Key, the Artefact of Power belonging to *her* city.

A wordless noise of wanting rose in Mercury's throat. Who cared about being dux? She needed that Key.

Keep reading:
AmyLaurens.com/books/kaditeos/castle